Praise for BLACK SITE

"A thriller that crackles with gut-wrenching action and authenticity." —*Publishers Weekly* (starred review)

"Fury is retired Delta Force, giving the action a rapid-fire, realistic air . . . Racer is locked and loaded for a series of adventures." —*Kirkus Reviews*

"*Black Site* is an amazing thriller from a new all-star in the genre. Packed with speed, surprise, and overwhelming violence of action, this is one book you will not be able to put down! Want to know what Spec Ops really look like? Read Dalton Fury. Simply put—nobody does it better."

—Brad Thor, #1 *New York Times* bestselling author of *Full Black*

"Step aside, Jack Ryan—Kolt Raynor is the true hero of the new millennium. Written with an authentic voice, the debut novel by Dalton Fury, *Black Site*, left me breathless and awed by its battlefield-hardened reality. I kept having to remind myself this was fiction. Here is a book to put you in the trenches, slogging with the best, armed to the teeth, challenging you to keep up. If you want to know what it's truly like to be a Delta Force operator, pick up this book today."

—James Rollins, *New York Times* bestselling author of *The Devil Colony*

"Dalton Fury and I came up in the Unit together, flip-flopping troops and missions from Afghanistan to Iraq. What makes his writing unique is not just the tactical accuracy—which this book has in spades—but his unique understanding of the geopolitical events that propel the plot. He is the real deal. If you want to know what it's like on the front lines of the shadow war, pick up this book."—Brad Taylor, *New York Times* bestselling author of *One Rough Man* and *All Necessary Force*

Praise for KILL BIN LADEN

"A riveting account of one of the most important—but also least understood—battles in the war on terror."

—*Time*

"*Kill Bin Laden* is one of the most detailed and informative descriptions of a battle forgotten by most Americans, but one that was truly the closest the West got to bin Laden since 9/11." —Military.com

"The best book ever written by a special operations insider. This guy Fury's men are the real-deal Delta Force operators. You need to know what happened at Tora Bora, and this great book will tell you."

—Colonel David Hunt, U.S. Army (Ret.), *New York Times* bestselling author of *They Just Don't Get It* and *On the Hunt*, and FOX News special ops and counterterrorism analyst

"Special Forces Operational Detachment-Delta is without a doubt one of the most fearsome military units ever assembled. Delta officer Dalton Fury didn't just take part in the battle of Tora Bora, he commanded all the special operations troops, both U.S. and British, who were there. *Kill Bin Laden* is a proud, riveting, warts-and-all account of that battle, one of the most important special operations missions of all time."

—Michael Smith, author of *Killer Elite: The Inside Story of America's Most Secret Special Operations Team*

"An important, must-read book about real warriors. A story that so positively reflects what on-the-ground decision making, professional acceptance of risk, and maximizing interagency cooperation can do. Dalton Fury shows us with amazing detail and insight what highly trained and motivated special operators can accomplish successfully in combat out of all proportion to their numbers."

—Cofer Black, former chief of the Central Intelligence Agency's Counter Terrorist Center

"The most compelling and comprehensive account of the Battle of Tora Bora that I have read, heard, or seen in any format."

—Colonel John T. Carney (Ret.), author of *No Room for Error* and President/CEO of the Special Operations Warrior Foundation

ALSO BY DALTON FURY

Kill Bin Laden: A Delta Force Commander's Account of the Hunt for the World's Most Wanted Man

BLACK SITE

A DELTA FORCE NOVEL

DALTON FURY

St. Martin's Paperbacks

For the Eagles on the wall

BLACK SITE: A DELTA FORCE NOVEL

For information address St. Martin's Press, 175 Fifth Avenue, New York, NY 10010.

Library of Congress Catalog Card Number: 2011033811

ISBN: 978-1-250-01419-1

Printed in the United States of America

St. Martin's Press hardcover edition / January 2012
St. Martin's Paperbacks edition / October 2012

St. Martin's Paperbacks are published by St. Martin's Press, 175 Fifth Avenue, New York, NY 10010.

10 9 8 7 6 5 4 3 2

PREFACE

In 2001, I was the Delta Force troop commander given the secret mission to hunt down and kill the most wanted man in the world—Usama Bin Laden. In 2008, I shared the untold story of that fateful mission in the book *Kill Bin Laden,* and recounted the twists and turns of the Battle of Tora Bora fought high in the mountains of Eastern Afghanistan. Soon after *Kill Bin Laden* became a bestseller, I started a new mission—a mission to craft a thriller series about classified "black" ops and operators, "real" fiction about real warriors.

But before I took pen to paper and rushed something out onto the already overcrowded action-fiction shelves, I realized that I needed to first do some deep soul-searching. Specifically, I needed to analyze and isolate the unique mental aspects of the Delta Force operator—all because of one simple but powerful word.

The year was 2004, and we were laser-focused on

anything and everything Abu Musab al-Zarqawi. The elusive Jordanian terrorist and leader of al-Qaeda in Iraq had just shot to the top spot of our high-value target list after Saddam Hussein was ferreted out of a smelly rat hole.

One night, we were moments from launching into the heart of Fallujah to service a time-sensitive Zarqawi-related target. We didn't have a lot of time to discuss it. Everyone knew what needed to be done. America expected us to launch, even if the intelligence was a little shaky. After all, we were Delta Force. Moments before heading for the vehicles and helicopters, a fellow officer looked me in the eyes and said, "Dalton, you are impetuous!"

I thought to myself at the time, "You are damn right I am!"

Hunting terrorists sometimes requires operating within a unique psychological spectrum that often rewards impulsive behavior, haste, or acting without consideration. A mind-set that places enormous value on intangibles like instinct, intuition, or a hunch often raises eyebrows in a risk-averse culture. For my novel *Black Site* to be plausible, Kolt Raynor needed to possess all these qualities and more.

But Kolt Raynor is a free-spirited Delta Force operator—not Superman. The guy is average height, weight, and build. He is also a mix of the unique talents, idiosyncrasies, motivations, and personalities of the real deal Delta Force operators.

He is more comfortable when operating with teammates than when operating alone, just like most Delta operators are. He has vision. He also has a passion for the profession, the mental stamina of a chess champion, and he does his best to ignore the red tape. The knock on Kolt Raynor is that at times he is borderline insubordinate, and he operates largely off of gut feeling. It was a modus operandi that garnered him widespread support within Delta's ranks, solidified his pad speed, and gave him enormous operational clout. And even though the generals didn't care much for his antics, they were smart enough to let it play out.

Just as important as Raynor's makeup, the story line itself had to be plausible—high-risk, certainly, as all Delta missions are, but a clear sense of nonfiction possibilities had to be captured inside a fictional structure. Moreover, the reality of the times had to be captured fully. Real-world issues, like the difficulty of garnering political support to operate over ambiguous borders, obtaining execute authority for high-risk missions, and the indescribable love of teammate that kindles a bizarre willingness to sacrifice it all to save a buddy or do the right thing had to resonate in *Black Site.*

For many years, Kolt Raynor got things done. Until one night when he pushed it too far. On a high-risk mission in the badlands of Pakistan, Raynor allowed his enthusiasm to cloud his judgment. It was a deadly mistake. And as things go in Delta Force, the fall from hero to zero is rapid, even for an operator of Kolt Raynor's stature.

Disgraced and off the net, Raynor turned to the

bottle. He tried to walk away. But there were too many strings attached. And, misgivings or not, the Unit soon realized they needed Kolt Raynor more than he needed them.

Dalton Fury

ONE

Three small boats skipped over the water on an intercept course with the colossal freighter looming in the afternoon haze. Coal black, sinewy Somalis and cream-coffee Arabian Yemenis, sixteen men in all, leaned into the wind, watched the ship grow on the horizon, and fingered their Kalashnikov rifles.

None of the sixteen was new at this. They were all experienced pirates.

The choppy waves and the small profile of their long narrow skiffs hid their radar signature as they closed on the stern with brazen speed.

To a man they were all high, but not high on sedatives or the like, drugs that would muddle their senses or diminish their resolve. They were instead doped up on khat, the amphetamine-like leaf chewed like tobacco across Africa's horn. They'd been chewing since late morning, and the full effect of the stimulant now gushed through their veins. The khat gave them extreme energy and near-superhuman confidence, but it also made them anxious, irritable, volatile.

With the loaded weapons in their hands and the promise of big money once they took control of the ship, the khat was a hazardous additive to a situation that hardly needed another unstable ingredient.

And one other dangerous ingredient, already well stirred in the pot, ensured that events soon to follow would not end well.

Their leader was out for revenge.

His name was Abdiwali. He was just twenty-two and already a veteran pirate of these waters. He spit khat-laced sputum into the foaming wake created by his wooden boat's bow as it churned through the green sea, gripped his AK with sweaty fingers, screamed at the old man operating the outboard motor, told him his mother was a whore if he could not make the skiff go faster.

Abdiwali looked ahead at the looming freighter, imagined workers on the deck milling about. Helpless fools. Infidels, no doubt. Soon they would see the approaching speedboats, and they would know they were being hijacked. If these seamen were like all the others on ships captured by Abdiwali, they would point a sound weapon and blast a loud noise that was annoying and painful, but hardly a deterrent. They also might spray the pirates with water that could easily capsize a slower or bigger craft, but deck hoses would not threaten Abdiwali's sleek and mobile skiffs. Finally, if the seamen on this ship were like all the others, when they realized their fate was unavoidable, they would slow the ship and allow the boarding. If they had time they would lock themselves in a safe room, a citadel, to remain protected from the pirates' guns while communication was established with the freighter's home office. Abdiwali and his men would demand ransom and then raid the officers' stores of liquor and meat. With assurances that no harm would come to the crew, the citadel's doors would open, and cigarettes would be passed around in a show of friendship. Tea would be poured and food would be passed about. The deckhands would return to their duties or retire to their bunks. In a few days, a few weeks if the home office felt the need to be obstinate, Abdiwali would have his money, and hands on the ship would be shaken. The pirates would return to their skiffs and race home to their mother ship, and the freighter, her men, and her cargo would continue on as if nothing had happened.

No. Not this time.

It had been a week since Abdiwali's brother's death. He'd led a similar hijacking, had made the mistake of targeting a Saudi tanker, and for this error had paid the ultimate price. The Saudis refused to negotiate. They sent armed helicopters from Jeddah, and the helicopters raked the deck of the tanker with machine guns, killing hijackers and hijacked alike, even gunning down the first officer of the vessel. Abdiwali's brother was ripped in two and kicked into the sea for the sharks. One pirate was left alive, picked up by the helicopter and delivered to the coast, to tell the others that they could hit ships in the Gulf of Aden to their hearts' content, as long as the ships were not Saudi flagged.

The freighter roiling the warm water before him was not Saudi owned, of this Abdiwali made certain, but his rage was real and his thirst for vengeance needed to be quenched, if only by proxy. With no real motivation other than impulse and wrath, young Abdiwali decided he would kill every last living thing on board.

Thirty-seven-year-old Kolt Raynor opened his eyes slowly, stared at the low ceiling above. The heat hung oppressively in his cabin. Sweat dangled in beads off his eyelashes. The stale taste of vomit in his mouth, mixed with the discount-store bourbon he'd been sipping nearly nonstop for the past six days, threatened to sicken him yet again. He rolled onto his side on his bunk, looked across the closet-sized room, out the portal at a blue sky.

Afternoon sunlight.

Shit. Kolt had slept since breakfast. He looked to his watch.

Three p.m.

He sat up, his head swirled, and he put his hands on his knees to steady himself. His baggy cotton warm-up pants were twisted up to his shins, his tank-top undershirt was smeared with greasy food, and his white socks were blackened at the soles. His uniform was pressed and crisp, but it was also hanging in the closet. He had not even taken it out of its plastic bag.

Kolt's soft girth filled his clothing. His love handles

seemed to be widening in the mirror these days. His beard and mustache had grown unkempt, and his hair hung past his collar line.

Not that he'd worn a collared shirt in some time.

He reached down to the floor, caught the rolling bottle that journeyed back and forth along with the movement of the ship. He found his plastic cup and poured three fingers of whiskey. As hot as it was in the cramped room, he served it up neat because he was too lazy to climb the stairs down to the galley on A Deck to get ice from the machine.

As he brought the drink to his lips the satellite phone wrapped in the sheets of his bunk chirped.

He found it on the third ring.

"Raynor."

"Kolt? It's Pete."

"Colonel? What time is it in Virginia?"

"Six a.m."

Raynor wiped salty sweat from his brow with his forearm. "Not a social call, then?"

"Son, have you been drinking?"

Raynor looked down at the bottle that he still held in his right hand. It was half empty. He'd snuck a case of booze on board, and this was the last of it. "Of course not. I'm operational."

"The captain says you've been puking off the side."

"It's a boat. People puke on boats, Pete."

"The captain also says you've been insubordinate."

"The captain is a jackass. We had a little run-in. No big deal."

"He said you were drunk and unpleasant to him."

"It's not my job to be nice to the captain. It's my job to . . . well, you know the deal. It's basically my job to sit here and do nothing."

"You are the security officer. You have many assigned duties, and you know what your duties are."

Kolt finished the plastic cup of bourbon and tossed the cup on the floor, knowing it would roll back his way soon enough. "Yes, sir. I am allowed to run the LRAD if we're attacked." The Long Range Acoustic Device was a sonic weapon that blasted high-volume pulses and, in theory, could be used to fend away pirates.

But in real-world situations, the LRAD had been little more than an annoying noisemaker.

"That's not all."

"I turn the hoses on at night to slow down boarding attempts from the side. I check to make sure the anti-pirate fencing is in place. Sixty minutes' work max, and work that a well-trained chimp could do. C'mon, Pete, this job is a joke."

"You are the one making it a joke. You should be thankful for a paycheck. Six months ago you were selling camping gear in a mall in North Carolina. Now you're a well-paid private security officer on a container ship crossing the Gulf of Aden. You *did* read the threat assessments I faxed you in Naples, didn't you?"

Raynor stifled a hiccup with the back of his arm. Brought the phone back to his ear. "I know about the threat. There are pirates in the gulf, and they are assholes, but statistically speaking, there is less than a one-in-three-hundred chance we'll get hit. Since NATO began patrolling the Gulf of Aden, attacks are down. And even if we do get hit, it's not like I can do anything about it. I'm a damn stowaway. I don't have any authority and I don't have any weapons."

"Our client's rules of engagement are strict, I can acknowledge that, but—"

"Rules of engagement? Their rules of engagement are 'Don't engage.' They won't let me do anything but handle the LRAD if we get hit, or handle the ransom transfer if we get boarded. The captain could do that as well as I could."

"Kolt, there is half a billion dollars' worth of cargo on that ship, and there is a poorly kept secret in the maritime protection industry that you should know. Jorgensen Cargo Lines, like many others, hires us to staff every ship making the Gulf of Aden run with a security officer purely for the reduction in insurance premiums. They are saving money by just having you sit on your ass and work on your tan. If you get boarded you just tell the guy with the biggest towel on his head that Jorgensen will wire ransom to any bank he specifies. Your job is crucial, it is easy, and it only requires you staying sober. Can you do that for me, Kolt?"

"Yeah, Pete." Kolt drank bourbon straight from the bottle now. He liked Pete Grauer. Appreciated the ex-Ranger colonel giving him security work when no one else would return his calls. Even if it was a piss-poor contract on a smelly ship cruising back and forth in the middle of nowhere.

Grauer continued. "Make a few more runs on the freighters, show me you can keep yourself together, and I'll find some cushy static work for you somewhere closer to home."

"Thanks, Pete."

"How's your back doing?"

"Aches a bit. Not too bad."

"You're damn lucky to be alive after what you went through. You do recognize that, don't you?"

Kolt thought back to a moment in the not too distant past, and the flood of emotions that filled his booze-altered brain made him feel anything *but* lucky. Still, he replied, "Yes, sir."

"You doing your exercises?"

Kolt gulped the bourbon again, leaned back in his bunk. "You bet."

"How's the crew treating you?"

"Other than the captain, they are fine. Norwegian officers, Filipino deckhands. My only incident so far was when one of the crew tried to turn in another for having a pistol on board. I talked to the culprit and he showed me the gun. It's an old pot metal .22 revolver he keeps for rats."

"Did you confiscate the weapon?"

"Hell no. This tin can is infested. I'd let him keep a belt-fed .50 cal in his bunk if he'd use it to assassinate rats."

Pete chuckled. "Okay. We'll let that one slide. Call me if you have any trouble."

Raynor snorted. "Statistically speaking, there is a one-in-three-hundred chance you'll hear from me."

"One more thing."

"Sir?"

Kolt listened to the cracks and pops of the satellite connection for several seconds. Grauer was a man rarely at a loss for words. "I understand . . . *everyone* understands that what you've been through these past three years has been tough. I can't imagine the guilt you deal with. But . . . no matter what happened, you need to turn the page and get past it. Those guys are gone, and your feeling sorry for yourself will not bring any of them back. You need to forgive yourself, and you need to pull those shoulders back, lift that chin up, and move forward. You have a life to live."

"Yes, sir." Raynor's VA shrink had been saying much the same thing for most of three years.

Grauer's tone changed a measure. From disappointed but empathetic father to taciturn commanding officer. "And I have a business to run. I can't have you causing problems with the captain. That's a lucrative contract."

"I understand."

"I expect the same professionalism from you that I got each and every day you served under me."

Raynor sat up straighter. He could not help it. Fifteen years in the military had created a Pavlovian response to such a commanding tone of voice. "Yes, sir."

"Good. Now, Major, put down the bottle. Clean yourself up. And no more fuckups."

Kolt looked to the near-empty bottle in his hand. "Yes, sir."

Grauer terminated the call.

Raynor dropped the phone and with it his shoulders. He rubbed the sting from his eyes, leaned forward on his bunk to stretch his aching back. He was hungry, filthy, sick from the booze, angry at himself for falling so far. He used to be someone, he knew it, and it sickened him to think about what he'd let himself become.

He'd been an Army Ranger, an officer, and then a member of Delta, the most elite fighting unit in the world.

But all that had ended three years ago.

Kolt shrugged, shook away the memories that haunted him, shook away just enough of the self-loathing to stand, and stepped into his sandals. He headed out the door and down to the galley to make himself a sandwich.

Five minutes later Kolt Raynor sat alone in the galley. He ate bread with cheese spread, wondered if he would vomit again. He felt queasy, like the room was moving, and he put his hands flat on the metal table to steady himself. His plate slid to the right, as did several other items in the room. He felt it now, unmistakable—it was not his nausea, and it was not his imagination. The ship was turning hard to port, still at full power. He knew they were far from land, it was broad daylight, and he therefore could not imagine why the captain was executing such a dramatic maneuver. There was no one around to explain why—all hands were working in other parts of the freighter. He grabbed a hunk of white bread and left the galley, climbed the stairs to the outside. He was one floor above the main deck, and he started for the stairs to go up to the control room. A middle-aged Filipino crewman in a tan jumpsuit and a red hard hat climbed a steep ladder to his level and ran past him, his thick rubber boots banging the cleated metal surface of the deck.

"What is it?" This man, Kolt knew, spoke only Tagalog, but he was able to convey a simple message.

"Pirates!"

Kolt stood there, said, "No shit?" through a lump of bread in his mouth.

TWO

Raynor didn't believe him. He kept chewing his bread as he climbed another steep flight of stairs to B Deck, two levels above the main container deck. He looked off the starboard side, out at the ocean.

Nothing.

He moved around to the port side of the superstructure, more curious than anxious. The ship had stopped its dramatic turn, and again it shot straight and true through the water. Just behind the ship, off the port side and well within its wake, he saw three small boats. Twelve-footers, fast movers, each full of men. He estimated fifteen in total, some black, some Arab. Most had AK-47 or AK-74 rifles, though he saw at least one RPG launcher. The small craft bobbed up and down, closed confidently on the massive ship.

"I'll be damned." They were too close for the LRAD, and Raynor had no time to get to the fire hoses.

These men would board the ship.

Raynor had already failed.

Though the pirates looked ominous enough in their turbans and with their chests full of rifle magazines, Kolt had studied the modus operandi of Somali coast hijackings, and he knew there was little chance anyone would get hurt in the transaction to come. Jorgensen Shipping would pay—these guys would know that already. Despite a few highly publicized violent clashes between pirates and naval forces in the Gulf of Aden, the vast majority of incidents turned out to be little more than a "taxing," where the gang would board the ship and require payment to be wired for the ship to pass through the waters.

Hardly the high drama of movies and TV shows.

Raynor thought about going back to the cabin to change into his uniform, clothing more representative of an agent of the shipping company. But he decided against it. Getting dressed up for a meeting with half-naked African pirates would just add to the absurdity of the moment.

The gunmen began boarding the ship with rope ladders hanging from long poles while Kolt made his way down the stairs and across the long deck. He'd tossed his bread in a garbage can, and he walked calmly with his arms to his sides. From a hundred yards away he saw several of the deckhands standing around near the pirates, even helping them aboard. Surely some of these guys had been in hijackings before: they knew the protocol. There was no time to get down to the citadel, the safe room several decks down in the bowels of the ship, so the deckhands just did their best to make friends with the men now in control. The Norwegian officers were nowhere in sight, maybe racing down to the citadel, though the gunmen at the bow would probably beat them there.

Wherever the Norwegians were, one thing was certain: they were leaving the negotiating to Raynor.

This was good news, actually, as Kolt knew his breath was ripe with liquor, and though he'd certainly been drunker at other times on this cruise, he was nowhere near sober at the moment. He decided he'd work with the pirates directly and stay as far away from the captain as possible. Captain Thomasson was not exactly Kolt's biggest fan, as evidenced by his tattletale phone call to Pete Grauer.

As more and more of the shirtless pirates began filling the deck in front of him, Kolt was surprised to see some of the bandits angrily pushing and shoving the Filipinos. They lined them up near the bow, yanked off their hard hats, and put them on one another's heads. Raynor continued to advance, but something inside him registered danger, something in the movements, something in the mannerisms of the attackers.

Kolt stopped in his tracks. The aggression showed by a few of these boy-men did not sync with what Raynor had been told about the standard operating procedure of a typical Gulf of Aden takedown. The gesticulations of one young Somali, perhaps the leader, were especially curious. His wide white eyes and screams at the Filipinos seemed wild and animal-like. He shoved men to the ground, hit them over the head with the butt of his rifle, kicked them while they squirmed on their backs on the hot metal deck.

Raynor quickly knelt behind a coil of ropes at the edge of a container bay, not forty yards from the melee. The sudden movement made his stomach roll and his body weight sway on his rubbery legs.

From this distance he could plainly hear the pirate leader. "I am Abdiwali. I am in charge of ship now! Where is captain?" the young man screamed in English. No one said anything. He pushed a young crew member toward the ship's tower to fetch him. Then, with a wave of his hand, he sent four of his men off in different directions, presumably to round up the officers and anyone else on board. As they moved out, the leader fired a half magazine into a yellow shipping container just over the heads of the cowering crew.

The American private security contractor did not know what to do. His job, on paper anyway, would have him walk toward the leader right now, assure him Jorgensen Shipping was ready to work together with their good friends the Somalis to come to some reasonable agreement on the tariff necessary to allow this freighter to continue on through these waters with its full complement of cargo and crew.

But Raynor had a very bad feeling about this, and the last thing he was going to do at the moment was saunter up to the pirates with a smile on his face and declare himself in charge.

Kolt turned, still in a low crouch, and ran.

* * *

The teenage Filipino deckhand sat on his tiny lower bunk on G Deck. In his hand he cradled the rusty revolver he'd bought in port in Athens to keep the largest rats at bay. He heard the crack of rapid-fire gunshots several levels below him on the main deck. He'd never fired the weapon in his hands, never even opened the cylinder to check the status of the ammunition that came with it.

The young man shook from head to toe. This was his first experience with pirates. He'd been told by his crewmates that there was nothing to fear, but the young man was simple, anxious by nature, and quite reasonably afraid of guns pointed in anger by shouting men. He began near convulsions as running footsteps approached from down the hall. His door latch clicked, and he raised the tiny revolver awkwardly.

"Walter, Walter, it's okay."

It was the American, the long-haired security man who stayed in his cabin all day and smelled of drink. The man who'd come to look at his gun on the third day out of Naples but with a chuckle had allowed him to keep it after learning why he'd bought it, made Walter promise to kill a rat for him someday.

Walter lowered the pistol with an audible sigh of relief.

"I need to borrow your gun."

The young Filipino held it out in his quaking hand. The American looked determined, confident. He took the weapon, spun it nimbly on a finger, slid forward a catch and dropped the cylinder, pulled out a round and held it up to the light. In under three seconds he'd put it all back together again, slipped the revolver under his undershirt in the small of his back, and turned to go back into the hall.

Walter called out to him. "Mr. Kolt! There are many pirates with big machine guns. You have only five little bullets. Five little bullets will not stop them."

The American leaned back into the cabin. The eyes that had watered with the effects of liquor for the past week now glinted sharp and bright with purpose. "No. But five little bullets just might buy me one of those big machine guns."

The American turned away again. His running footsteps faded down the hall.

Captain Thor Thomasson walked past the huge containers on the main deck. Two pirates flanked him and held his arms and waved rifle muzzles up in his face to spur him forward. He wore his formal coat buttoned up, held his head high and his nose up, kept a proud chin. He could hear his officers behind him as they were pushed along at gunpoint as well.

He was angry at these filthy brigands, of course. Considered them the vermin of the sea, the absolute scourge of a profession of great honor and nobility. But as angry as he was at these poorly dressed, sweat-dripping black and Arab men around him, he was incalculably more furious at that son-of-a-bitch American alcoholic security officer who should already have been on his satellite phone wiring funds to these cretins' Nairobi bank accounts.

Where the hell was that drunkard Raynor?

Captain Thomasson was led in front of the leader of the pirates and shoved down to his knees, which was a shock to the Norwegian mariner. He was screamed at in French and English and Somali and Arabic. Spit flew from the young pirate leader's mouth as he shouted and yelled and waved his gun around in wild arcs.

Thomasson had endured hijackings before, but this was clearly different. These men were whipped into a fierce rage, and they almost looked as if they *wanted* to kill.

Kolt Raynor ran down the stairs to B Deck, turned the corner, and all but crashed into two surprised pirates. Both men raised their rifles at him quickly. He could tell some drug was amping up their brains. Their jerking and ticlike movements were hard to judge. He put his hands out, palms forward, waist high.

And he smiled as he spoke. "Francais? Parlez vouz Francais mes amis?"

One of the men nodded and said he *did* speak French.

"Tres bien. Je suis avec l' societe de transport Jorgensen. Tu va bien."

Everything is okay, he assured them. He spoke politely and calmly.

In French he continued, "I have the authority to offer you payment for our safe passage. Look, my friends, I will show you my credentials."

Kolt's right hand slowly began to reach into his waistband. The men had spread apart warily, one on each side of the gangway, and each kept his AK on his chest.

They had been somewhat calmed by Kolt's words and his demeanor, but they were no amateurs, and they were no fools. As his right hand lowered to his side one of the men shouted at him to freeze.

Raynor's hand movement transitioned from slow and cautious to a whipping blur. He reached behind his back as he took a quick sidestep to his right. His hand appeared, and before either pirate could react, he shot the man on his left through the right eye. The second man jolted in shock, began to squeeze the trigger of his AK-47, but two rounds to the neck short-circuited his central nervous system and his finger relaxed.

Kolt returned the hot pistol to the small of his back, stepped forward, and gently took the rifle from the second dead man's hands even before his body hit the metal deck. This rifle he slung over his shoulder. He lifted the identical AK from the ground next to the first pirate, opened the collapsed wire stock with a snap, and continued walking toward the bow side of the superstructure.

"Go see what that was!" Abdiwali shouted to two of his men, and they started off at a run toward the ship's superstructure. Captain Thomasson remained on his knees, the hot metal burning his white skin through his pressed trousers. His fellow officers were lined up on their knees alongside him. The Filipinos stood behind the Norwegians. All were terrified by the erratic actions of their captors.

It wasn't supposed to happen this way.

Thomasson had offered money, money to be wired anywhere in the world. The pirate leader had laughed at him and told him they would kill them all and take their cargo and their boat and earn ten times the money his company would be willing to pay for their miserable lives.

Just then cracking Kalashnikov fire echoed off the large wall of containers behind them. The origins of the noise were hard to pinpoint. All the pirates, and all the captured crew, looked up at the superstructure. There, a lone man stood on B Deck, fifty yards away, holding an assault rifle over the scene.

Thomasson squinted in the glare of the sun off the windows of the superstructure. Finally he said, "Raynor?"

THREE

Kolt Raynor had just killed four men at close range, two with the pistol, and two more with a "borrowed" Kalashnikov. It had been easy. But now, at a distance, he found holding the sights on a small target extremely difficult. The ship rocked gently from side to side, Raynor had not trained with a rifle in years, and his physical condition had deteriorated to the extent that he was already winded from running a short distance and climbing a few flights of stairs.

And, there was no question in his mind, he was legally drunk.

But what he lacked in capability, he attempted to make up for in bluster.

He shouted at the attackers below him. "I've killed four of you already! Turn around and get back on your boats or I'll kill you all!"

The leader of the pirates screamed back at him. "I

will shoot the captain!" Abdiwali grabbed Thomasson by the pressed and starched collar of his uniform and pulled him up to his feet. Held the AK to the officer's neck and gripped him close, using the thick man for cover.

The punishing sun scalded Kolt's face. He squinted, sighted carefully across the top of his AK. The weapon rocked back and forth in his hands. Raynor was furious with himself for drinking on duty. At the same time, he desperately wanted a tall shot of bourbon to help calm his nerves. He worried about his abilities, and he worried about the weapon in his hands. Raynor had not sighted this weapon—he didn't know how accurate it was even in the hands of a stone-cold-sober shooter.

Still, it was only fifty yards. In his military service Raynor had routinely popped head-sized targets with iron sights at four times the distance. He told himself that fifty lousy yards, even buzzed and firing an unfamiliar weapon, would be no problem. He tightened his aim on the pirate's forehead, pushed the captain out of his mind, slowly and confidently pressed the trigger.

Boom. The weapon's recoil slammed the stock against his shoulder, and in his alcohol-addled state his knees were wobbly. It took him a long moment to refocus downrange.

The pirate leader remained standing.

Captain Thor Thomasson fell to the deck. He writhed on the ground, clutching his shoulder.

"Oh shit," Raynor mumbled.

Abdiwali screamed, "What is wrong with you? Are you crazy? I will kill everyone!" Quickly the pirates made human shields of all the ship's officers, and Abdiwali pulled the injured Captain Thomasson back to his feet and held him between the superstructure and himself.

Blood ran down the blue sleeve of the captain's uniform.

Kolt Raynor slowly lowered his weapon, dropped it to the deck, and raised his hands.

Abdiwali hit the wounded captain on the head over and over with the wooden stock of his gun while he waited for his men to bring the bearded man down from B Deck. He'd lost four men today, but he would take twenty-five lives as repayment. Then he and his surviving men would ransack the ship, and spend some time searching for loot. Then they would climb back on their boats and speed toward the coast before NATO ships or helicopters arrived.

This would be a fun afternoon, and Abdiwali would get it started by making the bearded infidel now approaching beg for his wretched life.

"Abdiwali!" shouted one of the pirates pushing him along. "He is American! He had Mustafa's rifle, and he had a pistol hidden in his pants." The pirate shoved the American down onto the hot deck at his leader's feet. The man went down on his hands and knees, began spewing vomit, ejecting sick bile on the pirate's sandals and bare legs.

First Abdiwali leaped back and screamed with anger. Then he raged forward, used the butt of his rifle to pound the top of the man's head. The two pirates flanking the disgusting creature followed suit, and all three began hitting him with their rifles as he rolled on the deck in his own effluence.

When they slowed their attack he crawled back up to his hands and knees. The man on his left raised his gun high to rain one last powerful blow down on his back. Suddenly the cowering American leaped up toward the descending rifle, spun his back to the pirate's chest, and grasped the AK as it swept down. The sling was around the Somali's neck—the American pulled the gun in front of him and yanked the choking pirate off his feet, spinning him around to his back and holding him off the ground while he kicked and gagged, strangling the pirate with the pirate's own rifle's sling.

Abdiwali frantically tried to turn his weapon back around from its butt-forward position, but the puke-covered infidel was too fast. The American stepped closer, still using the sling to choke the rifle's owner. The barrel of the AK pressed against Abdiwali's forehead, and it shoved him backward to the bow's railing. One more strong push and Abdiwali would fall two stories to the water below.

The Somali pirate leader dropped his weapon and raised his hands quickly.

All the pirates were shouting now, save for the leader, who looked wide-eyed at the barrel pressed just above his eyes, and the one who hung by his neck off Kolt's back. Raynor could not see the other men, but their screams and shouts indicated their location behind him and, more important, their indecision.

Kolt looked at the man at the end of his gun barrel. "If you say anything, anything at all, other than 'Get back in the boats,' I will blow the top of your head out to sea!"

The Somali hesitated, started to speak, but Kolt cut him off.

"Remember, *anything* but 'Get back in the boats,' and you are fish food, asshole!"

The pirate leader's forehead sweat dripped on the blued gun barrel. A fat drop trailed down past the front sight. The kicking of the strangling man on Raynor's back caused the rifle to jerk back and forth, and the sweat dripped off the underside of the barrel with the motion.

Abdiwali moved his eyes down the barrel, past the American's sunburned hands and arms, to his face. Into his eyes. They were watery and bloodshot, and Abdiwali was certain he could smell the sickly sweet scent of liquor in the rancid stench of bile on the man's face and clothes.

After a moment he said, in English and then Somali, "Get back in the boats!"

Kolt stepped back and raised the rifle just enough to let the choking man behind him drop to the hot deck, where he gasped for air like a fish pulled from the hot green waters.

The pirates climbed back over the side. They kept their weapons with them, but Kolt did not take his rifle's sights off of their leader's forehead until all of his men were back on the speedboats two stories below. Then, without a word, Raynor pushed Abdiwali to the railing, and he went over. Adroitly he climbed down the rope ladder they'd used for their ascent, and a wooden skiff pulled forward to meet him at the waterline.

The three boats began to accelerate away from the ship, the officers on the deck scrambled to attend to their wounded captain, some of the deckhands came forward to cheer and pat Raynor on the back, but he pushed them back, told them to run. They did not understand, grew more confused when the vomit-covered security man went down onto his knees under the railing, then lay prone with the pirate's rifle in front of him.

The boats were leaving. Why was he still concentrating on them?

Captain Thomasson lay nearby, moaning in shock and pain.

The blade sight of Kolt's AK weaved in front of him. He concentrated on the sight as best he could, but switched focus from time to time to the pirate leader in the middle boat. At one hundred yards, just as Raynor expected, the boat slowed and turned broadside of the cargo ship. Kolt concentrated all his diminished faculties on the front sight post now, tried to line it up with the jet-black man standing in the little boat. He ignored the waffle-patterned deck's heat as it reddened his skin, and he watched Abdiwali lift a rocket-propelled grenade launcher in the air in front of him, heft it to his shoulder, and point it at the ship.

Kolt knew the pirate could not sink the huge freighter with a few lousy RPGs, but he could kill crewmen and damage the vessel and cargo. Kolt did his best to aim for the distant man's head, thought he had him lined up in the sights, and fired a single round.

The pirate did not move, just held the RPG at the ready and took aim himself.

Kolt fired another round.

Another miss.

He could tell the Somali was about to let his rocket fly.

"To hell with this," said Kolt, flipping the selector switch to full-auto fire. He sighted perfunctorily on the speedboat and let it rip. Five, ten, twenty, twenty-five rounds blasted forth. The pirate leader lurched back, the RPG launcher raised, and a rocket streaked high into the air and flew harmlessly over the ship ahead of a white smoke trail.

The Somali pirate leader fell back into the water with the metal launcher still in his grasp. All but one of the other pirates on board the skiff jerked and spasmed and dropped dead along with him. Collateral damage. The sole survivor crawled low to the outboard motor and turned his splintered and bullet-ridden boat away. The other two speedboats left their leader and the others behind as they raced back to the safety of the coast.

Kolt climbed back up to his feet, staggered again a moment, and suffered a short bout of dry heaves. Captain Thomasson was being tended to by a ship's officer with a medical kit. The white-haired Norwegian captain stared angrily at the American while prostrate on the hot deck.

"You fool! Typical American cowboy! We have insurance to deal with these matters. They would have been reasonable if you had just offered them the money!"

Kolt turned away and toward the first officer. "Get the crew to throw the bodies and the guns overboard. Then I want you to show me how fast this boat will go," Raynor said. "I'll be in my room."

"Getting drunk?" shouted Thomasson, icy derision in his voice.

"Damn right, Skipper," mumbled Kolt as he headed alone back toward the superstructure.

FOUR

Raynor unlocked the door to his mobile home, stepped inside, and tossed his keys and wallet on the peeling Formica kitchen counter. He crossed the tiny living room and plopped down roughly on the mattress on the floor, grabbed the half-empty bottle of Old Grand-Dad he'd left there, and took a violent swig.

It had been a long afternoon with his shrink, and Raynor needed this drink. He was careful to avoid smelling like a honky-tonk bar when he went in to meet with Dr. Rudolph in his office just off base of Fort Bragg. He knew the interminable session would only become more insufferable if Doc got a whiff of the whiskey, and Kolt would do anything to just get in and get out, and get back home, where Old Grand-Dad, his true therapist, would be waiting for him.

As he swigged another mouthful, making up for lost time, he surveyed his worldly possessions. Kolt's mobile home looked like it had been ransacked around him, but in actuality it had been trashed by the occupant himself. Every dish in the trailer was filthy, stuck to tables or stacked high in the sink. Empty, nearly empty, and soon-to-be-empty whiskey bottles lay strewn around the kitchen and den. Adventure gear lay on the couch and floor, and backpacks with dirty clothes were scattered about, as if Kolt had just returned from one of his overseas security postings.

In fact, Pete Grauer had fired Raynor a month earlier, almost immediately after the pirating in the Gulf of Aden. Kolt didn't blame him. He knew Grauer had no choice in the matter. Most of the witnesses said that Raynor had doubtless saved lives with his actions, but every last one of them admitted he'd likely done it while intoxicated. Wounding the captain and then firing a full magazine into a boatload of pirates, all but one of whom were little or no threat to the freighter, didn't set well in maritime security circles, though Jorgensen Cargo Lines had done its best to cover up the matter. They removed Grauer's firm from future crossings and voided their contract with him.

Consequently, Grauer saw no alternative but to let Kolt go.

Kolt returned to the States and went back to his dingy trailer, his home since he had rented it with his best friend and Delta teammate T.J. seven years prior. It sat on a poultry farm a few miles from the north gate of Fort Bragg, away from the busy Fayetteville side of the post. The farmer who'd rented out the mobile home asked only two hundred a month, but that would have seemed a criminal rip-off to anyone not accustomed to the austerity of a special operations unit. The nearby chicken coops filled the air with the dander of old feathers and the musky stench of bird droppings, and training at the artillery range just across the road used to shake T.J. and Raynor off their mattresses at night. Still, the two friends had outfitted their pad with a big-screen TV, cardboard boxes full of clothes and canned food, and a computer. They trained together in Brazilian Jiu Jitsu in the dirt yard behind the trailer, they competed for hours on end overhanding throwing knives from distance into a head-sized target fashioned into a gnarled oak tree just outside the door, and they watched movies on the big screen.

And though it looked more like a dorm room at a Third World junior college than a home base for two of America's most elite commandos, once a month or so when T.J. and Kolt ordered a mixed-martial-arts fight on Pay-Per-View and filled the fridge with cheap beer, their dump of a home became party central for themselves and their Delta mates.

Raynor considered moving away when he left Delta—there was no reason for him to stay so close to Bragg. But he never really felt like he had anywhere to go, so he remained, waiting on some new direction or new plan to carry him away.

For the past month the former Delta major had done little but lie around and brood, avoid phone calls from his parents and from the media who had gotten wind of his shootout with the African pirates, and drink himself to near oblivion.

And he was drinking now. He lay back on the mattress, looked at the clock, and wished like hell that the night would not come so soon.

Most nights he had the dream. If he was drunk enough before the dream, the images would be muddled, less crisp, less real, less nonfiction and more fiction. But it was evening already, he'd fall asleep before successfully pickling his brain, and he knew that this inability to be sufficiently shitfaced before bed, plus Doc Rudolph's persistence in discussing the events of three years prior during today's session, all but ensured that tonight's dream would be stone-cold authenticity. History, not fantasy. Kolt would hear the sounds, feel the fear, smell the death.

Relive the guilt.

He chugged the Old Grand-Dad and began to cry. And he wished like hell he could stay awake all night so that he could avoid the motherfucking dream.

FIVE

Three Years Earlier

Four pairs of hiking boots dug for purchase on the narrow mountain spur. Four pairs of wary eyes searched the dark distance for threats. Four men climbed onward and upward, sucked lungs full of thinning air, and ignored the churning snow that wetted beards and clothing, adding to the bone-soaked chill of their own sweat. Heavy packs and load-bearing vests, buckles and straps straining with gear, compressed spines and hampered balance.

Though it was perilously steep and poorly marked, discovering this goat track had been a windfall for the team, even if using it was a gamble. Certainly crossing the mountains via an established trail was preferable to just humping overland, but the men had no illusions they were the only two-legged creatures on this path between Afghanistan and Pakistan. The Taliban, al Qaeda, donkey caravans of opium poppy or assault rifles, anyone with an illicit requirement to travel from one side to the other undetected, might well be just beyond the next rise.

With a craggy limestone wall on his left and a sheer drop-off to oblivion on his right, the lone officer in the silent procession stopped. Thirty-four-year-old Major Kolt Raynor looked ahead into the darkness and surveyed his team. Master Sergeant Michael "Musket" Overstreet clambered up the trail twenty meters on, decked head to toe in high-tech mountain clothing in blacks and browns. He sported an impressive salt-and-pepper beard and wore a pakol, the local wool cap favored by Pashtun men in the region. Though heavily burdened with equipment, Musket showed no obvious strain. He pulled himself up the incline, his gloved hands grabbing and then pushing off the mossy rocks on the wall to his left, and then he looked back over his shoulder. Noticing his major's halt, the master sergeant dropped to a kneepad and turned his attention to the wide valley arrayed off his right shoulder.

Looking back now through the darkness and precipitation, Major Raynor could just make out Sergeant First Class Spencer "Jet" Lee moving up the mountain trail fifteen meters behind. He climbed carefully, reaching out to steady himself as he stepped onto an icy stone in his path. Jet wore a Heckler & Koch 416 rifle over his chest and a fat Combat Casualty Response Kit on his back. A pouch on his chest rig sported a .40 caliber Glock 23 pistol. Jet served as the team medic, but he could shoot his long gun or his pistol as well as any of his colleagues. His beard, in contrast to Musket's, was short and scruffy and obviously hard-earned, and he kept his North Face cap pulled down below his eyebrows. He looked up and saw the halt in front of him, so he lowered himself and his sixty pounds of gear to the cold earth, took a knee on a broken piece of shale.

Raynor knew Rocky was up ahead on point, just out of sight but leading the way with his rifle cradled in his arms. Even though he was fifty meters ahead of his team leader, with his new third-generation NVGs, Sergeant First Class Carl "Rocky" Price would be able to cover the trail all the way back to Jet, at least when the trail was straight enough to get line of sight.

Kolt Raynor pressed the Talk button on his interteam radio. "Rock, you good up there?"

The reply took a moment. The labored breathing was audible in the transmission. "Just chillin'. Why we stoppin', Racer?" As expected, Rocky *did* have eyes on the team. Raynor was not surprised to hear the man struggling in the thin air. Although Rocky was the best pure mountaineer in the squadron, a serious sinus infection had sent him back to the States for recovery, and since his return he'd not yet fully reacclimated to the altitude.

"Let's break out the O2," Raynor suggested to all the men. "Huff 'em if you got 'em, boys. It's thinning out fast up here. We'll be heading down below eight thousand in less than a klick."

"Roger that, boss." Though he could not see him, Raynor knew Rocky would now be on a knee, pulling a tiny aluminum tank from his pack and inhaling heavily from its attached mouthpiece.

Raynor, Musket, and Jet had been in the mountains for nearly three months, and altitude sickness for them at this elevation was highly unlikely. Still, a few inhalations of pure oxygen sounded good to the major. He'd played it like he was making the offer for Rock's benefit, but he took this opportunity to reach for his own tank as well.

Raynor leaned his rucksack against the wall behind him to take some weight off his legs and hips. Though his fitness level was that of a professional athlete, this was no ball field. This was war. His conditioning of late had been of slight concern to him, but he hid it well back at base. He had no doubt whatsoever that he could fulfill this mission, and he would have done anything to avoid being left behind. Yes, he had let his training lapse—he was an officer, and his focus had been on the maps and the intelligence reports and the gear and the personnel and the logistics, and not sufficiently on his fitness. But Kolt Raynor had always considered himself a game-day player. He knew he'd rise to the occasion and suck it up, even if that meant sucking wind along the way.

This hit was too important.

Though they all held military rank, these were not soldiers. These were operators. Members of First Special Forces Operational Detachment–Delta. The public and the press called them Delta Force; the Department of Defense called them Combat Applications Group; inside Delta they often just referred to their organization as "the Unit." And when America needed hard men for hard duty in a hard land, America called Delta.

With all the shit holes and shit heads in this world, these days Delta did not go wanting for work.

When his men again stood at the ready, Raynor prepared to move out. He adjusted the sling on his short-barreled HK416 rifle so that it would scrape against a different patch of skin on his neck, and he took a swig from the nipple on the end of the tube running to the water bladder in his backpack. He checked his GPS, found his location, and noticed he was literally straddling the border. Though that was probably significant to some politician or diplomat far away, it did not really matter to him, because the border here was just a fantasy. The mountains held no signposts, no fence line, no markings at all. The British had drawn a stroke across a map over a hundred years earlier and named it the Durand Line after some meddlesome English foreign secretary, and since then it had been all but ignored by the millions of Pathans and Baluchis who lived on either side of it, and by smugglers of weapons and drugs, jihadists, and, on extraordinarily rare occasions, American commandos.

For Raynor and his three men sharing this stretch of trail there was no cause to be more vigilant now, entering the Federally Administered Tribal Areas of Pakistan, than there had been at any point during the previous three hours of their insertion. No, there was just as much danger five klicks behind them, in the hills of Afghanistan, as there would be five klicks ahead, in the hills of Pakistan. The Taliban did not consult a GPS, did not check their maps or check their fire. This entire region, deep verdant valleys and jutting snowcapped peaks alike, was the homeland of the enemy, and they outnumbered Raynor and his men one thousand to one.

Major Kolt Raynor, code name "Racer," turned his eyes back to the east, away from his procession of operators and toward his objective, though it was still hours off. He moved out and his men followed suit.

Nine seconds later in a darkened trailer at Creech Air Force Base in Nevada, the thirty-year-old pilot of an unmanned aerial vehicle spoke into her headset without looking away from the flat-panel screens in front of her.

Her voice was smooth and soft; a hint of Ohio infused her vowels. "Hunter 29 is over the border at Waypoint Charlie. Incursion time Zulu nineteen-nineteen."

In her headphones came an abrupt reply from her commanding officer. "Hunter 29 at Charlie nineteen-nineteen Zulu. Okay."

Air Force Captain Pamela Archer watched the feed from her variable-aperture infrared camera, tracked the four operators moving along the trail fifteen thousand feet below her MQ-9 Reaper drone as news of the cross-border incursion came from the GPS coordinates on the moving map panel mounted above the real-time image monitor. The Delta element showed as white hotspots on the monochrome display, hotspots with arms and legs, climbing and pulling themselves arduously up a mountain trail snaking along a wide canyon.

Although this morning's focus was on the Afghan-Pak border, Archer considered herself on the front line of this war as well. True, she did concede, there were conveniences on her front that were not enjoyed by the Delta boys. She had the fortune of stopping off at the base's Starbucks on her way to battle. Indeed, a four-fifths-empty quadruple mocha sat alongside the black joystick that controlled the flight of the UAV. The men on her infrared monitor, by contrast, had been humping through the mountains for hours, with only an occasional swig from their CamelBak water bladders to sustain them. And they had the frigid November air to contend with, thinned by the nine-thousand-foot mountain and whipped into brutal intensity by the high-walled gorges, whereas Pam lived in a middle-class apartment complex in a suburb north of Las Vegas, enjoyed daytime highs in the eighties and nights just cool enough for a zip-up fleece.

But from half a world away Pam Archer deftly piloted the aircraft from her station, communicated with the CIA/Delta command and control center at Bagram Air Base in Afghanistan, and, when so equipped and so instructed, fired the Hellfire missiles that hung on the wing pylons of her Reaper hunter-killer aircraft.

Pam did not control all the Reaper's bells and whistles herself. Two sensor operators in another room in the Ground Control Station ran the cameras and recording devices and other system monitors. An hour earlier these men had detected the goat trail over which the element now traveled, putting the operation back on schedule after an earlier delay with the helo insertion into eastern Afghanistan. This success earned Pam and her team some hearty "atta-boys" from Bagram, but these were strident professionals. They didn't bask in the moment.

Instead, the two sensor operators concentrated closer still on their screens, and Pam flew on to the next waypoint, watching over the Delta boys from above.

Pam's unit, the 17th Reconnaissance Squadron, often worked with CIA and Delta, providing the agency with remote eyes and standoff killing capability. Pam herself had flown her Reaper or a smaller Predator UAV into Pakistan forty times in the past year on reconnaissance operations, and six times on hunter-killer flights. She'd launched her Hellfires four times, once killing a minibus-load of al Qaeda jihadists, and twice taking out Taliban encampments.

Battle damage assessment of her other strike had been inconclusive.

Although UAV overflights of Pakistan had become so routine that many in intelligence circles referred to America's "unblinking eye" over the theater, actual ground incursions were quite rare. More often than not, *much* more often than not, the Delta boys working the border would get word that a strategic reconnaissance mission in their current area of interest was under consideration, and they would begin the process of prepping gear and transport, only to be told, invariably at the last minute, that the SR was a no go. The politics in Washington, the politics in Kabul, the politics in Islamabad. Somebody in D.C. would decide somebody somewhere else would get their panties in an especially tight twist if American troops were known to be waltzing around inside Pakistan. For every "boots on the ground" operation over the border that received sanction, fully a dozen had been proposed, and certainly fifty had been warranted.

But recently things had been heating up, and this uptick in OPTEMPO resulted in Pam Archer's bird roaming the western Pakistan skies over the four-man Delta element as they moved to a waypoint six klicks into South Waziristan. This foray into Pakistan's lawless tribal area by Hunter 29 had been given the auspicious title of Operation Infinite Reach 09. It was the sixth mission over the border for elements of Task Force 33, part of the larger joint CIA/Delta-run Operation Denied Redoubt, an eighteen-month-long campaign to target Taliban rally points on the other side of the border.

CIA intel sources had indicated that a way station for jihadists lay hidden in a dry gorge south of the Tochi River. It was more than just a hut for overnight lodging—intelligence reports told of a complex warren of tunnels and camouflaged structures, replete with an armory, a bomb lab, an infirmary, a barracks, even a mosque to administer one last inculcation of fervency in advance of the fighters' and suicide bombers' missions into Afghanistan. Five farewell cell phone calls from suicide bombers to loved ones in the Middle East coming from the area had been intercepted by signals intelligence crews in the last three weeks. Further SIGINT raised the stakes even higher. Word was a high-value target from Chechnya who had been operating in eastern Afghanistan for months had recently arrived at the way station to lick his wounds and plan another hit-and-run raid over the border. If Hunter 29 could get eyes on the HVT, then either they would take him out themselves with a sniper rifle, or, if the location was determined to be free of noncombatants, they could "request and clear hot" a launch from the UAV. Within seconds Pam Archer's bird could send a Hellfire or two down a laser's path and kill the Chechen AQ leader. Further, if Raynor and his men could reconnoiter the valley and determine the area to be of sufficient value to the enemy, then CIA/Delta command and control would send in two Chinook helicopters full of Delta assaulters the following evening to take it down.

Captain Archer tilted her control stick gently to the right. Instantly the image on her lower monitor turned, altering the infrared camera's viewpoint. She continued her bank until her Reaper's nose pointed due east. Now that she had monitored the border crossing, it was her job to fly on and surveil the path on the way to Hunter 29's next waypoint to locate any threats ahead.

SIX

"Hunter 29 for Eagle 01. Are you receiving, T.J.?" Raynor spoke softly into the microphone of the satellite radio. It was past 3 a.m. now, five hours since the helo insertion. The snow had stopped and Kolt had led his team down below seven thousand feet. Here at Waypoint Echo he'd had his men take a knee, and then he'd set up the small dish and adjusted the angle of the SATCOM antenna to the correct azimuth; now he waited for a response from the other side of the border.

"Eagle 01 reads Hunter 29. Go ahead, Racer."

"Hunter 29 is at Echo."

Racer and T.J. had been best friends since Ranger Selection, eight years earlier. Though they were both thirty-four years old, T.J. had been an officer since West Point, whereas Raynor had begun his service as an enlistee and only entered Officer Candidate School in his midtwenties. Consequently T.J. was a lieutenant colonel to Raynor's major, but their friendship negated the need for much ceremony. Josh Timble—his initials had inexplicably been reversed to form his code name—referred to Kolt as "Major" only when he felt the need to condescend, and Kolt called Josh "My Colonel" only as a smart-ass platitude.

Now T.J. and his Eagle 01 element were billeted in a safe house just twelve kilometers inside Afghanistan, where they served as direct command and control of Operation Infinite Reach 09. They communicated directly with Racer's element, Hunter 29, and relayed commands to Delta/CIA Joint Operation's command in Bagram, who in turn was in contact with Archer's UAV team in Nevada.

T.J.'s voice came over the satellite. "Racer, you're not going to like this. Just got word from Creech that something on the UAV went tits up and it has to turn back for Bagram. Seventeenth Recon has another bird on the way, so just continue on to the edge of your next waypoint and lay up until it gets on station."

Raynor leaned his head back against the pine in frustration. "So much for 'Infinite Reach.' "

A pause. Then, "Just carry on to Waypoint Foxtrot, take a load off, and stand by." T.J.'s voice was clipped, clean, and disciplined. Raynor knew their communications were being monitored by generals, Delta colonels, and intelligence technicians, as well as by CIA and others back at the JOC. T.J. was surely as frustrated as his friend—he was just *much* better at hiding it than was Raynor.

Raynor looked to his watch. He replied with his best

display of radio protocol: "Understood, Eagle 01. Uh—we've got just about two hours till BMNT." "Beginning of morning nautical twilight" was Armyspeak for dawn. "Request we continue to the objective. If we don't press on we'll have to lay low till nightfall." While he waited for his friend to respond over the radio, Kolt pulled out his GPS.

"Negative, Hunter 29. Get to the next waypoint and find a ROD." A "remain over day" site was exactly what Racer wanted to avoid.

"Uh, roger all, Eagle 01. We'll monitor and check in on schedule. Send weather update ASAP. Hunter 29, out."

Raynor shut down the sat link, reached into a pouch on the right side of his load-bearing vest. He pulled out a satellite phone, switched it on, and swiveled a cigar-shaped antenna into position. He knew his request for a weather update would mean T.J. would be calling, and within ten seconds a light flickered on the phone. Major Raynor brushed tree bark off his neck as he answered.

"What's the deal, T.J.?" Both men carried Globalstar satellite phones that were not monitored by other parties. These were used chiefly for mundane logistics communication and weather updates, but Raynor knew he could speak freely to his friend over the Globalstar, and he did not hesitate to do so.

T.J.'s voice was different now that he was not being listened to by others. "Here's your weather update, bro. It's gonna turn dark and stormy over your head if you don't check your tone. Smart-ass remarks over open comms aren't gonna win you any friends."

"Yeah, sorry. Just came out. Apologize on my behalf."

"That's what I'm here for." T.J. was pissed, his radio protocol of a few minutes ago was long gone.

"What's up with the Reaper?" Raynor asked, changing the subject.

"I don't know. It's gonna be a couple of hours before they can replace it."

"Look. Foxtrot gets us less than two hundred meters from a decent overwatch on the target. We can go ahead, make it before BMNT. If we lay up two hundred lousy meters short we'll shove the entire timetable back twenty-four hours. That's twenty-four hours where something can go wrong."

"If you find a good ROD nothing will go wrong."

"I can think of a half-dozen things off the top of my head. The HVT might leave the target area. Taliban spotters might hear the UAV and get spooked enough to double security. A Pashtun farmer might stumble onto Rocky while he's taking a leak. Some suit in Washington might pull the plug on the whole op. Every minute we sit around short of target is another minute this whole thing can go south. I know. I've been here before." Kolt had led this same element over the border on Infinite Reach 02 and 04, and both times he'd been ordered to turn around for reasons never made clear to his satisfaction. He took it personally.

"Wait for the UAV."

"We've only got two hours to dawn."

"Yeah. I've got a watch."

"It's just two hundred meters."

"Yeah, I've got a map, too."

Raynor gritted his teeth. T.J. always was the more careful one. "Fortune favors the brave."

"Fuckups favor the brave too, Major. I don't want to have to fly down there and save your impatient ass." In the event of an emergency there was a Ranger Quick Reaction Force up in Bagram and a pair of Chinooks prepared to fly them in over the border to extract Raynor and Hunter 29. But Raynor knew that T.J. was closer, and Raynor also knew his best friend would move mountains to get to him if he needed him.

Raynor blew out a long sigh. Waited a little longer than necessary to respond, just to show his friend that he thought the order to find an ROD was stupid.

"Understood, Colonel."

In Nevada, Pamela Archer cussed into her mike. "We've got a team over the border and they're pulling us offline for a software glitch? The bird flies. The cameras see. This is crazy!"

"Come on, Pam. We've got two sensors showing ice buildup," barked back her commanding colonel over the radio.

"She's not freezing up! I've seen those readings before. Everything else is in nominal range. De-ice controller is working. Flight characteristics are unchanged. It's just the software misreading the fluctuating air pressure on the wings. It thinks the antifreeze is blocked in the weeping holes."

"If those wings ice up—"

"They won't."

"You want to risk losing the bird?"

"You want to risk losing the men?"

"Damn it, Captain! We fly inside operational limits. On a mission this big I'll let you fudge it a bit here and there if I have to, but two simultaneous ice readings take this UAV offline. I'm not going to let a Reaper go down in Pakistan. We've got another crew that can have their ship there in three hours. You bring yours back to base ASAP! This discussion is over!" The colonel left the conversation. Pam imagined him ripping his headset off and throwing it down as he paced back and forth in the UAV Operations Center a few hundred yards from where she sat.

Pam's earpiece was silent for several seconds. Then a tinny voice came through from the next room.

"Great job, Pammy. An hour ago we *were* the shit, now we're *in* the shit."

"It's just stupid, Myron." Myron was one of the Reaper's two sensor operators. "Is she flying like her wings are iced?"

A pause. "Negative."

"Exactly. My four boys are blind down there facing every Taliban and AQ fighter in the region. They *need* us." The emotion in her voice revealed more than just frustration over the order. She was genuinely concerned about the men. This was her third flight over the element with the call sign Hunter 29. She hated leaving them alone in enemy territory.

Myron's voice chided her over the mike. "You're not their mother. They're Delta—they can handle it till another crew gets overhead."

"I hope so." She watched the GPS coordinates change on her navigation monitor. As her bird crossed back over the mountainous border between Pakistan and Afghanistan she said aloud, "Good luck, Hunter 29. You're on your own."

SEVEN

First light dawned at five thirty. Racer, Musket, Rock, and Jet lay spread out over ten meters of tall snow-covered brush on a ridgeline overlooking a small gorge. Below them a dry stream bed narrowed to the south, but widened to the north as it snaked around a bend away to the east. A lower hill rose in front of them, and ended a hundred meters to the north to form the southern bank of the stream bed's curve.

Just on the other side of the little hill, intel suggested, the sprawling enemy complex lay camouflaged on the floor of a larger canyon.

One hundred sixty meters away from Hunter 29's layup point.

"This sucks," barked Raynor. Vapor from his breath turned to wisps in the frigid morning air.

All four men rested while they surveilled the area through their night vision goggles. As they did so some dug into First Strike Rations, a pared-down Meal, Ready to Eat for ops when even MREs were too bulky. Raynor sucked energy gel from a foil pouch, squeezed the calories and caffeine and sugar into his lean body, washed it down with water infused with small amounts of salt to aid in hydration.

Rocky replied to Raynor's comment with one of his own. "It's dead down there."

Jet asked, "If the Reaper comes back during daylight and clears to the next waypoint, are we going forward?"

Raynor shook his head though the men could not see one another in the brush. "I doubt it."

"So we just hang out here all dang day," Rocky said, and followed the comment with an audible spit.

Raynor hesitated. Then said, "I don't like this place as an ROD. What do you think, Musket?"

The oldest of the team at thirty-eight, Mike Overstreet was also the ranking NCO of the troop. He had nearly twice the time in Delta as his major. His voice was low and gravelly. "Could be better. These bushes aren't much cover."

"Yeah," agreed Racer. "Did you see a better spot anywhere behind us?"

"Not that we can get to before sunup."

Kolt nodded. "What about those trees on the crest ahead? That would be a better ROD."

Overstreet did not respond.

"Musket?"

"You askin' me or tellin' me, boss?"

"Asking."

Racer heard the man shrug. "It's a better spot than here. But Eagle 01 said to sit tight."

"Yeah, he did, but that *is* a safer spot up ahead. We don't need a UAV to tell us that this ravine is clear. We can cross, summit to that little saddle on the hill, and lay up there. If we should happen to get an overlook position—well, I'm not going to cry about it."

Musket had been silent but now he spoke. "What's Eagle 01 going to say about that?"

"Sometimes it's better to ask forgiveness than permission," said Raynor.

Rocky's and Jet's chuckles permeated the hide.

For another thirty minutes they lay there, searching the nothingness of the gorge as it slowly filled with enough clear morning light for them to stow their night vision equipment. Kolt Raynor scratched his short black beard and rubbed his gloved fingers into his temples, briefly flattening the deep creases formed by sun and wind and austere living, most of it spent outdoors. Like a coiled spring his pent-up energy refused to dissipate until released.

Kolt Raynor was known in the Unit for making the most of his abilities. He wasn't the fastest, the strongest, the smartest, or the most disciplined, but he was always there, always getting the job done by hook or by crook. The knock on him was that his confidence had gotten him a lot farther than his talent would ever have taken him. He was a risk taker, but even though he liked to do things his own way he was by no means a cowboy. Delta operators were team players and Kolt knew the strength in the Unit was the experience and skill of its cadre of NCOs. All in all it had served him well. That said, it certainly didn't hurt that his friend T.J. was one of the most brilliant and dedicated officers in the Unit, and T.J. trusted and appreciated Raynor enough to run interference for him when his mouth or his exploits pushed the envelope of Delta standards and norms.

By 6 a.m. nothing had disturbed the stillness of the gorge. White rocks, thin pines and firs, patchy snow that rose into the air and then resettled with the comings and goings of a light breeze. Raynor thought of waiting another eighteen hours for just the *potential* of ID'ing the target location, only a few minutes' hump away. At any time the al Qaeda HVT could leave the area, move deeper into Pakistan or cross into Afghanistan by any one of a number of routes. U.S. military outposts just over the border had been taking a beating recently, most likely due to improved training and tactics of the Taliban fighters in the area. Fighters trained by assholes like the HVT who, according to the intel reports, was close by, but just out of reach.

Kolt knew that if he and his men sat right here, at any moment the recall order could come, forcing him and his team back and ending what was likely to be his last incursion over the border before rotating back to Fort Bragg in a few weeks.

No. That would not be acceptable.

Raynor spoke into his mike. "Musket, what do you think?"

"About?"

"Can we make it across this little basin without being compromised?"

"I reckon." Musket's minimal small talk was typical of the man from the backwoods of Tennessee. More often than not his answers were punctuated with a spit of tobacco juice.

"You think we can find a hide in the trees on the crest of that hill that might get us overwatch on the target?"

A slight pause. "Don't see why not."

"You know that Chechen HVT could split at any time."

"I reckon he could do just that."

"I'm thinking the risk would be worth the reward."

A considered pause now. "Your call, boss."

Raynor hesitated a long time, weighing his options. Finally his chin rose slightly in the tall grass. "To hell with this. Let's go take a peek."

"Right on," said Rocky. All four rose to their feet.

"I'll straighten it out with T.J." Raynor winked at Musket.

"You always do, Racer," replied the master sergeant as he turned to lead down the hill.

"Fortune favors the brave," declared Raynor, and then, "Rock, you and me first. Musket and Jet cover."

The major and the sergeant descended the hill carefully. Under the watchful glass of their two teammates they crossed the low thick foliage on the western bank of the stream bed, negotiated the sharp shale and quartz of the bed itself, and ascended the steep rise on the other side of the ravine. Ten minutes later they dropped low in the hill scrub near the summit and scanned the little gorge behind them while Jet and Musket followed in their tracks. When the element rejoined on the eastern hillside they spread out and ascended to within a few yards of the crest. They moved in a crouch now near the summit. Raynor spoke into the mike of his MBITR inter/intra team radio. "Sit tight. I'm going over to find a spot in the trees where I can get glass on the area."

Musket said, "How 'bout I go grab us an overwatch, Racer? You can come over when I call you."

"No worries. Low and slow, I've got it." Raynor doffed his pack, scooted forward on his belly with his rifle slung tight across his back and his spotter's scope in his left hand.

Musket's calm southern voice came over the MBITR. "Don't get too far ahead, boss."

"Yes, Mother."

At the crest itself Raynor found the snowy brush too tall, so he turned to the right and lowered back behind the saddle, came back up at the small grove of pines. Here he could not get eyes on the valley either, because the high trees ran down the hill in front of him. So he advanced a few meters more and went prone again. He began moving west on the hillside. "Drop rucks and wait at the top of the ridge. As soon as I get an overwatch I'll update you."

Raynor scooted forward. He estimated he was twenty meters below the crest now, farther away from the relative safety of the saddle than he would have liked, but the shrubs were lower with each meter of his descent, providing more opportunity for a clean view of the valley. He knew he was pushing his luck a bit, but his concerns about the HVT slipping through their grasp and slipping into Afghanistan to kill Americans drove him forward. When he finally did get line of sight ahead he realized the hillside had a military crest a little lower. Only from the military crest could he see the entire floor of the valley. He began crawling down, but Musket spoke again into his ear, his tone more emphatic now.

"That's far enough, Racer. I can't see you. Come on back and we'll try again farther south."

"I'm almost there. Ten meters and I'll have the entire gorge in sight."

Forty meters from the ridge and his team, Raynor found a good spot in a tuft of snowy brush on the edge of a small outcrop of feldspar that hung over the valley. He settled in and brought his scope to his eye.

The 40 mm aperture did not provide a wide field of view, but its variable 10- to 20-power zoom gave him all the enhancement he needed. He studied the canyon floor, saw it to be nothing but a continuation of the winding dry stream bed that he'd crossed back on the other side of the hill, though now it widened to the width of a small river.

"This isn't right. This looks like it fills with runoff during the rainy season. I don't see how there could be an enemy fortification on the floor here."

On the far bank the terrain rose sharply, nearly vertically in some places, to fully twice the height of the hill he was now on. Searching through the narrow glass he saw ledges and defilades on the hill, scanned them carefully though they were still well covered in shadows. He looked up at the glowing sunrise to the east—it would be an hour before he'd get a good look at that hillside.

"Could be something on the far wall. We'll have to wait on the light."

"Boss, how bout you exfil and we get back to the first ROD? We can make it work. We'll come back tonight and look for a better overwatch, hit it from another angle. Shouldn't have any problem finding enemy signatures with NODs."

Raynor could hear the agitation in the master sergeant's voice. Musket didn't like it that his officer was so far ahead of the element over the target area. Raynor felt sure he wouldn't be compromised here in his hide, but he also didn't want to create any friction between himself and Musket.

"Roger that, Musket. I'm heading back."

Raynor kept low, turned around on his knees, and began climbing off the shelf of rock. He'd gotten no more than five feet when his right boot broke off a thin plank of stone. The loud crack echoed in the wide gorge. Raynor tried to hook his boot onto the broken shale to keep it from falling away, but it slipped, slid lower across the outcropping, and fell off, into the gorge. The flat rock cracked and crunched against others as it smashed its way down. The noise was unrelenting for several seconds.

"Damn it."

"You okay?" asked Musket. "You want me over there?"

"Negative, stand fast. I'm heading back."

Raynor started to climb once again, but a faint noise caught his attention. He looked back over his shoulder at the canyon. There it was again.

Thump. Thump. Major Raynor cocked his head. It came from far away, but it almost sounded like—

Musket shouted over the MBITR. He recognized the noise. "Mortars!"

A brief whistling and the hillside just below Raynor erupted in flash, smoke, and blasted debris. Rock and clumps of frozen dirt rained down on him.

"What the—"

More *thump thumps,* right before the second salvo landed on top of the first. Raynor knew a third was in the air, though he had no idea from where they were being fired. He rose to his feet and, crouching, climbed the hill toward the pine trees. A few meters to his left a sizable chunk of bark snapped off a thick trunk. Echoes of a high-powered rifle's report followed. Kolt sprinted up the steep hill now, ran for the protection of the saddle as he shouted into his mike, "I got snipers!"

More crashes of mortar impacts behind. Directly on the overwatch Raynor had just vacated. As he climbed he saw his three-man team rise from the snow on the saddle above and to his right, scanning for targets through their weapons. Musket fired off a couple of rounds—whether he was shooting at an actual enemy or was just trying to keep heads down on the opposite hillside, Kolt had no idea.

"Bug out!" Raynor shouted to his men. Their fire was meant to cover his escape, but he wanted them to get the hell off the saddle and clear of the hornets' nest he'd just stumbled into.

He reached his team as their rifles spat fire. He felt the overpressure of their rounds as they whizzed inches from his head toward some unseen enemy behind him. He passed Rocky at a sprint, crossed the threshold of the ridgeline, and started down the other side. He slowed and turned to provide covering fire for his team's egress, unslung his short-barreled HK416 from his back and faced the valley. He lost his footing on the steep frozen earth and brittle shale and stumbled, just raised himself and his weapon back up when a mortar's thunderclap slammed into his chest. Light and heat enveloped him and he saw his boots leave the hill, his legs rise out in front of him, and he felt his head spin backward. He had a notion of just missing one of his team members' dropped rucksacks on the ground as he spun, crashed into the steep gradient and then bounced up, twisted sideways now and slammed onto his shoulder, rolled end over end down the hill, just missing boulders the height of automobiles and dragging down with him rocks the size of bowling balls.

Downward he rolled, no control as his arms and legs flailed in the air, the centrifugal force of his spin more powerful than his own muscles. His rifle twirled away from him and continued on its own descent, gear flung off his load-bearing vest and bounced along beside him, the rifle magazines and grenades that remained in their Velcro pouches buried themselves in his rib cage with each strike of the earth as he picked up more and more speed.

Close to the floor of the gorge now he suffered through one more whipping forward revolution, bounced awkwardly off his legs this time, and went completely airborne for several meters. He rotated through the air toward his back to try and cushion the impending blow.

His lower back and tailbone slammed into a massive stone, taking the full weight of his body and the full force of his motion.

He skidded off the side of the boulder and dropped four feet down to the cold earth, ending up on his back and staring at the sky.

Raynor heard the cracking of bones in his back and hip with the first impact, felt the continued crunching inside him as he came to rest.

Disoriented for several seconds, it took him a while to realize it, but as he tried to get up he found he could not feel his legs.

EIGHT

Kolt Raynor opened his eyes. He'd lost consciousness, he was sure, though he had no idea for how long. Frantically he reached out with his gloved hands in all directions. His fingers dug at the frozen dirt, wrenched brown grass out by the roots, slapped the sun-blanched boulder on his left hard while searching for his HK.

His rifle was gone, lost somewhere up the hillside.

His boots pointed toward the hill he'd just tumbled from. He lifted his head with a wince and scanned for his men. Tried to speak into his MBITR, but his microphone had been torn from his head in the fall.

He felt nothing below the waist, and with each frantic breath he registered unnatural movement in his rib cage.

A ringing in his ears subsided enough for him to realize that the mortar barrage had ceased. A new sound grabbed his attention, just louder than the crunching of his broken ribs as he took labored breaths.

Footsteps approaching.

Raynor pulled his Glock from the Velcro holster on his vest. Raised it toward the noise down by his feet.

Jet appeared around the edge of the boulder and dropped to his knees at his major's side.

"Damn it, Jet. I broke my back. Can't move my legs." Raynor thought Jet had come to render aid. He expected him to dive into his Combat Casualty Response Kit, but he did not.

Instead, Jet carried two rifles. Held the weapon in his left hand out for Major Raynor. It was a long-barreled HK416. Covered slick with thick red blood.

"Rock's gun?" Raynor asked as he took it, but he knew. Price painted yellow tick marks on the butt stock, one for each month he'd spent in Iraq or Afghanistan. Forty-one yellow lines showed from under the blood smears. "Where's Rock?"

"Dead. Can you fight?"

Kolt continued to battle the vertigo acquired during his fall. He fought confusion. "Fight? Fight who?"

"We got company."

"Company?"

"Bad guys. Me and Musket will hold the northern approach. Cover the ridgeline in case they try to flank us from the east."

"Roger that." Raynor was officially in command, but he lay on the cold dirt, flat on his back and bleary-eyed. He had no problem relinquishing authority to the two ambulatory operators still in the fight.

Jet disappeared back around the boulder.

For a moment all was quiet. Raynor squinted into the sun, now just barely rising above the hill in front of him and beaming into his eyes. He had Oakleys stowed in a pouch somewhere, but he did not bother to search for them. They were probably either crushed or lost up on the hill. Instead, he just lay there, tried to slow his breathing and to use what senses he had available to acquire threats.

Small-arms fire erupted to his left, hidden from view by the big stone that had shattered his back and pelvis. Multiple AKs burped at full auto and HKs snapped return fire in short controlled bursts or cracked single shots. Musket shouted out, an order barked to Jet. The medic answered back. Raynor could tell the two operators had positioned themselves far apart to divide the enemy's fire and attention and to cover for one another.

"Reloading!" shouted Jet after a minute.

"Covering!" replied Musket authoritatively.

Raynor raised himself to his elbows, tried to inch his way backward to get around the boulder to help. He felt so impotent positioned here, covering a quiet snow-dusted and brush-strewn hillside, with his two men screaming and battling for their lives just thirty meters off his left shoulder. After no more than a foot he dropped again, weakened by the agony in his back and rib cage. He looked down at Rocky's weapon. Raynor's gloves were stained bloodred.

The AK barrage picked up considerably. The rifle fire echoed through the gorge and bounced from all directions toward Kolt. It sounded as if a world war had erupted around him. A pair of low explosions that he recognized as golf ball–sized Mini Belgian frag grenades thrown by his men answered back.

The fighting continued for another minute. Then Musket called out. "Jet! Jet?"

When there was no response Kolt cried out to Sergeant First Class Lee as well. "Jet, you good?"

Then he shouted, "Musket! I'm coming around!" Major Raynor made it back to his elbows. Reached back and dug them into the dirt and shale, pulling himself another half foot. He dropped again in a cold sweat.

"Racer, hold fire," Musket said, and he appeared around the foot of the white rock. His nose and beard dripped blood from a cut between his eyebrows, but he moved quickly and confidently. Raynor just looked up at his master sergeant.

"Jet?"

"He's gone." The NCO slung his rifle and knelt down over his officer. Reached for Raynor's belt and began unbuckling his hip rig. "I'm gettin' you out of here."

"We can't leave Rock and Jet."

"And I can't carry all of you, Racer! Help me get your gear off."

"Comms?"

"Not down here in the basin. Now work with me, Raynor!" Just then, AK fire cracked to the north, and 7.62 mm rounds smacked against the boulder next to the two operators. "Wait one," Musket said. He stood and fired over the top of the boulder. Quickly dropped down to a squat behind the cover and reloaded his rifle as bullets whizzed over both men.

"How many?"

"Too many. Let's go." Master Sergeant Michael Overstreet made to reach under Kolt's armpits to lift him up, but Raynor pushed the hands away.

Raynor said, "No good. It'll take you twenty minutes to get me out of here. They'll be on us in two."

Overstreet looked down to Raynor. Nodded. "Right. Okay. You keep them off the hilltop. I'll take the north."

"No, Mike. Help me around the rock. I'll keep them back while you bug out. You can't help me."

"Negative, Racer. We'll hold out for the Rangers."

"Bagram doesn't even know we're in contact! Get the hell out of here!"

"I'm not leaving you, boss."

Raynor slammed his gloved fist into the cold dirt. "That's an order, Musket!"

"Then I guess I'll see you back at Bragg at my court-martial." Overstreet reached into Raynor's vest. Pulled a fresh mag from a pouch and reloaded Rocky's bloody weapon for Kolt. He lowered the gun back to Raynor's chest and held the half-empty magazine out for him to see. "Partial mag by your right hand." He placed the magazine on the ground on Raynor's right.

"I messed up, Mike."

Overstreet said, "These are tier-one AQ and that mortar fire was too accurate. They were expecting us. This was a trap."

"And I led us right into it."

"Yeah. Yeah, I reckon you did, but it was a fair call

you made." He spit into the snow. "Screw it, Racer. You and me. Blaze of glory and all that shit. Let's make 'em hurt."

Racer blinked cold salty sweat from his eyes. Nodded. "Roger that. Help me around the boulder."

"Just watch the hill." Musket spun away, headed back around the boulder in a crouch.

"Mike! Help me around the boulder! Mike!" Raynor called out in vain.

The shooting began immediately.

For a full minute Raynor listened to the long salvos of Kalashnikov rifles, followed by higher-pitched, staccato bursts from Overstreet's HK416. Twice Raynor called to the master sergeant but Musket did not reply. Twice Raynor tried to get around the boulder, but the pain in his back was too excruciating to bear.

With a sudden thought Kolt lowered his rifle to his chest, reached for a cord around his neck. On the end of it hung a morphine self-injector. He bit off the red safety cap, pushed the pen-sized injector against his thigh, and smashed the black plunger with his thumb. Instantly 20 milligrams of morphine entered his bloodstream.

In seconds he felt a wave of relief course through his body. The pain remained, but the edge had been taken off.

It was at this time he realized that the AKs, still belching steadily to the north, were no longer receiving answering fire.

"Musket? Musket?" No response.

Raynor winced with pain, lifted his HK over his

head, pointed it at the edge of the rock on that side, holding the weapon's grip with his left hand. With his right he hefted his pistol and pointed it at the other edge of the rock. This way he had both approaches around the boulder covered, though he could not look both up and down at the same time. The muted pain in his pelvis pulsed with his frantic heartbeat.

"Musket? Talk to me!"

Without sound nor warning a black-clad Arab leaped around the edge of the rock at Raynor's feet. The turbaned man's eyes widened and his short-barreled AK rose toward the prostrate American invader just two yards away.

Kolt's pistol cracked and jumped. Acrid wisps of smoke ejected behind three .40 caliber cartridges. The Arab's head snapped back and away and he fell to his knees. Slumped dead on his back.

Raynor sensed the second man, though he had heard nothing. With barely a glance the Delta operator fired a three-round burst from his rifle back over his head, spinning a similarly clad gunman 360 degrees before he fell facefirst, his rifle clanging against the sun-blanched boulder on the American's left.

As the AK came to rest next to him, another figure appeared at his feet. Raised a rifle toward him. Raynor's reaction time suffered from the morphine. He'd let his Glock sag to the ground but he lifted it and fired.

But the al Qaeda fighter fired first.

The Arab held his Kalashnikov at his hip and at three yards' distance blasted a burst that sent dirt and rocks and snow into the air between Kolt's splayed legs.

Raynor felt his right leg kick up and caught a brief glimpse of splattering blood in the air through the gun smoke of his own weapon.

Raynor pressed his Glock's trigger once, twice, five times before the enemy fell back and away screaming shrilly as he dropped dead in the snow.

Without taking time to check himself for wounds Raynor looked back over his head, expecting another attack from the west side of the boulder. Only when it did not come for several seconds did he look back down to assess himself.

Propped on his elbows he saw the red hole torn in his boot at the instep, a growing pool of blood forming in the snow just below his knee, and a third blood-speckled gouge on the outside of his right thigh. The AK-47 had stitched up his leg, though even with the horror of this realization the professional in Raynor was thankful to see no gushing arterial spray.

Though he had already been incapacitated, he was now even more so, surrounded and alone and bleeding and weakened by the morphine. He dropped down on his back and looked up to the sky. There, on his back, he executed a tactical reload, topping off his pistol with a fresh magazine. The action was accomplished through pure muscle memory.

He was furious for allowing himself to be shot. Furious with the dead man at his feet who'd shot him. "Son of a bitch!"

Now he heard noises on the other side of the rock. They were converging on him. Three at least. Perhaps many more. Raynor dropped his pistol and reached into his vest. Pulled a Mini Belgian frag. First he fumbled with the duct tape securing the pin, his doped-up dexterity making even this petty action a complicated chore. He concentrated his diminished faculties and finally freed the pin. Then he tore it out of the grenade with his teeth.

"Frag out, Musket!" He let the spoon fly, and the explosive sputtered a moment in his trembling hand as he let a few seconds cook off. He lobbed it over the rock.

The explosion on the other side sent brush and snow over the top of the boulder.

Raynor lobbed a second and then a third grenade. Each one a little farther away. Each time he called, "Frag out!" If any of his teammates were still alive, maybe they would be able to scramble to cover.

When he had lobbed all his frags he hefted his pistol again and covered both approaches, expecting at any moment a dozen men to converge.

Thirty seconds, and nothing.

A minute, still no attack.

This was good, and it was also standard operating procedure for the enemy. The Taliban and al Qaeda both were well acquainted with American close-air support tactics. Their attacks were furious and intense, but they were virtually always short-lived. They had learned to expect that if they stuck around in a firefight, within a matter of minutes, death would rain down on them with a vengeance.

Raynor holstered his pistol on his chest rig and slung Rocky's rifle around his neck. Back up on his elbows, he scooted backward with all the strength in his shoulders. Most of the pain in his back was gone now, adrenaline and morphine masking the wreckage of his body for the time being. Kolt took advantage of the lull in his agony and reached back with his elbows to find wedges between the white stones of the dry stream bed, and then pulled himself backward by his elbows. In urban terrain he wore hard-plastic elbow pads, and he wished he had them now. Three times he looked down to his feet and saw that some of his blood had smeared across a sun-whitened river stone. And three times he scooted forward, grabbed the stone, and flipped it over or tossed it to the side. He knew he could not remove all evidence of his evasion route, but hiding or dispersing the most obvious markers of his trail was better than nothing.

As he crept backward, his elbows shredding against the hard stones, Raynor kept his eyes on the northern approach. He saw a dozen or more bodies strewn along the dry riverbed, the rocky bank, and the grassy hillside. Among them would be Jet and Musket and Rock, but Raynor did not dwell to pinpoint his dead men. The enemy had backed off for a moment, but he knew they would likely regroup and attack again in force when no planes appeared in the clear sky. After he'd traveled twenty-five meters he reached the far bank of the stream bed. He continued, and though the exhaustion in his shoulders slowed him, he did not stop his pathetic retreat. Without looking back he made his way into some thick brush, pushed through it until his feet were covered with foliage, and continued on until he reached the beginning of the hillside. Here he stopped, lay back under the meager protection of the snowy thicket, and feebly attempted to dress his thigh wound. The holes in his shin and his foot would just have to bleed. He could not reach them and he could not lift his legs up closer to his hands.

The morphine put him slowly to sleep. Shortly before losing consciousness he heard voices across the dry stream. Arabic and Pashto. Men shouting out in exultation, praising their god for their blessed victory. The unmistakable cry of "Allah-hu Akbar!" God is Great!

NINE

Major Kolt Raynor realized he was in a helicopter from the vibrating sound and the prevalent smell of fuel, but he had no idea how he had come to be there. Turning his head slowly from side to side, he saw mud-slicked tan combat boots. When he tried to lift his head to look around, he realized he was on the floor and strapped onto a backboard with a neck brace. He was wrapped in a blanket, and tubes ran into his arm. His right leg lay outside the blanket. A medic knelt over him and bandaged his foot. His thigh and shin were already shrouded in dressings.

He'd been administered IV drugs, this was clear, because he felt no pain, only the cold in the thin air and the vibration of the helo's engines. A dozen Rangers sat around him on the floor, their backs pressed against the thin walls of the aircraft. Their uniforms and gear were government-issued, in stark contrast to his own clothing and equipment. The Rangers looked impossibly young and clean-cut in the red light of the cabin.

He looked down and realized that the man treating him was Benji, a baby-faced Delta operator from Raynor's squadron. He then noticed another operator looking out a portal of the Chinook with his rifle cradled in his arms. Master Sergeant David "Monk" Kraus stared into the night. Behind Monk, on the floor of the helo, Raynor saw three black body bags stacked one on top of the other.

He blinked and looked away.

Benji must have noticed that his patient had awakened. He shouted over the chopper's engines. "How you holding up, Racer?"

"Can't feel my legs." His words felt fat and slow in his mouth, an effect of the drugs coursing through him.

"Yeah, your lumbar is broken. Most likely the snap just bruised your spinal cord. If you're lucky you'll get your feeling back in a few days. You also caught three in the leg. Lost two quarts of blood, but we're filling you back up. You're outta here. Going to Ramstein as soon as we get up to Bagram and get you on a transport."

"Where's T.J.?" Raynor asked. Although T.J.'s Eagle 01 element was not part of the Quick Reaction Force, they had been staged three hours closer to the border than this Ranger/Delta QRF. Raynor had assumed that if anyone had been able to rescue him, it would have been his friend.

Benji looked down at Racer. Said nothing.

Now Monk appeared over Raynor's immobilized head. Dropped down on his kneepads, leaned closer still. Even in the dim, red-tinged cabin, Raynor could see malevolence in the master sergeant's eyes. He and Musket were best friends.

But there was something more.

Monk said, "The JOC ordered up the QRF at 0900 after they intercepted AQ radio traffic saying the Taliban engaged American commandos. But T.J. didn't want to wait. He talked an Mi-17 chopper at his safe house into taking Eagle 01 over the border to your ROD. They couldn't find you, so they flew to your rendezvous point. On the way the chopper took an RPG to the prop. They tried to make it back over the border, but they lost control. They went down hard in the Tochi River four klicks north of where we found you. The UAV overhead didn't see anyone surface. We asked the Pak Army to help us search for survivors, but they're plenty pissed about the incursion, and it's not like they've got control of that area of operations. The river is fast and deep and runs through a hundred miles of bandit country. We've been told we're to make no more cross-border incursions unless we have positive proof of life. We've got two UAVs overhead, but it looks like T.J. and the rest of Eagle 01 are dead, along with the two Agency pilots."

"Oh my God," Raynor said.

"God didn't have anything to do with it. Did you vacate your ROD site, Racer?"

"We were ambushed."

"In your ROD?"

Raynor looked up at the ceiling of the chopper. For

the first time since puberty, tears welled in his eyes. "Negative. I moved us forward."

"Then all this shit is on you."

Kolt nodded slowly. Closed his eyes. He knew his reasons for moving ahead had been sound, but it did not matter now. "I know," he said softly.

Monk turned away, returned to his seat by the door.

After a week of intensive care in the hospital at Ramstein Air Force Base in Germany, and a further three months of inpatient treatment at Duke Medical Center in North Carolina, the majority of Raynor's physical wounds had healed. Surgeons fused two vertebrae, and sensation and mobility returned to his legs. But while in the hospital, it was hard not to notice that visits by his chain of command were nearly nonexistent, and visits by teammates in-country were few and far between. He knew his decisions in Pakistan would be harshly criticized, but he also knew the OPTEMPO of his squadron kept the boys busy. He assumed it was the latter that was keeping his comrades away. But his mates who did drop in to check on him shared very little about their current activities, and this Raynor found strange. Strange that after three and a half months, he knew little more about what had happened to Eagle 01 than he'd learned from Monk on the recovery helo.

Soon enough it became clear to him. He was no longer "one of the boys." As a Delta troop commander, he had always been audacious and aggressive. His superiors and subordinates had admired the ease with which Raynor seemed to fall into the shit and crawl back out smelling like a rose. But this time it was too much. Lieutenant Colonel Josh Timble and the five men who went down with him were missing and presumed dead, and when he finally returned to Fort Bragg, Major Kolt Raynor found his wall locker in his team room cleaned out and a maelstrom of incrimination and charges awaiting him. That he would be cashiered from Delta was never in doubt. No matter the extenuating circumstances, he had disobeyed a direct order and nine men had died as a result of his insubordination. A court-martial was considered, but all agreed that Raynor should be dismissed from the Army, quietly and quickly.

The Army he could live without, but the Unit declared him persona non grata, and this devastated him. Four months to the day after his ill-fated operation in South Waziristan, Major Kolt Raynor became, for the first time in eighteen years, simply Kolt Raynor, a man who had lost much more than a title before his name.

TEN

Three years later Raynor lay on the mattress on the floor of his trailer. Dressed only in his underwear, his body was covered in sweat that stank, though he didn't notice, so accustomed had he become to his own stench. Morning light poured through the blinds in bright linear shafts and he recoiled from its sting. His long hair hung askew and his T-shirt retained the colors and smells of the microwavable Chinese dinner he'd polished off just before nodding off the night before.

He looked across the room at his clock, squinted to bring the green numbers into focus, and determined it was either ten after six or ten after eight. If it was the former he could go back to sleep; if it was the latter, he was in trouble.

He had to get up and go to work this morning.

Shit. Kolt closed his eyes.

His money had run out and with it all but the last of the booze, so now it was back to his old job, selling sleeping bags and climbing equipment at an upscale sporting-goods store in Southern Pines.

He had to be at work at nine, and he had either slept through his 6 a.m. alarm or forgotten again to set it, and now he was too hungover to even tell the time.

A knock on the door caused him to lift his eyes, but not to get up. He hadn't heard a car pull up the gravel drive to his trailer, but in his current state his senses were hardly at their sharpest.

It came again. A pounding this time. Kolt rolled onto his side, his head hanging off the edge of the dirty mattress. He wasn't expecting company, didn't have any friends or owe anyone money.

"Hang on!" he shouted, fought with his covers to try and sit up.

With a crash the aluminum door flew in, a big black leather boot behind it, the cheap plastic blinds fell off the window, and the entire trailer rocked as if it had been hit by a bus. The upper hinge of the door broke free. The lower hinge held, but the door sagged deeper as the soft aluminum bent.

Raynor bolted upright.

David "Monk" Kraus stood in the doorway. Kolt hadn't seen the Delta master sergeant since the night over western Pakistan, three years earlier, but he looked exactly the same, save for his clothes. Gone was his military uniform. Instead he wore a rust-colored flannel lumberjack shirt and faded blue jeans. He stepped inside and cleared the doorway, and Benji entered behind him.

They both looked down at Kolt, at the bottles on the floor, at the shitty living arrangements.

"What the hell?" was all Raynor could think to say. He remained on the mattress against the wall.

"Get your ass up," growled Monk.

"What's going on?"

"We're taking you to see somebody."

Kolt did not move, recovered a bit from the shock of the intrusion. "And if I don't want to go with you?"

"Nobody is asking what you want." Monk kicked a bottle out of the way as he approached. It was a short walk to the opposite wall of the trailer.

Raynor made it to his feet, wobbled a bit. "I don't know who the hell you think you are, but—"

"Are you drunk?"

"What? No. I'm a little hungover, but I—"

Monk looked to Benji. "Find the bathroom, start the shower. Ice-cold." The baby-faced blond-haired operator disappeared up the tiny hall to the little bathroom. The water started in seconds.

"Back off! I can take my own damn shower. Just tell me what's going—"

But Monk grabbed Kolt by the arm, turned him toward the bathroom, and pushed him forward.

Kolt could have fought—even in his present state he was no shrinking violet—but Monk had him beat in speed, size, and sobriety. In fact, the master sergeant was so overbearing that Raynor found himself intimidated, and did what he was told.

Three minutes later, with Benji and Monk standing by the door and watching his every move, a shivering

Kolt Raynor kicked around in the clothes on the floor, found a pair of khakis that were not too wrinkled and a sweater that was not too stained. He pulled them on, toweled off his shaggy hair, and grabbed his wallet, cell phone, and keys off the tiny kitchen counter. The icy cold shower had awakened him, but a pang of nausea in his chest and stomach remained. He wanted to lie back down, but instead he followed the two Delta operators out the broken door and down the drive to Monk's pickup truck.

In the cab no one spoke for several minutes as Monk drove south. Kolt assumed he was being taken into Fort Bragg, though he could not fathom why, unless it had something to do with what had happened off the coast of Somalia. But when the truck headed east on Highway 1, passing the turnoff to go south to the base, Raynor began with the questions.

"Where we going?"

"I told you," said Monk. "Somebody wants to talk to you."

"But not somebody from the Unit?"

Benji broke in. "Just sit tight, Racer."

"I haven't done anything."

Monk chuckled angrily. "That's for damn sure."

Soon they were heading north on Highway 22. It was a clear and cool September morning. The green hills rose and fell on both sides of them. For a moment Kolt thought they were taking him to the Moore Country Airport, but the truck shot on by the turnoff at seventy miles an hour.

"What's in Carthage?" Kolt asked. It was the next

town to the north, but it was small, and Raynor did not really suspect it to be their destination.

So he was surprised when Monk responded, "Somebody who wants to take a look at you. If he doesn't like what he sees, and I expect he won't, we'll take you back to that shit hole you call home and drop you off. You can fix your own damn door."

Shortly after 9 a.m. they turned into a cheap motel just off the road. Monk drove around to the back and pulled up next to the only two cars in the lot. Benji got out of the cab, motioned for Kolt to lead the way to the door just in front of the two cars.

Kolt found the door unlocked.

He entered, followed by the two Delta operators, but only after they scanned the parking lot and the grove of trees behind it for several seconds. Once inside the two-bedroom unit, Monk shut the door, enshrouding the three men in low light.

Kolt stood in front of the TV and looked around for some explanation of what was going on. Monk and Benji just stood there with him in the dimness. Raynor said, "If you guys start taking your clothes off, I'm going headfirst out that window."

Benji burst out in surprised laughter. Monk rolled his eyes, opened his mouth to say something, but a gentle rapping at the access door to the adjoining room interrupted him. Monk pushed by Raynor and opened the door.

Benji flipped on a lamp on the table between the beds.

A man in jeans and a denim work shirt entered the

hotel room from the next unit. Kolt's body stiffened immediately.

Colonel Jeremy Webber, the commander of Delta Force, stood in front of him. Raynor had not seen Webber since court-martial proceedings against him were dropped. He'd never seen him out of uniform, and he'd never seen him off base unless they were deployed in a combat zone. Standing in a fleabag motel and wearing clothes that looked like they had been bought at a discount store only added to the shock and confusion of this morning.

Behind Webber, Pete Grauer, Kolt's former Ranger commander, and former employer, stepped into the room.

"Take a seat, Racer," Webber said. He did not offer his hand. His voice was gentle for a man obviously fit and formidable, but the fifty-year-old's eyes were stern and serious.

Raynor sat on the edge of the bed nearest the door. The other four men in the room remained standing over him.

Webber eyed the former major for a long time in the shadowed light. Looked him up and down, as if Raynor were on sale at a cattle auction. "Worse than I thought."

Kolt said nothing.

Grauer observed, "He's definitely out of shape."

Monk nodded. "He's a waste case, sir. He's useless."

Colonel Webber frowned, gave a half nod. "You could be right. I must admit I wasn't expecting this level of . . . decay."

Kolt looked back and forth at the men. "I'm sitting right here. You want to tell me what's going on?"

Webber said, "I brought you here to beg you to do something, but now I think I need you to beg me to *let you* do something."

Kolt shrugged. "Whatever it is, I've got to get to work."

"At the camping store? Expecting a mad midmorning rush on tent pegs?"

He shrugged again, defensively. "It's a job."

Grauer asked, "How much are you drinking these days, son?"

Kolt didn't answer.

"How's your leg?" This time it was Webber.

"Fine."

"How's your back?"

"It hurts."

Webber reached into the front pocket of his denim shirt, pulled out a few folded sheets, and opened them up. Kolt got the impression that this was all just for show, that Webber knew what was printed on them. "Your doctor says, 'Mr. Raynor's post-op radiography is consistent with a complete recovery, but patient complains of persistent midline LBP.' " Webber looked up at Kolt. "Low back pain, I suppose." Then he continued: " 'His refusal to comply with physical therapy seems to be the basis of his continued discomfort.' " He looked up at Raynor again. "You don't do your PT?"

Kolt shrugged, slowly. "I get the feeling the VA didn't send you to check on my back."

"No, they did not." Webber put the papers back in his pocket. Sat down on the bed across from Raynor, so close that their knees almost touched. Grauer and the two Delta operators remained standing. "Son, how would you like to go back to Pakistan?"

Kolt chuckled, shook his head. "No, thanks." But after a hesitation, he asked, "Why?"

The colonel leaned closer still. "Racer, you and I have had our disagreements in the past. That may be putting it mildly. I think you screwed the pooch in Waziristan, and I did what I had to do to get you out of my outfit. But whatever your faults and past mistakes, I have always considered you to be a man of principle and character."

Raynor just stared back at him.

"I say all that to say this: What I am about to tell you does not leave this room. You never came here today, and you sure as hell did not meet with me today. I want your word that you will keep this to yourself, no matter what."

"Yes, sir."

Webber nodded, sighed. "Here is the situation. Langley, the Pentagon, and the White House have known for the past eighteen months that most, if not all, the members of Eagle 01, Lieutenant Colonel Timble's element that went missing on the SAR mission for you . . . are alive and being held in captivity in Pakistan."

Kolt sat on the bed. His eyes flicked from Webber, to Grauer, and then to Monk and Benji.

"T.J.?"

"Was alive as of three months ago, and is thought to remain so at present."

"Mother of God."

ELEVEN

Raynor began to stand, stopped, sat back down. "How do you know?"

"About a year after your ill-fated operation, our Predator attacks on Taliban and al Qaeda leadership started picking up. We . . . well, the Agency mostly, was making significant progress on killing their tier-one guys, leadership and military-wing operatives. The drones were hitting them pretty hard, and pretty successfully, for a good six months. Then a package arrived in the mail at our consulate in Lahore. Inside, we found pictures of all four of our missing operators and one of the Agency pilots who disappeared with them. Proof-of-life photos. Holding newspapers, guns to their head, Taliban standing behind them. All that nonsense."

Raynor looked down to the ground, balled his fists. "You are saying this intelligence came to us a year and a half ago and we haven't gotten them back yet?"

Webber held a hand out. "Settle down and listen up. The message that came along with the photos was clear. They were going to drag our men along in chains wherever AQ or senior Taliban leadership was. A Predator strike just might kill them."

"Human shields," Kolt muttered.

"Exactly. And to tell you the truth, it worked. The Agency kept up the rate of Predator hits, but the target matrix changed. Instead of hitting leadership we started taking out Toyota vans full of AQ foot soldiers and second- and third-tier Taliban, local commanders, political-wing guys. Logistical convoys were targeted, small-potatoes stuff that we calculated would not jeopardize the captured operators. We backed off on targeting the big fish, and consequently the Taliban and AQ in Pakistan have grown in both power and quality over the past eighteen months.

"When the SEALs got bin Laden in Abbottabad, we were afraid that our boys would be killed by AQ in retaliation. But it didn't happen. We suspect they were in the hands of the Taliban at the time, or else, and this is still a concern, the AQ leadership has some other plan for Eagle 01.

"Of course, we were prepared to go in after the boys if we spotted them. And we did. A Reaper drone got a positive ID of Eagle 01 eleven months ago. They were being held by the Taliban commander of Swat Agency in a compound near the city of Mingora. We put together a ground operation, Langley put assets in place to help out locally, and we were ready to go. Our objective was to keep Pakistani intelligence out of the operation, but the White House wouldn't hear of it. We were forced to work with the ISI, and by the time we hit the compound, the Taliban had melted into the city with our men."

"Shit."

"The next day the four Agency assets were shot to death in their car in Mingora."

Kolt remained stone-faced as he shook his head slowly in frustration.

Webber said, "Pakistani intelligence says it was a random act of street crime."

"Bullshit."

Webber shrugged. "Five months ago Eagle 01 was identified by human intelligence up in Chitral. This time we weren't allowed in. Instead the Pakistani army went after them."

"And?"

"And they walked into an ambush. Thirty-one Pakistani forces killed versus no more than five Taliban. Our boys weren't there. Probably never were."

"Sounds like a setup."

Webber nodded. "From the get-go. They are not only using our men as human shields, they are also using them as bait. Drawing us, or in that case the Pakistani army, into fights they know they can win.

"We've had close to a dozen sightings or indications of the hostages' whereabouts over the past five months, but nothing actionable by the standards of the White House."

"But we think they are still alive?"

"We're just about sure of it."

"Go on," said Kolt. There was a reason he was here.

Webber turned to Grauer, and Grauer spoke. "As you probably know, my company, your ex-employer, Radiance Security and Surveillance Systems, has a large operation in Afghanistan."

"Sure. At Jalalabad."

"Right. We also have some assets over the border in Pakistan, working under cover."

"Private spies?"

"After a fashion, yes. Just a few men. Ex this and ex that. They report to me and my analysts and provide us with information that helps us fulfill our contracts with the Afghani government. One of these operatives is based in Peshawar. Recently he received some intelligence indicating that T.J. and his men are being kept at a warlord's compound nearby."

Raynor nodded. That sounded pretty thin.

"We have a couple of Predator drones in our fleet. Two nights ago I sent one over the border, thirty miles into Pakistan, to check out this compound."

"And?"

"The UAV pilot found the place, found it crawling with possible Taliban, but we were unable to get eyes on the prisoners."

"Then go back. Try again."

"We've been back. We can't be sure this is the place from overhead images. The human intelligence that says the prisoners are being kept there also indicates that the men will be there through the coming winter, so we do have a little time to keep an eye on it."

Raynor was confused. “So why didn’t the Agency send their own Predators over?”

Grauer answered. “They’ve burned the agent in Peshawar who works for me. Deemed him unreliable, so they aren’t putting stock in what he says. Moreover, the Agency and the DOD are letting Radiance work on this. Nothing in writing, of course, but they are allowing us to use our resources to fish around western Pakistan.”

“So you need more intelligence on this warlord and his compound. What do you know about him?”

Webber said, “His name is Zar. He’s an Afridi Pashtun tribal leader. He runs a militia. Three hundred or so strong, not huge, but one of the biggest in the Khyber region. They aren’t Taliban, per se, but Zar has aligned himself and his force with the Taliban when it suits his needs.”

“Who cares whether or not he’s Taliban? If he’s holding Americans—”

Webber shook his head. “It’s too big an if for the White House. In order to get authorization for a Delta hit on Zar’s fortress we’re going to have to produce more evidence than secondhand info from some Agency washout and an illegal overflight by a private security drone.”

Kolt leaned back slowly. Looked at Colonel Webber. “What are you looking for, exactly?”

Webber stared at Raynor for a long time. Softly he said, “Eyes on that compound. Proof of life of our men.”

“But Delta can’t do it, because you guys can’t go over the border.”

Webber nodded.

"Radiance?"

Grauer started to speak up but Colonel Jeremy Webber shook his head. "They don't have an asset with experience in that type of covert recon work."

It all came together completely for Kolt in a heartbeat. Like on the last page of a confounding mystery novel, the pieces fell into place and he knew why he was there, what his role would be in all of this. He said, "*I* am going over the border. Aren't I?"

Webber shrugged. "That was my original thinking. We need someone who can jump in from altitude, get into the valley, meet up with Pete's contact, get eyes on the compound, and remain there for several days. Looking at you now . . . I'm not sure how feasible that would be."

Raynor spoke without an instant's hesitation. "I can do it."

"He can't. *I* can, sir. Send me," Monk barked from behind in the dark.

Webber didn't even turn to look back. "We've talked about this, David. You are active. No active operator is going over the border without White House sanction."

"I'll resign from Delta."

"The hell you will." Webber addressed Raynor now. "We've got a bit of a time constraint. Weather will begin to deteriorate in Khyber in about a month. Plus key Radiance personnel are due to rotate home for Christmas. It's the slow time of year in the Afghani poppy-eradication industry, I guess. We could keep a couple of guys in place, but if everyone changed their holiday travel plans at the last minute, then that would raise eyebrows that we don't want to raise, both on our side and on theirs."

"So when am I going?" Kolt asked.

"*If* you go . . . you'll need to be over the border in three to four weeks."

"I'll do it tomorrow. You *know* I will. Let's get on with it."

"Calm down, Racer," Webber admonished. "If we decide that you are our man, then we have time to give you, say, three weeks of training: PT and firearms, altitude acclimation, language, time to get you reacquainted with the mission-specific gear you'd be using. Then another couple of days to get you in theater and briefed on the specifics of your operation."

"Plenty of time."

"No," interrupted Monk. "For Raynor, three weeks is not enough time to train for this job. Doubt we can even have him sobered up in three weeks."

Kolt was tired of Monk's constant barbs. His friend was out there in the badlands of Pakistan, and no one was going to stop him from going to help bring him back. He stood up and stepped forward. Monk moved to meet him, and Kolt stood face-to-face with the master sergeant. Raynor spoke in his long forgotten officer's voice, channeling his Ranger career more than his Delta career.

"What is your problem with me, Kraus? If the colonel says I can do the job, then I can do the job!"

Monk balled his thick fists, did not shrink from the voice or the gaze of the former major.

"Settle down, both of you!" Webber shouted. Kolt sat back down slowly; Kraus relaxed his fingers, but did not back up. The colonel continued, his voice having regained its previous tenor. He turned to Grauer, the former Ranger colonel. "Pete. It's your mission. It's your call."

"Kolt certainly isn't my first choice, but he *is* my first choice among the available operators."

"Thank you, sir," said Raynor, still staring angrily at Monk.

Webber nodded gravely. "All right. Kolt, if you are in, you are in all the way. I will give you one more chance, right now, to back out. If you tell me that you want to go ahead, then you are with us—your free will will be on hold until the reconnaissance on Zar's village is complete. Monk and Benji will train you, push you to your very limits, much further than you would be able to go *without* their boots on your ass. You can just consider yourself back in Assessment and Selection. We need to see if you have what it takes."

Raynor took a long breath, let it out slowly, and nodded again. "That's the only way this can work, Colonel. I will do my best."

Monk said, "Your best isn't going to get it, Raynor. I'll get more out of you than that."

Webber admonished his operator. "That's enough, Monk. Racer is going to give you everything he's got, which means the ultimate success is *your* responsibility."

"I will not let you down, sir," said Kolt, and then he looked at Grauer. "Either of you."

"Then it's settled," Colonel Webber said.

Raynor nodded, said, "Not that I really care, but is this a one-way trip, or is there a way out of Pakistan for me after I do the recon?"

Grauer thought about his response for a few seconds. He replied, "That all depends on you. We can get you in, and we can get you out if you don't get compromised while you're there."

"Delta is going to come in and get me?"

Webber said, "Absolutely not. This recon operation has nothing to do with the Unit. I need you to be one hundred percent clear on that, son."

Kolt nodded, but said, "You can forgive my confusion, sir, seeing how there are three Delta men in front of me laying this all out, and one of them is the current commander."

"I am not here. I have not spoken to you since your court-martial hearing. Benji and Monk are on personal time, and will be for the length of your training."

Pete Grauer said, "When you are in Pakistan you will be handled by Bob Kopelman, a Radiance employee."

Kolt nodded. "The guy in Peshawar?"

Webber nodded. "The ex–CIA case officer that I mentioned."

"And you mentioned he was a washout," Kolt answered back.

"*You're* a washout too, Kolt. We're going to do this with what we have available to us."

Raynor nodded with a shrug.

Grauer added, "Kopelman is low pro there, operating

for Radiance while holding down cover employment. He's a bit of a rogue, but he's a good man. He'll get you back home."

Kolt nodded. "Sounds good."

Webber stood. "Kolt, regardless of what happens, you and I won't be speaking again. Good luck. Go get eyes on our men, so we can get the go-ahead to pull them out of there."

Raynor stood and the two men shook hands. It wasn't particularly warm, and Webber looked like he had more reservations than resolve regarding the entire scenario. He turned to Grauer. "Colonel, he's all yours." Without another glance at Kolt, Colonel Jeremy Webber left via the access door to the next room.

Grauer said, "Monk and Benji will handle your day-to-day training. I'll have a language instructor work with you on your Pashto."

"Yes, sir."

Monk stepped forward reluctantly. "Don't suppose you've been in any altitude recently?"

Kolt just shook his head.

Monk sighed. "We'll need to get you up to about eight thousand feet, get your body used to it. Send you up higher after a few days. We'll do your training at that altitude, make you ready for Pakistan."

"So we're going over immediately then? To Afghanistan, I mean?"

"Nope. We'll train in Wyoming."

"The Hole?" Kolt had done his high-altitude training with the Unit in Jackson Hole.

"No. We'll take you to a place about fifty miles southeast. The Wind River Range. Know it?"

Kolt shook his head. He'd done a ton of camping, climbing, and backpacking in his life but had never made it to that part of the Rockies.

"Rough country. Khyber without the hajjis. There's a boarded-up dude ranch in a valley at eight thousand feet. The peaks all around are between eleven and fourteen thousand. We have a relationship with the owner. Three weeks running your fat ass up and down those mountains will get you back in shape." Monk paused. "If it doesn't kill you, I mean."

Master Sergeant David "Monk" Kraus had a hopeful glint in his eye that filled Raynor with unease.

TWELVE

Five hours later Kolt was at thirty-five thousand feet over Tennessee, sitting shoulder to shoulder with Benji in the back of a Maverick Cruiser, a five-seat VLJ, or very light jet. The diminutive aircraft was flown by a civilian pilot, and Monk sat in the copilot position. The plane was owned by Grauer, and it wore the Radiance Security logo on its tail.

The emotions going through Kolt's mind during the day had kept him from thinking about himself and his own needs. But as he sat in the leather cabin chair, his head back on the rest and the humming of the engines relaxing him for the first time since he'd been rudely awakened that morning, his thoughts turned inward. He worried about how he'd be able to handle the training, the mountains, the lack of cheap bourbon. Any sacrifice would be a small price to pay for helping to get T.J. and the boys home—it was not a risk-versus-reward conversation going on inside him. No, it was a true question of his own capabilities, now, after so much time had passed since he'd been at his best.

And he wanted a drink.

A touch on his right shoulder caused him to open his eyes. Benji leaned in close, a toothpick hanging from his mouth, and a serious look on his boyish face.

"Hey, Racer. You ready for lunch?"

"Are you the stewardess?"

Benji grinned. "Well, Monk thinks he's a copilot, so yeah, guess so." The master sergeant shrugged. "Nah, I just want to make sure you got some food in you before we touch down. It's a couple hours' ride in a 4×4 from the airfield. Ain't gonna be no Mickey D's along the way."

"Is this good cop, bad cop?"

"What do you mean?"

"Monk wants to rip my throat out, and you want to make sure I'm eating right."

Benji nodded thoughtfully. "I like you okay. Monk doesn't. That's real. We ain't paid enough to do no acting."

Benji turned in his seat to face Raynor in the tiny cabin. Then he looked over his shoulder at Monk to make sure he had his headset on and could not hear. "Look, man. Kraus hates your ass."

Kolt stared at Benji with feigned shock. "Really? He hides it pretty well."

"I'm serious. Mike Overstreet and him were as tight as they come. 'Bout like you and T.J."

"I know."

"I figure it sticks in Monk's craw that his job is to get you prepped to go help rescue T.J., when Musket's pushing daisies up at Arlington."

Raynor just nodded.

Benji continued. "Don't get me wrong. He wants those guys back . . . just doesn't like the fact that they are using you. He's going to push you past what's necessary." Benji hesitated. Then said, "He wants to hurt you, bro."

Kolt looked out the tiny portal; clouds below obstructed his view of the land. "Well, I guess the next three weeks are the perfect opportunity for him to do just that." He smiled ruefully to himself. "My ass is his."

They landed in Dubois, Wyoming, a little before two in the afternoon. A muddy white four-wheel-drive Ford Expedition was waiting for them in the small parking lot. A fit-looking young man stood at the open tailgate. He shook hands with Benji and Monk, handed them heavy winter coats though the temperature hovered in the high forties. He was introduced to Raynor as Tim, but they did not shake hands. Tim turned to shut the hatch, then climbed back behind the wheel. Kolt took a moment before getting into the car. To the east he could see the incredible mountain range reaching with its sheer peaks into the expansive gray sky. It looked like Afghanistan. Like Spin Ghar, like the Khyber Pass. Kolt had been to the Rockies numerous times, and he practically lived in the Smokies. This range before him hit the nail on the head as a stand-in for Pakistan in a way the others did not.

It looked like danger.

They drove for nearly two hours, first on a highway, but that soon gave way to a paved road with switchbacks like ribbon candy as it ascended into the foothills. Wet pines and firs and steep gray rock cliffs took over the view out the back window next to Kolt as they entered the Wind River Range. He was offered a package of Mexican rice from a standard MRE and he took it. His body began to tighten in anticipation of the beginning of his training, which he assumed would get under way the following morning. Already he could feel the altitude in his chest, knew he would be weaker for the first few days, and hoped he'd be given a reasonable amount of understanding from the cadre of trainers in charge of prepping him for his mission.

The fatigue set in quickly, nearly lulling Kolt to sleep in the back of the warm truck as it bounced and splashed on rocky off-road trails that had clearly seen better days. It was no wonder to Raynor that the hotel/dude ranch that would be his home had ceased operations. It was no easy feat just to get to the place.

Finally the ranch appeared off the nose of the truck, lower in a wide valley of brown grass and long, wide swampy lowlands. It was a large complex, built log-cabin style but sprawled across a gentle rise. It was still a half mile off, but Monk told the driver to stop in the road. To the left of the truck was a relatively steep earthen incline dotted with pine trees that went up a hundred yards before the gradient lessened. Beyond that a thirteen-thousand-foot snowcapped mountain disappeared into the mist. To the right of the truck was a thick pine forest; the clearing with the ranch began just ahead.

Monk opened his door and slid out. Looked into the tinted window at Raynor without speaking, until finally Kolt popped his door latch and climbed out himself. He stood with his hands on his hips in front of the master sergeant on the muddy road.

"We aren't going to the ranch?" Raynor asked, confused.

"The truck is. You aren't," declared Monk. "The cadre training you for the next three weeks will be staying there. You will have language study and a three-hour class there each day related to the mission. But no, you won't be bedding down in a hotel. You think you're heading to a B and B in Pakistan?"

Kolt did not answer.

The master sergeant stepped to the back of the Expedition, dropped the tailgate, and rolled a huge rucksack out of the back. He let it fall into the pooled rainwater and icy mud in the road. "Here's your shit, Raynor. Same shit, more or less, that you'll have in Khyber."

Kolt looked at the pack but made no move toward it. Monk continued. "I want to find your camp up above the snow line tomorrow morning. Have some coffee ready for me and Benji at 0600."

Raynor had no idea what was in the rucksack, but he hoped like hell there was some sort of a coat. It was down into the thirties already, and his jeans and fleece sweatshirt would not keep him alive overnight.

Kraus climbed back into the front passenger seat, but rolled down the window. "By the by, there's an AK and a Glock in the bag. Mags loaded with Simunition ammo. I suggest you arm yourself ASAP and get some eye-pro on. You could be hit by opfor at any time." The window rose and the muddy white truck began rolling forward toward the ranch.

Huh?

Kolt knew Simunitions were training rounds that fired from real converted weapons but left only a nasty and painful blister and a big splotch of paint on their target. He didn't know what Monk meant by an opposition force, but assumed his training would include force-on-force encounters with some sort of simulated enemy. As the truck disappeared around a bend down the hill he knelt over the big brown bag and unzipped the main compartment. Inside were basic camping and cold-weather gear and, as promised, two converted weapons, both stripped down to their component parts. Raynor dragged the big ruck of gear off the side of the road to a flat rock and began laying it out, hoping to find bulky things that he could discard before heading up the mountain. He'd just slipped a thin but warm wool base layer thermal over his head when he heard a noise a few yards behind him. Like metal scuffing against rock.

Then the pop of a small explosion. White smoke billowed into the air on the road.

A smoke grenade.

What the hell?

He turned and saw, maybe fifty yards back up the road toward Dubois, four men moving toward his position. They wore the black garb of the Taliban, and they carried Kalashnikovs.

A wave of panic swept over his body. In an instant he was back in Pakistan, facing the enemy that had nearly killed him.

Quickly Kolt slipped polycarbonate glasses over his eyes. Being shot in the eye with a simulated round would cause almost as much damage as a real bullet. A second later he focused on the pieces of the Glock pistol, not because it was the best weapon with which to engage four men with rifles, but because it had fewer parts and he could assemble it quickly. He grabbed the frame, the slide, the barrel, and the slide spring and forced his numbing fingers to pinch and slide and snap the weapon together. He noticed a tremor in his hands as the men came closer.

The crack of a rifle, his pack on the rock shuddered, a three-inch splotch of red dye appeared as a simulated round slammed into it.

Kolt dropped to the ground, crawled behind the stone, and finished assembling his Glock.

He found himself terrified.

Shit. Shit. Shit!

Kolt retrieved a loaded magazine from the top of the rock and charged the pistol, rose, and fired several rounds, hitting one of the men in the road with a gut shot as the others scrambled for cover, not thirty yards away. The "hit" man lowered his gun to the ground and slowly lay down next to it.

Kolt used the pistol to keep the three remaining men's heads down while he worked on putting the AK together behind the low stone. His pants were soaked with the wet mud all around him. He worried now about getting away from these faux Taliban, getting to a campsite, and starting a fire before the cold in his extremities sent his body into hypothermia.

This "training" was life-and-death.

He heard a noise off to his left, on the far side of the muddy dirt road. An attempt to flank by the three men to the east? No. They were all still there, firing sporadically. It was another unit of opfor, and they opened up on him from close range, long AK volleys raking his position as he loaded a magazine into his rifle.

Within seconds Kolt went down hard with the impact of four paint rounds slamming into his chest. They stung and throbbed instantly.

Damn it.

He tossed his rifle to his side and lay in the mud. Above him the gray sky was darkening with the onset of dusk. He was sore and dejected and embarrassed by his performance. And he was cold, and already the altitude was affecting his joints as well as his energy.

He heard men approaching. Within seconds they were above him. Their Taliban dress was realistic, almost certainly because it *was* Taliban dress, gleaned from prisoners or the dead back in Afghanistan. Having seven Taliban standing around his prostrate form was horrifying. Fear was added to his long list of uncomfortable sensations.

He focused on one of the men. The man was, without doubt, Middle Eastern. He shouted at Kolt in Pashto, and though Kolt could barely understand him, the tenor of the language brought him closer still to that event in his past that had so changed his life.

A crunch of boots on gravel to his right, and then seconds later Monk stood above him with a rifle hanging off his chest. Raynor blinked hard behind his eye protection. Sergeant Kraus had obviously climbed out of the truck at the first turn and dressed himself in the traditional Pashtun salwar kameez clothing and a pakol cap. Monk looked at him with complete derision. "You managed one kill, Kolt. *One* kill." It was unquestionably an admonition. "You're going to have to do a lot better than one damn kill."

Kolt sat up in the mud. "I know."

"Now get the hell out of here. You can expect to get hit a minimum of twice a day, every day, for the next three weeks."

Damn, thought Raynor. The pain from the Simunitons hurt, but he could tell they'd left nothing more than bruising and shallow cuts across his chest. But a round in the right place could break a nose or a rib, no question. He needed to get a hell of a lot better very, very quickly just to *survive* forty more enemy engagements like this. He climbed to his feet, shook mud from his cold, red hands. Silently he began putting items carefully back into his rucksack, but after no more than five seconds Kraus raised the barrel of his AK slightly and fired a burst into the mud at Kolt's feet. The gunfire was painfully loud in Kolt's unprotected ears. "Move!"

Raynor scooped up everything in the bag, grabbed the Glock and the AK with his fingertips, and lugged it all awkwardly up a thin trail on the hillside.

Behind him the AKs cracked again, tearing brush and dirt on both sides of him.

Kolt stumbled several times before disappearing from view. Behind him he heard the chants of "Allahu Akbar," and panic threatened to overtake him as he struggled upward.

THIRTEEN

Kolt had a fire built not long after dark, and by 9 p.m. he was warm and dry and fed, to the extent that rice and warm water could sustain him. Kolt had always found comfort in the wilderness. But this altitude was seriously sapping his strength, and he knew he needed sleep. His body craved alcohol—this cold-turkey method of drying out made his head heavy and his stomach twist with nausea. He found it hard to get comfortable, but finally he dozed on a thin bedroll near the fire, under a camouflage tarp erected as a tent. His rifle lay by his side, his pistol on his chest.

He awoke twice to stoke and feed the fire. Each time he tossed and turned and thought of booze before finally falling back to sleep.

A third time he woke, and instantly he knew something was not right. He reached for the Glock on his chest and found it missing. He felt out for his rifle and it was gone too. A heavy boot stepped on his searching hand and pinned it into the soft earth by the fire. His left arm was grabbed by a figure under the tarp with him, and someone dropped their body weight down on his legs.

He was pinned to the ground, and the blows came hard and fast, to his stomach and his bruised chest. Boots kicked his legs. The tarp disappeared, torn in the melee. Men shouted in Pashto—he had no idea the number of them, only that they were above him and they had him and they were making him pay for leaving the fire burning, announcing his position to the entire valley.

Someone slapped ice-cold mud into his face, forced it under his lips and into his nose.

And then, suddenly, the attack ceased, and everyone on top of him dispersed.

Monk knelt over him now. Kolt could not see his face, just recognized the silhouette in front of the fire, and his low voice.

"Haji won't be so kind to you. You've got thirty-nine more engagements with us, Raynor. Are we going to kill you *every* damn time?"

Kolt said nothing. He pulled his arms in tight to his body, as if to ward off the blows that had already fallen. Monk stood and muttered something to his men. Immediately they began kicking at the fire, extinguishing the flames and the warmth with their boots. When nothing remained but a low pile of smoldering coals, two Taliban-dressed men grabbed Raynor by the shoulders and dragged him off his bedroll, pushed him up into a kneeling position, and slid a thick and wet wool bag over his head. Monk flipped the safety catch down on his Kalashnikov and stepped behind Raynor in the dark.

Raynor shouted out through the wool. "Monk! You know AQ and Taliban don't execute soldiers in the field!"

Sergeant Kraus's reply came just as fast. "You're no soldier, asshole."

A single gunshot cracked and the back of Raynor's head ignited in fiery pain, his neck snapped forward, and he fell facefirst into the mud. Agony and shame and cold were prevalent in his mind. He did not move for a minute as he breathed wet wool.

When he did move, when he finally sat back up and took off the bag, he felt at the back of his head, fingered the knot at the base of his skull. They'd put the bag on him to keep the simulated round from doing even more damage. Still, it hurt like a bitch.

He turned around to yell again at Kraus, but all the men had melted away on the dark mountainside.

Kolt Raynor crawled on his beaten hands and knees back to his bedroll, pulled the torn tarp over himself like a blanket, rolled into the fetal position, and moaned.

"Two friendlies, coming in!" The shout came from down the hill, the voice muffled by the thick firs and pines and by the snowfall that drifted lazily toward the wet ground. Raynor sat on his pack and stoked the fresh fire in front of him, lifted a collapsible metal pot out of the flames, and poured instant coffee into three tin cups on a flat rock near the fire.

"Friendlies, my ass," he muttered softly.

Raynor had bandaged his head to keep the mud out of the shallow swollen wound at the base of his skull. He'd also wrapped his two smallest fingers on his left hand together to reduce swelling in a sprained knuckle, and put antibiotic medicine and gauze on the oozing scrapes where the AK Sim rounds had broken the skin on his chest. His ribs and extremities were sore from the beating he'd taken the night before, and the cold had done nothing but stiffen his body further.

On either side of him, close by, were his weapons. He'd cleaned them at first light, their chambers were loaded, and spare magazines rested at the ready in a shoulder rig by his side.

Monk and Benji appeared from the wood line near the camp. They wore camouflage fatigues and small backpacks, and they sat down in the dirt by the fire, each taking a cup of black coffee from Kolt as they came to rest.

Kolt opened the conversation. "No chance I can get a couple of days to get acclimated to the altitude? The air is thin and—"

Monk interrupted. "No chance."

Kolt rubbed the aching bulb on the back of his head. "Who is in the opfor? Other than you, I mean?"

"Haji we scarfed up in Konar Province. You may recognize one or two if you look close enough. Radiance Security hired them to come to the States. Bet they figured they'd be riding rides at Disneyland and not just exchanging one cold-assed valley for another. I'm in charge of them."

"Yeah, I put that together when you executed me."

Benji laughed into his coffee cup, stifled himself after a second. Monk just stared out over the foggy morning valley.

Raynor looked to him. He started to complain, to tell Kraus that throwing him up here at ten thousand feet in the snow and pummeling the shit out of him was not the training that Webber and Grauer had promised. But he held his tongue. Kolt knew better than to whine.

Monk would enjoy that, and Kolt did not want to give the big sergeant the satisfaction.

Kolt fought the urge to bitch, and instead just asked, "So, what's on today's lesson plan?"

Monk sucked the steaming coffee down his throat. He motioned to all of Raynor's gear. "Today you're going to get all this on your back, descend the valley, cross the floor, and then ascend to nine thousand on the other side."

Raynor just looked off at the mountains on the far edge of the valley, thinking about his sore ribs and the heavy straps that would soon be cinched tight across them.

"You'll make camp, and then come back down the mountain and meet us at the ranch. We've got some gear lists to go over, some maps to memorize, codes and radio freaks, shit like that. Then, after dark, you're heading back up to your camp."

"Where I'll no doubt get jumped by you and your gunners."

Monk smiled for the first time. "No doubt at all."

"Is there a medic at the ranch?"

"Sure is. You hurt?"

"No. Just planning ahead." He thought a moment. "I need some O2."

"No. You're good. We won't start pushing you for a couple more days."

"Look, Monk. I'm more amped up than anybody about getting T.J. back. I just need—"

Monk tossed the dregs of his instant coffee over the fire. Stood up. "The problem is, Raynor, that you need to be switched on, *not* amped up. Your good intentions aren't going to amount to jack squat in Hajiland. We are going to make it uncomfortable for you now, miserable for you in a couple of days, impossible for you before the week is out. You aren't going to make it through this; you are going to fail, fall by the wayside, and then Webber and Grauer can move on and find a qualified former Unit member to do this job."

"So you think I'm just wasting everyone's time here?"

"Yes, I do."

"This is because I was an officer, isn't it?"

"In some ways, yeah, that's what this is about. What has to be done in Khyber has nothing to do with being an officer."

"Bullshit. I led men into combat. I have fought—"

"Yeah, and that last batch of men you led into combat are dead, so you don't have anybody left to lead. What is needed now is a man who can lead his own body, and Raynor, you don't seem to exert the same kind of control over yourself that you did on others."

"Then tell Webber I'm unsatisfactory, and then we can all move on!"

"I would love to tell him you are unsat, but he isn't going to take my word for it. You'll have to quit or drop dead on this mountain. So either you get your shit together and get ready for this mission, or by God I will do my damnedest to drop you dead on this mountain. *If* T.J. and the boys are over there, *if* they are alive, then you can be damn sure we aren't going to get a second chance to prove it. I have been against you going from the very beginning, I know you are going to fuck it up, so the best thing that can happen is you fuck it up in Wyoming, so you don't compromise a real attempt at a rescue. Your failure is the best thing to increase this mission's chances of success."

Kolt stood angrily, began breaking camp. It was going to be a long day, and arguing with David Kraus wasn't going to make it go by any faster.

FOURTEEN

Kolt was "killed" again five hours later. He'd spent an hour at the ranch meeting and getting started with his Pashto instructor, a middle-aged woman in a hijab face covering who did not know his name; nor did he know hers. An hour later the Afghani opfor hit him on a mountain pass at nine thousand feet, a typical L-shaped ambush, and Kolt knew he should have seen it coming. He marveled at the ease with which these Afghans could handle the altitude, and he wished he was as thin-blooded as they. After the hit he struggled higher up the mountain, and he made it through the night without another attack.

But when he was hit again the next morning on his way down to the ranch, he managed to shoot three enemy and break contact, sliding and splashing and rolling down a hill until the opfor gave up the pursuit.

Day three found Raynor with a serious head cold.

The altitude and the low temps had swollen his sinuses shut, his weakness growing worse instead of better. By day four he was on a cot in the ranch, getting injections of antibiotics and vitamins from the doctor. Though sick as a dog he kept his language training up. That, he felt, would be the extent of his work until he got back on his feet, but he was wrong. Monk and his Taliban attacked him in the building itself—they did not give him a day off just because he was sick. He was pulled from his cot in the hallway, pushed back down into the kneeling position, covered with the hood to absorb some, but not enough, of the impact from the Simunitions round, and "executed" again by the Delta master sergeant.

After being cleared by the doctor he was led down to the front door. His pack was waiting for him outside in the rain, and he hefted it with tired and sore muscles and staggered off into a mountain storm. "You're discharged from the hospital," growled Monk as Kolt stepped out into the weather.

It got worse before it got better, but it *did* get better. On day eight, just after a grueling one-hundred-foot rock-climbing ascent with Benji, four of Monk's Afghans attacked in a pincer move, attempting to pin Raynor against the rock wall. But Kolt took down the two men on his left, flanked the others as they moved in for the kill, and destroyed the rest of the opfor arrayed against him.

His physical and mental strength began to grow with each passing day. Not in a straight line—day eleven had him back under a doctor's care, and day fourteen had him on the verge of quitting after he was executed by Kraus yet again while sitting at a picnic table studying Pashto with his teacher. But by day seventeen he'd dropped twenty pounds of fat, revealing lean muscle that was hardening by the day, and his body was sufficiently acclimated to the altitude for him to operate the entire day without teetering on the edge of collapse. He also improved his Pashto, practiced with the gear he'd be taking with him over the border, studied maps of the FATA, and finally took down all eight opfor, when Kolt found a hide above their staging area for an attack on his camp, and then sniped them one by one with his AK at sixty yards as they struggled to pinpoint the origin of fire.

Two days later he "killed" all eight of his opponents again, the last two in hand-to-hand combat that ended with both Taliban tapping out, and with muscle spasms in their necks and bruises on their backsides that would nag the fit young Afghans for days to come.

On his final full day in Wyoming, Raynor staged another surprise attack on Monk and his forces. Most of the Afghans had long tired of the hunt, especially after they found themselves, as often as not, the prey. They were just leaving the ranch in the early-morning darkness, with a plan to set a dawn ambush in the tall grasses a kilometer up the trail Kolt would take into the valley. But their quarry had come down during the night, positioned himself by their 4 × 4s, and ferociously attacked and killed every last man as they sleepily began to lace up their boots and load their guns on the front porch.

Monk made it into the front door of the lodge, but Kolt chased him back inside, rushed right past Benji and the doctor, and kicked Kraus's pistol out of his hand the instant he raised it to fire. The master sergeant put his hands up in surrender, smiled, and began complimenting his pupil on how far he'd come in three weeks.

"I gotta hand it to you. I didn't think you had—"

"Shut the fuck up!" barked Raynor, a hard, wild look in his eyes. He spun Monk around, turning his face toward the paneled wall of the huge great room. Kicked at the back of the older man's knees until he dropped into a kneeling position.

"Benji, you better get Monk a padded hood."

Kraus's hands were still up in the air. Furious, he shouted, "Americans don't execute prisoners, Raynor!"

"American *soldiers* don't, Sergeant. But, like you said, I'm no soldier." Benji rushed over with the hood, put it over Monk's head, and Kolt shot David Kraus in the skull with the powerful simulated round. Knelt down over him afterward.

"You made me, asshole. No one to blame but yourself."

Raynor stood, turned, walked back out the front door, past the awed stares of Benji and the eight "dead" men watching through the windows of the front porch.

FIFTEEN

Pakistan

The four men shackled to their rope cots awoke to the sounds of vehicles outside their door. Two trucks by the sound of it, 4×4 pickups, because nothing else would survive the trek through the valley.

Three of the four rolled over and went back to sleep. They were not healthy. They tired easily and woke slowly. They were given next to no exercise, very little natural light, and a diet that, while recently much improved over what they'd lived on for the past three years, was by no means well balanced.

The man who remained awake was the leader, and his responsibility for the others meant he would not let himself go back to sleep. Josh Timble cocked his head and listened carefully, trying to pick up clues about the new visitors from any sounds. He had become an expert in the art of deriving intelligence while imprisoned.

The sound of a vehicle, the mood of his guards, the change in the weather or in the quality of the bits of vegetables mixed in with his rice . . . everything was a potential source of information to be gleaned. He spoke more of the local language than the others, and he'd used this and his minimal Arabic to make friends with some of his captors over the years. This, too, was a crucial means of gleaning intel.

He'd already pegged the two trucks as Toyota Hiluxes, but this was no great feat. He'd been in this compound for two months now and had not heard a single engine larger than a tractor's that was not connected to the ubiquitous pickup truck in Pakistan, the Hilux. During the day T.J. and his men were unchained and free to walk around the small room, and a high window slit in the stone-and-poured-concrete wall was accessible by stacking two of the beds on one another and then climbing up and stretching oneself. He'd done just that dozens of times he'd heard engines, and he wished he wasn't shackled right now, so he could see if these trucks were Taliban or al Qaeda or just local vendors or allies of the warlord who ran this little valley fiefdom.

He pulled against his chain until his wrist burned, then let his arm drop back to the rope cot.

Hearing no more noise outside, he looked around his dark cell.

The room was twelve feet square, with dirt floors and reinforced concrete walls. It was featureless save for the four cots made of wooden posts and woven rope, and a two-foot-square indentation in the dirt in one corner from which a three-foot pipe made from empty mortar shells led out to a drainage culvert along the wall of the compound.

This was their "shower," the corner where they poured the bucket of hot water over each other once a week.

The rest of the time the men kept a rock over the pipe to keep the bugs and rats out.

The window slit above his cot showed him it was morning, maybe six thirty. He sat up and rubbed his eyes. Only the tiniest slivers of light came from the window slit and from below the heavy metal door to the room, but these served as their clock in the morning, the first indicators of daylight. Soon, T.J. knew, he would hear the steady thumping sound of the women pounding the morning bread behind the main building, and that told him it was an hour or so until breakfast.

The conditions here at this compound, run by a man they knew as Zar Afridi, were actually not all that bad. In the past three years they'd been kept in caves, in urban cellars chained or caged like monkeys, in dank underground bunkers, and even tied to trees on more than one occasion. They'd also been force-marched, or stuffed like cordwood into the backs of trucks, each man's full body weight pressing down on whichever unlucky compatriot had been tossed in first.

No, this compound of Zar's was not Club Med, but it was much better than anywhere they'd been before. They even got a tiny smattering of exercise during the evening walk. One at a time, each man was taken from the one-room stone hut that served as their prison and led, under guard and with hands chained in front of him, from the northwest corner of the compound, fifty yards to the east, where the simple outhouse stood in front of a copse of trees.

One hundred yards of strolling a day was not much exercise, nor was it much fresh air or solitude, but it was something.

The most interesting aspect of their imprisonment here in Zar Afridi's compound was the arrival of the doctor at the beginning of their stay, and his decision that all the men immediately begin taking medicines to help wean them off the heroin they'd been given for years. The drug had been cruelly administered to debilitate the elite war fighters and keep them compliant and addicted.

Josh had no idea why the decision had been made to clean them up. At first he wondered if they were to be released, but he'd gotten no wind of that rumor whatsoever from his captors. Some of the guards were, in a word, stupider than the others, and they spoke a little too much, revealed things to T.J. without realizing what they were doing. There was no discussion by these simpletons with guns about setting the Americans free. No, if there were discussions about the politics of their captivity it always centered on a tug-of-war between the Taliban factions on one side of the rope and the foreign al Qaeda forces here in FATA on the other.

T.J. and his men were, of course, the rope itself.

Just when Josh was about to lie back on his bunk, footsteps approached the shack and Josh forced his mind to awaken and clear. At this time of the morning it was still early to see Zar himself, though he would be by to deliver the morning meal. It was an interesting dynamic of Pashtunwali, the local tribal code, that the owner of the property saw to the care of his prisoners. The warlord, while certainly of no importance on a global scale, was unquestionably the local strongman, the big fish in the little pond that was this valley. Zar had personally been bringing food for the men each morning. The other guards saw to them the rest of the day, but Zar came and in a polite, if not friendly, manner asked after the men's comfort and needs.

Timble took advantage of this, asking for fresh water and medicine for his men to help with the near-constant diarrhea they were suffering from. Sometimes it was delivered.

Sometimes not.

The chain outside the iron door was unlocked. This made a distinctive sound that stirred the other men in the room. Then the door opened, cutting the still dark air with a bright shaft of light.

The three men in the doorway looked like giants in silhouette before they entered. They were bigger and broader than the Pashtuns around here. They stepped inside, and Josh Timble blinked hard and rapidly.

Three American soldiers in full battle dress. Helmets on their heads, sunglasses over their eyes, and rifles slung across their chests.

Their uniforms revealed them to be Army Rangers.

Josh turned to look at his three cellmates, to make sure they were seeing the same vision. All three sat up quickly, rattling their chains with the movement.

T.J. had long thought of rescue, dreamed of it, but he wasn't dreaming now.

Could this be?

No. Something did not add up. He knew good and well that there had been no firefight outside in the compound, and he could not believe Zar's men had just evaporated into thin air.

He hadn't heard a helicopter, hadn't heard English-speaking voices. The women outside began pounding the bread flour. The start of a normal day.

No, he did not believe these three Rangers had just walked in the front gate without anyone noticing.

Still, he could see the light hair and skin on the three men, he recognized the Wiley X sunglasses, the Casio watches—the guns and gear all looked general issue.

They wore Colt M4 rifles across their chests.

His emotions overrode his logic. "Holy shit, guys. Where the hell did you come from?"

One of the men smiled and nodded. Gave the thumbs-up sign.

Spike sat on the cot next to T.J.'s. "Thank God!" he shouted.

The other two men just stared dumbfounded at their three rescuers.

But T.J. spoke quickly. The military officer in him was taking over from the captive he had been. "There is a hurja on the opposite side of the compound, that's where the tangos are billeted. Probably a dozen-plus, all armed, there will be more in the main build—"

He stopped talking as more men stepped into the doorway, blocking the light from outside.

Two long-haired Pashtun gunmen, Taliban perhaps, an al Qaeda man in a trim beard and eyeglasses, and an older European-looking man with gray hair and a dusty white suit. They all entered the room behind the Rangers. The floor of the cell was flooded with men now; the four Delta captives just sat shackled to their rope cots and stared up at the bizarre scene in front of them.

T.J. muttered, "What the hell is going on?"

One of the Rangers removed his helmet and scratched his head while turning back to the men behind him. He wore a standard military haircut, well kept and tapered. Light brown hair stood no more than a half inch on the top of his head.

The al Qaeda man stepped farther into the room, out of the doorway, and addressed the man in the suit in English. "Good. Very good." He then turned to the Rangers, spoke to one of them in Arabic. The man took his M4 rifle from around his neck and held it out for T.J. to take.

Josh just stared at the man. No one held a weapon up in any threatening manner. He was being asked to take hold of a rifle?

Bouncer said, "Don't touch it. It's a trick."

Roscoe disagreed. "Take it, boss. Shoot these sons of bitches."

One of the Taliban produced a key and unlocked T.J.'s restraints. He stepped away and Josh Timble stood, reached out, and took the gun from the Ranger's hands.

Everyone in the room stared intently at him.

Josh immediately dropped the magazine, looked into it, and found it empty. He pulled the charging handle back and found the weapon itself empty.

He looked up at the men. They continued to stare at him like he was a monkey in a cage.

"What the fuck?" asked Spike.

Timble racked the charging handle again while he looked at the men. A third time. He looked down at the weapon for a moment, rotated it in the bad light, then held it back up to the crowd in front of him.

"It's a fake." He tossed it roughly to the al Qaeda man in the wire glasses, who struggled to catch the empty gun. Then T.J. reached out to the Ranger, put his hand on the man's chest rig, ran his hands across the stitching of the plate carrier on his armor, and looked back up to the men in his cell. "Phony. All this gear is counterfeit."

The al Qaeda man deflated somewhat. The suited man seemed to grow defensive. He began moving forward to speak, but the al Qaeda man stayed him with a raised hand. Instead, he spoke in English to Timble. "Why do you say this?"

T.J. did not answer. Instead, he looked at Roscoe. "You still remember your Russian?"

"Sure, boss."

He pointed to the oldest-looking man in a Ranger uniform, a cold-eyed blond of about thirty-five, who stood five feet in front of him. "Tell this motherfucker that I just called him the son of a Chechen whore."

Roscoe translated, and immediately the "Ranger" leaped at T.J., knocked him down on the cot, and reared back to smash his fist into the face of the weakened American. The al Qaeda man shouted in Arabic, the Ranger's raised fist froze above his intended target, and he climbed back up slowly. His face remained red with fury.

Josh sat up on the bed, shook his head at all the men

in front of him. "Don't know what your plan is, but unless you're heading to a costume party in Mullah Omar's cave, you're going to get your dumb asses killed." He laughed cruelly. "You didn't fool me, and you won't fool anyone else." The faces of some of the visitors to the cell, obviously the ones who spoke English, contorted with fresh anger. All the men filed out and the door slammed behind them. In seconds the sound of the chain and the padlock, and then retreating footsteps and arguing.

Raised voices.

T.J. tuned into the voices, and for an instant he was certain he heard English with a German accent.

He had stopped smiling the instant the men turned away from him. His smile had been as fake as the faux Americans and their equipment.

"How did you know, boss?"

"Educated guess. AQ has used light-skinned Chechens or Nuristanis before. These guys didn't look like any of the Nuristanis I've come in contact with. Not all Chechens speak Russian, but I figured if they *were* Chechen, the oldest guy would know enough to get the gist."

He looked to his men now, still sitting on their cots, their eyes still wide in shock at all they had just seen. "Damn it, boys. That shit was fake, but it was close enough to get them through any security checkpoint I've run across in Afghanistan."

They all understood the ramifications, and these men's mood sank as they imagined what horror would befall their unsuspecting comrades over the border.

SIXTEEN

Pamela Archer stood on the tarmac, just a few hundred yards away from the runway at Jalalabad Airport. The U.S. Air Force controlled the airport and runway, but Pamela's employer, Radiance Security and Surveillance Systems, had its Afghanistan base here, adjacent to the U.S. military installation. There was also access, via this tarmac and taxiway, to the runway itself, and here Pam stood among a large group of Radiance employees.

She was the only female.

All eyes were on the Radiance 727 landing in the hazy morning. It touched down, applied its reverse thrust, and kicked up a swirling cloud of dust behind it. Soon it turned onto the taxiway and began slowly heading in their direction.

While she awaited the arrival of the aircraft Pam Archer looked off to her left, toward her Predator drones. Her two babies sat sleek and still on the tarmac in front of their hangar. Pam allowed herself a little smile. Before joining Radiance Security and coming out here to Afghanistan she'd served twelve years in the Air Force, and many of those years were spent flying drones from Creech AFB in Nevada. But in the Air Force she and her birds were rarely in the same hemisphere, much less so close that she could walk over and touch them.

And these days sometimes she *did* touch them. She couldn't help it. They were beautiful, and they were hers. Well, they were hardly hers in any legal sense, but she was in charge here, and she liked that. This wasn't the Air Force. She called the majority of the shots when it came to the UAVs; she had her own team of systems officers and mechanics, but still she was the only drone pilot here at Radiance Afghanistan.

So, to her, anyway, they were hers.

She'd even given them pet names. "Baby Girl" and "Baby Boy." Baby Boy had an additional nub that protruded from its belly, hence the distinction between the two.

But this was not the day to be sentimental, she told herself as she stood in the mass of beefy men while the stairs rolled up to the side of the 727 and the cabin door opened. An operation that had been in the planning and development stages for the better part of two months was about to be put into action, and although she was an integral part of the operation, although she had worked sixteen-hour days preparing for it, although she was determined to play her role and do it well . . . she did not like it at all.

Men began filing out of the 727. She recognized many

of them. They were Radiance paramilitary operators, and each man seemed to be carrying his own weight in gear. The first guy was an ex-SEAL who'd hit on her tirelessly all summer long in the base cafeteria. The second man was an ex–Army Special Forces medic; the third was also a former Green Beret, a quiet man from upstate New York whose bunk was decorated with artwork created by his young children. A couple of ex-Rangers followed, young guys who'd done well for themselves earning the larger pay of a PMC, a paramilitary company, compared to what they would have been making if they were still in the Army. A former marine followed these Rangers out onto the stairs.

All these men had been based here at the Radiance compound in Jalalabad, but they had flown off to Wyoming a month ago, all to help prepare the last man off the aircraft. A large contingent of Afghani nationals had flown off with them, but they were not on today's plane. Radiance had allowed the men a week of sightseeing and shopping in Denver before they would return on the same aircraft. Peter Grauer had arranged this not out of the goodness of his heart, though the eight sore and tired Afghans would certainly enjoy a once-in-a-lifetime experience. No, for the purposes of operational security Grauer had decided he didn't want the Afghans popping out of the same plane as Raynor here at Jalalabad, and shuffling around the same base from where the op into Pakistan would take place in just a few hours.

Pam kept her eyes on the cabin door of the jet, waiting to catch her first glimpse of the man she knew only as Racer. When he appeared she knew immediately, even though she had never seen a photo of the man. He stood there at the top of the stairs for a moment, looked around at the base, and sucked in the jet fuel–infused air that must have brought back memories of his troubled past.

She'd been told beforehand that after a few initial rough patches, he'd aced his training in Wyoming, and he'd done it at the expense of his Afghan opposition. She smiled wryly with the mental image of eight dark, bearded men hobbling through the food court of a Denver shopping mall with bruises and lacerations, after spending three weeks playing the role of the Taliban force pitted against the man in front of her.

Racer was filthy. Someone had mentioned that morning that he had refused to shower, refused to eat American-style food in the time between the end of his first training evolution and the beginning of the operation. He wanted to stay dirty; he wanted his insides as well as his outsides to fit into the Pakistan border region where he would be operating. They'd said he'd spoken very little English, only communicated through his Pashto instructor, the woman in the veil who followed him out of the aircraft now, and down the stairs.

Pam Archer regarded the man as he stepped up to the crowd of men around her, the operational leadership of Radiance Security and Surveillance Systems. He shook hands and nodded with them, said a couple of soft words to Pete Grauer, her boss and the president of the company, and then he stepped up to her. She shook his hand; the skin of his palm was coarse and cracked and his fingernails were blackened. She was introduced to Racer by Grauer as the flight director of the Predator drones, and Racer thanked her in advance for her support of him.

It was surreal to be face-to-face with the man she had thought about so much in the past three years. To see him as she thought of him, as a human being. Not a code name. Not a number. Not an infrared signature on a television monitor five thousand miles away.

He seemed even more human, more flesh-and-blood, more fragile, than she had envisioned. He was smaller than most of the Radiance security guards around. More slightly built as well. It occurred to her that she could walk right now to the front guard post and grab the first man she saw, and he would be more the image of the commando that she had in her head than the man who stood in front of her.

Pam Archer had put the pieces of this man's biography together, and knew that he'd been cashiered from Delta after an op that went bad three years earlier. She knew, without a shadow of a doubt, that this man had been the leader of the Delta team that she had failed three years ago just a few hours south of where they now stood together.

Racer was ushered into an SUV with Grauer and they rolled off toward the Operations Center. Pam climbed into another truck and followed behind with a group of egghead analysts. She would be front and center in the meetings between Racer and this group, she'd do her job during the operation to follow, and she'd do her best to hold her tongue about her opinions.

But she didn't like this op one damn bit.

She could not help but think that Racer was on a one-way suicide mission, another well-planned date with disaster, and she would be there, in the sky above, watching over it all.

Kolt Raynor said good-bye to his translator at the entrance to the Operations Center. She'd be returning almost immediately to Kabul, and for the rest of the day, English would be the language of necessity. She had helped him greatly with his Pashto; he certainly could not pass five seconds' scrutiny posing as a local, but he would be able to understand much conversation and get his point across in most circumstances, and that would have to be good enough.

He was processed by security and issued a large red badge that he hung around his neck. The security director of the base himself warned Racer that if that badge ever came off, "even if he was in the crapper," then Racer would immediately be considered hostile and would be treated as such.

There was zero tolerance around here for lax security.

A morning meeting would be held in the Bubble, a secure conference room in the OC that was scanned every morning for listening devices. The Radiance base was not as reliant on foreign workers as the adjacent American military base here at Jalalabad, where citizens from literally dozens of nations worked every possible job from fixing satellite equipment to ladling gravy onto mashed potatoes. Still, they were in a foreign nation, they dealt in and discussed highly classified information, and they were therefore cognizant of the need to adopt counterintelligence measures.

Pete Grauer offered Kolt a soda once they got into the conference room, but he declined. Instead, he sucked water from a CamelBak bladder that he held in his lap. There was a minute of small talk, and then Pam Archer entered the room and headed for a seat across from the men.

"You've got one hell of an operation here," Kolt said to Grauer as she sat down.

"You better believe it. Our contracts cover the gambit. We've got reconstruction and development money, drug-interdiction money, black-fund money from the Agency. We are juggling a lot of balls over here at this base."

"What kind of contracts are you guys working?"

"You name it. We are the biggest private security and surveillance firm in Afghanistan. We provide security, both mobile and static, for development and reconstruction projects."

"And you have your own Predators?"

"Sort of a lease arrangement with the Air Force. But we have one of the best drone pilots running the show here in Ms. Archer."

Pam nodded politely as she sipped coffee.

Grauer continued: "We use them primarily along the Pak border monitoring poppy farming for the Afghani government."

"On both sides of the border?"

"Yes, but unofficially."

"And what do the Afghans do with that information?"

Kolt caught Pam rolling her eyes behind her coffee mug. Pete just shrugged. "Not enough, unfortunately. Opium is a hell of a cash crop around here. We're doing the legwork, and Washington is applying the political pressure, but heroin is going to come out of the mountains and plains of Af-Pak a lot longer than we'll be around to monitor it."

Raynor nodded. He'd heard this same lament three years earlier, the last time he was in theater.

Colonel Grauer looked at his Predator pilot. "A few months back Pam and I went to Kabul to meet with some high-ranking officials, basically to report on our progress. Ms. Archer joked that we could equip the drones with defoliant-extruding devices, sort of turn them into unmanned crop dusters, and she could low-fly the poppy fields for three months and thereby cut opium production in half."

Pam Archer looked at Grauer. "I wasn't joking."

Grauer said, "The Afghans looked terrified. I thought we were going to lose the entire contract." Grauer didn't look too happy about Pam's plan.

"Sounds like a good idea to me," Kolt remarked.

"Hell," Grauer said, "we have to strike while the iron is hot. There's no guarantee we'll have any contracts around here this time next year."

"Why's that? White House wants to start sending troops home. I would have thought fewer U.S. forces would mean more work for you guys."

"It should. But the Afghani government is courting the Taliban, trying to come to some sort of truce, if not an outright peace. There's going to be a big peace jurga next spring between the government and the Afghani Taliban, and a lot of people think the leadership in Kabul will accept some Taliban terms to give them a measure of regional control. If that happens, God help them, and God help us."

"No shit," said Kolt. He'd heard about peace talks with the Taliban. To him it sounded like insanity. Making deals with a loose coalition of religious zealots who bombed girls' schools and were prone to violent and protracted clashes against one another did not sound like a recipe for lasting peace.

It sounded more like madness.

More Radiance personnel entered the room. Kolt noticed that the open seat on his right was the last to be filled on his side of the conference table. He assumed that was because of his foul odor. Soon a crisp white sheet of paper was placed in front of him and he smudged it immediately with his soiled hands. It was his itinerary for the day. The first line under the heading said, "10:30 a.m. Initial Briefing—Bubble." He looked at his watch and saw the readout flick from 10:29:59 to 10:30:00.

"Good morning," Grauer instantly barked to the dozen men and one woman arrayed around the table. Just like during his days in the Ranger battalion, Raynor thought to himself. Colonel Grauer was on the ball.

Kolt recognized that he was just a cog in the system, though he also recognized how important a role he played. He knew that other than the pilots who would be dropping him over the border, no one else around here was running the risk of death if this op went tits up.

SEVENTEEN

Grauer quickly introduced those at the table, a bit more of the meet and greet, and each person's role in the operation was explained for Raynor's benefit.

Grauer then began discussing the support Racer would receive from Radiance Jalalabad while over the border. They'd be watching him via the Predator feed, they had a solid contact man to help him on the ground in the FATA, and they had a brilliant ex-CIA operator working from Peshawar to help him get out when the job was done.

After a few minutes Kolt began to detect a certain defensiveness in Grauer's tone. It was almost as if the details and discussion were all lined up to put his mind at ease, to let him know that he was not just being dropped in the wind, that he was not on his own.

But by going so far out of his way to assure his operator that he had their full backing, Grauer was, to

Raynor's way of thinking, underlining the fact that he'd be the one taking the ultimate risks.

As Grauer spoke a man appeared at the door to the Bubble. He looked like a Pashtun businessman in his fifties or sixties. He was heavyset, he wore a long and threadbare white kameez shirt with a dark vest and local salwar pants, his beard was gray, and his hair, what there was of it above his high forehead, was curly, salt-and-pepper with a lot more salt. Kolt was surprised that this local had made it this deep into the Operations Center without being shoved facefirst onto the linoleum tiling, zip-tied, and dragged back outside by one of the many base security men.

Then Kolt noticed the red badge hanging from his hip. It had been folded up in his baggy pants. Somehow, in some capacity, this guy belonged.

Grauer pressed a button and the door opened. All conversation in the room stopped while the "security seal" was broken on the Bubble, and the gray-haired man in the salwar kameez entered.

Pete Grauer stood, crossed around the large conference table, and shook the man's hand. "Racer, I'd like you to meet Bob Kopelman."

Instantly Kolt felt he was being sized up—just as he was doing the same to the ex-CIA officer who, quite literally, held Raynor's life in his hands. Kolt thought the man looked a bit like pictures he'd seen of Ernest Hemingway in his later years, big and heavy and past the prime of life, but someone you definitely did *not* want to fuck with.

Yet, still, he definitely could pass as a local.

Grauer continued. "Bob acquired the contact who will get you to the target village, and Bob will be your go-to guy as long as you are in-country."

Kopelman was four inches taller and easily sixty pounds heavier than Kolt. The big man looked him over slowly and carefully, and made a short proclamation.

"You smell like a goat. Excellent."

Kolt relaxed. He could work with this guy. They shook hands.

Kopelman plopped down across from Raynor, next to Pam Archer, and he declined the coffee he was offered, instead asking for green tea with milk. He was a man just in from the field. Kolt could tell by his choice of beverage.

Grauer spoke up. "Okay, let's get down to the mission itself. Lights, please." Someone flipped off the overhead, and a screen lowered on the wall behind Grauer. The athletic fifty-eight-year-old stood and stepped to the side, and flipped on the laser pointer in his hand.

Great, Kolt thought with bitter sarcasm. *Just what we need to save T.J. A damn PowerPoint presentation. Some things never change.* He kept his opinions to himself and picked up a pen.

A satellite map of Pakistan appeared on the screen. Almost immediately it zoomed in on the western side of the country, to the Federally Administered Tribal Areas near the border.

Grauer said, "Target location Gopher."

Kolt Raynor knew the general area well, and he'd been dumped into many places code-named Gopher.

The map image zoomed again, and the center

focused on the Khyber Agency, smack in the middle of the FATA. It was striking to see how close he already was to his target—Raynor could see Jalalabad, where he now sat, in the northwest portion of the screen.

"Khyber," Pete Grauer said with his customary brevity.

The satellite image zoomed one last time, to an area near the center of Khyber, and a pair of mountain ranges that looked like arthritic spines, between which a narrow river wove through lower green hills.

"The Tirah Valley. Full of Pakistani Taliban, Afghani Taliban, AQ, and local militia who pinch-hit for the Pakistani Taliban. This mountainous region, just south of the valley, is rugged, it is secluded, and it is absolutely off-limits to foreigners."

Now the screen changed again; a village built along a hillside. This image was not from a satellite—it was clearly taken from a drone. Kolt assumed the young woman sitting across the conference table from him had piloted the eye in the sky that captured this picture.

"Shataparai village, deep in a valley, twenty-six klicks southwest of Peshawar. This is your target."

It was beautiful. The hillside was verdant and the terra-cotta-colored block village buildings looked like toy houses. An idyllic blue-green river ran at the base of the dwellings with a narrow stone bridge spanning it.

At the top of the hillside, abutting the village but looming above it, was a large walled compound. Functional and cold, it marred the splendor of the hillside.

A new image appeared, the compound in much more detail, again photographed from a Predator. There were easily a dozen buildings inside the high stone walls. Between them were groves of trees, open spaces, and a road or driveway that ran from the front gate to the main building.

"The home of Zar. He's an Afridi, one of the many Pashtun tribes. He has his own militia but he's nominally aligned with the Pakistani Taliban."

"Nominally aligned?" Kolt asked.

Grauer said, "He's allied with the Taliban at the moment, but there are so many factions in play, it's complicated. We don't have a picture of him, he's a bit of a mystery, but this *is* Zar's compound." Grauer used his laser pointer to indicate features. The pointer circled the largest building in the compound, two stories high and the size of a basketball court. "We know this is his main residence." Then he indicated an open fenced-in area near the rear wall. "Obviously this is a corral, so we can assume this running next to it is a stone barn. We think the long structure running along the south wall is a hurja, a guesthouse. It's likely this is where his sentries are billeted. It only stands to reason. Several sentries man the walls and patrol the grounds. See the shadows of the armed men here, here, and here?"

Raynor nodded. He caught his right leg bouncing up and down. He was ready. He wanted to go, *now.* To get eyes on the men so Webber and his men could come in and get them.

He kept quiet still, but inside he was screaming. *This is where the guys are! Let's stop all this PowerPoint bullshit and move our asses!*

But Grauer continued calmly. "These smaller buildings here at the northwest corner of the compound? Anyone's guess. An armory? Dry stores? A prison?"

Kopelman spoke up. "My contact goes into the compound twice a week. He is only allowed on this road up through the main entrance and up to the main building. He reports sentries patrolling, but he has not seen any static guarding of any of these outbuildings, at least from what he can see on the outside."

Kopelman looked at Raynor. "Understand this, son. Just because my guy doesn't see them on the outside, that doesn't mean there are not a half-dozen SOBs with AKs inside the walls of any one of these stone or concrete buildings."

"Understood," Raynor replied, not taking his eyes from the large screen. Then he focused on the southern wall of the compound, and on what lay just outside it. It was another building, square, with a large open courtyard. "Is this part of Zar's place?"

"Negative," said Grauer. "Our analysts have been calling that the Playground. It's interesting: in a land where girls don't go to school at all, and boys are taught in a madrasa, this location stands out as a complete anomaly in the region. All day long it is full of children. We think the kids might be serving as some sort of cynical way to prevent Hellfire attacks on the compound. See how the Playground is just on the other side of the wall from the hurja? The hurja is where Taliban or AQ stay when they are visiting the compound."

"So the kids are also human shields, just like T.J. and his men?"

"These bastards love their human shields," Kopelman muttered behind his mug of hot tea.

Pam Archer chimed in. "We don't know where the kids go at night. There is enough space inside the building to bed down, so no Langley drone would ever be cleared to fire missiles at this location."

Killing terrorists would mean killing children. Raynor sighed. It had been like this for a decade.

The image on the screen changed again, the entire village came into view, and Grauer's laser pointer ran east away from Zar's compound at the top of one hill, across the small stone huts and dirt roads and mud-walled buildings of the village, across the tiny river, and then up a terraced and cultivated hill on the other side.

"We see this as the optimal vantage point for you to lay up. You'll be about twenty meters higher than the compound's walls, four hundred meters away on the far side of the river. With the optics you'll be taking in, you should have no problem getting eyes on everything that moves in the compound. Looks like good cover here just above where the poppy fields end. We need you to go here, tuck yourself in tight, and watch the compound until you see something interesting. Film it with the cameras you'll bring in, send it to us, and wait for Kopelman's man to come pick you up to get you out of there."

"If the Predator hasn't been able to find the men, what makes you think I will see them from four hundred meters?"

Pam spoke up. "You will be there twenty-four hours a day for three days. I sneak over to overfly the village only on rare occasions, but the Agency, the Air Force, the Pakistani government, and likely even the Afghani government will get word if I spend twenty-four hours doing lazy eights on the Pakistani side of the border. I will be overhead for your insertion and your exfiltration, and probably once more each day. I'll do what I can, but the majority of the time you will be on your own monitoring Zar's fortress."

Kolt nodded. He'd momentarily forgotten that this mission was supposed to be carried out even below the radar of friendly forces.

Grauer said, "We are looking for signs of American prisoners. In order to take this information to the next stage—meaning a Delta hit on the compound—that means nothing less than you getting a visual on any one of the six missing men. We need you to do what the drones can't."

Kolt wasn't totally satisfied with this plan. "If you can get me this close to the vill, then why don't I try and infiltrate the vill, and if I can, the compound itself?"

Grauer spun in his chair, away from the screen and toward Kolt. "Negative, Racer. You aren't going into the village. That would be too risky. And you aren't going into the compound, because that would be suicide. You are going to the other side of the valley, four hundred meters away, and you'll have the gear you need to get a nice, close-up view of the compound."

Raynor nodded, then swiveled his chair to face Kopelman. "This source. The guy that's going to get me into the area. What can you tell me about him?"

"Jamal? He's reliable. He lives in a camp near Peshawar, but he delivers potable water and other goods to

Zar's compound every three or four days. He will pick you up near your infiltration and get you all the way to within a few hundred yards of your layup position."

Pam Archer spoke up. "There are two checkpoints along the track that you and Jamal will have to pass before arriving at Shataparai. These are Zar's militia. On-again, off-again Taliban, as everyone keeps saying. There are also other Taliban forces in the area that move around, travel on the same road. There could be rolling checkpoints anywhere and at any time. The vehicle you'll be traveling in will be searched multiple times with you inside it."

Kopelman said, "Jamal will get Racer through the checkpoints undetected."

"How?" Pam asked. It was an odd question from the drone pilot. It had nothing to do with her mission responsibilities.

Kopelman looked at her a moment, then turned his head slowly to Grauer and cocked it in surprise. Still, he addressed her concerns. "Jamal had been using his own tractor pulling a cart to get water and goods into Shataparai. A few weeks ago I outfitted him with a Toyota Hilux pickup. It's common in the region, and damn near indestructible. This particular truck had been used by dope smugglers on the border with China. There was a stash compartment behind and below the backseat. Access is from an invisible hatch beneath the removable rear seats. It wasn't quite large enough for a person, but I had a metalsmith in Lahore enlarge the compartment and the hatch. Racer *will* fit. His gear will go in another compartment hidden under the driver's seat. The locals are used to seeing Jamal and the truck. At the roadblocks they'll give it a once-over, but we don't expect any problems at all."

He finished, drummed his fingers on the table, and looked at the female UAV pilot. "Anything else?"

Pam met Kopelman's gaze. Shook her head.

"So," Grauer moved on. "We'll be dropping you in about fourteen hours."

"If this village is only twenty-six klicks from Peshawar, and you can get Bob into Peshawar, why don't I just fly into Peshawar and infiltrate on the ground?"

"One thing the Pakistani army does well is maintain the checkpoints into the FATA. Foreigners aren't normally allowed. Could we get you around that? Yeah, probably, but they will check the truck a lot harder in Pesh than the guys who already know Jamal will check it out in the FATA. We could get you phony documents to cross in, but we are at the very end of our weather window for the year. In a couple of weeks it will start getting really cold. Best we simply drop you out of an aircraft just this side of the border and have you HAHO into the area to meet up with your contact."

"Works for me," Kolt said, though he wasn't crazy about jumping into the night over mountainous Taliban country. A HAHO, or high-altitude, high-opening jump, required a lot of precision. He'd done it many times, but there were so many variables and factors involved that he knew it wouldn't be easy.

Grauer pushed an intercom button and summoned three men waiting outside the Bubble. In seconds the flight crew of the 727 that would fly Kolt to the border entered and went over details of the drop. Ten minutes later they left. They did not possess "need to know" for the rest of the operation.

Grauer turned back to Raynor to continue the briefing. "The U.S. military does have a presence in western Pakistan. Right now there are roughly two hundred SF men in the FATA. They work with the Pakistani military, training, compiling information about the needs of the people in the area."

"What are our guys teaching them?"

"Pakistan's army has been focused on India, not on a counterinsurgency. Our SF guys are showing them how to combat insurgents. We did it in Iraq, we're doing it in Afghanistan, and now we're helping them do it in Pakistan."

"Dangerous work," Raynor commented.

"And they've lost some good men doing it."

"Are any of them around the Tirah Valley?"

"Negative. The U.S. has never had anyone anywhere near Shataparai. This village is really out in the boonies. The Taliban and local warlords allied with them are in control. They are fighting it out with the Paki army. Estimates say seven thousand dead a year in the fighting in the FATA, but that also includes Taliban bombings and other terrorism."

Kolt said, "Back when I used to go over into Waziristan the Pak army had a unit called the Frontier Corps that came and went in the FATA. They any more effective now than back then?"

Grauer just shook his head. "Not really. They are good guys, staunchly anti-Taliban, really our best allies in the region, but they won't be where you are going. The Frontier Corps operates on main roads, in some of the main cities. But when you get in the mountains, in the farms, out of the cities . . . it's the Wild West."

Raynor looked off into space. He'd been in Taliban country many times before.

Grauer noticed his man's unease. "Be under no illusions, son. We will be sending you into a shit storm. But if you do your job and don't take any unnecessary risks, we all feel good about your chances for success."

Pam Archer looked down at the table, away from Raynor. Kolt had noticed her watching him intently throughout the meeting. She held a pen in her right hand and it tapped up and down on the table silently. He got the impression she was planning on speaking up on some topic important to her, but she held her tongue. She'd answered a few times when some operational detail relevant to her mission was questioned or brought up, but never did her eyes leave Raynor until now. He had found it disconcerting to have this woman stare him down like this, but now, just after Grauer assured him that the mission was doable, she would not look his way, and this he found even more troubling.

EIGHTEEN

Just after noon a logistical coordinator for Radiance escorted Kolt to a team locker room that was made off-limits to the rest of base personnel. There, splayed out on the floor in front of a plastic chair, was a massive array of gear.

Every last bit of it was for Raynor. He'd jump with it all, and then, assuming a safe landing on terra firma, he'd hide the chute and schlep the rest of the gear across the badlands and up a mountainside for nearly a mile before meeting with his contact.

Raynor's lower back ached just looking at it all, but he nodded and sat in the chair while the loggie waited silently behind him.

First Kolt unpacked and then repacked his parachute. Then he reacquainted himself with the oxygen equipment he'd need on his high-altitude departure from the aircraft.

He played with the GPS unit, looked over a lightweight binocular outfit that switched between straight daytime lenses and night vision. Also, he saw he would be carrying a thermal monocular with variable range and a high-powered spotting scope on a mini tripod. All of these optical devices had memory cards built into them, giving him the ability to record hours of high-resolution video.

As far as food and water he noticed immediately that he'd be going in light. There were energy bars stowed throughout his kit, enough to keep his calories up, but not enough to stave off hunger. Four days of laying up would, under normal conditions, necessitate four gallons of water, but Raynor would jump in with only two. He had water-purification tablets to make any found source drinkable, but he didn't really plan on this being a hunter-gatherer-style camping trip.

There were two weapons, but he harbored no illusions of either of them getting him out of any real trouble. Grauer wasn't sending him in to fight, that was clear, but at least Grauer wasn't sending him in empty-handed. He looked over an old but well-maintained Makarov pistol that he could stow under his clothing in its bandoliered holster. There were two extra magazines, and a four-inch fixed-blade knife of local origin that attached to his belt in a leather sheath.

Piled next to these items Kolt found a multitool, camouflage netting, and a supply of extra batteries.

Last, Raynor popped the lid on a rubber tub and found it full of local clothing. It was well worn and dirty; its drab appearance and malodorous stench matched

Raynor's cover perfectly. Surveying it quickly by stirring it around in the container he found the ubiquitous salwar kameez outfit, a bulbous pakol cap, a heavy gray knit sweater with various holes and runs in the stitching, and a patoo, a wool blanket that was often worn across the chest for warmth like a backward cape.

He then reached deeper into the tub and pulled out a cellophane-wrapped package. Opening it, he found brand-new and expensive-looking camouflaged long john tops and bottoms. He held them up in confusion and mild amusement.

The logistical coordinator noticed his surprise. "That's to control your scent. It's lined with silver, and kills bacteria and eliminates human odors. It won't make you completely invisible to dogs, but it sure as shit will help."

"My clothes are already covered with my human odor."

"Yeah, but when you are scared you give off a different scent, and those pooches over the border will alert to that in a heartbeat. That's what we're trying to avoid."

Kolt nodded and put it aside. That made sense. Dogs out here in Pashtun country were big, dangerous beasts, violent in their tendencies and hostile to strangers. The last thing Kolt wanted to deal with, on top of all his other threats, was an angry mutt who could smell his fear.

The afternoon was one long intelligence briefing, with Raynor and Grauer being the constant attendees as others entered, then departed, the Bubble at their scheduled times. An image analyst and a cartographic analyst spent a couple of hours discussing the terrain he would face. Together the men looked over satellite and drone images and topographical maps, talked about what to do if he missed his drop point, and spent some time working with him on the handheld GPS he'd be taking with him.

Next a former Green Beret survival expert discussed the conditions Raynor would face spending several days on an alpine mountainside. Kolt was no stranger to the outdoors, but the SF man did have some insight on camouflage that the former Delta officer found useful.

Even a meteorologist came in to provide an up-to-the-minute weather briefing for the next five days in the Tirah Valley. His presentation could have been summed up in seconds. Cool, sunny days and chilly nights. Misty in the mornings and evenings, but nothing that would cause any problems for the mission.

Bob Kopelman returned to give the last briefing of the day, a presentation on the area, the Pashtun culture, the village, and Zar's fortress. The compound intel had been passed on from Jamal, the local agent that would insert Raynor in just a few hours.

Kolt sat silently through most of it and paid close attention to everything, and when he did ask questions, they were short and relevant.

Kopelman looked at the filthy spy in front of him. "Do you know what Pashtunwali is?"

Raynor looked at Grauer, then back at Kopelman.

"This isn't my first rodeo, Bob. Of course I know what Pashtunwali is."

"All right. Then humor me, cowboy. Tell me what you know about it."

"The way of the Pashtun. An honor code among the tribes around here. Nine main principles, or ethics, including the right of asylum, hospitality, bravery, justice, a woman's honor . . ." Kolt hesitated. "Uh . . . and some other stuff."

Bob nodded, not unimpressed. "You hit the important parts. Zar is Pashtun. He will protect a guest at his home from all comers."

"But he's with the Taliban, so he's not protecting T.J."

"There is gray area when it comes to Pashtunwali. Zar may rationalize his holding the men captive as a way of providing them with security. He won't let them go, but neither will he let them be taken away and killed by others. I just want you to remember, it's all Pashtunwali with the tribes, but not with the Taliban, and certainly not with al Qaeda. The foreign AQ dudes in FATA look at these local Pashtuns like they are from another century, which they are. They are using them for their own devices, but often AQ, the Taliban, and the rogue militias battle between one another, Pashtunwali be damned.

"People call this the lawless tribal region, but don't believe that for an instant. It's *not* lawless. It has a *very* strict code. Pashtunwali. It's just not the law of the Pakistani government, the Taliban, or AQ. And it's not a law that we are familiar with."

Raynor just nodded. He knew all this, as he had been

in and out of Afghanistan much of the last decade. His mission, if successful, would not have him in contact with any Pashtuns other than this agent of Bob's, Jamal. He hoped he didn't need to know too much about the ins and outs of the social mores of the region he was about to sneak into.

It was 9 p.m. and Raynor's finger-smudged itinerary sheet told him he was to be sleeping right now, but instead he sat outside in the cool evening, on a bench near the outer fence. He wore a blue tracksuit with the Radiance logo, and the all-important red security badge hung around his neck. A thousand yards to his east Air Force aircraft took off with regularity. It wasn't the pace of operations he remembered from a few years earlier, but still, for as little as Jalalabad, Afghanistan, made the news Stateside these days, it sure as hell looked like there was a lot going on over here.

A Radiance sentry had appeared a few minutes earlier; he'd used a flashlight to check Kolt's pass, but then apologized for bothering him. The guard didn't know who he was, but knew enough to know he wasn't supposed to know who he was, so after warning Kolt about occasional mortar attacks on the base, the guard left him alone, and continued his lonely patrol through the night.

Even these static security officers at Radiance were top-notch. Kolt realized that the security guys had a job Raynor himself wouldn't have been able to wrangle just a month earlier. It made him laugh for a moment, but he also knew the only reason he was the catch of the day was because he was the only one motivated enough—some would surely say dumb enough—to go on this operation.

He heard the crunch of distant footsteps on gravel, someone approaching from behind. He credited the three weeks in Wyoming, nearly all of it under the peril of imminent attack, for allowing his body and his ears to tune so quickly and acutely to movement and sounds or threat. He looked back over his shoulder, and was surprised to see the drone pilot coming toward him from the UAV area, a series of mobile buildings set up in a parking lot near the Operations Center.

"You are supposed to be in bed, mister." She said it in a matronly way, but he recognized that her sarcastic tone was pointed toward Grauer's to-the-minute itinerary.

He shrugged. "Would you be able to sleep?"

"Hell, I'll be flying a remote aircraft seven miles over you, and I can't sleep. So I don't blame you at all."

Kolt nodded, looked back out to the mountains to the south.

"You mind if I sit a minute?"

"Not at all. I'm sorry . . . Is it Pat?"

"Pam," she said as she joined him on the bench.

"I'm not too good with names."

"No problem, Racer." They sat in quiet for a moment. She said, "Every now and then we get hit with mortars . . . usually about this time of night."

Kolt nodded. "I've been warned. I can haul ass if I need to."

Pam laughed. Then stopped when she realized Kolt was looking at her.

"I feel like a monkey in a cage," Kolt said.

"Why is that?"

"The way you were eyeing me in the meeting today. The way you are looking at me now."

"I . . . I'm sorry." Archer looked off into the distance herself.

"Is there something you want to tell me?"

A new sentry passed by, shone his light on the two sitting in the dark. "Hi, Pammy."

"Hey, Jay." She held up her red badge and Raynor waved his.

"Good evening, sir."

"Evening," Kolt said.

The light turned off and the sentry continued on. After a long moment Pam turned to Kolt. "Three years ago I was in the Air Force, based at Creech."

Raynor smiled politely. "Vegas."

Pam did not return the smile. "Right. Anyway, I was on one of the Reapers. I worked Af-Pak missions . . . cross-border ground incursions."

Kolt's eyes widened in surprise. He held up his hand and cut her off before she could say another word. "Pam, I don't think we should—"

"I know who you are."

His hand lowered. "No you don't."

"I *do*. I know you led your team into Waziristan in November 2009. Hunter 29. I know you got hit. I know you were the only surviv—"

"I'm not having this conversation." He started to get up from the bench.

"I was overhead. I piloted the drone that turned back.

The one that left you and your team in the black, just before you guys were attacked."

Raynor was standing now, but he did not leave. He did not say a word.

"It was me. I let you guys down. I . . . I don't know why it matters now, but it's important to me that you know."

Raynor blew out a sigh. He shrugged and lowered himself back to the bench. "Small world, huh?"

"Small community."

Kolt looked back to the mountains to the south. Waziristan was off in that direction. "I heard there was some sort of problem with the bird."

Pam shrugged. "The Reaper was fine. False reading. I fought it at the time, I did not want to turn back, but I was overruled."

Raynor shrugged again. "Shit happens."

"I should have fought harder. I should have insisted—"

"Pam. You didn't do anything wrong that day. *I* did. I accept that, and I don't need anyone to share the blame with."

The comment hung in the cool air for a long moment. Then Pam asked, "Do you even know why you are here?"

Raynor was confused by the question. "Of course. In three hours I'm going to drop into—"

"No . . . I mean, why you?"

Kolt smiled. "Because I am the only man in possession of the skills necessary to do this job."

Archer just stared at him.

"I'm kidding. Of course, I get it. I am here because I am the only one who would risk it. Because of what happened before. Because of my responsibility in what happened before. There are a shitload of ex–Unit operators more qualified than me, but Webber and Grauer knew nobody in his right mind would take this job, except for the guy who's responsible for those boys being over there in the first place. I understand that."

"So you understand they are using you."

"I am willing. I want this. I *need* this."

"Look, the ground portion of this mission is not my part, obviously, but I've been around enough to see what's written between the lines. Langley, JSOC, or any organization with any self-respect would never send a man out on an op like the one that you are about to go on. I can think of fifty things that can go wrong in the next twenty-four hours."

Kolt knew she was right, but he was nevertheless surprised to hear it. "For example?" he asked.

"For example: this Pashtun contact, Jamal something. Did you know that his reliability is rated at only twenty-five percent? Who puts American lives in the hands of a contact with that level of trustworthiness?"

It was a rhetorical question that Raynor did not answer.

"And when was the last time you did a HAHO jump, or any kind of jump, for that matter? Your record says it's been nearly four years."

"I can handle the jump."

She shrugged. "I sure hope so, but even if you land right where you are supposed to, we know so little about the security setup in and around Zar's village that you won't be sure you're safe. We've counted as many as thirty men in close proximity to his compound, but there are reports that there are as many as three hundred in his militia."

"Well, you haven't seen three hundred in the village, have you?"

"Of course not. But things can look significantly different from forty thousand feet compared to how they really are at ground level."

"I trust the op to get me in."

"Maybe so. If you can make the jump, that is. They've spent a hell of a lot of time on working out your infiltration. But your *exfiltration* is the most poorly thought through component of this operation. Why do you suppose that is?"

"I am to ride out with this Jamal guy, just like I got in."

"Yeah, and then go to Peshawar? Sounds fine on paper, but that's a half day's drive. You're going to be in an iron box next to a truck engine the entire time? And if you're caught, you're dead. I don't just mean the Taliban who are holding Eagle 01. There are other groups running around the Tirah Valley. Taliban factions, AQ affiliates, warlords whose men would kill you outright, bandits and smugglers who would sell you to the Taliban or AQ, who would behead you as a spy."

"I know all this."

"Then you have to know this is pretty close to a suicide mission. Grauer and Webber need you to do this, they hope like hell you can get proof of life on the missing men, but nobody really expects you to survive long enough to get home."

Kolt understood this in a general sense, but having Pam Archer lay it out in such stark terms made him blow a long stream of steam into the night air.

"I can do it," he said. Telling her. Telling himself. "I better go get suited up."

She kept looking at him in the same disconcerting way. He could tell she was frustrated that she hadn't been able to get him to rethink his mission. Finally she just said, "Good luck."

"Thanks. Keep an eye on me from above."

"As much as I can. Sure wish my birds were armed, though."

Kolt stood, shook her hand. "I'll be fine." Shrugged in the dark. "Just help me get our guys back, okay?"

"Okay, Racer."

Kolt Raynor turned and walked off in the dark.

NINETEEN

Raynor sat in the back of the aircraft, his gear strapped to his body. The flight would be short—they were already so close to the border that the flight path would have to take them north, away from his target, to climb to the correct altitude. From there it would turn, hitting a couple of waypoints on the map along the way, and then turn south, flying along the border just east of the infamous Tora Bora complex, where Osama bin Laden slipped through the noose in December of 2001.

Immediately after a turn back to the west, a Radiance loadmaster would drop the aft stairs of the 727 cargo craft, and Kolt Raynor would drop out into the frozen black sky.

Raynor sat quietly, thinking about the moment when he'd feel nothing but the wind against his body and the pinch of the straps holding the gear tight to him, but his meditation was interrupted. It was the big ex–CIA spook, Kopelman. He'd lumbered aboard the aircraft, and he shouted over the engine noise that came through the open door. He stuck out a hand. "Just came to wish you good luck."

"Yeah. I'm gonna need it, right?"

"It's all on your shoulders. If you can make the jump, my guy can get you to the village. If you can lay low and not get compromised, he'll be back to pick you up four days after that. If you can make it back to Peshawar, I can get you out of the country. Easy as pie!" Kopelman said it with a smile.

"Right," Raynor replied. He leaned over and adjusted the laces on his right boot where they were biting into his calf.

Bob seemed to notice something in Racer's tone. "You have any particular concerns you'd like to voice at this late hour?"

"Just a few. Like this contact of yours."

Bob shrugged. "Jamal is solid."

"Twenty-five percent solid?"

Kopelman's bushy eyebrows rose, and he sat down on the mesh bench next to Raynor. "Where did you hear about that?" Raynor did not answer. Kopelman shrugged again. "That's Langley's assessment, not mine. Jamal was a walk-in; he had a hell of an interesting story, but that's all he had. The brain trust on the seventh floor took a pass on him, but a buddy I have who's still with the Agency slipped me the lead. He knows what we're working on, and he thought this guy's story was worth us knowing."

"What's the story?"

"This kid has been making his living delivering goods up into the less accessible parts of the valley with a tractor pulling a wooden cart. Eight weeks ago he was in Shataparai, and one of Zar's men asked him into the compound. Told him they required a weekly delivery of purified water. No local in Khyber pays money for water. They all drink the rotgut shit they get from their streams and wells. But Jamal didn't ask questions. He made his first shipment, and was searched up and down like he was heading into Fort Knox."

Raynor nodded, picturing the scene.

"The compound was full of Zar's men, no surprise there, but there were a couple of foreign guys. Westernized assholes. Turks, he thinks. Jamal thought the water might be for them, but there was too much of it. After his third trip to Shataparai he was contacted on his cell phone, ordered to go to a pharmacy in Peshawar, pick up a package, and deliver it to the compound. He sneaked a peek as he was bringing it out. It was antibiotics. Western stuff. Not something that would normally be used around here, or even known about around here."

"That's it?"

"No. One of the guards is kind of a dolt, apparently. Five weeks ago the guy was making conversation while Jamal was hand pumping water into their tank. The guy said there were some Westerners in the compound, they were prisoners, and the Taliban and al Qaeda were fighting over them. Zar protected them from both factions, but was trying to rid himself of the burden of the prisoners. He followed Pashtunwali, but he didn't want to get in the middle of a fight between those two goon squads.

"The next day, Jamal went to the U.S. embassy."

"So neither you nor any Western intelligence agency has ever worked with Jamal before that?"

Kopelman did not answer directly. Instead, he said, "I've been working with Pashtuns since I was a zit-faced punk passing them Stingers in the eighties to knock down Russian Hinds. I *know* the Pashtuns. I've looked in this kid's eyes. He's telling the truth. He's a loyal agent."

"Why would he work with us?"

Kopelman just looked off into the empty space toward the rear of the aircraft's cabin. "He's got his reasons. Good ones." A pause. "Jamal is as solid a source as I've ever had. I'd stake my life on it."

Or mine, at least, thought Kolt.

Just then the loadmaster leaned into the conversation. "We're ready to go."

Kopelman stood, shook Raynor's gloved hand again. "See you in Pesh."

"Expect it," replied Kolt with a tone that conveyed both the intensity brought on with his game face and his continued annoyance that Bob had been less than forthright about some of the details of this operation.

Kopelman's large body turned away. Behind it Raynor saw Grauer leaning inside the side door of the aircraft.

He had to shout over the three spinning Pratt & Whitney turbofans. "Good luck, Racer!"

Kolt just nodded to his former commanding officer. Said, "I'll get it done."

"I know you will." Grauer turned away. The loadmaster shut and sealed the hatch, and then put on his headset to communicate with the cockpit crew.

Kolt Raynor suddenly felt extremely alone.

He rehearsed his actions in the air over and over inside the plane. Old habits learned years earlier in a Delta recce troop were hard to break, and this time he was his own jumpmaster. He stood up on the shiny cold metal flooring and recited the jump commands. His black assault boots grabbed the floor like glue. Underneath the flight suit and the black Patagonia long underwear, Kolt was drenched from head to toe: a combination of nerves, altitude, prebreathing on the oxygen console, and the double layer of clothing he knew he would need at twenty-five thousand feet over the Pakistani badlands.

He spoke aloud, but he alone could hear his words. "Fly flat and stable, keep legs slightly bent, don't backslide, check altimeter, check left, front, and right, clear my immediate airspace, check altimeter, wave off fellow jumpers, arch back, pull rip cord, brace for severe jolt, and pray for good canopy."

Kolt thought about what he'd just said. "Wave off fellow jumpers?" Kolt looked toward the loadmaster, who was busy stowing seats and snapping into his safety line. He wore an Army olive green flight suit and green Nomex gloves similar to Kolt's. But he also wore a large gray helmet with a full plastic face piece to protect his eyes. Kolt was pleased he hadn't heard him say that. The engine roar all but drowned out his entire voice.

Kolt lost himself in his thoughts. His memory bounced back several years to his last high-altitude jump. The skies over Iraq treated him well back then. He prayed for the same this time around, even though, this time, he would be jumping alone. He much preferred the feeling of heading into harm's way head-on knowing he had a team of professionals heading in with him.

Soon the loadmaster shook Kolt's shoulder and signaled it was time to go. He unhooked Kolt's green air hose from the oxygen console and hooked him to the bailout bottle on his left hip. Kolt stood and moved aft as a set of stairs lowered into the slipstream below the tail of the 727. He turned around, facing the front of the plane, and gave a brief thumbs-up to the loadmaster, before slowly backing down the stairs until he could no longer see the man or the cabin. He stood by at the bottom of the stairs, enveloped in the incredible noise of the wind blast. He held tight on the rail, kept his eyes fixed through his goggles on the caution lights next to him.

Red. Red. Red.

Green.

Kolt pushed backward, kept his head up, dropped a few feet until his legs hit the slipstream, which slammed them back and up, turning his body horizontal. The wind smashed into his face and chest, the cold blast against his oxygen mask and goggles biting through the seams like fat needles puncturing his skin.

He fell facedown toward the black badlands below him.

Even in the hottest of summer months, the temperature at this altitude can send icicles through a jumper's veins. This visit was in early November. At his current altitude he was floating in twenty-degree weather.

Out of habit, Kolt counted out loud. His words vibrated behind his oxygen mask up to his earlobes. "One thousand, two thousand, three thousand, four thousand, five thousand, pull!" Kolt arched his back hard, kept his left arm half bent out in front of his head to maintain balance, and reached back to his right shoulder for the silver ripcord handle. He gave it a vigorous tug, pushing out and away at 60 degrees.

Thankful for the good canopy above him that blocked his view of the stars, Kolt reached up high for his left toggle, pulled it down to head level, and arced in a 180-degree turn. He turned his head to the left to see the 727's lights being swallowed in the distance by the dark night. The big bird would be on final approach over Jalalabad not long after Raynor's boots touched the earth. A few seconds later he checked his small compass on his right wrist to confirm he was heading due east.

At twenty thousand feet above the tribal region of Pakistan, just east of the Afghanistan border, Kolt easily identified the lights of Peshawar in the far distance. So far so good.

Kolt's next waypoint was the lights of the small village of Landi Kotal, off his left shoulder. He strained under a moonless night to locate two more scattered towns along the N5, the highway through the Khyber Pass to Afghanistan. He thought he might be a little north of his route, so he pulled on the right toggle and shifted to the right twenty degrees.

Kolt turned his left wrist over and checked his altimeter—thirteen thousand feet. Suddenly, Kolt's left side dropped as if he were no longer being suspended from above. He felt like a puppet with only one string. Kolt struggled to right himself, but before he could manage a hold on his left riser he started spinning rapidly clockwise. A free-fall parachutist might experience a partial malfunction of his parachute once in a lifetime. But Kolt had been there before. In fact, he had experienced the same malfunction years earlier during his initial operator training. He knew he had to act quickly or risk losing consciousness due to the violent uncontrollable spinning.

A dozen of his left suspension lines had snapped. He didn't have to check his altimeter to know he was losing altitude fast. With his right hand he reached up to where his right shoulder and chest met and grabbed the red cutaway pillow. With his left hand he reached up to his left breast and found his oval-shaped ripcord. With solid grips on both Kolt yanked the cutaway pillow in his right hand from its pouch and immediately pulled his reserve cord with his left hand.

Kolt's main chute separated and floated away as Kolt felt the obvious sensation of free-falling in an upright position. In a second, his reserve silk caught air, causing his leg harness to snap him vigorously in the groin.

Feel pain. Still alive. Must be a good chute.

Kolt checked his altimeter again. He had lost four thousand feet during the escapade. He quickly toggled to his left toward his drop zone, still several miles distant. He'd never make his rendezvous with Jamal on time now.

But Kolt had no time to worry about that—he had to

concentrate on his landing. He reached for his right toggle, drew it down to waist level, and executed a tight right-hand turn, heading back into the wind in the opposite direction. At one thousand feet Kolt made his final turn.

He knew he was in the mountains, which meant there was little chance of his landing on level ground. He pulled the quick-release strap holding his big rucksack to his body, allowing it to drop the length of the fifteen-foot tether. Looking down now, he could see nothing in the blackness below him, but he had to keep his body ready for the moment when the—

For the third time on this jump, a violent tug to his harness jolted his body and burned into his skin between his legs.

Raynor lurched to a sudden stop, but his feet had not yet touched the ground.

He was stuck in a tree. Instantly he began swaying with a cold valley breeze.

There was no moon, and his night vision equipment was stowed in the pack that had been hanging far below him. He had no idea how far he was from the earth, or what sort of terrain he'd find when he hit it, so he spent a couple of minutes perfectly still, intently focused on the sounds around him. Satisfied that he was alone here, he retrieved a small flashlight from a pocket on his shoulder. It had a filter which emitted a lower-intensity red light, and he switched this on.

Pausing a few more seconds, he scanned below him with his light.

He was less than five feet from the ground.

A few seconds of jerking and heaving helped him the rest of the way to the pine-covered earth. The chute was tangled but he tore it out of the tree in under a minute, all the while thanking God that his jump was over.

TWENTY

Kolt buried his olive gray silk reserve parachute, harness, altimeter, oxygen mask, boots, and a small survival shovel in the forest. He unzipped his flight suit and let it drop to his knees before he hurriedly stepped out of each leg. He pulled off the Patagonia base layer as well. He retrieved his local canvas pack from the jump bag, and quickly donned his local garb.

He opened the jump bag and pulled out a pair of old ragged leather sandals that tied around the ankle and had a single loop hole for the big toe with a one-inch-wide band behind it, closer to the instep. The soles were made of several layers of tanned camel hide, and were as authentic as the rest of his clothing, with the exception of the hidden scent-reducing long johns.

When everything he no longer needed was well hidden he sat on a bed of pine needles and covered his head with his patoo, the capelike wool blanket that is wrapped either around the front of the body or over the head like a hood. He used it as a tent to cover his work, and then fired up his GPS. It took a moment to receive the signal from the satellite, but once the GPS got a fix on his position, he realized he'd landed three miles south of his original drop zone.

Three miles would not have seemed so bad, if not for the topography illustrated on the GPS. He'd landed in a pine forest down in a small basin, and to get to his destination he would need to head sharply uphill. There was no possibility of making his rendezvous with Jamal on time, but that wasn't the end of the world. Kopelman would have warned his agent that he could expect unavoidable delays to the pickup window.

Raynor shouldered his backpack, wrapped himself in his patoo, and began walking north. His eyes took in what light they could, but he struggled to see through the darkness in the thick pines, hoping like hell he'd run across a path before long.

He stopped to rest on a cold rock at 6 a.m., after three arduous hours of constant uphill trudging. There was still no light and he'd not yet broken out of the pine and fir-covered hillside, but he had covered a respectable amount of ground considering the conditions.

He'd found a disused logging trail. It was level and cleared of brush enough to be useful, and it was completely devoid of traffic. This wasn't unexpected during the middle of the night, but he did consider himself fortunate. These rural parts of the Tribal Areas were full of locals who regarded each and every outsider with utter suspicion, and a stranger walking through this valley would attract a *lot* of attention. He needed to get to his meeting point with Jamal as soon as possible, but he knew from his slow progress that he would not make it to the rendezvous until several hours after sunup.

He took a long swig of water from his hidden Camel-Bak and began marching once again up the hill.

The first living creature Raynor encountered in the Tirah Valley was a rail-thin cow, standing alone in a clearing of freshly cut cedar trees along the side of the trail. The animal startled him with its movement in the dawn's light, but Kolt recovered quickly, passed the field of low stumps, and then made out other cattle milling in the distant mist.

He entered fallow fields, then left these behind him by following the trail along the side of a steep gorge, and found that the gorge and the trail spilled out onto the valley floor, where a village lay shrouded in fog. He smelled cooking fires, knew the women would be up preparing the morning meal even before the first prayer of the day, and he wanted to give this village a wide berth. He left the trail, climbed the steep hill to another clearing. Here he entered an orchard of peach trees, their branches bare this late in the year. Looking back behind him he eyed the village through the vapor. He saw baked mud buildings, all single-story, with flat roofs that made them look like the mortarboards of college graduates.

He wanted to stop and rest again, but he fought the urge and turned away, moved on up the trail.

A waterfall trickled off a cliff side and fell into a stream, and Kolt followed the stream down into a valley via man-made steps that ran alongside it, because a quick peek at his GPS told him to do so. The decline did not last, however, and soon he was climbing again, leaving the trail behind as it wound back to the northwest.

His legs ached and burned as the incline increased even more now. His lower back tightened under the weight of his heavy canvas pack. His three-year-old war wound ached, the fused vertebrae protesting every step.

Soon the terrain rose so abruptly that he was forced to his hands and knees, pulling his way upward by grasping the trunks of firs and carefully setting the soles of his smooth leather sandals on rocky outcroppings before pushing himself higher.

Just off his right shoulder a long wash ran up into a saddle of the hill above him. He knew the going would be smoother there, if just barely. He began moving laterally but stopped when he heard a noise. He froze in a copse of wild mulberry trees in the fading mist, and listened hard again.

The sound repeated. He cocked his head.

A group of men chanting softly.

There. In a small flattened-out section of the wash just above him, at the limits of his eyesight in the vapor, a group of a dozen men knelt on their patoos and prayed aloud.

At their sides, next to their ersatz prayer rugs, Kalashnikovs and rocket-propelled grenade launchers rested on the ground.

They were either local militia or Taliban—either way, he'd come within thirty seconds of wandering out into the open right in front of them.

It had been too easy so far, and the long lonely walk was lulling him into false confidence.

Come on, Kolt. This isn't the damn Smokies. This is Indian country.

He tucked deeper into the fir trees, continued on up the forested hill, slowly and silently, and passed to the left of the armed men, leaving them behind to complete their morning prayer.

By the time the mist burned away completely he had reached a highland plain, where he passed an opium field. The poppies were dormant this late in the season, short sticks preparing themselves for the winter cold.

Now he could see to the distant west and north. The land was green and lush, and the tall mountain peaks of the Kurram and Khyber ranges were snowcapped, sharp and beautiful in the distance back toward the Afghan border.

It reminded him of Wyoming.

For the first time he was thankful for the training he'd received in the States. He'd climbed, crawled, and walked for over seven hours, and his muscles, joints, and back ached, but his lungs had no problem with this altitude.

He was surprised to find himself feeling good as the first warm rays of the sun beamed onto his face.

But he knew this would not last.

TWENTY-ONE

Jamal Metziel turned the key back toward himself, silencing the rumbling engine of his old truck. It was daylight already, he'd arrived to the rendezvous point late, but an exact time was nigh on impossible with the terrible condition of the track that he'd been forced to drive for the past three hours. Quickly he leaped out of his Toyota Hilux pickup and lifted the hood, coated his hands with grease and grime from the air hose, and then wiped the evidence of his "truck repair" across his light blue kameez shirt. He pulled some tools from his truck bed, dropped onto his back, slid on grass and dirt under the vehicle, and waited there.

The ticking and clanking of the hot metal kept his attention for a moment, relaxed him to the dangers around him, but he knew he was not safe here.

The American would come soon, maybe any moment, and at that point the true perils would begin.

He was no fool—he knew the stakes. If he was caught helping a Westerner he would be killed.

But he did it anyway. He had made the difficult decision to help the Americans, and whatever came after that, Allah would decide. He would survive, inshallah, or he would die.

Inshallah.

Unlike most others here in western Pakistan, Jamal was motivated neither by tribal affiliation nor by religious precepts. His allegiance to America was personal, born out of his own experience and his own loss and his own pain, and this motivation rivaled anyone's here in the FATA, from the most devout Wahhabis to the Pashtuns deeply instilled with the honor code of Pashtunwali.

Already Jamal had seen more death than most men his age. The Afghan was near thirty, and his every memory was laced with visions of blood, bribery, and backstabbing.

He did not remember the Russians attacking his village—they came just a few years before his birth—but he grew up with stories of the helicopter attack that killed his cousins and uncles.

He did, however, remember the bombing of his hometown as the Soviets left in 1989, and again around the time the Afghani Communists collapsed a few years later at the hands of feuding warlords. As a child he would squat in the corner of his home at night, unable to sleep as the bombs rained down on the hills surrounding Kabul.

Then the bombs stopped falling, but the danger had only begun. Because then the Taliban came.

As a teenager, neighbors spoke of Jamal having been blessed with his father's hands. While most kids peddled tainted gasoline on the side of the road or pushed a cart of hay, Jamal learned his father's trade, repairing and building weapons. It was honest work, not smuggling guns or harming anyone. No, Jamal's father did a thriving business restoring everything from seventeenth-century swords and shields to mid-eighteenth-century muzzleloaders.

But the Taliban were in charge of Kabul now, and the Taliban had enemies. They demanded firepower, not souvenirs.

Soon Jamal's father was put to work for the Taliban. His new masters reasoned that if he could make an old bolt-action Enfield look showroom new, then he could certainly file the iron sites on a Kalashnikov properly.

Jamal knew his father wasn't happy. But he also knew it was healthier to submit to the pressure than to resist the bearded and black-turbaned fighters who visited his small back-alley shop every few days. Jamal vowed to make it as easy on his aging father as he could. He sat cross-legged on a soiled green pillow and delicately sanded and filed the trigger mechanisms of the AK, the most prolific Eastern Bloc rifle in the world.

And then the Americans came.

By the time of the terror attacks in the United States on September 11, 2001, Jamal had all but inherited his father's shop. Within weeks the Taliban fled Kabul and the Westerners arrived. Jamal noted the incredible interest the foreigners had in Chicken Street just up the road from the old abandoned American embassy. He wanted in. Reluctantly, his father agreed to move the shop two streets over to the back room of a carpet vendor. Jamal wasn't looking for a secretive location, but it was all they could afford.

Jamal was astonished by the new and insatiable desire for junk weapons. Americans were willing to pay top dollar and in U.S. currency for the same rifles he contemplated leaving behind in the old shop during the move. Jamal worked hard, restoring weapons for these polite and well-to-do foreigners, and within a year his shop was well known throughout Kabul.

Jamal Metziel did harbor concerns that Taliban spies would notice the profits he was raking in from the Westerners. Kabul had fallen a year earlier and the ruling shura had moved across the border to the Northwest Frontier Province, but that did not mean there was no Taliban influence on the bustling streets of the Afghanistan capital.

The beards and black turbans were gone, but the Taliban's henchmen were not.

Jamal liked the Westerners and feared the Taliban, but one night black helicopters landed in the square near his shop, and green-eyed soldiers poured out. Jamal, his two teenage brothers, and his ailing father were snatched up by American Special Forces. He was surprised the women and children in the compound weren't shot on sight. He had heard the stories of how the Americans valued only the fighting-age males and would kill the women during these roundups. But the women were left alone. *Must be another group of Americans,* he decided. He and his brothers and father were classified as PUCs—persons under custody—and flown to Bagram for lengthy interrogation.

Jamal was surprised that he wasn't tortured. He had figured his father certainly had been, as the interrogators only seemed to want to know about his father's relationship with the Taliban and where Osama bin Laden was. They must have believed them all because within three weeks they were given new clothes, one hundred dollars each for their trouble, a bottle of water, a new Koran, and a nighttime helicopter ride to Kabul airport, where they were curtly released without so much as a wave good-bye. In talking with his father and brother on the way home he was astonished to learn that no one had been beaten by the Americans.

The very next night the Taliban came to their shop. Jamal's father was taken in the night by a half-dozen armed men. Jamal and his brothers were knocked around a bit as they tried to come to their father's aid, but they were left behind. It was clear the jihadists had questions of their own. What had Jamal's father told the Americans?

Jamal was in the shop when he heard the news. His father's body had been hung by its bare feet from a telephone pole in the western part of Kabul. His head was found stuffed inside a bloody burlap sack a few feet from the pool of blood that had drained from the headless torso.

Jamal was crushed and confused. His father had always done exactly what the Taliban asked. He never openly resisted, only in private to his family at home.

The young Afghan sold the shop to the carpet vendor for practically pennies. He didn't care—he just wanted to get out of Kabul and protect his brothers and mother. They packed their meager belongings and headed east toward Jalalabad. But before they could settle in there they learned that the underground Taliban was alive and well in Jalalabad, so they continued to Pakistan and a refugee camp on the outskirts of Peshawar.

Jamal took on odd jobs for enough money to help his family. Soon his cousins and uncles arrived at the camp, and they found menial work in Peshawar and nearby Darra Adam Khel.

On a Monday evening in April of 2010, while Jamal drove his recently purchased tractor-pulled delivery cart through the less accessible valleys of Khyber Agency, Jamal's mother and his youngest brother were purchasing items in the Qissa Khawani Bazaar in the heart of Peshawar. Items Jamal had sent them to fetch. Items he would resell on his next run to the FATA. A protest in the market hampered the movements of the two. Seconds later a bomb exploded in the crowded street. Jamal's mother and brother were blown into tiny bits of unrecognizable flesh and skin and hair.

Al Qaeda took credit for the bomb.

Once more the jihadists had taken members of his family from him. He was devastated, he was consumed by anger, but he still had to make money to survive, so he continued his delivery runs into the FATA.

* * *

A compound out of town and in the hills needed potable water once a week. Jamal thought that was odd. He didn't know why the people living in the compound couldn't drink the same murky stream water that everyone else did, but he wasn't complaining. He needed the work.

Jamal drove his tractor to the compound once or twice a week past armed guards on the edge of the road. He also thought it odd that he was always made to climb off the tractor and raise his arms to be frisked. He was never sure if the armed men were Pakistani Taliban or maybe even foreign jihadists now under the al Qaeda banner. When he arrived at the compound a funny-looking black wand was waved around his body. It ticked slowly. After Jamal was checked, several men searched the tractor before he was allowed to pump the water into the large drum.

He saw a pair of foreigners, al Qaeda from Turkey, he decided, and then his suspicions were raised further about the goings-on in Shataparai when he was sent to pick up antibiotics at a pharmacy and deliver them to the compound.

When, on his third week of deliveries to the compound, a bored guard mentioned Western prisoners, he decided what he would do.

The next day Jamal Metziel rose from his afternoon prayers in Peshawar and took a bus to the U.S. embassy. After waiting in lines outside the building for hours he was led into a hallway. Here he asked to speak to someone in the Central Intelligence Agency. A Pashto-speaking American woman treated him with more respect than any government employee he'd ever met, either back home in Afghanistan or here in Pakistan. He told her his story, and she took notes. Then she asked him many questions about himself: his family, his history, his motivation.

He was told to return in two days, but when he did return, he was told by the same woman that someone would contact him at his home.

As he left the bus stop to return to his tiny flat, a big, burly, white-haired man dressed like any other local on the street called out to him from his small car. Within minutes they were driving together through the city, and the man revealed himself to be an American.

Jamal had no clue that "Mister Bob" was not, in fact, in the Central Intelligence Agency.

TWENTY-TWO

Jamal waited by his "broken-down" truck for hours. Mister Bob had told him that the agent would come out of the sky, but Mister Bob had also said there were many factors in play and he could not promise that the man would arrive on time. Only once during his wait did Jamal encounter others on the broken road. Four men with pack mules loaded with cans of tainted gasoline passed by at eight thirty in the morning. And well behind the men, two women in bright blue burkas shuffled along, carrying heavy loads in their hands. Jamal wished the men peace, and avoided glancing at the women so as not to offend the men, and the procession moved on.

At 10:30 a.m. he was ready to leave. It was another three hours from here to the village of Shataparai, and he had to make his delivery at the compound of Zar Afridi, even if he had to go on alone. And even if the

American spy arrived right this second and they set off immediately, he would not make it back to Peshawar before dusk, and the roads into Khyber were dangerous after dark.

Jamal looked up into the clear blue sky and prayed to Allah, willed a man in a parachute to appear.

Shortly after eleven, Kolt arrived at a low rise that, according to his GPS, should put him just above his rendezvous point with his contact. He dropped his backpack in a copse of low bushes, crawled forward on his hands and knees, and crested the rise.

Down below him, not more than fifty yards, he saw the old yellow truck. It had pulled off the rough dirt track, and the driver had the hood raised. The beige plastic water tank in back was full of water, and the rest of the bed contained boxes and cartons and other items a traveling merchant might transport.

Then Raynor saw his contact. Jamal was thin. He wore a prayer cap and a blue kameez under a gray vest, and had a short scruffy beard. The man looked up to the sky, and even from this distance, Raynor saw the nervous expression on his face.

He didn't blame the contact for being scared or, for that matter, being pissed off. Kolt was three hours late. He quickly scooted back down the hill to retrieve his backpack, thankful that his strenuous walk/climb was almost over. A minute later he crested the hill again and headed toward the truck.

Jamal turned to him as soon as he appeared, but he looked utterly confused.

"A sallum aleikum," said Kolt.

"Wa aleikum a salaam."

The men shook hands, but the Afghan did not smile. He spoke in Pashto, because other than some Dari and a little Arabic he knew no other language. "I have been here for many hours. I thought you were coming from the sky."

Kolt answered in his halting Pashto. "I *did* come from the sky, but missed my landing. Thank you for waiting for me."

"It is a big problem. I will be late for my delivery."

"Then we should go."

Kolt and Jamal hid the American's rucksack in a hollowed-out area below the driver's seat. It barely fit, and then only after much pushing of the seat by both men and some colorful cursing by Raynor. Then Kolt climbed into the backseat, and Jamal shut the hood and fired the engine.

For the first twenty minutes of the journey Raynor rode in the back of the little truck's cab, crouched next to the stash compartment behind the folded-forward seat. He spent the time asking Jamal about the lay of the land around them. He was interested in the area, of course, but mostly he was trying to get a feel for this agent. Was he as reliable as Bob promised?

As Jamal answered, sweat beads dripped from the tip of his hooked nose, and Kolt did not take this as a good sign. He had no problem with the kid being scared of the Taliban. But was he, in fact, afraid of Raynor? Afraid the American would figure out what treachery he had up his sleeve?

Kolt did not know. He kept up the conversation, searching for any clue as to what was going on in the Afghan's mind.

"Not much of a road, is it?" Raynor commented. The path they traveled on was rutted and narrow; large boulders had to be avoided or carefully driven over, Jamal attacking each obstacle one wheel at a time. Even with the big tires and the four-wheel drive, the truck threatened to bottom out several times on the hard dirt track.

Jamal said, "It is a mule trail. It is difficult for this truck, and I can only do it this time of year, after the rains and before the snow. Normally I drive my tractor."

Kolt nodded.

"You speak the language well," Jamal complimented. He was visibly nervous, checking his rearview, checking both sides of the road.

Kolt himself looked around before saying, "Thank you."

"But you do not sound like a Pashtun."

"I know. I do not plan to deceive anyone."

Jamal nodded. "Good. You will fail. You are not *that* good."

Raynor kept his head low but his eyes just high enough to see out the front of the dirty windshield. He wasn't sure what he was looking for. The steep hills all around, the low scrubland, the rocky dirt road, everything looked the same in all directions. His GPS told him they were headed southwest, which was correct, but other than that, he had no idea if he and Jamal were following the same plan.

For all he knew this skinny, scruffy young man was

going to sell him out to the Taliban just around the next turn.

This part of the mission, Raynor knew, he'd just have to go with the flow and hope like hell that Bob Kopelman was a better judge of character than the CIA.

The late-morning temperature was nearing seventy-five, and the sun shone directly on the unair-conditioned truck cab. Raynor was tucked tight behind the front seats, and his legs were near cramping. Still, he realized the box he'd soon be forced to climb into would be tighter and hotter and much more stifling.

"How close are you going to get me to the compound?"

"Mister Bob did not tell you?"

"He told me. I want to hear it from you."

"It will be less than one kilometer away. There is a turn in the road just before the village. Two weeks ago Mister Bob told me to stop there and check the hill. I climbed into the trees and found a good place from where you can watch the compound."

Raynor nodded—he'd play along—but he'd make his own arrangements once Jamal dropped him off. He wasn't sure where he was going to find overwatch on Zar's buildings, but he was damn sure *not* going to go exactly where this unproven contact expected him to be hiding.

"How long will you be in the compound itself?" he asked the Afghan.

"Normally thirty minutes."

"And you will pass by the same road when you leave the village?"

"Of course. This village is very small. There is only one road to Shataparai."

Soon Kolt slid around and got his feet into the stash compartment behind the passenger seat, and he struggled to slide his body inside. The space in the stash was large enough to accommodate him, with difficulty and discomfort, and it was black as night and hot as hell. He found a bottle of water that Jamal had placed there for him. He assumed the liquid would be somewhere just short of boiling, but he appreciated the gesture. Kolt had his CamelBak and he'd wet his patoo and placed it around his neck. When Jamal slid the metal door up he mercifully left the hatch open a half inch. He then locked the left rear seat back into position. Kolt would have to shut it tight soon enough, but for now the dusty and diesel-infused air was the most beautiful part of his world.

Every bump and bounce in the road seemed amplified here down low behind the cab, and Raynor cursed the lack of infrastructure in the FATA, and added a curse for Jamal, as they rocked and rolled slowly toward the west. When the truck drove through a stream that reached up to the frame of the cab, Raynor heard splashing on the bottom of his metal coffin, and then water squirted in on his leg through a seam in the box that had not been well soldered. Kolt fought a brief bout with panic—he'd surely drown here if the truck got stuck in the stream. But seconds later they were back on dry land, and with that came the banging rocks, the dust and the fuel fumes that made their way through that slight gap in the corner weld, and the infernal stifling heat.

The truck never got out of first gear, but Raynor felt it slow down even more than normal, and he quickly sealed the sliding door tight with his right elbow. This, he assumed, was the first of the two outer checkpoints, just a few kilometers from Shataparai village. The engine remained idling. It sounded rough to the American down there seated just behind the engine, but a breakdown was only one of his many worries. He lay on his side in the fetal position, not moving or even breathing deeply. He pictured Taliban guards looking into the cab and under the truck just now, and he hoped like hell they didn't look too closely.

After less than a minute they were moving again. Kolt had heard no voices during the stop, but he felt confident they had just made it past their first obstacle.

He felt the urge to slide open the hatch again, to suck the dirty but cooler air. But he fought this urge, remained in his coffinlike box and sipped warm water through the tube every few minutes, well aware that his lack of a need to piss, while damned convenient considering his present circumstances, was nonetheless disconcerting. Dehydration would come soon. His body would be unable to retain the salts it needed to function. He had salt tablets in his ruck, but his ruck was secreted away under Jamal's seat, and getting to it was not an option.

The second stop came just after two in the afternoon. Raynor lay perfectly still. His perspiration wet the entire floor of the iron box, and he worried it would drip out through the thin crack and draw attention to anyone checking the underside of the vehicle. It seemed unlikely, but Kolt could do nothing at the moment but lie there and worry, so his mind worked in overdrive.

This time Jamal turned off the engine, and this time Kolt heard voices. Several men spoke. Their words were not loud or angry, but there was a discussion of some sort. Raynor heard Jamal, seemingly speaking from behind the wheel, as the other men walked around the truck.

There was a scuffing sound on the ground below him. Someone was on his back under the vehicle. This man spoke out, and now Kolt heard. It was Pashto.

The truck moved slightly on its suspension. Jamal climbed out and shut the door behind him.

Raynor had pulled his pistol out of its holster just after climbing into the stash compartment. It lay pressed against his body, but it was near his hand and he would be able to wield it if absolutely necessary.

He crouched there for a long time. He pictured Jamal and the Taliban or Zar's militiamen crouching around a fire and sipping chai, and he wondered if the Afghan's nerves would show with a jittering hand or fleeting glances back at the truck. He did not know this guy. Even if he *was* solid, as Kopelman had insisted, could he keep cool under the pressure he must be feeling right now?

The door opened and shut, and the engine fired up again with a cough.

Soon Jamal had them moving again, rolling forward, breaking and turning and slowing in accordance with the conditions of the rough dirt trail.

Kolt's appendages were numb and the stifling heat was cooking his brain, but he was thankful this Afghan agent was not rushing. Not pushing his luck. A breakdown would be catastrophic, not only because they would be stuck out here, but also because others would come to help, and Raynor did not want a dozen locals hanging around this truck, crawling under it to fix something. It was one of those Murphy's Law–type scenarios that derail operators in the field from time to time, and Kolt hoped he was lucky enough to avoid that particular eventuality.

By three in the afternoon Kolt Raynor was literally choking on dust and diesel fumes in his hot box below and behind the cab of the truck. He had no sensation in his lower legs, and the back of his neck hurt from three hours in his contorted position. His water was gone, and the knuckles on his hands were burned where he was forced to position his fists against the scorching metal of the box.

He pictured Bob Kopelman, back at the auto shop in Lahore where this stash compartment had been enlarged. In his mind's eye he saw the big, burly sixty-year-old peering into this tiny metal coffin and nodding. "That looks perfect."

Raynor wished he could just shove one-third of Bob's big ass into this hellish glove compartment right now.

Mercifully the truck came to a stop once again. He prayed it was time for him to get out, and within a couple of seconds, his prayer was answered. Jamal popped up the seat and slid open the hidden access plate to the stash compartment. The seventy-five-degree air rushed in like an arctic gale, and the daylight singed Kolt's eyes when he poked his head out. Jamal had already flipped his driver's seat forward to remove the rucksack, and softly but hurriedly he spoke to the American. "You must go. There is a caravan of donkeys and merchants behind me in the road. Ten men or more. They are only minutes away."

"Okay," Kolt said as he tried to pull himself up and out of the box, but his legs were not cooperating, his upper body had to extricate the rest of his body, and this took a half minute of grunting and twisting and pulling. Jamal had taken this time to pull the American's pack from the bottom of the smaller metal box below his seat, and he heaved it out of the cab and let it fall in the dirt next to where Raynor tried to climb out from the backseat.

Kolt slid out gingerly and stood up as if wearing a new pair of prosthetic legs.

"Mister Racer. Please go. This way." He pointed at a steep, wooded hill, marked by limestone outcroppings that ran from the rutted dirt track up toward the sky.

Jamal helped Kolt get the pack on his shoulders, and then the young Afghan literally pushed the American forward to the hill. "Hurry, please. It is not safe here."

"I'm going, dude," Kolt replied in frustrated English, and with a gait hindered by numb legs and sixty pounds of gear, he made it to the hillside, then began hauling himself up off the road by pulling on handfuls of thick foliage. Just seconds later he heard the truck's transmission pop into gear, the machine start back on its way up the trail, and the driver's-side door slam shut soon after.

Jamal was getting the hell out of there, and Kolt couldn't say he blamed him.

TWENTY-THREE

It took over an hour for the infiltrator to find and establish his hide site. Over an hour of arduous climbing and hauling his tired and sore body up and over rocks, belly-crawling in the scrubs alongside open fields, fighting his way through thick pines and tall brush. All the while he followed his GPS map toward the hide Pete Grauer's analysts had determined was the best place for him to get eyes into the compound. The location he ultimately chose was thirty yards or so from where Grauer had indicated on the satellite and UAV images back at Jalalabad. Raynor had hoped to get even farther away, maybe find something higher up on the hillside, in case this Jamal character sold him out to the Taliban and a crew of gunmen came up the mountain looking for him. But when he arrived at the general location of his overwatch, above the terraced poppy fields stepping down all the way to the banks of the river, he realized his options were few. Most places that gave a view of the compound four hundred yards away were exposed—open meadows—or else they were so steep and sheer that he could not get to them. He finally made his way above a large pine that grew out of a wall of broken limestone, and then used the thick needles as cover as he lowered himself down onto a ledge of rock with thick moss growing on its surface. The outcropping jutted away from the hillside just farther than the length of his body, and there was a slight incline toward the village. This and the thick tree above would keep his body concealed, with only his head and his spotting scope exposed to the far side of the valley.

It was a great hide, unless he was detected, in which case he'd be in trouble, because he had absolutely *nowhere* to run. If he found it necessary to bug out in a hurry he could leave his gear behind, scale up the ten feet or so of rock behind the tree, and then make his way toward higher ground. But if he was sighted and men came up to root him out, they would be above and behind him before he knew it, and his little Makarov pistol wouldn't do him a hell of a lot of good.

Unless, of course, he jabbed it into his mouth and pulled the trigger.

In the Operations Center at the Radiance base in Jalalabad, Pete Grauer stood next to the conference table with his hands on his hips and his gaze fixed on the monitor. Around him a half-dozen analysts and technicians adopted the same stance. They could no longer see their man on the screen. He'd shimmied down a rock wall behind a thick pine tree and was now undoubtedly hidden below it.

UAV pilot Pam Archer, while flying the Predator she dubbed Baby Boy from a trailer a hundred yards away from the OC, was nonetheless present in the room via an open radio link. Grauer had only to speak aloud and a microphone on the table would pick up his voice and transmit it directly into Archer's headset.

"It looks like he's found his hide," Grauer said. Raynor had been under the tree for five minutes.

"Roger that," replied Archer. "I show him about thirty-five meters south of where you instructed him to position himself. Is it possible his GPS is not functioning properly?"

"Negative," replied Grauer. "Racer just found a spot he likes better. We all need to get used to him doing his own thing on this op. He's played as fast and loose with his orders as possible since he was a second lieutenant."

"Roger that."

Grauer rubbed his hands through his thinning hair. "Okay, Pam. Good work. Best you get your bird out of there before anybody gets suspicious."

"Yes, sir. Baby Boy is returning to base."

Grauer punched a single number on his satellite phone. He waited thirty seconds or so for the call to make the requisite connections into near space and then back down to Peshawar, seventy miles away over the Pakistani border. "Yeah, Bob? It's Pete. Our man is in position outside of objective Gopher. A few hours late, but his hide looks solid. Phase One is complete."

* * *

By the time Raynor got his hide organized, his scope set up on its minitripod, and his thin layer of camouflage netting over himself and all his gear, the sky had faded to black and a thick mist began to grow over the river. With the naked eye he could still see the village—cooking fires lit up the hillside like match glows through the growing vapor. Far below him at his one o'clock position, the stone bridge across the river was manned by a group of armed militia. Jamal would have crossed over this bridge to deliver the water and other supplies to Zar's compound, and he would have regressed back over it, all while Raynor crawled up the hill. By now Jamal should be halfway back to Peshawar, no doubt thanking Allah for getting him through this stressful day.

Raynor was exhausted, but he took the time to look through his thermal monocular to scan the north–south limits of the valley. He took note of any heat signatures wherever he found them. A flock of sheep was across the water to his left. A small encampment of men were on his side of the river, but on the far side of the road to his right there were deer and foxes and wild boars up and down the steep forests on both sides.

He lowered the thermal and lay there, breathing in the pine- and cedar-scented air, feeling the moisture on his filthy skin, letting his naked eyes take in the starlight and the firelight and the wide expanse of the evening alpine vista.

The tranquillity of the scene fascinated him. Here he was in the Federally Administered Tribal Areas, not one hundred klicks north of the most horrific and harrowing experience of his life, surrounded now by enemies too numerous to count and hell-bent on evil too ghastly to contemplate.

And yet it was beautiful.

The valley was fucking beautiful.

Kolt shook his head, covered himself in his patoo, and went to sleep on his thin mat, his bone-tired body covered by the camouflage netting.

His eyes opened slowly, blinked, and then focused on the GPS he'd positioned on the moss just a few inches from his face. The clock on the device indicated it was not yet 7 a.m., there was hardly any light yet in the sky, but he knew instantly that something had awakened him.

A soft but persistent thumping in the distance, like someone banging on a door.

He'd heard that sound before, in Afghanistan. Women up early, beating flour on the millstone, making the morning bread.

Kolt rolled onto his belly and stretched. "I'll take mine with a big cup of black coffee." A pause. "And a double shot of Jack Daniel's."

Kolt's body felt cold and tight. His muscles, from his calves to his thighs, throughout his lower back and all the way up high in his shoulders, were stiff and sore from the climbing and pack hauling the day before, and the hard surface and cool night had compounded the complaints his muscles now sent him via his central nervous system.

He looked across the valley. The village was just

beginning to awaken. A rooster crowed, and smoke from morning fires drifted up in the morning mist. Soon there would be movement on the alleys and dirt roads of the steep village, and by then there would be enough light to use his optics. He wondered what all the people who farmed the poppy fields did between growing seasons. He imagined there would be some men in the village for whom this was the only convenient time of year to be a member of the warlord's militia.

And then he wondered about T.J. Was his best friend, the man he'd thought dead for three years, really only four hundred yards away from where he now lay?

Perhaps so, but four hundred yards had never seemed so great a distance to Kolt.

The fog burned out of the valley shortly after nine in the morning. He had used the time to eat cold rations and sip water. He tucked behind the lip of the rock and did a slow set of push-ups to warm his body a few degrees, and then, with the daylight and the clear view across the river valley, he crawled forward to his spotting scope and looked at the compound at the top of the village.

He had a good view over the eastern wall. Through his lens he could see armed sentries walking on the road that ran from the main gate, to his right, toward the main building, in the center of his field of view. The hurja, the guesthouse where it was thought the al Qaeda operatives and Taliban soldiers slept, was to the left, higher on the hill, and the barn was just on the other side of the wall nearest to him.

In the distance, still partially obscured by mist drifting up from the grasses that grew there, were several buildings back near the far wall of the compound. Grauer's analysts suspected the prisoners were housed in one or more of these simple stone-and-poured-concrete structures.

Raynor peered through his spotter's scope at these buildings, looking for any indicators of use. Were they storerooms, tack rooms for the horses' and donkeys' gear, sleeping quarters for the guards? Or were they prison cells?

For hours he busied himself with the study of these structures, pausing only to quickly scan other parts of the compound or the village, or to give his eyes a brief rest from the strain.

Throughout the day he learned nothing that Pam Archer had not already discerned from the cameras on her drone.

Shit.

TWENTY-FOUR

The fog rolled back in around five in the afternoon, earlier than the day before. It was thicker, coiling wisps above the river, heavy wet clouds drifting lazily through the cedars and mulberry trees on the hillside. By six Raynor could no longer make out the compound, his night vision gear was useless through the vapor, so he had to switch to his thermal.

A thermal monocle illuminates the signature from any heat source. Besides showing car engines, stones warmed by the sun, animals, and any other generator of warmth, it displays a silhouette image of a human body, but it does not show the identity, as everyone looks essentially like a white or black ghost through the optic. He could see men in the compound through the mist, but the device was utterly useless for his task, obtaining proof of life of six specific men.

He began to worry that this fog might be a serious

problem for his mission. What if the prisoners—assuming they were in the compound—were let out only in the late evening? If that was the case, and the mist pattern of the day held for the next two, then how the hell was he going to get eyes on T.J. and the guys?

Frustrated by what he saw as a wasted day in his hide, he decided to call it off for the night, to hope for better weather conditions in the morning.

He had just started to move his eyes out of the thermal sight when new movement caught his attention. From the northeastern corner of the compound, two men walked toward a shack in front of a copse of trees along the north wall. The Radiance analysts had determined the small stone building to be a latrine for the guards. Kolt could tell that the man in back held a flashlight in one hand, and he illuminated the way forward for the other.

It took a moment to be certain, but soon Raynor realized that the man in front had his hands clasped together like he was handcuffed.

Through the thermal sight he was unable to identify the prisoner. Raynor could only watch while he stepped into the latrine, and the guard waited outside. The militiaman seemed extremely relaxed: his weapon was turned upside down on his back, and the man strolled off a good twenty-five yards from the front of the outhouse while he waited. But he turned sharply and suddenly, and walked purposefully back to the latrine, as if the man there had called to him. The man in shackles appeared again, and the two returned to the buildings in the northeast corner.

Five minutes later the scene repeated in Raynor's thermal scope. Again, the man in front was in irons. It was clearly the same sentry as before—he walked with the same relaxed gait, swinging his flashlight as he wandered around the open area between the latrine and the road from the gate toward the main building.

These two disappeared again in the distance, and then a third time the event was replayed. This man in front was taller and thinner than the first two. He was definitely not T.J., but one of the first two men certainly could have been.

Thinking back as he waited for the next man, Kolt felt certain that the posture and walk of the prisoners were Western. Maybe American, maybe not, but the men *seemed* like Westerners.

Kolt waited for the fourth man on the team to come out to the latrine, but after another half hour of pressing his eye into the rubber lens cap of the thermal device, he realized that the show was over for the evening.

He switched off the scope to save battery power, rolled onto his back, and stared up into the impenetrable fog that hung around him like a cold wet blanket. He knew now, with absolute certainty, that there *were* prisoners here at Zar's camp. But that was something they were already reasonably certain of. Kolt also determined they were likely Westerners being held, but again, by Jamal's deliveries of fresh water and medicine, this was already suspected.

"Shit," Kolt muttered. He was going to need more than three thermal signatures across four hundred yards of fog to get a rescue mission approved for this compound.

He resigned himself to sleep. Tomorrow he'd have to do better. He could *not* take his eyes off that damn hillside.

But the second full day began as a virtual replay of the first. The fog hung in the air well past sunup, and then the village and the compound came alive with activity, but there was no sign of the operators of Eagle 01.

Men came and went. Women peered from the windows of their homes or traveled with male family members while completely ensconced in burkas. The villagers moved about the buildings of the village, and along the banks of the river, shepherds tended their flocks on meadows to the south of Kolt's hide, and small children gathered tinder for firewood throughout the forest.

There was activity on the narrow logging road. Mule carts with supplies passed slowly; some stopped in the villages, while others continued all the way up the steep path to the compound.

Kolt could not see down into the area Grauer's analysts had dubbed the Playground, the large courtyard building on the southern side of Zar's fortress, but he noticed activity on the roads around it, so he assumed it was full of children, coming and going, just like in the Predator images.

These kids were unknowing and unwilling impediments to the military and intelligence forces of the United States of America just blowing the hell out of this fellow Zar and all his houseguests.

Kolt did not want to waste the day lying there in vain hoping that T.J. and his men would just appear, so he used the time to carefully plot the movements and rotations of the guards around the compound, and to pick out every static sentry in sight. He wrote it all down on a small notepad. All this would be crucial for a successful mission if a Delta hit was ordered up, but there would be no hit if Kolt didn't get some real intelligence sometime soon.

Nevertheless, he busied himself with this work. He timed all the movements and even mapped out the potential fields of fire from the guard tower at the front gate, the men on the roof of the main building, and the forces manning the bridge.

The fog came in thick and heavy in the afternoon, just as it had the day before. Raynor was on his thermal scope before 6 p.m., pissed and frustrated, because this meant another day without identifying Eagle 01. In the hillside village ghostly beings appeared as if from thin air as they stepped out from behind buildings, the hovels warmed by fires shone as lighter gray than the colder dark gray facades around them, and the compound's sentries continued their patrols, although now they appeared as ethereal beings floating through the air on the other side of the valley.

This was useless. Kolt put his head down on his patoo and cursed. Wished he had a shot of whiskey to warm his bones and calm his frustrations.

The first prisoner appeared again at 10:30 p.m., just like the previous evening. Again, he was escorted by an armed guard. This time, one by one, four men were led out into the cold, into the darkness, into the thick mist, delivered to the latrine, and left alone for five minutes or so to take care of their business.

Kolt was more convinced than the night before that these were the missing Delta men. The last man in the group even moved like T.J. No, he could not be certain, but he had an incredible sensation that he was looking directly at his old friend as he shuffled, hands together, across the compound to the latrine, and then back again.

Raynor switched off the thermal sight for the evening and dropped his forehead to his mat. He saw this entire mission falling apart because of this fucking fog. He'd do his four days here, he would obtain no video recording of the men's faces, nothing would be seen, no actionable intelligence would be derived, and then he'd be pulled out. There would be handshakes and backslaps and the clucking hens in the intelligence community would say, "Well hell, of course we did all we could, we even had a guy from a PMC go to the site and spend four days there and he didn't see a cotton-picking thing, so what else can we do?"

This was the sort of thing that had driven Raynor crazy back when he was in Delta. Missed opportunities. Failure.

It was also the sort of thing that had caused him to push forward that morning in Waziristan, getting his men killed in the process and creating this disaster.

Kolt tried to sleep, but cold, worry, and frustration kept him up through most of the night.

* * *

The flaw in the compound's security setup revealed itself to Kolt Raynor on the morning of his third and final full day, right after the mist swirled up and out of the valley with the arrival of the sun's rays.

Zar spent much effort protecting himself, but Raynor identified the Afridi warlord's Achilles' heel.

It seemed like Zar's biggest worry was Hellfire missiles from Predator drones, and there was but one way for Zar to counter that—place himself as close as possible to large numbers of civilians. This he had accomplished with the compound on top of the village, but Zar had gone one better with the construction of the Playground. He packed kids up against his fort like sardines, put them on display during the day, and then tucked them into their beds at night, still well within the blast radius of any missile hitting the main building of the compound or the hurja where al Qaeda and the Taliban sought shelter when they were in the valley.

That was his anti–air-to-ground ordnance plan, and, Raynor conceded, it was pretty damned foolproof.

Zar's next biggest concern would be the threat of American commandos being choppered directly into his compound. But Raynor had searched in vain for anything that would preclude Delta from assaulting, fast-roping out of Black Hawks inside the compound walls, directly in front of the main building and the hurja. Yes, there were men with light weapons inside, but Kolt had seen nothing in the past forty-eight hours that would rule out a rescue attempt by helicopter, should he be able to identify the American prisoner.

It would be tough, and it would be bloody, but an assault on the compound would, in Kolt Raynor's estimation, be doable.

Just below this on Zar's threat matrix would be fears of a ground attack. The logging trail that led into Shataparai was guarded by men with guns in fortified positions. They would have radios and they would be in contact with Zar's militiamen all over the valley. If invaders appeared, even kilometers away, there could be more security in Shataparai itself in moments, meaning the steep village pathways toward the compound would be one fatal funnel after another ready to repel a ground attack from the road. The stone-and-concrete walls of Zar's lair were twelve feet high, and the main gate was steel with a guard tower alongside it—any ground assault would be met with a wall of lead outside the walls of the compound.

Yeah, Zar was ready for the Frontier Corps or the militia of a rival Pashtun strongman charging straight up the middle toward his fort.

Clearly the warlord who ruled over this area had a lot of enemies, and a lot of fears, but one thing he did not seem to guard himself against very well was the potential for a lone man infiltrating his compound under cover of darkness.

The Playground, this newish construction pressing up against the southern wall of the compound, was the key. In his attempt to make his home and guesthouse safe from missiles, Zar had unwittingly damaged another aspect of his security. The hillside south of the Playground was steep and thick with alpine trees, but it was free of other structures and not patrolled by anyone

Raynor had seen through his binoculars during the day, or through his thermal scope during the night. Certainly no large force would be able to scramble alongside the sheer valley wall undetected. But one man, one man possessing enough skill and daring, could make his way right up to the Playground, over the wall of its large courtyard, and then sneak right up to the wall of Zar's fortress.

But what about the patrolling sentries inside the stronghold? Kolt had spent thirty-six hours, on and off, monitoring and recording and mapping their movements, and he had come to a conclusion: the answer lay in the time frame—one minute, thirty-seven seconds.

One minute and thirty-seven seconds was the minimum amount of time between patrolling perimeter guards passing a particular point inside the compound at any time of the day or night. Sometimes it took them longer, but they were never less than one minute, thirty-seven seconds apart.

Any potential interloper into the fortress would need to get over the wall after one guard passed, and then find a hide or move out of the path of the next man, all within a minute and a half.

It would not be easy. Shit, it would be the most challenging thing Raynor had ever attempted. But he felt he could do it. With the dark of night, with the thick evening fog, with his training and his gear . . . yes. He could get in there and get eyes on T.J. and the boys.

And he knew he had little choice.

Jamal would return for him the following day, and

Kolt had no illusions that the fog that had fallen the past two nights would not be back this evening.

Damn it, Kolt. Are you really going to do this?

He lay there and thought about it throughout the day, but by midafternoon he knew what his decision would be.

It was obvious.

He was going into the compound.

Grauer would be pissed, but only if he failed.

And he would not fail.

The Playground was the way in, but figuring out how to infiltrate from the southern wall would be tough. He could get across the river, he could skirt the village, he could come to the Playground from the wooded hillside to the south, but he did not know if the kids and their supervision would be in the courtyard or not. If not, if it was just a big empty dirt patch, he'd be in good shape.

But if it was full of sentries or dogs or even kids, he'd be in serious trouble.

In the late afternoon women shrouded in their burkas appeared on his side of the river. There were two dozen in total, moving in small groups of two or three up the fallow stepped fields closer to his position. Kolt was not worried about being seen. Even from the highest of the terraced fields, there was still a hilly tree line and then a sheer limestone cliff between his position and the women. They strolled all the way to this tree line, and they began to gather armloads of small sticks and branches, kindling for their fires.

In his intelligence briefing with Kopelman back at

Radiance's Operations Center, Bob had told him that if he saw women working in the fields or gathering wood, then it was a good bet that there was not a strong Taliban presence in the area, because the Taliban did not allow women to work outside of the house, even to gather fuel for their fires.

A good bet. Yeah, that sounded so much better to Raynor in a conference room on the other side of the border. The women before him now indicated something *might* be the case, but was he ready to risk his life on it?

Kopelman had also warned him that the women would know how to shoot Kalashnikovs, and many would be better shots than the men. He didn't see weapons hanging off the outside of the burkas, but even without weapons the women of this village would be a danger.

The two dozen women filled their arms, their backs, and, in some cases, their heads with kindling and firewood, and they returned over the bridge and back to their village. The cooking fires began burning as the mist fell in late afternoon. Kolt caught the scent of gently wafting wood smoke through the moisture long after the village disappeared from view.

He ate a little of his rations and sipped water, preparing himself and waiting until nightfall. His stomach turned with nervous energy and concern, but despite his fears, he was determined, and Kolt Raynor was a man who acted on his resolve. He knew he'd be heading for the compound as soon as the village went to sleep.

TWENTY-FIVE

"Pete, are you seeing this?" It was Pam Archer calling into the Operations Center. Her disembodied voice was louder than the murmured conversations between the analysts and senior staff in the room. Her aircraft had just arrived on station over the Tirah Valley, here for her nightly checkup on Racer. It was just after 9:30 p.m. and she'd zoomed her thermal camera in on his hide, but there was no man-sized heat signature to be found. An empty black void showed on the monitor against the wall.

Grauer had not been looking. He'd been talking to a pair of analysts on the far side of the table. When Pam's voice filled the room he immediately walked over to the monitor, his men trailing behind him.

"Where the hell is he?"

"No idea." Pam's voice quivered with concern. "I'll adjust the image scale."

With a series of flashes the monitor's image took in more of the valley now, the cold river curling like a black snake through the center of the picture. Rocks on both sides of the valley that were large enough to keep a measure of the day's warmth this late into the chilly evening showed up as fuzzy light gray spots. The houses in the village shone nearly all white where dying embers of the cooking fires and the body heat of the locals and animals radiated.

But there was no sign of Racer.

Archer took her Predator to the other side of the hill, a few kilometers behind Racer's last known position, on the theory that he might have felt he was compromised and needed to escape. But she saw nothing but some large cattle, some sheep and their shepherds, and an encampment of men, probably members of Zar's militia. She then traced the road with her camera, followed it ten or more kilometers back to the east, in the direction of Peshawar. But she found very few men or vehicles on this stretch of the dirt track, and nobody that she did find was traveling alone.

After ten minutes of searching, each moment more worrisome than the last, Pete Grauer's square jaw rose slowly, and he spoke through clenched teeth. "Pamela. Search the river crossing a couple of klicks south of the village."

"The *crossing*?" she asked.

"Affirmative. There is a spot where the river bends and it's bisected by boulders. A fit man could cross the river there if he was careful."

A brief pause before acknowledging her compliance. "Roger that."

Grauer's jaw muscles flexed as he waited for the drone to move into position nearer to the natural stone pathway that spanned the river like a rocky dotted line. The water was swift here between the rocks, but a motivated and sure-footed man could make his way from one boulder to the next and cross the river here without having to use the guarded stone bridge in at Shataparai.

Pam centered on the river, zoomed in, and enhanced resolution on her thermal camera.

Nothing. "Negative heat signature," she said.

"All right," replied Grauer. "Now I want you to scan all the way from this crossing point to Zar's compound. Check the hillside, not just the riverbank."

A long pause from Pam. "Are you saying you think he—"

"Humor me, Pam."

"Yes, sir."

The camera zoomed out and then began tracking along the hillside toward the village of Shataparai. Twice Pam stopped panning and focused on heat registers. Both times they were animals in the forest. When she was just a few hundred yards from the village she continued panning but said, "Negative contact."

"Keep going," ordered Grauer. He had a feeling.

Nothing for a moment more. And then there it was. Just a tiny white splotch moving through the trees at this magnification. Archer centered on it and then zoomed. Then zoomed again.

Walking along the steep hillside, slowly and stealthily, not more than fifty yards from the southernmost structures of the village, was a single individual. He was well secreted in the trees, but the thermal camera picked him out easily.

"Oh, shit," said Pam Archer into her mike, violating the normal protocol in her transmissions.

"Son of a bitch," muttered Grauer. "Someone . . . *please,* tell me that Racer is not attempting to infiltrate Zar's compound."

The analyst on his left just shook his head slowly. "What the hell is he going to do?"

"What do *we* do?" asked Grauer. No one spoke. No one knew.

Then Grauer growled, "Get me Kopelman on the secure line."

Kolt Raynor hoped like hell that the UAV hadn't come to check on him tonight. He hoped to get in and out of here and back to his hide, with more information than he would have been able to get from across the valley, well before daylight tomorrow. Further, he would much rather Pete Grauer did not know what he was up to until he could tell him about it, after the fact. He did not want Grauer to think he was on some crazy solo mission, because that's not how Kolt saw this. He could call this off at any moment: if guard dogs alerted to him, if sentries changed up their patrols, if villagers remained in the alleyways this late at night. There were a dozen or more indicators that could convince him to back off for now, but he was not going to just lie on his belly across the valley from T.J. for three days and then exfiltrate the area without getting proof of life.

No, he *had* to try.

There was a camera on his tiny GPS unit and he'd brought this along, kept it stowed in a pocket of his salwar. He'd left his spotting scope, his night vision gear, and all the other recording devices back up in his hide. His thermal monocular would be his main piece of equipment to get him to the prisoners, but once there, he'd pull out the GPS camera to get proof of life.

Raynor made his way to the southern wall of the Playground. He was reasonably certain that the courtyard would be empty, though he was equally certain that the building adjacent to it would contain kids, families, or at least sentries. He hid himself for several minutes in the brush across from the rusty iron gate that led into the dirt courtyard. He kept his eyes and ears open and tuned to any human noises.

Nothing from the dirt road. Nothing from the courtyard in front of him. Everything was dark and still.

At 10 p.m. he moved toward the Playground.

He did not try the gate. He assumed it was locked, and even if it wasn't, the iron hinges would creak loudly upon his opening the door. He instead walked along the baked mud wall, up the hill, until he reached the corner of the building. Here, a man-sized stack of old tractor tires leaned against the wall, and this looked like his best bet. He checked it for stability, then made his way up with one hand on the brick wall and the other pulling himself gingerly up the tires, using his feet in the same way—one on the tires, the stack held steady with his hand, and the other getting purchase only by wedging the tip of his sandal into recesses in the brick wall.

In ten seconds he was standing on the tires, looking over the wall into the dark courtyard.

As near as he could tell it was empty. He looked through his small thermal monocular back toward the Playground's main structure and saw no warm bodies in the windows, which he took as a good sign.

He dropped into the courtyard, immediately saw that a long colonnaded hall, with a tiled floor and an open wall to the Playground, stretched away from him on his right. He checked it with his monocular. No signs of life. He moved along the wall to his left, low in a crouch, and approached the common wall with Zar's compound.

A door opened on his right, twenty-five yards away. Kolt dropped flat on his face and looked toward the movement. Torchlight in the hallway behind silhouetted a lone figure, a man with a rifle. He stood in the doorway, looked around at the dark open courtyard for twenty seconds, and then reshut the door. Raynor saw no hint of tension or concern in the man's movements, supposed he was just a guard in the building who patrolled lazily during the night.

After waiting a minute to make sure the man would not return, Raynor climbed back up to his crouch and continued on.

He made it to the wall of Zar's fortress thirty seconds later. He heard dogs barking in the distance, but they were too far away to have alerted to his scent.

Scaling this twelve-foot wall would not be a problem for Raynor. Sandstone blocks had been inlaid into the wall, and these blocks were used to hold buckets to collect rain. Kolt stepped up on one and hoisted himself to the top of the wall.

As silently as possible, Raynor dropped down into the darkened compound, with the hurja just fifty feet off his left shoulder.

"Holy shit, Racer is *inside* Gopher!" an analyst behind Grauer said, but Pete was watching the monitor, and he could see for himself. There was little definition to the monitor's image other than the warmth of Racer's body and some slight residual heat retained in the wall he'd just dropped from. Pam pulled back on the range, and several more heat signatures appeared, inhabitants of the fortress. The closest ones were on the far side of the hurja's roof, thirty yards away from Racer, but they would not be able to see the infiltrator through the thick vapor hanging in the air.

Racer's image turned away from the hurja, but it continued hugging the wall as it moved east toward the southeast corner of the compound.

Grauer stared at the screen, the footage from Pam Archer's Baby Boy displayed in front of him. "Obviously he is going to try and go around the entire property, behind the corral, cross over to the north side before he comes to the main entrance gate, and then try and get eyes on the prisoners in the northwest corner."

Pam Archer's disembodied voice filled the conference room. "Pete, do you want me to stay on station?"

Grauer hesitated, said finally, "Negative. You are

going to draw too much interest on radar if you hang out here much longer. Why don't you pull back across the border and return to the Tirah Valley in an hour? Just try to make it look . . . random."

"Understood. I'll wander back across the border into Khost and then swing back to Gopher in sixty mikes."

Grauer and his analysts watched the angle of the image change, the UAV leaving the airspace, and moments later Archer flipped off her thermal camera.

The president of Radiance Security and Surveillance Systems was angry. His man was dangerously off mission, and he jeopardized everything with his actions. Still, there was nothing he could do about it now from here in Jalalabad except root him on.

Pete spoke softly. "Good luck, son."

TWENTY-SIX

Things had been going smoothly for Raynor, and he appreciated it, but he knew it would not last. As he turned at the southeast corner of the compound's wall and began heading north, he took a moment to look through the thermal optic he carried in his right hand. A white image appeared in the darkness through its lens, directly ahead. It was a sentry, he was in the way of Kolt's progress to the latrine, and he wasn't moving. The man leaned against the wall, twenty-five yards ahead of the American. He guarded a wooden door in the wall that must have led to the alleyway that ran along the east wall of the compound. Kolt had not been able to see the door or the sentry from his vantage point, as the door was shielded by the roofs of village buildings on the hillside, and the sentry was shielded by the wall. He suspected this door was for the comings and goings of the women of the fortress. Kopelman told him women were generally not allowed to use the main gate, but if they were clothed in their burka or at least a chador, and accompanied by a man, they could leave through the women's door to go to the village market.

Shit. He'd been on the lookout for static guards while surveilling from across the river, but he'd missed this guy. Now some asshole stood directly in his path, and it didn't look like he was going anywhere soon.

Kolt tucked himself tight against the wall, secreted the majority of his body in some brown weeds that grew in thin tufts there, and looked down at his watch.

0220 Zulu. 10:20 p.m.

Shit. The nightly toilet procession would begin soon, and he was 150 yards away from where he needed to be and pinned into a corner.

At ten thirty Raynor used his thermal monocular to try to get a look into the distance where the latrine stood near the northern wall, but his view was blocked by the large corral and barn and a low rise.

His options were few, and they were bleak, but it was time he made a decision. Unless the guard wandered off right this minute, Kolt wasn't going to be able to sneak past him. He could try to go around him, but that would entail walking through the center of the compound toward the latrine, and even in his disguise, even with the darkness, and even with the fog, Raynor would need an incredible amount of luck, and he wasn't prepared to trust his fate to the stars to that degree.

He could sneak close to the sentry at the door, pull out his four-inch blade, and kill the man without a sound.

Right. Then what? Continue on with his mission, a mission that would keep him here in the compound at least another half hour, and then somehow cover up the fact that a guard had been slaughtered so he could get out of the compound and back to his hide site with no one being the wiser?

No. The wet alternative wasn't going to work here.

That left one thing. Calling it off. Backing out, making his way back over the wall into the Playground, hopping one more wall, and then getting back into the hills, crossing back over the river, and climbing back up "home." Four hours of grueling effort, absolute risk, all for zero gain.

Raynor hated failure. He took it personally. As he squatted there in the grass, dropping to his belly now as a patrol wielding lazy flashlights headed up the center road, past the big house and toward the hurja, Kolt decided he had no choice but to exfiltrate. He'd already missed the beginning of the latrine march; there would be no sense waiting till it was over and then heading to the row of buildings and knocking on doors looking for prisoners.

No, this night was a blown opportunity. All because of this jackass at the little side door. Kolt looked at him through his thermal optic one last time before heading back in the other direction.

The man moved. He pushed off the wall and began walking toward the patrol, twenty yards in front of him.

The guard called out in Pashto: "Wait." He kept walking. The flashlights stopped on the road. He continued, clearing the way forward for Raynor. Kolt followed the sentry with his eyes as he stepped up and began a conversation with the three patrolling guards. Kolt had no idea what they were talking about or how long this little get-together would last, but in an instant he decided to go for it. He quickly pulled off his sandals and held one in each hand, dropping the thermal sight into the pocket of his salwar. With a last glance toward the lights in the fog, their beams pointed toward the earth as the men stood and talked, Kolt Raynor rose out of the brush like a runner on the starting block. And in bare feet he ran forward into the darkness, his shoulder never more than a couple of feet off the baked mud wall on his right.

He neared the small door in the wall and kept running, did not look left or right, his entire body tense in fearful anticipation of the shout of a man or the crack of a Kalashnikov. He passed the door and within just a couple of seconds he was behind the long stone barn. The perimeter wall and the barn wall created an alley not six feet wide, with open gates in the barn that gave access to a row of closed stalls inside. Raynor kept running, a little slower now because he could not see his hand in front of his face here in the alley, as the barn shielded all of the ambient light from the sky.

Just a few minutes later he had crossed the main road, fifty yards from the entrance gate. He'd taken the time to account for all the sentries there, to make sure no one was positioned with a good view inside the compound. He crossed the road at a normal pace, his sandals back on his feet and his patoo back on his head. In the wet, hazy distance he was just one of the boys heading between two points at this time of night. No reason for anyone to stress about a single unarmed man walking here.

Raynor made it into the copse of woods behind the latrine. The fog was thick like strings of milky cobwebs between the pines. He lifted his thermal monocle to his eye several times as he neared his destination.

It was ten forty-five—he was fifteen minutes past the start of the bathroom trips. He only hoped one of the prisoners was constipated; otherwise he'd missed the entire thing.

Just then he saw movement through the thermal lens. From around the front of the latrine, a man moved forward, away from the outhouse, his hands fastened in front of him, the armed guard behind him.

Kolt moved forward quickly and quietly, opened his eyes wide to take in all the light he could.

But it was too dark to make out the man in the shackles.

Just then the prisoner turned back to the sentry to say something, and the sentry's flashlight swept across his face.

Raynor knew him instantly.

It was Spike. Staff Sergeant Troy Kilborn, from Lincoln, Nebraska.

One of T.J.'s teammates.

He looked like he'd lost thirty pounds, but there was no doubt Kolt had found a missing man from Eagle 01.

Yes! I've done it, Raynor said to himself.

But the moment of euphoria evaporated quickly.

Just what had he done? He'd gotten "eyes on," yes.

But that wouldn't do anyone a lot of good if he didn't find out where the team was held, if he didn't ensure they were all together. And he wouldn't do anyone a damned bit of good if he didn't make it back out of here.

He closed on the back of the latrine, put his hand out, touched the rough stone wall, knelt down, and checked around the side toward the main house with the thermal monocle. In the distance, fifty yards away or more, three armed men stood at the front of the two-story building. He saw signatures of two more on this side of the roof.

They would not be able to see him here, so he knelt by the side of the latrine. Kept his monocle pointed toward the west, where the next prisoner would come.

Unless that was it for the night.

In seconds he saw a single white blob. In a few more moments it separated into two, as the men in the distance neared. Quickly Kolt moved around to the front of the latrine, pushed open the wooden door, and stepped into the room, shutting the door behind him.

It smelled like shit. Two black plastic buckets sat in a trough dug in the dirt. A three-legged wooden stool in the corner held a lit oil lantern that gave out more shadow than light. Kolt pushed himself tight into the space behind the door, across the eight-foot-square room from the lantern.

He took a few slow breaths in an attempt to calm himself, and he waited.

Within a minute he heard shuffling footsteps in the dirt outside. The quick flare of a flashlight's beam as it shone through the cracks in the doorjamb and the space through the hinges.

The door opened inward, shielding Raynor, and then it shut.

In front of him the back of a chained prisoner. He did not have to look for more than one-half second. He knew.

It was T.J.

With all his other worries about making this clandestine approach to the property, Kolt hadn't spent any time thinking about what he would do or say if he actually managed to make contact with one of the boys. Now his knees weakened in terror as he frantically planned the next few seconds. He could think of only one way to be certain that he could do this quietly. He waited until Josh took a full step closer to one of the buckets, and then Raynor took a step forward, reached in front of his friend's body, and yanked him tight. His hand covered T.J.'s mouth as he yanked him back onto his heels.

Raynor had expected much more of a fight. Back in the old days the two men would train in Brazilian Jiu-Jitsu for hours at a time, and the winner was never predetermined. All things being equal, the two men were almost perfectly matched physically. But the past three years had taken a shocking toll on Josh Timble. His body was thin and bony and his reaction to Kolt's attack was slow.

Raynor wanted a quick and quiet surrender, but his friend's instant supplication was disquieting.

For three seconds the two men were locked together in the blackness of the smelly latrine. When Raynor was confident he'd get no noise or fight in return for his sneak attack, he leaned into the other man's ear and said, softly, "Josh . . . it's me. It's Kolt."

TWENTY-SEVEN

No response. For a brief but horrifying moment Raynor worried that he'd misidentified T.J. and grabbed some random Paki goon taking a break to run to the john.

No, even in the dim light he could tell this was his old friend. "I didn't mean to scare you. I'm going to take my hand from your mouth. Just be real quiet, cool?"

A slight nod.

Kolt moved his hand.

T.J. turned around and faced him. Kolt could barely make out his outline in the darkness. Five seconds. Ten seconds. Kolt started to speak again but T.J. said, "I thought you were dead." Slowly he stepped forward and gave Raynor a weak hug.

Raynor felt bones again under his friend's dirty pajamas. The shadows in the room only accentuated the deep hollows in Josh's bearded cheeks, the rings around his recessed eyes—malnutrition had taken a toll on his buddy's face.

"I thought the same about you, brother."

T.J. backed up just far enough to reach out a hand. He put it right on Kolt's face. Confirming that the person in front of him, the person he'd just embraced, was not some sort of dream-state apparition.

"How long can you talk?" Raynor asked.

T.J. shook his head. He was recovering from the shock, albeit slowly.

"Colonel. I need you to snap out of it. How much time do I have?"

"Not long. Couple of minutes." Even in the darkness Kolt saw the whites of his eyes widened in utter amazement. "You *can't* be here. They patrol the compound and—"

"I'm here to establish proof of life. We're going to get you out." Quickly Raynor grabbed the GPS and fired it up. Began filming with a quivering hand.

T.J. shook his head again. Then he said, "When I leave, the guard will follow me back to the room. There won't be anyone over here except for the patrols. If you can make it to the northwest corner of the compound, there is a narrow drainage culvert behind the concrete shed. That's our cell. Sentries don't patrol down in the culvert. A drain runs from our floor into the culvert. It's only about three feet long. We can talk through the drain."

"Okay. I'll be there as quick as I can." The two men just stared at each other for another ten seconds. Kolt thought Josh wanted to tell him something.

"Uh . . . dude?"

"Yeah, brother?"

"I kinda need to take a dump."

Raynor smiled. *Good ole T.J.* He turned off the video camera. "Who's stopping you? This latrine isn't much less private than our trailer."

"Good point. That place was a shit hole."

"Still is," Raynor said, and Josh smiled.

Two minutes later a shackled T.J. left through the wooden door.

It took twenty minutes for Raynor to make it out of the outhouse and back into the little grove of trees, crawl to the wall of the compound, and scurry the eighty yards or so to the northwest corner. As promised, a three-foot-by-three-foot indentation ran the length of the western wall, a dirt drainage ditch to control runoff at the back of the compound during the rainy season. Brush and grass grew wild down here, which Raynor knew would help provide cover from above. He also knew it would hide rats, and he heard tiny footfalls of scurrying creatures all around him in the dark culvert.

He found the pipe sticking out of the mud wall just behind the single-room stone shack. The pipe seemed to be fabricated from empty Russian mortar tubes stuck together. A glow just barely shone through it. A lantern inside the room. Kolt looked inside but could make out nothing for a moment. Then the opening at the far end darkened, and he heard the soft whisper of his old friend through the pipe.

"Racer?"

"I'm here."

A pause and the sound of shuffling. If anything the tube amplified the sounds of the room. He could hear other voices, excited, behind T.J.'s words.

"They'll come to lock us down to our bunks in a bit. We don't have much time."

"Roger that."

"I didn't think you made it out of Waziristan."

"I would have come after you years ago. . . . I just found out you guys were alive."

There was a long pause. "I'm surprised. The Taliban have been showing us off to UAVs for two years."

"Yeah, I heard. Look, man, we're setting up a hit on this place. I was sent in to get intel, but we're going to—"

"Negative. Forget about a rescue. You guys hit this valley and it will be a massacre. The warlord says they are ready for it, and I believe him. They've got mobile heavy machine guns hidden in caves around here just waiting for the sound of choppers in the valley. I don't know how you got in here, but you need to back your ass out the same way. This valley is going to light up like Christmas at the first thump of rotors, and anybody coming in on the road will be chewed up before they can get five klicks from Shataparai."

Kolt thought a moment. "All right. Then we're leaving tonight. I'll find some keys and get you guys out—"

"No. We couldn't make it out of here together. We're all weak. Skip, the chopper pilot, is still detoxing from the heroin they've been giving us for two years, plus he's being held in the main building. They always house one of us away from the others so we don't try and escape. We aren't walking out of here."

"Shit," muttered Raynor. While he sat in the brush of the open drain he heard footsteps above. A steady, relaxed cadence. A sentry patrolling the grounds. In thirty seconds the footsteps receded into the misty night.

"Okay. I'll report the situation back to Radiance, see what we can come up with."

"Who is Radiance?"

"Sorry. It's a private security outfit run by Pete Grauer. They are the ones looking for you. I'm with them."

"You're not with the Unit anymore?"

"No."

T.J. did not respond.

"It's complicated. Delta knows we're here. Webber is involved, Monk and Benji trained me for this op, but officially I'm working for Radiance. We got intel that you guys were here. The Agency thought it was either bad intel or another trap, but Grauer figured it was worth sending me in to get proof of life and a feel for the defenses here."

"Kolt, me and the guys are a commodity. A lucky charm to be loaned out to wear. A get-out-of-hellfire card. There are over a dozen Taliban leaders who can request us. We've been on the move for a year and a half. Until we came here, we were always traveling with some leadership group or being used as bait in a trap."

"But you're here now. Whatever the risks, we can't afford to lose this opportunity."

T.J. spoke again through the pipe. He was more

emphatic now. "Promise me you won't even think of hitting this compound. This whole village is a hornet's nest. On top of that, a group of Chechens arrived the other day. I don't know how many—they aren't staying here in the compound, must be down in the village somewhere. They are trickling in and out of the main gate all day long."

"What are they doing here?"

"We don't know, but it's big. They showed us some U.S. Ranger uniforms to gauge our reaction to them. They were copies, but good copies. Fake weaponry as well."

Raynor kicked out at the sound of a rat scratching down near his sandaled feet. "They're going to try and infiltrate one of our bases?"

"That's what we figure. Where and when, who knows?"

"Damn." There had been a few small-scale false-flag infiltrations by insurgents during the Afghanistan War, and others during the Iraq War, and they were typically bloodbaths.

"There is an AQ operation in the works. We are guarded by Zar's men and a unit of Paki Taliban, but AQ foreigners are staying here at the hurja. Zar's men hate the AQ guys, so they tell me bits and pieces of what's going on. They say the al Qaeda guys have Zar in their pocket."

"Zar is al Qaeda?"

"No. Look, Zar is a malik, an important elder in the Tirah Valley, but for us he is just the innkeeper. He's the one holding us here. He was supposed to keep us here while we detoxed from the heroin over the past few months. He's fed us well and treated us well, given us the meds we need."

"Why?"

"I don't know, and neither does Zar. He's under orders from al Qaeda, but he's also a Pashtun, and the Pashtun take care of their guests, even if their guests are their enemy."

"Any idea when this AQ op is going to happen?"

"Negative, but I know who *does* know. The key to this op is a German guy who was here in the compound. I only saw him for a minute, but he had a German accent. Balding, silver beard. He was not an operator. He looked miserable and scared shitless meeting with us. Zar's guards said he came from Peshawar, so hopefully he is still there. Have Grauer tell Langley. Maybe they can find this guy and unravel this mess."

Kolt was happy to see Josh had not forgotten how to give orders. He nodded and said, "I'm on it."

T.J. said, "I heard we nailed bin Laden."

"Yeah, last year. Right up the street from the Pakistan Military Academy."

"*Please* tell me the unit did the hit."

Raynor shook his head. "It was Six."

Timble groaned a little. "Well, that's a damn shame."

"Yep."

"Now, Racer, don't press your luck. Get out of here."

"Okay." He paused a moment. "Hey, I've talked to your mom and dad a couple of times."

A long pause. "How's Mom?"

"They are both okay. It's tough, but *they're* tough."

"Yeah."

"And tell Bouncer he's got a baby girl. Two and a half now, I guess. His wife named her Hope."

"He'll appreciate *that* piece of intel. Now take off, and that's an order. You've gotten everyone excited. You getting killed on the exfil would really darken the mood around here."

Raynor smiled a little. Same old T.J. "I'll see what I can do to keep my ass alive."

"Good luck."

Kolt hesitated. Then said, "Don't jinx me, bro."

A slight chuckle from the other side. "Right. I forgot. Go out and make your own luck, brother."

"Will do. And Josh? Thanks for coming for me back in Waziristan. Sorry I made you do it."

"It was a setup, Kolt. The Taliban were trying to sucker one of our ground incursions into a fight. They were ready for us."

"Yeah, and I was the sucker who fell into the trap."

T.J. said, "Someday you and I can have a good cry over a couple of beers, but why don't you skedaddle for now?"

"Roger that. Y'all take care."

"You, too."

Raynor turned away from the pipe reluctantly.

Theoretically, he had just accomplished his mission. But in reality, he was far from claiming any success.

Kolt started heading south along the western wall, thinking he could take the culvert all the way to the southern wall, then make his way behind the hurja and back over into the Playground. But after no more than fifty yards he realized that this plan would not work. Ahead of him in the mist he could hear barking dogs. From the optics at his hide site and the photo reconnaissance by the Predator, he knew that straight ahead would be the rear of the main building. Apparently it was also where the kennel was located. The Kuchi dogs ubiquitous here in western Pakistan were deadly. A form of Central Asian shepherd, they were big and strong, growing to thirty-two inches at the withers. And though they were not vicious by nature, here they were nurtured to be aggressive to outsiders. He did not know how close he would have to get to the Kuchi dogs if he kept to this route. For all he knew the culvert was fenced in and part of their kennel.

Hell no, he thought. *Better backtrack and give those monsters a wide berth.*

This change of plans cost him a half hour. He had to retrace his steps, go all the way back behind the cement building where the majority of Eagle 01 was held, turn along the wall, and then make his way through the trees behind the latrine, crawl on his hands and knees to the main road through the compound, and then, after fifteen minutes waiting for a patrol to appear in the mist and then disappear behind him, cross the forty feet of open ground with his heart in his throat.

On the other side he made his way down to the eastern wall, turned south, walked low along it through the blackness, and headed toward the alley behind the barn.

More sentries passed on the road to his right, but he

heard them in plenty of time to tuck down behind a stack of bags of mortar stationed there next to where a new poured-concrete building was in the process of being erected. As he waited for them to pass he checked his watch, saw that it was well past midnight now. After a minute lying low, he rose, took one step, and then heard a voice ahead in the mist.

He dove to his face, made himself as small as possible, and waited.

The voice grew louder. It was Arabic, not Pashto, this Raynor could easily discern. A man appeared in front of him. He was not as tight against the wall as was Kolt, but still he would pass close. He spoke into a handheld radio. Raynor could see the short-barreled AK-74 hanging low on the man's chest. As he came within thirty feet Kolt saw that the man wore dark blue or black clothing and a white skullcap.

He was most definitely one of the al Qaeda men Josh had warned him about. He passed to Raynor's right, ten feet or so on the other side of the stack of building materials. Kolt could hear an Arabic transmission over the radio. He expected the sound to dissipate as the man walked on, but instead the conversation continued at the same volume. After a half minute or so Kolt climbed to his knees, carefully looked over the bags of mortar, and saw that the AQ operative had sat down on a stack of building stones, facing toward the road, away from Raynor. There the man continued his conversation over the radio.

The two men were only ten feet apart. Kolt hated to

chance it, but he also did not want to just sit here and run the risk of being spotted. He shouldered up to the eastern wall, stayed as low as possible, and crept off into the darkness and the mist, away from the Arab.

He moved slowly now. The large barn was just ahead. Kolt headed for the dark alleyway between the barn wall and the fortress wall. Just beyond was the door that had been guarded by the static sentry earlier. Checking it through his thermal, he saw no sentry there now. There were heat signatures from cracks in the stone of the barn, but Kolt knew they would be animals: horses and goats and chickens, and whatever else Zar's men kept there. He entered the narrow alleyway. Any tiny bit of light his well-adapted eyes had been pulling from the sky's glow through the mist disappeared. He heard a bit of shuffling from the goats and donkeys through the openings in the barn as he walked forward, and he smelled the creatures too, but he much preferred these farm animals to the hyperalert dogs on the far side of the compound.

As he walked he kept his eyes fixed on the door in the wall ahead. Kolt would love to use this exit to get the hell out of the compound, but he dared not. He did not know much about the village itself—the narrow roads and alleyways on the steep hill around the mud and stone structures would be like a rat's maze in the dark.

No, the wall to the Playground was how he got in, and that would be how he'd get out.

Raynor walked forward, passed in front of the last opening in the stone barn, and heard a noise on his right.

He thought it must have been a donkey, shuffling there in the straw. He peered into the near-impenetrable darkness as he passed.

And found himself eye-to-eye with a bearded man carrying a Kalashnikov rifle.

In a fraction of a second Kolt determined he was Taliban.

TWENTY-EIGHT

The sentry was clearly as startled as Raynor. A faint shaft of soft light reached from the open area at the end of the barn, just enough for each man to be aware of the presence of the other.

"What are you doing?" asked the guard in Pashto.

As a response, Kolt drew his black knife and plunged it forward, low at the man's stomach, but it clanked off a rifle magazine in one of the pockets of the sentry's chest bandolier. The Talib began to cry out, but Raynor launched on top of him, and covered his mouth with his hand and then his forearm as the two men crashed into the hay in the barn.

They kicked at each other while locked in violent embrace. Here, deeper in the barn, light from the entrance to the fenced-in corral reached just to where the two men fought in the straw.

Around them the animals stirred: a bray from a

donkey, the fast shuffling left and right of horses in their stalls, the clucking of a hen. Kolt shoved his forearm deeper into the mouth of the sentry to keep him quiet, expending just as much effort and concentration on this task as he did on desperately trying to kill the man with his blade.

After a moment more Kolt got his knife positioned again above the sentry, but the man's strong torso pushed the American to the side, and he lost his advantage.

Goats in the corral stirred with the movement now, but the American kept his forearm in the Pashtun's mouth to stifle his shouts. Kolt realized in an instant that the sentry was trying to fire his weapon to raise the alarm. Raynor needed both hands to simultaneously cover the man's mouth and prevent the rifle from firing. He dropped the knife into the deep hay. The gun was positioned between the two men, its barrel pointing harmlessly at the side of the corral, but a single squeeze of the trigger would call out the enemy cavalry, and Raynor could *not* let that happen. The Talib had just jammed the safety down to unlock the bolt, but Raynor forced his thumb over the safety of the weapon and flipped it back up to where the gun would not fire. He pulled at the rifle but could not get it out of the other man's hands, so, with his hand still on the rifle's receiver and the thumb holding the safety lever up with all his strength, Raynor threw all his weight forward, jamming the gun between his body and the Taliban man's face. The impact stunned the bearded man for a moment, just long enough for Kolt to pull the rifle away, heave it against the wall of the barn, grab the knife in the dirt, and then fall forward with it, plunging it into the sinewy but yielding throat of the sentry just as he began to shout.

The man kicked and writhed in panic and pain, but Raynor covered his mouth again, and pushed and turned the long black blade until every last twitch had ceased.

He crawled off the dead guard quickly, immediately worried about the noise the two of them had made while locked in their death grip here in the darkness. Raynor hefted the Kalashnikov, took up a prone firing position in the bloody hay. His wide eye peered through the notch sight toward the main building of the compound, lost somewhere out there in the mist.

After a few seconds the animals quieted back down, and the only sound remaining was Raynor's heavy breath.

He took his eye from the rifle's sight, looked back at the body lying next to him. "Shit, shit, shit, shit," he whispered over and over.

What now?

He could not leave the dead man here. It would be clear in minutes that an infiltrator had been in the compound and had escaped. Had he seen the Americans? The AQ men in charge of the operation would pull T.J. and his men out of here immediately, before a rescue mission could be mounted. This opportunity to repatriate Eagle 01, as implausible and tenuous as it was already, would evaporate completely.

Kolt had to come up with something fast. He looked down at the dead man; around the body, steam rose from the blood glistening on the straw.

"Shit," he said again.

Unless the compound was ready to believe this man had committed suicide by nearly decapitating himself, the entire mission had just been compromised.

Unless . . . Raynor's head swiveled to the right.

Maybe.

On the other side of the barn, back the way he had come, was twenty yards of open ground. Then there was the small stone building under construction.

And sitting there had been the man from al Qaeda.

Yes. He'd have to hurry, but it was the only option.

Kolt Raynor stepped back out into the darkened alleyway behind the barn.

Three minutes later the al Qaeda operative finished his conversation on the radio, shut the radio off, and stowed it in his vest pocket. He stood and began heading back to the hurja across the compound.

Kolt took him from behind as he walked, used his rock-hard arm muscles to cut off air and blood and any sound, performed this trifecta while lifting the man's feet off the dirt and whipping him into the air toward the back of the partially constructed building.

They fell together, and Raynor realized this man was not half as strong as the Pashtun guard. Maybe he lived a city life, came from Riyadh or Baghdad or Cairo. True enough, Kolt had this man in a more compromising position—the Arab's options were few with a man squeezing the life out of him from behind. Still, the al Qaeda operator did not possess nearly the functional strength of the Taliban sentry.

And Kolt could not have been happier about that.

In under twenty seconds the man was out cold.

If this worked the way Kolt hoped that it would, that animosity T.J. had mentioned between the Taliban and al Qaeda around here was about to get ratcheted up a couple hundred notches.

Kolt heaved the unconscious Arab onto his shoulder, struggled to walk with him back toward the corral. He heard footsteps and conversation on the main road—a patrol of sentries no doubt—so he picked up his pace and hoped the darkness and the fog would aid him one more time tonight.

He made it behind the barn, lowered the man to catch his breath, and then hefted him up once again. It took another two minutes to get the man inside the barn, where Kolt leaned him against the stone wall in a sitting position across the dim room with the hay-strewn flooring. A donkey was tied by the neck to a wooden support beam, and Raynor smacked its haunches to move it out of the way. When the donkey ambled around to the other side he placed his knife in the unconscious man's right hand. Then he crawled back over to the dead sentry. He picked up the AK, set the Safety/Selector switch to fire, and raised the rifle toward the Arab.

Kolt hesitated. He lowered the rifle and went back out the back of the barn, stepped softly all the way to the women's entrance, and tried the door latch.

It was locked from the inside with a large lever lock. He released the lock, opened the door, and checked to make sure the lock would reengage when the door shut again. He left it cracked open.

Breathing a sigh of relief for thinking to check it, he returned to the barn, stepped over the dead Talib, and raised the AK.

Just then a radio chirped on the sentry's belt.

Kolt Raynor sighted in on his target and then closed his eyes to retain his night vision. He fired a single round into the neck of the unconscious terrorist. The gunshot hammered the still darkness with an earsplitting crack and a flash of fire. In a single motion Raynor dropped the rifle at the side of the man with the knife wound to his throat, turned, and made for the open gate.

The compound was alive with barking dogs and braying donkeys and shouting men by the time the rifle's report echoed back from the valley walls.

TWENTY-NINE

The village came alive as well as Raynor sprinted blindly down narrow streets, turning left and then left again and then right, leaping over a mud-brick water trough and ducking low under an awning of irregular-sized wooden beams that jutted out into his path. The black night began to sparkle all around him as oil lamps and torches twinkled to life in doorways and burlap-covered window openings.

The way was steep, and though his escape had no specific direction, he knew that the fastest way out of the village was to descend the hill. He hurtled downward, flew down a flight of stone steps in three loping bounds, nearly tumbling as his arms windmilled through the air to keep just enough balance to avoid face planting into a wall at the bottom of the stairs.

He moved as fast as he could for thirty seconds, was a good hundred yards from the compound wall when dark figures waving flashlights turned into his path ahead. He slowed to a fast walk before they shone on him, then turned his back to the light and pivoted down a dirt path to the left, and the light moved on. His clothes and his demeanor fit in with the village, so there was no reason for anyone seeing his back at distance to suspect him of having anything to do with the single rifle shot up inside the compound.

He began running again as he neared the river, and now he heard men's shouts and broadcasts from walkie-talkies in all directions. The entire village was awake, angry dogs barked and howled, and as he passed a small hovel, a pair of young kids shot out into the alley in front of him. A woman came out behind, her face uncovered. She grabbed the children, then looked up at Kolt Raynor, not more than five feet in front of her. Their eyes met. It was extremely dark in the alley, but still Kolt saw her eyes widen in fear.

With a scolding shout at her kids she lifted them into the air and turned away, disappeared back into the dark doorway.

Damn it! thought Kolt as he moved on down the hill, turning to the right to continue his descent. It would take only one witness to foil this hasty plan of his, and he'd just been spotted. He hoped the woman would not be certain of what she'd seen in the dark, or else would be too scared that her husband would find out she'd shown her uncovered face to a male who was not in the family.

That could get a woman beaten or killed in this part of the world, and Raynor prayed the woman's fear of the Taliban's strict enforcement of Sharia law to subjugate women outweighed her fear of white-skinned interlopers.

He came out of a cluster of low mud buildings and found himself at the road running along the river's edge. Most of the activity was well above and behind him now, but he could see a group of armed men on the bridge to his right. He didn't know if they were Zar's militia, Taliban, or even al Qaeda, but he knew he had zero friends in this valley, so he turned in the opposite direction.

After fifty feet he heard an engine start up directly in front of him, maybe fifty yards ahead along the river's edge. The hillside on his left was a sheer wall of rock fifteen feet high, so he stepped into the frigid water and ducked into the marsh grass growing there.

The shock of cold to his body, the additional stress on his already pounding heart, were nearly too much to bear.

The engine belonged to a tractor, which rolled closer up the road. Raynor tucked himself down in the water to his neck, and though the grasses tickled his nose, he remained perfectly still. As the tractor passed he realized it pulled a long cart with a mounted Russian Kord 12.7 mm machine gun. Four men on the back of the cart stood alongside it. Two held powerful flashlights that illuminated the way ahead.

The tractor passed Raynor and continued on toward the bridge.

Damn, thought Kolt. *That* big gun had not shown up on the Predator's images. A couple of those weapons hidden in the woods and caves around the village and then moved into position by a tractor or even a team of donkeys would spell disaster for any helicopters diving into the valley on a rescue mission.

T.J. was right. Hitting Zar's compound from the air or over land would be impossible without devastating losses to the attacking force.

Raynor remained neck deep in the water. The current pulled him away from the bridge and the village, and he felt his feet, ankle deep in rocky mud, slipping out of their sandals. He fought it for a moment, grabbed the reeds around him to combat the flow of cold water pushing against him, but soon enough he allowed himself to be taken away by the current.

He knew there was no way he could make it back upstream to his crossing point, and he sure as hell was not walking across that bridge to get back to his hide site on the other side of the valley.

The river was the quickest way out of here, so he allowed it to carry him away. As he floated into deeper water in the faster-moving center channel, he pulled his heavy sweater over his head and let it go. He felt the numbness already in his fingers and toes. Soon his joints would be deadened by the icy river, then his appendages. Shortly thereafter enough body heat would leave his torso that he would run the risk of hypothermia.

But to Raynor, that was a problem for fifteen minutes from now. Getting out of the area and preserving this operation was paramount. Everything else would have to work itself out afterward.

For the first time tonight he hoped like hell that Pam Archer was somewhere above him.

When Racer stepped into the cold water, he disappeared from the thermal monitor in the Ops Center.

"Switching to infrared," Pam Archer said calmly into her microphone. Her words were broadcast in the OC shortly before the image on the main monitor flipped. Through the fog it was difficult to see the man in the water. He disappeared for several seconds at a time. Occasionally he passed under trees or large boulders sticking out from the cliff walls, and she lost him altogether.

"He's going to freeze in that river." Archer said this into her microphone as well, and those in the OC knew she might be right.

Grauer rubbed his hand through his hair. He'd done it so often in the past day that he was certain he'd ripped out hair by the roots.

And he had Kolt fucking Raynor to thank for that.

"Okay . . . how cold is that water?" he asked the room.

"Can't be over forty-five degrees."

"Hypothermia in how much time?"

"Fifteen mikes . . . twenty tops," came an answer from an analyst who sounded like he was guessing.

"I need hard-and-fast answers, damn it! And figure out where he will wash up. And get me Bob Kopelman on the phone."

A hand with a satellite phone in it appeared in front of his face. "I've got him, sir."

* * *

Kolt lay on the rocky riverbank, shivering uncontrollably. Every inch of his body was cold and wet, the sun would not be up for hours, and there was no way in hell he was going to give his position away with a fire, even if he'd had the means to start one. His pakol hat had come off while he was running through the village, and his Makarov pistol had washed out of his pocket while he was drifting down the river. The thermal was gone, he'd left his knife near the dead al Qaeda operative, and, looking down at his numb feet, he realized he was barefoot.

The GPS! Raynor felt in his pockets in a panic. No. He flipped onto his stomach and reached all around him, picking up stones in the dark, then tossing them away when he realized they weren't what he was looking for.

The GPS with its camera was gone and, with it, his proof of life.

Kolt rolled back onto his back and stared into the mist.

He'd floated for no more than ten minutes but he suspected he'd covered roughly three-quarters of a mile. He sat up slowly, then climbed to his feet, wrapped his arms around his shivering body, and looked around. He did his best to get his bearings. He could only use the fact that the river flowed to the northeast to plot his location. He was northeast of Shataparai, on the wrong side of the river from his hide, and he had neither the energy nor the gear to get himself across the water, find his way back up several hundred feet of alpine hillside, and get back to his hide.

He decided the only way to stay alive, to keep his body's core temperature high enough to ward off hypothermia, was to begin jogging along the river, and to move away from the compound, away from his equipment, away from his mission. He thought that if he could only find a village or a road or a horse or a donkey, he'd have a chance to make his way toward Peshawar.

After that, he did not know.

He was hobbled by the fact that his feet were bare, and the muddy, rocky riverbank was hardly ideal for a run, but he kept on. He stumbled in the darkness, but he knew he could not stop, could not rest, could not sit down for a break, for fear he would drift off and then drift away.

He looked up into the impenetrable fog, and it occurred to him that if Pam Archer was not watching over him right now, he might well not make it out of this alive.

Which meant T.J. and his men wouldn't either.

At ten minutes past four in the morning, Pam Archer detected a heat register, fainter than normal, but unmistakably the image of a single individual moving twenty-two thousand feet below her. She zoomed on it, saw a hobbled man staggering along the riverbank. He fell at the water's edge, splashed on his hands and knees, and then pulled himself to his feet and regained his earlier slow but steady pace.

"Pete?" she said into her mike. Grauer was still in the OC, but his head was down on the conference table. He was catching a few minutes' rest.

"Pam?" came his surprised reply.

"I think I have him. Check the monitor."

Pam banked the drone gently and the image-stabilization computer corrected for the buffeting of the winds at altitude.

Grauer stared at the screen. It did not take long for him to feel sure the UAV had found their asset. "Yeah. You got him!" Pete Grauer exclaimed loudly through her headset. "I'll call Kopelman and have his man go out and pick Racer up. Let's hope saving his ass turns out to be worth the trouble."

Jamal Metziel yawned deeply, looked up briefly at the late-morning sun. After a call from Mister Bob, he'd raced out of his tiny shack at four thirty in the morning and run three kilometers in the dark to a nearby garage. Bob met him there and unlocked the door, and now Jamal drove his large red Euroleopard 650 tractor and towed an iron-and-wooden cart behind him. He left the yellow Hilux in Bob's other garage west of Peshawar because the route he would have to take to pick up the American spy would take him over broken ground and dry riverbeds that even the formidable 4 × 4 pickup could not negotiate.

For a time he puttered along the Khyber Agency Road. This was a virtual highway, the single piece of efficient infrastructure for dozens of miles in every direction. The tractor just barely made fifteen miles per hour. The few cars and trucks running in this area at this early time zipped by him like he was standing still. Finally he exited the road and turned south onto the flatlands north of the Tirah, passing bare orange orchards and simple factories and towns and military garrisons that were buttoned up like sealed Tupperware containers, providing no security to the villagers whatsoever from the highway robbers, the Taliban, or any militia who decided to set up a roadblock to exert dominance on the area, even if for only a few minutes at a time.

But there were neither bandits nor zealots on Jamal's path this morning. The young man with the scraggly beard and the junky tractor moved along at low speed, bumped up and down on the rutted trails, headed south like a man on his early-morning run to pick up goods in the FATA to take back to market in Peshawar or Hayatabad.

He hoped any brigands in the area would deem robbing him not worth the trouble.

But Jamal did have one possession of value, and he had secreted it below the torn vinyl seat, between rusted-out springs.

A Hughes Thuraya satellite phone.

He called Mister Bob twice in the two hours after leaving Khyber Agency Road. The burly American gave him updates on where he should go to pick up Mister Racer. Bob also begged him to go faster, but there was nothing Jamal could do about that. He had to refill his tractor's gas tank twice from the metal jerricans in the cart, and that took time. And he was forced to go twenty minutes out of the way after taking a small mountain spur and pulling up behind a colorful bus that had thrown a wheel crossing a rock bridge. Jamal maneuvered out of the line of traffic and up to a shallow portion of the stream that he could ford in his Euro-leopard.

It was straight-up noon when he used the phone for the third time, then pulled the tractor over on a hilly mule track and turned off the engine. Bob answered immediately, and said there was a Predator above him right now, and the American spy was just a hundred yards away, lying on his back under a cedar tree. Jamal jumped from his tractor and headed to a copse of cedars and found the man huddled there, awake and aware, more or less, but completely worn out. The Afghan helped him to his feet.

"Salaam aleikum." The American's voice was weak. He looked dehydrated and cold and gaunt.

Jamal walked him back to the cart behind his vehicle and guided him in, grabbed an extra patoo, wrapped it tightly around the American, and helped him sit up. His clothing was no longer wet, but still Jamal helped him take off his kameez, and replaced it with an old green sweater that was a few sizes too small for the American's frame. He pushed a pakol hat on his head and helped him toward the front of the cart, facing backward. A plastic canteen of water was placed in his hand—Jamal assured him it was safe for him to drink—and then a flat loaf of bread appeared. The young Afghan leaped up to the tractor's seat and refired the engine. The machine lurched forward, found a wide enough place in the trees to turn, and then began heading back to the northeast.

The tractor had been a necessity for this part of the trip—the truck would not have made it ten kilometers on these steep, rutted, and narrow spurs—but, unlike the Toyota truck, there was no good way on the tractor or in the cart behind it to hide the American for the return trip to civilization. With Mister Racer's beard and clothing he would not look in any way suspicious to passing donkey caravans or men on foot, and this stretch was normally too disused for the Taliban to establish roadblocks. Still, Jamal would not be surprised to pass a small Taliban convoy or two heading toward the Afghani border, and then his fate would rest on the whims of the unit's commander and whether or not he was in the mood to stop these two locals or to continue on to the war just over the mountains.

Jamal and Bob had decided that they would not press their luck and try to make it all the way to Peshawar. Mister Bob's cover was as a logistics coordinator for an aid group called World Benefactors, so he was allowed outside of the city of Peshawar as far as a relief supply warehouse just west of the city of Jamrud. If Jamal could stay out of sight of the heavily traveled Grand Trunk Road, he just might be able to deliver his human cargo to Mister Bob's warehouse, where the two Americans could ride together back to Peshawar in a large World Benefactors truck.

Everything hinged on the next three hours. If they were stopped by a Pakistani army patrol they would be arrested. Mister Racer might be expelled after an international incident, but a poor young Afghan refugee caught in the perpetration of international espionage would likely just disappear.

And if they were stopped by the Taliban or al Qaeda fighters who camped in the area to organize and train locals for the jihad, there was not one shred of doubt that they would both be killed.

Mister Racer could communicate in the local language to a degree, but he would not last through three seconds of questioning. Jamal could claim his "friend" was from Nuristan, a province of Afghanistan in the Hindu Kush mountain range populated by Muslims with lighter skin, and it was not common that a Nuristani would speak Pashto. But this cover story was thin. To check this legend one would just need to ask this foreigner to drop down onto his janamaz and pray.

Racer would reveal himself as a nonbeliever, and Jamal would thereby be revealed as a conspirator with the nonbelievers, and that would be that.

THIRTY

They made the first hour of their return trip wholly without incident. The American lay swaddled in blankets in the back as it bounced and shook and shuddered behind the loud tractor. He was all but hidden below the wooden lip of the cart, and the various odds and ends Jamal had hurriedly tossed back there at 4 a.m. to give the appearance that he was a merchant or a laborer served well to conceal his stowaway. It had been Bob Kopelman's idea that Jamal half fill the cart, so the young Afghan had tossed items from the garage where he kept the tractor. There were some hammers and nails, a shovel, a pick, blankets, water jugs, and four large jerricans full of fuel.

The items rattled and bounced, and they gave the vehicle and the driver an air of purpose.

Just after safely crossing the Khyber Agency Road, Jamal stopped in a deep valley and turned off the engine so he could refill the tractor's gas tank from a can in the back. He also took the opportunity to make a quick call on the satellite phone. Mister Bob answered immediately, reported that he was already on the Grand Trunk Road, west of Peshawar, and heading toward the warehouse. He reported seeing many Frontier Corps convoys on the main thoroughfare through this part of Khyber Agency, which was no great surprise, but he was making good time and expected to arrive at the rendezvous point well ahead of the Euroleopard tractor negotiating the arduous terrain to the south.

Soon the American climbed up onto the vinyl seat next to Jamal. Jamal wanted Mister Racer to remain hidden in back, but the valley here was steep on both sides and anyone approaching would have to do it from straight ahead, so he was less worried about being surprised by strangers.

Jamal asked, "Are you feeling better?"

In broken Pashto the American said, "Yes. Thank you. And thank you for coming to get me."

Jamal shrugged. "I came because Mister Bob asked me to. This was not the plan. I was going to pick you up tomorrow where I left you."

"I know. I am sorry."

Jamal just repeated himself. "I came because Mister Bob asked me to."

Racer said, "I understand the danger you are in, friend. If you are caught—"

"Caught? I would not have to be caught. I only have to be suspected of helping you and my life will be over. If the Taliban suspect me for one second you will find me hanging in the square by my hands, and my head will be hanging by a rope between my knees."

That image lingered in the dusty air while they made their way over a dry hillock low in a valley. Finally Raynor asked, "So why do you do it? Is Bob a good salesman?"

Jamal took a moment with the question; apparently he did not recognize it as a joke at first. When he did, he laughed.

"No, no." He thought before speaking. "I have been living at Kacha Garay camp outside of Peshawar. But Mister Bob has helped me, and now I help him. God willing, someday the Taliban will be gone, and I will be a truck driver."

"That is your dream?"

"Yes. Not the truck you saw the other day. That is for thieves and men who travel off the highway. Inshallah, I will someday own a proper truck. A semi truck. I will move back home to Kabul and deliver goods all over my country."

"Do you want a family?"

Jamal shook his head. "I am too old to take a wife."

"How old are you?"

"I do not know." Racer had met many Afghans who were not certain of their age. "But I must be thirty."

"That's not too old."

"This is not America. It is very different in my culture. Here I am an old man."

Racer did not speak again. After a moment he patted Jamal on his sweat-soaked back, then climbed back into the cart behind the tractor.

* * *

Jamal and Kolt entered the plains of Kohat just after noon. They traveled almost due north along narrow farm tracts running alongside fields of winter wheat and grasses and fallow farmland. Mud-walled compounds and simple houses dotted the hilly landscape, and trees and brush alongside the roads helped conceal them from great distance.

They skirted far to the east of Sara Garhi, a city legendary for an epic battle in 1897 when twenty-one Sikhs under British rule fought to the last against ten thousand Pashtun attackers, killing hundreds before being wiped out.

Things had been going well, but Jamal made his first mistake by leaving the low mountains and heading instead farther to the east; he had been searching for a smoother trail, but he'd followed a promising spur that took him all the way out onto a ridge that ran above the flatlands to the east. Off in the far distance, a mile away or more, was the Hyatabad–FATA road, and as soon as Jamal realized he could be seen by anyone with binoculars at the Frontier Corps outpost that would inevitably be located there, he knew he'd screwed up. He felt completely exposed for a quarter mile, then took his first opportunity to leave the mule trail by following a dry stream bed back due west.

Mister Racer was in the back and unaware of the danger. Jamal did not want to tell him, because he worried the American would be mad at him.

Five minutes of bone-jarring travel on the stream bed was about all Kolt could take. He heard the iron bolts in the wooden cart bed cracking the oaken beams, and he was concerned that the cart at least, and perhaps even the big tractor itself, would fall to pieces if they continued on this terrain. Jamal seemed to be taking the rocks and boulders much faster now than earlier, and Kolt sensed a problem from the driving technique of the young man. He rolled up to his knees to ask Jamal why they had left the dirt track, but as soon as he did this, the tractor lurched to a stop. Racer flew forward into Jamal's back before righting himself and looking up the stream bed.

Four men stood in dappled shadows under a massive cherry tree twenty-five yards ahead.

Black turbans were piled high on their heads. Folded-stock Kalashnikovs swung from slings around their necks.

Beards hung to their breasts.

These were Taliban, and Raynor knew it.

Jamal let out a slight high-pitched gurgle from his throat that Raynor could hear even over the rumbling engine.

Kolt did not see a vehicle, but assumed these guys wouldn't be this far out in the boonies on foot. There would be horses, donkeys, or a four-wheel-drive pickup somewhere close. Perhaps more Taliban as well. These men weren't set up for ambush—perhaps they'd just been resting and drinking tea—but they'd obviously heard the tractor from a distance and had moved away from their camp to come investigate.

Kolt thought quickly. Options? Vehicle or not, he and Jamal weren't going to outrun these guys or their rifles on a damned tractor, and Raynor did not even possess a sidearm to fight them with. The Makarov was back at the bottom of the river, and his knife, impotent as it would have been against four men with assault rifles, had been left as a prop back in Zar's compound.

Options? What options?

"Keep going, Jamal. Maybe they will let us pass."

Jamal reached down to shift the Euroleopard back into gear. His hand shook, and that, combined with the perspiration on his palm, with the terror coursing through his body, caused him to stall the vehicle. Quickly he reached down to restart it, but Raynor patted him on the back.

"It's okay, friend. Just relax."

The four Taliban hefted their weapons and approached the tractor. Jamal sat in the seat and Raynor knelt in the cart behind, facing the men with the rifles.

"As salaam aleikum," said the driver of the tractor. Twenty-eight-year-old Abdul Salaam did not reply; instead, he held his rifle up, snapped his fingers, and motioned for his three men to spread out around the tractor and do the same.

Abdul and his three cousins were in hiding here in the hills west of Hayatabad. They had been part of a larger unit that had killed a French aid worker and his six Pakistani army bodyguards nearly a month ago up in Chitral, and the group had broken apart to avoid capture. Abdul Salaam and the other three had been heading slowly south. Their plan was to make it to Parachinar, where they would join a donkey caravan that would head west all the way to a crossing point through the mountains into Afghanistan, where, God willing, they would fight and kill more infidels.

Abdul Salaam did not know who these men were on the big red tractor. They could be locals. They could be smugglers.

They could be spies.

Abdul Salaam would find out.

"Wa alekeum a salaam," he said finally. "Where are you going, friends?"

While he waited for the driver to respond, he checked to make sure his cousins had their weapons' safeties off, and they surrounded the vehicle in an arc that did not endanger one another with gunfire from their own weapons should the need arise to kill these men. Yes, good. These three would be good fighters over the border. They would kill many infidels. Many Americans.

He looked back at the driver of the tractor. The man was afraid. He had not spoken.

"I asked you where you were going?"

"To Peshawar."

Abdul Salaam suspected instantly that the man was lying. "In this riverbed? There are roads to Peshawar. Where are you from?"

The driver in the light blue salwar kameez looked down to his hands. Abdul Salaam checked them—they were empty. The Taliban leader took a step forward and his cousins followed suit. They closed to within fifteen feet of the front grille of the big tractor.

"I am sorry, sir," said the man. He sounded like an Afghan. Perhaps from Kabul. "We have been delivering goods, and are returning to Peshawar. We wanted to avoid the Frontier Corps on the main roads."

Smugglers. Abdul Salaam nodded slowly. *Hardly unusual out here.* "What goods did you deliver, and to where?"

"Hashish. From Kabul to Mingora."

"You and your friend?"

"Yes. Yes, that is correct."

"What is your name?"

"Jamal."

"And your father's?"

"I am from Kabul. My father's name was Muhammad Metziel."

"Jamal, the Koran does not allow for the consumption of narcotics. 'Make not your own hands contribute to your destruction,' it clearly says. Are you not a follower?"

The Afghan said, "Yes, brother, I am a follower. I do not use the drugs. I am only trying to make a living."

"By profiting from the suffering of others? The Koran says, 'Anyone who believes in Allah and the Last Day should not hurt his neighbor.' "

"I . . ." The man in the seat of the tractor said nothing else. He was shaking now.

Abdul Salaam enjoyed making men shake in fear. Not just infidels. Anyone who defied the law of the Koran.

He turned his attention to the man in the back of the cart. "Do you speak, friend?" This man looked different. He was lighter in complexion and older, and, unlike his friend, he appeared calm.

The one called Jamal said, "He is my associate from Nuristan. He does not speak Pashto."

"I see," said Abdul Salaam.

Kolt Raynor desperately tried to picture a map of the FATA in his head. With all the other concerns and calculations going on up there in his brain, the geography was difficult to get his mind around. Still, he didn't think Jamal's story added up. They were traveling west when he made it as if they were going east, Mingora was way too far south to travel from by tractor, and while Kolt could manageably pass for a lighter-skinned Muslim, a non-Pashto-speaking Afghan from Nuristan Province would not be of much use as a drug smuggler down here in the Pashtun tribal FATA.

Yep, Raynor thought, *these assholes are about to call bullshit on twitchy Jamal's story, which means one thing, and one thing only.*

Raynor may have been the first here in the stream bed to figure it out, but he knew it wouldn't take the others long to catch up.

This polite conversation was just about over, and a fight was just about to start.

Raynor's right hand slid down to the bed of the cart, where his fingertips began walking along the oaken floor, searching for anything within reach that could be used as a weapon.

Abdul Salaam did not believe the frightened Afghan's story. Moreover, these men might have money, food, or other goods that he and his cousins could use. They'd long spent the French aid worker's cash. He would search them, he would relieve them of their belongings, and he would either kill them or send them on their way. The decision would be made by Allah, meaning that if the men showed they were good Muslims, if they could pray and recite the Koran to Abdul Salaam's satisfaction, then he would let them leave on their tractor with the clothing on their backs. If not, he and his cousins would shoot them here and now.

"Get off your tractor. Both of you." He turned to Dagar: "Check the cart for weapons," and then to Jandol: "Get them down from there."

Abdul Salaam covered the strangers with his AK. He took just a moment to unfold his stock to bring it to his shoulder, looking down for a split second to do so. When he looked back up he was surprised to see the Nuristani in the back of the cart standing up straight, quickly, and something appeared in his right arm. It was not a rifle, but it was long. He swung it like an ax at Jandol, who had stepped to the left of the cart. Abdul Salaam recognized it as a shovel just as it slammed into his older cousin's face. A clang of heavy steel against hard forehead echoed through the low creek bed, Jandol's head snapped rearward, and his body dropped limp onto the white stones.

Abdul Salaam's eyes widened in shock and his finger began to pull the trigger of his automatic weapon. As the first round cracked out from his AK's barrel, he saw the Nuristani sling a long instrument directly at him with his other hand. It cartwheeled through the air, directly at him. Abdul Salaam ducked as he fired, rounds shredded limbs and leaves from the trees above and behind the tractor, and he landed hard on the stones of the stream bed as an iron hammer whirled by, narrowly missing his head.

In panic Abdul held the AK's trigger down hard and saw sparks on the grille of the red tractor. The recoil of his weapon pulled his fire up high and to the right, and the Afghan in the blue kameez seemed to be propelled backward through the air and into the cart behind him.

Kolt Raynor dropped the shovel and grabbed Jamal by the collar of his shirt, yanked him off the seat of the tractor and out of the way of the gunfire with all his might, almost pulling the young man out of his sandals. Together they fell back in the cart and rolled all the way off the back of it, falling hard together onto the stony surface of the stream bed. Jamal would be safe back here for the next five seconds, so Raynor launched himself up and off Jamal and shot low to the right of the tractor, knowing he would find a gunman there. The lone Talib on this side of the cart had his weapon high over his head and was firing down over the side wall of the wooden cart. He was shocked to see the man appear at ground level to his left, and he swung his weapon at this fast-moving threat.

Kolt took the man down with a tackle that would have made the defensive line coach for his high school football team proud. He slammed his right shoulder into the slight man's solar plexus, the rifle flew into the air, and the American used his momentum to drive his body down through the Talib as they both hit the rock-strewn earth. Kolt heard ribs crack but he did not even look at his victim. Instead, he lunged for the AK-47, scooped it off the stream bed, and rolled his body three times to the left, into the space between the big right rear tire of the Euroleopard tractor and the right tire of the wooden cart. Now he was directly under the cart itself, and he searched for a target on the other side. Gunfire rattled in the stream bed and beat off the surrounding hills. Immediately he aimed at the legs of the man running past on his left. With a five-round burst Raynor dropped the Talib to his knees. He could see the bearded man's pain- and shock-stricken face now below the cart, and he fired one round into his chest, blasting him dead on his back.

There was one threat remaining: the leader, the man who had spoken, and the first man to fire. Raynor did not know how much ammo remained in this salvaged Kalashnikov, but he had no time to drop the magazine or check for a round in the chamber. He began rolling to the left again, his body came out from under the cart on the opposite side of where he had rolled under, and he stopped only when he bumped up against the man he'd just killed.

Quickly he trained his weapon forward.

The leader of the Taliban squad was in a low crouch. He had just reloaded his weapon and was bringing it back up to his shoulder.

Kolt Raynor lay flat on his chest, snap-aimed the automatic rifle's iron sights at his target, and pulled the trigger back hard.

A single round popped from the gun and then it ran

dry. The spent cartridge ejected in a smoking arc over his right shoulder, and Kolt rose quickly to his knees.

One shot was all he'd needed. The Taliban leader lay crumpled in a heap, facefirst on top of his gun.

Raynor found the man he'd tackled still alive on the other side of the cart, but the Pashtun was out of the fight. He lay on his back and stared at the infidel above him. His breath came in short wheezes, the broken bones rattling in his chest along with the raspy breath.

Kolt quickly searched him for more weapons, found a rusty Makarov pistol, and shot the man through the forehead with it.

There was no way he would leave a survivor here to tell others what had happened.

He then found Jamal right where he'd left him, lying facedown in the dry creek behind the wooden cart. Instantly Kolt's heart sank. Smears of blood on the young man's clothing, and on the rocks around him, convinced Raynor that the agent who had come to save him had been shot in the first barrage by the Taliban leader. But Raynor quickly ran his hands all over Jamal's body, and found him to be free of serious wounds, and also very much alive. Jamal climbed back to his feet, seemingly as frightened by all the rough and inappropriate touching by the American spy as he had been by the dozens of bullets fired in his direction.

Kolt found the source of the blood soon enough. His own knees, elbows, and forearms were cut from the rocks of the stream bed. His local clothing was tattered and torn. He felt not one iota of pain at the moment—a near overdose of adrenaline saw to that—but he knew his bruised and abraded appendages would sting and burn like hell in no time.

Considering the other possible outcomes of the event that had just transpired, he was thrilled to find himself only banged up and dripping a small amount of blood.

But there was no time to celebrate. Two of the tractor tires had been pierced by AK rounds and were now flat. Kolt knew they had to leave the vehicle behind and get out of there before others came to the sound of the gunfight. He grabbed the thin Afghan by the arm, then pulled the satellite phone from under the seat.

The phone was in pieces. It had taken a 7.62 mm round directly into its body. Raynor crammed the pieces into his pockets nonetheless.

"Is there anything on this tractor that can be led back to you or Bob?" Kolt asked it in broken Pashto, and his pronunciation and bad grammar, coupled with Jamal's shock and ringing ears from all the gunplay, slowed the response.

Finally Jamal said, "No. There is nothing."

"Good. Let's go!" Kolt instructed. He grabbed the Kalashnikov from the dead Taliban leader, and the two men ran up the dry creek bed toward the trees and hills to the north. Kolt had gone no more than ten yards when he felt pain in his feet. He stopped, looked down, and realized his feet were bare.

He'd forgotten that he'd lost his sandals in the river the night before. He tiptoed over to the closest dead Talib and removed his sandals. They were a tad too small, but they were better than racing barefoot through the woods.

THIRTY-ONE

Bob Kopelman stared blankly out a window covered with clay dust, out past the front gate of the warehouse compound, out past the busy Grand Trunk Road, and toward the mountains to the south. The sun was setting off to his right, his men were hours overdue, and his dozen calls to Jamal's phone had gone unanswered.

He'd been in contact with Pete Grauer over the border in Afghanistan and asked for a UAV overflight of the route he expected Racer and Jamal to take, but Grauer had demurred until evening, wanting to bring less attention to his drone activities at the base and over the border.

So Kopelman sat there, staring out the window, worrying about his men, worrying about encountering bandits on the road himself if he had to go back to Peshawar after dark, worrying about thieves hitting this warehouse, since he'd sent the security detail home hours earlier so that they would not see the American spy.

Worry came with his line of work, but the importance of this operation and the thin resources allotted to him caused him to agonize on this afternoon more than on almost any other job in his long career.

A big colorful bus slowed on the road in front of his gate, pulled to a stop on the gravel right in front of it. Gold and silver mirrored baubles adorned the bus like Christmas ornaments, and they caught the setting sun and sent it like laser beams into Kopelman's eyes. He turned away from the grimy window for a moment, and when he turned back, the bus was pulling back out onto the road.

Jamal and Racer stood at the gate.

"It's about time!" Bob exclaimed as he reached for the keys on the desk and shot outside into the swirling clay dust.

Once back inside the warehouse office, Bob greeted Jamal with a traditional Pashtun greeting consisting of a squeezing of the arm by the shoulder, with the other hand placed on the chest.

While still holding on to Jamal's arm, Bob regarded Raynor. The ex-Delta man looked like hell. His clothing was torn and streaked with blood, and the exposed skin on his filthy body was covered with cuts, bruises, and scratches. "You need a doctor?" Bob asked.

Raynor just shook his head.

"No? Well, you just might when I finish kicking your ass."

Kolt cocked his head like he did not understand.

Kopelman turned away, reached over to a single-eye electric burner, and hefted a metal pot. He poured hot green tea into a cup for Jamal. He sugared it heavily and poured in a long stream of hot milk from a shallow pan, and stirred it some more. Jamal thanked him and sipped greedily. The American ex–CIA man then reached into a little fridge and tossed a bottle of water to Raynor.

Kolt guzzled the cool water, poured a little on his long matted hair, and let it run down his back, where more cuts and bruises from the river adventure and the shoot-out in the dry creek bed were hidden under his kameez.

Jamal began speaking as soon as he'd had a few sips of tea. He told Bob about rushing in the tractor to rescue the American, about discovering him half conscious under the cedar tree, about the run-in with the Taliban and the fight that ensued, or at least what he saw of it, which was nothing but the end result. Four dead, the last one by execution.

Then he spoke of the forced run for much of an hour, all the while with the American prodding him onward. Then hours of walking, with no rest, no water, no tea. Then the arrival at the bus stop, the stress and fear of Mister Racer doing or saying something to reveal himself, and finally the connection to the bus that brought them there.

Kolt didn't understand half of it, but he got the gist of the message Jamal was trying to impart to Bob Kopelman.

Mister Bob, working with Mister Racer sucks!

Kopelman took it all in. He sipped sweet green milk

tea himself while the story unfolded. Finally he turned and looked at Racer. Just stared at him for a long time like an incredibly annoyed father. "Pete told me I'd have my work cut out for me with you. Would it have been too much for you to just accomplish the mission we agreed on?"

Raynor was defiant. "I did a lot more in a lot less time."

Kopelman snapped back. "By risking everything! It's not just your life to piss away, kiddo. Jamal could have been picked up at any point on that retrieval, and Jamal can be connected back to me! I have other associates who would have then been rounded up. Don't try to sell me that 'I'm a one-man army' bullshit, because I've heard it all before, and everyone who ever said it either is dead, or else suddenly learned to sing the praises of teamwork when it came down to getting a team of operators together to extract him from whatever shitty situation he'd managed to fall into all by his lonesome! You had a simple, manageable mission to accomplish—"

"That wasn't going to get us eyes on the men!"

Bob started to shout again, but instead he just slammed his hand against the metal table. The sound exploded like a bomb in the tiny room. Jamal stayed out of any argument, looked off into space, and sipped his tea, holding his hot cup with his thin fingertips. His hands still jittered from the events of the day.

Raynor may not have expected a ticker-tape parade once he'd made it back out of the valley, but he also had not expected this washed-up CIA geezer's vitriol.

He said nothing, just sipped water and brooded.

After a moment Kopelman seemed to regain some composure. "Nevertheless. You are here now. . . . Did you find the American prisoners?"

Raynor nodded.

"At least you accomplished that."

At least?

"Are you okay?" he asked in Pashto.

Kolt nodded. "Yeah, just some scrapes. I got banged up when—"

"I am talking to Jamal."

"I am okay, Mister Bob."

Kopelman addressed Racer. "We'll stay here tonight. It's not safe on the road after dark. I'm going to let *you* contact our associates over the border. I am sure Pete will be interested in talking to you."

Kolt drank an ice-cold Coca-Cola, his feet propped up on a couch in Kopelman's small but secure one-room office. Bob had gone up the street to another World Benefactor warehouse to retrieve a large aid truck. Once back in the building, he'd clear out the contents of one of the large packing crates in the cargo hold. He would use this to hide Racer during tomorrow morning's return to Peshawar.

Jamal had walked up the street to grab a dinner of rice and vegetables for all three men.

Raynor was instructed to lie low, to not answer the door, to not do anything but sit there in the room with the shades drawn and rest.

And call his boss.

"Hey, Pete," he said when the connection was finally made through Kopelman's satellite phone.

"Racer, it's good to know you made it out."

"Thanks to Bob and his local contact. And, I assume, thanks to Pam Archer and her Predator."

"Affirmative. We had the UAV over you for much of your . . . mission."

Kolt sighed. *Shit.* "How much did you see?"

"I think the UAV caught just about all of the most exciting parts last night."

"Right. Okay."

"Quite a thriller, watching all that in real time. None of us here, however, saw you doing much of anything that we talked about you doing."

"Yes, sir. Had to make some game-time changes to the op."

"Game-time changes? It was almost like you were playing an entirely different sport."

Kolt did not respond.

For a moment neither did Grauer. Finally he said, "Pam checked on Zar's compound. There is no sign of any changes to the force structure. Killing the two men seems to have worked. They don't seem to be aware their compound was infiltrated."

"That's good news."

Grauer cleared his throat. "You found them, didn't you?"

"Pete . . . I shook T.J.'s hand."

"My God."

"All four guys on the team and one of the helo pilots survived the crash. All five of them are still alive. Skip Knighton, the Agency Mi-17 pilot, is sick, but the rest are okay."

"Proof of life?"

Kolt paused. Sighed. "I filmed part of my conversation with T.J."

"Good work. Upload your file to—"

"I lost it in the river."

A short delay from Grauer. "Shit, Kolt. That's why you went in."

"I know. I'm sorry."

Grauer sighed. He was not pleased, but he recovered and moved on. "Did you find out which building they were in?"

"Yes, sir. But it's complicated."

"Explain."

Raynor told Grauer about the hidden Kord machine guns, and the fact that Zar kept one of the prisoners sequestered from the others as an insurance policy. He then told him the odd story of the counterfeit Rangers, the German, the phony gear, and the power struggle between the Taliban and the foreign al Qaeda contingent that T.J. had mentioned.

"What in the name of God are they up to?" was all Grauer had to say. He had Kolt on the speaker in the Operations Center. Immediately analysts began speculating about what this new information meant. The conclusions were the same as those Kopelman, T.J., and Raynor had suspected. Al Qaeda was planning some sort of infiltration-type attack in Afghanistan, and with good equipment, it was highly likely they would be successful.

Finally Grauer said, "Okay, son. You're going to need to sit tight on that side of the border for a bit. Bob will look after you. I'm going to go to my contacts at the Agency, as well as Colonel Webber. Our job was to find the men, and as far as I'm concerned, we've done our job. But with everything you just told me, I don't think anyone is going to be too interested in hitting that compound. We'll just wait to hear back from them and take it from there."

"Yes, sir. I thought maybe Bob could check with some of his contacts in the area, see if anyone knows anything about this German guy."

Grauer answered back immediately: "I was thinking the same thing."

THIRTY-TWO

At first light the next morning Jamal left the World Benefactors warehouse on foot. He walked along the road to the west until a passing bus stopped and picked him up. He'd been told by Bob to go back home and await further instructions. He was also to contact Zar's camp and tell them his truck had broken down, so he would not be able to make his delivery that day.

Again Kolt Raynor had to cram his body into a tiny space. A crate that had shipped milk powder had been emptied, and that was to be his accommodations for the short ride back to Peshawar. Raynor was stiff and sore from the past four days in the field, so even though the crate was a little larger than the stash compartment in the Hilux, it took Kolt longer to fold himself inside. Kopelman actually hammered the wooden lid back on, a bit too tightly for Kolt's liking, and soon the ex–Delta officer heard the truck's rear door slide down and lock into place.

The truck's engine coughed and then roared to life, and soon they were on their way.

Bob had told Raynor that it was a thousand-to-one chance that the contents of the World Benefactor vehicle would be inspected at the border crossing from the FATA into Peshawar, but Bob had also said there was no reason to roll that thousand-sided die. Kolt would hide out and deal with his cramping muscles, and he would shut the hell up about it.

And Kolt Raynor did what he was told.

They arrived in Peshawar just after 9 a.m. The truck stopped and the rolling lift door opened and finally the lid of the milk powder crate was pried off and Raynor struggled to stand back up, to step out of the crate, and to stagger out of the truck. He found himself in a garage. Bob had already disappeared through a doorway, and Kolt followed him through, climbed some stone steps, and entered a small urban home, nondescript and utterly devoid of anything that looked American or even Western.

Bob stood in the tiny kitchen, already putting on a tea kettle, and this time he placed two cups on the table and pulled milk from his fridge.

They sat in silence for a few minutes while the water boiled, a few minutes more while the tea brewed. Kolt had regained sensation in his extremities after the tight confines of his uncomfortable morning ride, and he was ready to begin the hunt for this mysterious German somewhere around Peshawar. Sitting quietly over a pot of steeping tea seemed like an absurd waste of time, and he started to mention this to Bob, but the burly bearded man just held his hand up before he could speak.

Bob seemed to get pleasure in this local custom, and he did not want to be disturbed.

Tea was poured, sugar was spooned, milk was added, and the concoction was stirred, all by Bob Kopelman. Raynor thought the man looked and acted nothing like an American here, in this house, performing this foreign ritual.

Finally, Kolt took his cup and brought it to his mouth. Bob sipped his own, and then spoke, as if the two men had just stepped into the room from opposite ends of the house to find one another.

"Big day today for me. Not so much for you to do. I'll work the phones, maybe run out and have tea with a couple of my local contacts, try to find this Kraut working for al Qaeda."

"I can help you—"

"You can help me by finishing your tea, heading into my spare room, and plopping your ass on the bed. I put a first aid kit in there for your boo-boos, and I've got a shitty battery-operated AM radio on the desk you can entertain yourself with, but other than that, I don't want you to do jack squat."

"Bob, at least let me—"

"You can take a shower, but the water won't be hot. The electrical grid around here is overtaxed—there are brownouts throughout the day, and always at this time of the morning. The Taliban bomb the power stations and transformers pretty regularly, and the locals don't really fight back anymore, so don't expect much electricity during your stay."

Raynor knew when he was beat. This guy would get his way. He'd sit tight, and his blood would boil while doing so, but Bob was running this show.

Raynor spent the day in the guest room of Kopelman's house. He'd eaten well, rehydrated his body, coated the worst of his cuts with antiseptic and bandaged them, and gotten a little sleep. He spent the rest of the time waiting for the call from Grauer, the call that would let him know what to do next.

Kopelman spent his morning on his phones. He had at least five different mobiles, not including the satellite, and he sat in his office, across the main living space of the house, and mumbled into one phone after the next. Raynor heard English, but he could not understand much of it because the old CIA man whispered and spoke in short, terse sentences. Then he made a call and conversed in Dari. Raynor barely knew a word of it, but he recognized the tenor and tone of the language. Then there were a half-dozen conversations in Pashto. Raynor understood that Bob was trying to track down the German man, but he had no idea whom he was calling or where he was focusing his search geographically.

Then Bob made a call and spoke Dutch. Raynor gave up trying to figure out the big man's game plan; instead, he rolled back on the bed and tried to go back to sleep.

His full stomach churned with the worry and the guilt.

Kolt had just dozed off when Bob leaned into the spare bedroom. "Racer, I'm meeting a guy at the Pearl

Continental Hotel. He may have a lead on the German."

Raynor sat up quickly. "I'll come with you."

"No, it's going to be just me and a contact sipping scotch. I don't need a Delta shooter on this run."

Racer did not want to sit here, but he did what he was told. "Okay."

Kopelman leaned a Kalashnikov rifle against the wall inside the door of the guest room. Sternly he said, "You won't need this." Then he shrugged as he turned away. "Unless you do."

Kolt heard Bob leave the house about 3 p.m., but he did not hear a car start or the garage door open.

Raynor lost track of time. He felt better physically, lying there in the quiet house, with only distant but persistent street noises to keep him company. But this downtime after his operation into the Tirah Valley was tough on his mental state. He worried and brooded, wondered if something he had done might just lead to the failure of the operation to rescue the prisoners. He wondered if these five men, men who had finally been located to a fixed area so that a plan could be concocted to go in and get them out, might already be gone. Might already be on the road, chained together, hidden for the winter season, only to reappear next with the spring offensive, once again to serve as human shields for the Taliban and al Qaeda.

Raynor lay there on the bed, his mind full of worry about his decision to enter Zar's compound. Zar was no fool. He'd made it this long in power in the valley. It would just take a hint of danger for the warlord to have his captives moved or, God forbid, to get rid of them permanently.

Shit, Kolt thought. What if his actions got the men killed? What if by him coming here he'd actually done more harm than good?

Kolt heard a key in the front door. He leaped to the Kalashnikov, hoisted it to his shoulder, flipped down the safety, and began moving up the hallway toward the main room.

Bob Kopelman locked his front door behind him, and turned to Raynor. Kolt lowered the rifle as he noted an expression of utter glee on the face of the other American. "A grand total of *one* German fitting T.J.'s description in Peshawar, and I found his ass!"

Thank God. A lead, an objective, something to shoot for. "Who is he?" Kolt asked.

"Helmut Buchwald."

"Okay. *What* is he?"

"He's an armorer. A gun maker. He worked for Walther, then Heckler & Koch. He got fired from HK for poor quality control. An internal investigation found out he was sabotaging rifles headed to the U.S. military, but they fired him quietly and never charged him with a crime. Apparently he's a big-time anti-American. He's married to an Iraqi woman who was picked up in Baghdad for insurgent ties. I guess he's playing for the other team now."

"And he's here?"

Bob nodded eagerly. "I met with a guy who gets foreigners the papers they need to travel through Pakistan. Reporters and spooks, mostly, but I had a hunch that he would cross paths with this German. I was right. He'd helped Buchwald find some real estate here. He showed up in my contact's office six weeks ago with a Turk. My contact says he pegged the Turk as AQ almost immediately."

"Real estate?"

"He rented a warehouse in Darra Adam Khel about a month ago. He's also rented a factory not too far from his warehouse. Illegally, of course. The government doesn't know he's here, and even if they did, they don't have much say in Darra Adam Khel."

"Why not?"

"Darra is called 'the Gun Village.' It's a lawless warren of tiny one-room factories and a smugglers' bazaar of guns, ammo, and dope. The Pak government doesn't run the show down there. It's Taliban all the way."

"Shit. What's the German guy going to do with a factory and a warehouse?"

"I know a guy who knows a guy. Buchwald has hired local talent, highly skilled armorers, less-skilled metalworkers, also tailors and painters, and he's made purchases in the bazaar here in Pesh. Fabric of different types. Plastic, steel. Everything he's snatching up would fit with someone building up an operation to manufacture counterfeit military clothing and personal equipment. Copies of U.S. general issue gear, perhaps?"

"That's our man."

"There's more. According to an armorer who worked in his place, Buchwald oversaw the manufacture of four dozen local copies of M-4 rifles."

"Four dozen? Holy shit!"

"Yeah, the scale of this is bigger than your friend suspected. T.J. may have seen only a few Chechens, but with an entire factory churning out clothing and gear and guns, we could be talking about an enemy operation of fifty tangos or more."

"A platoon of Chechen jihadists posing as Rangers."

"Looks like it."

"But why?"

Kopelman shrugged. "I don't know. And I *hate* when I don't know something. So I was thinking we might go down to Darra Adam Khel and find out."

Raynor answered immediately. He couldn't take another day sitting on a bed and going stir-crazy. "I'd like that a lot."

Although Kopelman made it sound easy, two Americans traveling to Darra Adam Khel was anything but. It was only a forty-minute drive south on the Peshawar–Kohat road, but distance was not the obstacle. Westerners, especially Americans, were not welcome in the winding, narrow village. The Pakistani government demanded that all foreign travelers there apply for and receive a day pass and hire a local guard and driver.

It was not simple kindness that drove these rules. No, it was simple economics.

Dead travelers, even foolish imbeciles who did not have the sense to avoid a town as lawless and uninviting as Darra Adam Khel, were bad for Pakistan's already devastated tourist industry.

Bob knew he wasn't getting down there in his World Benefactor truck with his WB credentials. No, he'd have to travel low-profile, taking his personal car, a filthy and dented Opel two-door that would arouse neither suspicion on the road nor suspicion in the town, and he and Raynor would have to have their pakol hats low and their game faces on.

It could be done—Kopelman had been through the Gun Village several times before in the black—but it would be a risk.

One way to both mitigate the risk and increase the chance for a positive haul of intelligence was for Bob to call up the useful Jamal Metziel and ask him if he would be willing to help. Jamal had spent years in the village, he had family living and working there, and as an Afghani Pashtun, he could go where he wanted to go with his head high and no risk of suspicion, unless he strayed too far into the realm of real spying.

Jamal tacitly agreed immediately—he wanted to help—but he relaxed and assented in full only when Bob assured him that even though Mister Racer would be tagging along, he would not be in charge of this mission.

The three men met late that evening at a Radiance safe house in the center of Peshawar. Kopelman explained to Raynor that he trusted Jamal, but not enough to give him his home address. The conversation was in Pashto, and Kolt knew this would keep him out of much of the planning, as his command of the language was not one-fifth of Bob's, or one-tenth of Jamal's. But Raynor understood, and he kept quiet. He did not know this town, these rules, the players in this game. On the singleton mission in the Tirah Valley he had felt in his element, even though he was surrounded by enemies. But here, in a city of hundreds of thousands, with checkpoints and papers and smugglers' bazaars and villages filled with criminals and devoted wholly to the manufacture of guns . . . no, Kolt recognized that the two dudes who knew their way around, who knew how to keep their heads low, were the two dudes who needed to do the planning on this op.

So he kept quiet, concentrated as best he could on the discussion, and even refilled the chai cups of the two men while they talked and looked over road maps and a satellite map of the city.

Kolt did ask one question. "Can we get Pam Archer to fly the UAV over us while we're there?"

Bob shook his head. "Nope. This is too far inside the border. The Predator can't travel this deep without everybody knowing about it. You and me and Jamal? We are on our own."

The plan for the next morning was finalized around midnight. Kopelman handed Jamal an encrypted walkie-talkie and sent the young man back to the garage where his truck was kept. Jamal would sleep there, in the cab, and then meet up with the two Americans the next morning just south of Peshawar.

Bob and Kolt returned to Kopelman's home to attempt a few hours of nervous sleep.

THIRTY-THREE

The two Americans rose early in the morning. Bob brewed tea while Raynor dressed in his salwar kameez and did his best to thicken his beard with his fingertips. Together they drank in silence as the morning call to prayer was cried out by the muezzins from the minarets of the half-dozen mosques within earshot of Kopelman's home, smack dab in the Old City of Peshawar.

Next they went out to the garage and stocked the Opel with a full case of bottled water and two full gas cans. Kolt checked the spare tire and the jack. Bob checked the oil.

A breakdown on the road to Darra Adam Khel for some reason that could have been avoided with a touch of preventive care would be an outrageous and unacceptable failure for the two well-trained operatives.

Murphy's Law could not be eradicated, but with some effort, it could be mitigated.

Then Bob threw in three walkie-talkies, extra batteries, and his Hughes satellite phone. He slipped a key in a long metal footlocker on the floor of the garage. Once it was opened, he retrieved a wooden-stocked AK-47 and an AK-74, its wire stock folded tight against its body, dramatically shortening the length. For these weapons he grabbed two extra magazines, and all this he put on the floor in front of the passenger seat. Upon it all he tossed a patoo.

Kolt was surprised to see they'd be going into the town with all this incriminating gear. "Bob, if somebody searches the car, they are going to find the guns and the sat phone. Isn't that going to raise suspicion?"

Kopelman looked at Racer for a long moment in the dim of the garage. "If somebody searches the car, they are going to find *you,* which is going to raise a shitload of suspicion, at which point the rifles may come in handy."

Raynor nodded. He never complained about having access to a weapon when heading into danger, and he sure as hell was not about to start now.

They met with Jamal, as planned, just after 9 a.m., and with the yellow truck in the lead they headed south on the Kohat Road to Darra Adam Khel. Raynor mentioned he would have felt better with a night op, but Kopelman knew the area, and he knew that the little town was packed full during the day. The three of them walking around in plain sight would not be noticed nearly as easily as they might if they skulked around the closed-up shops and factories in the dead of night.

As they drove south Kopelman spoke a seemingly prepared statement to his younger colleague.

"Now listen up, Racer. You were sent on one reconnaissance mission this week, and you managed to kill six guys in the process. That's not a recon. That's an assault. We don't need an assaulter today. I need a guy who can mind his manners and do what he's told. Do you think you can play that role for a few hours while we poke around town?"

It was the same as ever with Raynor—he did not like being talked down to or second-guessed. "So if we run into Taliban hell-bent on killing us, I'd better just keep my cover while they lop off your head? That's the plan?"

"We do this correctly, smart-ass, and nobody will know we're there. The guns are a last resort, and *I* will make the call if they are necessary. Understood?"

"Shit happens, Bob. You think I went looking to get into a tussle with those Taliban?"

"To tell you the truth, I don't know. I respect the work you paramilitary guys do at JSOC, but you characters are wound up a bit too tightly for my taste. I think sending in guys who've been trained to do nothing but fight just about ensures you're going to get a fight. I didn't want you on this mission in the first place. No offense."

Kolt looked out the window and shrugged. He'd heard *that* before. "Why on earth would I take offense?" he muttered sarcastically.

"Don't get me wrong," Kopelman continued. "*I* wasn't going up in those mountains with nothing but the word of an untested Pashtun agent, so I'm glad Pete found somebody dumb enough to do it."

Before the mission Kopelman had gone to great lengths to assure Raynor that Jamal was a reliable source. Kolt just shook his head in disbelief at the new assessment he was hearing.

Kolt kept staring out the window. A long adobe wall ran along the right side of the street. When it ended he looked across a wide plain that ended where the mountains began to the west. Just two days earlier he and Jamal had run into the small squad of Taliban encamped in the creek bed running very near that ridgeline in the hazy distance.

Movement on his left got his attention. He turned to look at Kopelman, who had, with much rocking and shuffling from his large frame in the small car seat, managed to pull a metal flask from under his salwar kameez. As he drove with one hand he put the flask between his knees and unscrewed the metal cap with the other. He tossed the cap into the backseat and took a long swig on the flask. Instantly Raynor smelled whiskey in the tight car.

"You have got to be kidding me," he said in shock. It was nine thirty in the morning, they were mere minutes away from an extremely dangerous mission, and his lifeline home was swigging booze.

Bob winced like he'd done something wrong. "You're right, kid. Where are my manners? Should have offered you the first pull." He held the flask out to Kolt.

Raynor had not had a sip of alcohol in a month. He'd *wanted* his booze, had been almost crazy at first with the withdrawals, but the operation was too important.

Kolt turned away from the flask, and a second later he heard Kopelman swallow another long sip.

"Are you going to get drunk?" Kolt asked.

Bob just chuckled. "Boy, I'm 250 and my liver is about pickled. It's gonna take a lot more than this flask to get me drunk. I'm just softening the nerves a bit. Helps with stress, makes me smoother when I need to be smooth, relaxed when I need to not show fear. The Pashtuns can smell fear."

Kolt kept his eyes on the back of Jamal's truck up ahead through the dust of the Kohat road. He asked the older American, "Isn't there a law that people in the private sector can't work as spies?"

"Yes, there is." He gulped a little more whiskey and stowed the half-empty flask between his knees. "But there is a gray area, and that's where I live. Atmospherics, they call it."

"Environmental assessment is the term we use in the Unit."

Kopelman nodded. "Yep. Same thing. Private citizens can report on atmospherics, the general feeling of the population, mood on the street, disposition of the police, general crap like that."

"And that's what you do for Radiance?"

"Officially, yes."

"And unofficially?"

Kopelman laughed. The smell of whiskey, so recently something that comforted Raynor greatly, now made Kolt want to retch. "Unofficially? Unofficially, I pull overzealous American operators out of the badlands and do my best not to punch their lights out for going off mission and then asking too many questions."

Raynor smiled.

"Among other duties, that is," said Kopelman as he swigged from his flask yet again.

"How do you get booze into Pakistan?"

"It's my front company."

"I thought World Benefactors was your front company."

"Right. The WB gig gets me into some places, but importing black-market booze from China gets me into other places."

"Radiance owns a front company to smuggle liquor into Pakistan?"

Kopelman shrugged. "It helps me make and keep contacts with influential expats, journalists, foreign embassies, hotel employees, and other folks with their pulse on what's going on. There's power in the bottle, even here in the land of Allah." He thought about what he had said. "*Especially* here in the land of Allah."

Raynor just nodded. It made sense. Hell, it was brilliant. A legend that got him out into the refugee camps, around the Pashtuns, to gain intelligence from them. And then a secondary legend, the relief coordinator who also makes a few bucks smuggling in liquor, thereby granting him access to virtually all the non-Arabs in Peshawar. Like Berlin in the Cold War, Peshawar was ground zero in the War on Terror, or whatever the hell it was called these days.

Kolt respected this cagey ex-Agency dinosaur. He had to ask. "So, how the hell did you get canned?"

Kopelman answered by waving the flask in the air and then tugging on his long beard.

"Booze. Okay, I get that. What's wrong with your beard?"

"They said I'd been in Pashtunistan for too long. I'd lost my objectivity."

Kolt understood now. "The Agency doesn't mind a drunk as much as it minds a case officer who's gone native."

Kopelman barked back. Obviously this subject struck a nerve with the old spy. "Yeah, well, it happens. They want you to fake it as good as a native, but don't you dare go too far." Kopelman shrugged. "I went too far, apparently." Bob raised an aggressive finger toward Raynor. "Doesn't mean I won't kill those AQ bastards with my own hands. I've spent the past ten years targeting al Qaeda and Taliban with behind-the-lines legwork, not UAVs and piss-poor third-hand walk-in intel that's more likely to result in a Hellfire landing on the dance floor of a wedding party than on a terrorist safe house. I've done a damn fine job for my country, and the heads at Langley said, 'Yeah, but he likes whiskey *and* chai, he looks and smells and acts too much like one of them, so we can't use him anymore.' "

"Pete respects you."

Kopelman nodded thoughtfully. "Colonel Grauer gets it. He knows how to fight this war. Too bad his job is to protect the gear in the rear and hunt poppy farms from the air, and he's not in charge, doing the kind of shit that needs to be done."

Raynor agreed. Bob seemed a little loony to him, but most of the nonofficial-cover CIA operatives he'd met in his career seemed like they were teetering between worlds.

That was tough work, for which the Langley suits and Washington in general offered little thanks.

Kolt watched Kopelman finish off the flask and then toss it into the backseat. Quickly he swigged water from the bottle between the seats, rolled down his window, and spat it out on the road.

Just then a long burst of automatic-weapons fire from the road ahead drew both men's attention.

Bob turned to Raynor. "We're here."

"Contact front," said Kolt. He didn't see the shooters, but he lifted his AK over the dashboard and—

Bob slapped the weapon back down. "Calm down, cowboy! This is Darra. They call this place the Gun Village for a reason. People come here to buy weapons, and the salesmen just walk them out in the street and let them dump a couple of mags into the surrounding hills."

"You've got to be joking."

"You'd better get used to the sound of gunfire up close. It doesn't mean you're in any danger down here. Hell, if the shooting *stops,* then you need to be worried. Automatic fire here is normal."

Another burst ahead—it sounded to Raynor like an automatic shotgun blasting 12-gauge loads. He tucked his head down in his neck instinctively, then resolved to fight this very natural and quite rational urge while in the village.

Darra Adam Khel appeared on both sides of the twisting valley road, buildings and shacks and fences and alleyways moving up the hills. As Jamal's truck and Bob's car snaked along the road, the traffic intensified around them. The noise of the street, the bustle of the bazaar, the smells of livestock and diesel fuel and cooking meat and coal-burning furnaces in the tiny factories, overwhelmed Raynor's senses.

Jamal's voice came over the walkie-talkie. "There is a checkpoint on the road ahead. I'll go through it, but you turn down the alleyway on the left. Follow it around—it goes through to the back of the arcade. No one will stop you there if you don't pull back onto the main road. I'll stay on the road and meet you there. Five minutes."

"Got it," said Kopelman.

Jamal spoke again. "Don't let Mister Racer get out of your car, Mister Bob. It is very dangerous here."

Bob spoke in English before pressing the Talk button. "No shit." Then he transmitted in Pashto, "Don't worry."

Kopelman turned down the alleyway as instructed by the young man who had lived and worked in this very village for several years. It was no surprise that Jamal knew how to weave through the back alleys to avoid roadblocks.

But Jamal's comfort level around Taliban was greater than Kolt's. Almost immediately Bob had to stop his vehicle to allow three armed men in black turbans to cross from one doorway to another. They stopped in the alley, looked at Kopelman's car and then at the men inside it. Kolt stared back at them, wondered how this was going to play out. He avoided any sudden movements, but his hands gripped the weapon between his knees.

The three did not leave the alleyway in front of the

idling car. Bob acknowledged the men with a gracious bowed head, and they turned to Raynor. Stared at him. Five seconds passed, and Raynor just stared back.

The men did not leave the alley.

Kolt's Kalashnikov sat between his knees, its muzzle resting on the floorboard, and his hand tightened around the grip. As the three men glowered at him, Raynor used his trigger finger to snap the safety down one position, getting his rifle ready to go full auto.

Bob heard the click of the metal lever. Softly he said, "Easy, son. Just give them a nod, not quite a bow. Let 'em know you are no threat. They just want you to recognize them as superior."

Kolt did as instructed. He hated taking his eyes off of the three men even for the half second necessary to lean forward.

The three men soon turned away, moved into the open doorway in front of them.

Bob put the car back into gear, headed slowly forward through the narrow alley.

"Watch your eye contact, boy!" Bob was pissed. "I know you've worked covert ops. You know better than that."

Raynor wanted to argue. He did not handle reprimands well. But he knew the older man was absolutely right. "Yeah. Sorry. Just a little on edge after the past few days. That felt like a situation that was about to go loud."

"Most of the time, whether or not it goes loud is up to you. You don't keep your eyes low and your body language looking like you're ready to kiss some tail, and you won't last the day out here in the middle of these assholes."

"Understood. I'll ratchet down the testosterone."

Driving through the alley got serious again seconds later, when a donkey overly laden with loose unloaded rifles was led out into the passage behind one of the larger factories. The donkey's owner made no effort to move the animal out of the way so that the little four-door could pass. After a half minute of waiting and another fifteen seconds of honking, Kopelman climbed out from behind the wheel, went over, and began talking to the man.

Raynor was impressed. He sat there stone-faced in the car, did all he could to avoid bringing any attention to himself. Meanwhile his "partner" integrated himself into the street scene without a second's hesitation. Kolt knew he stood out more by trying to stay back, in the shadows, than he would in a crowd. The Pashtuns' penchant for communication between one another made his hiding of his language skills more obvious here than if he were trying to go undercover in some Western nation where he did not speak the language. He knew he could go months or even years in Switzerland without talking to passersby on the street. But here, in the middle of "Pashtunistan" as Bob had called it, a quiet man keeping to himself was almost as out of the ordinary as an American spy.

He'd never felt so utterly out of his element.

THIRTY-FOUR

They linked up with Jamal's truck back on the main road and continued to the east through the thick village. The arcade was predominantly on their left: hundreds of stalls where weapons were made and sold ran up and wrapped around the undulating features of the brown hill. On their right were some more shops and factories, but a warehouse district ran up these tiny hilly streets. Jamal took a right turn at an intersection full of motorized rickshaws and Toyota Hiluxes and tiny two- and four-door cars, and the Americans followed. They went up one incline, followed a narrow road with twists and turns like a boiled noodle, and eventually made their way onto another fairly straight east–west thoroughfare.

Another five minutes' driving time brought Bob to the waypoint he'd programmed on his GPS. He spoke into his walkie-talkie in Pashto. "Jamal. This is it."

The truck in front of them slowed. "Okay . . . On the left here?"

"No. This long brown fence on the right."

Jamal stopped the vehicle in a wide cul-de-sac on the opposite side of the street from the entry gate. Kopelman stopped along the sidewalk twenty yards behind him.

"Mister Bob?"

"Yes, Jamal?"

"This . . . this warehouse. It is the one here on the left?"

"What did I just tell you?" This Bob said in frustration, and in English, but he switched to the native language before transmitting. "On the right. The big building. Do you copy?"

No response from Jamal.

Bob looked at Racer. Then spoke into the walkie-talkie: "Is there some problem, my friend?"

A hesitant answer from the man in the yellow truck in front of them. "Well . . . no. I thought maybe there was a mistake."

"What's wrong?"

A pause. And then, "My uncle . . . he owns this building."

Bob Kopelman's big head lowered and rested on the top of the steering wheel. "Shit." He said it to Racer. "Shit!" He yelled it this time, banging the steering wheel with a force that startled his passenger. He turned to Kolt. "Pashtunwali. If his family is involved in this, then he will *not* turn on them."

As if Jamal could hear Bob's worries, his voice

came through the speaker of the device in Bob's hand. "My uncle . . . he only cares for money. He is not involved with politics. He has no interest in jihad. He is not a terrorist."

"Okay, son," Kopelman responded. Raynor could tell the big man did not believe Jamal for a second, even if Jamal himself was convinced his uncle was not part of the plot. "What do you want to do, Jamal? Do you want to leave?"

"No. It is okay. Perhaps my uncle rented space to the German. My uncle may be there, or one of his workers. I can go in now and speak with them. We will have tea. I can tell him I need a job, ask him if he can hire me to work."

Bob shook his head, looked to Racer. "I don't like it. Either he'll get himself into trouble, or he'll turn on us."

Kolt looked at Bob and snapped. "Funny how when just *my* ass was on the line you assured me this guy was up for the Secret Agent of the Year Award!"

"He *was* solid. But if his uncle is working for the German, and the German is working with AQ . . . Jamal is tainted by the strength of family ties."

They talked it over for a moment, but ultimately, they didn't see that they had any other option. Bob considered approaching the warehouse himself, under the guise of a World Benefactors logistics coordinator looking for additional warehouse space to rent, but that seemed like a transparent lie. Aid groups did not work in Darra Adam Khel, the warehouse owner would know that his building would be firebombed as soon as he started working with a Western aid agency, and he'd think the logistics coordinator was either childishly naive or, and perhaps more likely, a spy.

Bob leaned into his walkie-talkie. Paused for a long time. "Okay, Jamal. Go into the warehouse. Do not take any unnecessary chances, but if you see anything interesting, use the phone I gave you to take some pictures. They could be very important."

"You will wait for me in the place you are right now?"

"Of course."

Racer immediately protested. "If you think he's going to turn on us, why are we going to just sit and wait right where he knows we are?"

Bob replied, "We aren't. We'll keep moving, but I'm not going to tell *him* that."

They watched through the dirty windshield, across the dusty and congested street, as Jamal stepped out of his yellow truck and approached the front gate of the building. He spoke with a guard, there was a greeting of familiarity, and soon Jamal Metziel passed through a door by the gate and disappeared from view.

Immediately Bob Kopelman started the engine of the Opel sedan and headed up the street, passed the truck, and turned into an alleyway. A group of corrugated-metal-walled buildings ran along the shadowed alley, and Bob backed his car into a recess between two of them. It was just deep enough to hide the car in the shadows and to give a slim view of the truck and the front door and gate of the warehouse from the right side of the front windshield.

"Be right back," Bob said, and he left Raynor alone in the car.

"What the hell?" Raynor said to himself. He did not like sitting here alone, and he hated not knowing what his "partner" was doing. It was ten full minutes before Kopelman returned, opened the car door, and plopped heavily back into the seat. Kolt felt the Opel sink with the strain of the man's heavy body.

"Where did you go?"

"I asked the shopkeeper around the corner if I could park here for a little while while I wait for my friend to do some shopping in the arcade."

"That took ten minutes?"

Bob shrugged. "We had tea."

Kolt was still impressed. "You can pull off a local accent, just like that?"

"No, they'd see through that. If they ask I just tell them I'm a Nuristani, born in France to immigrants, who's lived in Kabul for fifteen years. It's both convoluted and plausible, and it does the trick."

"You can pray like a Muslim?"

Bob looked at him. "Of course. I went native, remember?"

Bob and Kolt got out of the car, and when no one was looking, Bob made several adjustments to Raynor's clothing, making him appear more authentic by changing the angle of his hat and the drape of the patoo over his chest and shoulders, even by scratching dust into the skin around Raynor's eyes. "Stay close to me. Don't talk, don't make eye contact, and don't ask anybody directions to McDonald's, 'cause there isn't one." Then the two of them began walking at a steady pace through the streets, even though they had nowhere to go. This movement would give them the look of purpose here in this bustling market town.

Every twenty seconds or so gunfire crackled in the streets around them, causing Kolt to tense up. The shooting was just the gun makers and gun salesmen, handing loaded weapons to prospective buyers, who simply walked a few feet from the tiny wooden stalls, pointed the rifles or pistols into the sky or at one of the sandy hilltops ringing the valley, and squeezed off a couple, or a couple dozen, rounds. It occurred to Raynor that although strolling around here, surrounded on all sides by men who would love nothing more than to kill an American, could not in any fashion be construed as "safe," long-range reconnaissance of the warehouse from a hilltop outside of town would arguably be even more dangerous, as that's where many of these bullets were striking.

The gunfire crackled continually, but long and sporadically enough for Kolt to know that there was no real threat to the sound, and he began to relax.

An hour passed with the men walking up and down any street that gave them a sight line to Jamal's yellow truck. Occasionally they would pass Bob's Opel to check on it, but otherwise they were just strolling through the crowds, doing their best to blend in. Kolt noticed how incredibly comfortable Kopelman seemed around the Pashtuns. He had no problem making eye contact with men and bowing to them in a friendly manner as they passed; he even stopped to look at some chickens for sale hanging from the back of a donkey in small wooden cages.

Raynor, on the other hand, kept his head on a swivel. He watched people pass—all men, most of them armed, and practically all of them threatening in appearance. He thought he'd been in the belly of the beast in Zar's compound, but here, surrounded by Taliban fighters, seemed almost surreal to him.

On one trip back to check on Bob's little car, they discovered that a motorized rickshaw towing a wagon had parked right in front of their vehicle. The driver had effectively boxed them into the shadowed recess of the wall and was now nowhere in sight.

Kopelman ordered Raynor to wait for him inside the car while he went looking for the driver. Kolt watched him disappear up the alley through the dirty windshield. He hoped like hell Bob's Pashto and his mannerisms, clothing, and actions would continue to pass muster. Raynor knew his own situation was even more dire than before because he had no one who could do the talking if some tribesman came tapping on the glass of the car. What could he do? Pretend to be asleep and hope the man went away?

Play dead?

These were the only options that came to mind. He shook his head and asked himself how he'd gotten into this lousy predicament.

Twenty minutes later Kopelman returned. Apparently his language and cultural skills had passed muster, because he carried several items he'd obviously purchased at the market. Once inside the car he sighed. "Couldn't find the driver of the rickshaw, which means we might have to walk out of here." He fished through a canvas bag. "So, if worse comes to worst, I bought you this."

He handed Kolt a powder blue garment made of thin silk.

"What the hell is—"

"It's a burka. You might have to wear it before the day is done, so I hope you like the color."

Raynor told himself there was no way he'd be donning a damned burka. Still, he tucked it inside his baggy trousers.

Kopelman had also bought some fruit, and together they ate grapes and pomegranate as they stared out the front windshield, through the dust and the glare of the afternoon sun, and waited for Jamal to reappear.

Minutes later Jamal Metziel stepped through the front gate of the warehouse and returned alone to his truck. The Opel was still boxed in by the rickshaw and the cart, so Bob could not just follow him out of town. He and Kolt had discussed trying to unhook the cart on their own and rolling it out of the way, but Bob had decided that this act would likely draw attention. Not angry or curious men. No, just as bad, it would attract men who would gather to help. The last thing either of these Americans wanted to see was a gaggle of armed local goons forming to assist them with their work, and then inviting them to a tea stand for pleasant conversation afterward.

If you were in Pashtunistan and you were not a Pashtun, Pashtunwali could get you killed in so many ways.

"What do we do?" asked Raynor.

"Screw it," Bob said. "Pete Grauer can buy me a new car. I'm not sitting here all night. Let's go." Kopelman grabbed a few items from around the car: his sat phone, his laptop, a backpack to stow them in.

Kolt asked, "What about the guns?"

Bob reached down and grabbed one AK, then nodded at the other. He pulled the canvas satchel with the extra mags and slung it over his neck.

"Yeah, we definitely take the guns. I find out that Jamal turned on me, I'm sure as shit gonna put a few rounds in his chest before I check out."

Shit, thought Raynor. Bob had been so high on this contact a couple of days ago; now he was actually entertaining the possibility of killing him.

Jamal's eyes widened when he saw the two men walking toward him in the street. Quickly he motioned them over to his truck. Both Americans climbed into the cab, and Jamal nervously looked up and down the street before climbing in himself. He drove east to a more secluded part of town. Several times Bob asked him what had happened and what he'd seen, but Jamal just muttered some little prayer over and over.

The kid was scared. Bob and Kolt both saw this, and they both worried silently that the kid might well be leading them into a trap.

After some more stern prodding from Bob, Jamal's head cleared enough to explain. "My uncle and some of my cousins were there. We ate lunch together. Slowly they began to talk about the people who are renting the warehouse space now."

"And?"

"And they are foreigners. From Yemen and Turkey."

"Not from Germany?"

"Yes, the man from Germany was with them."

"What else did you learn?"

"They have their own security there. Ten men or so. But my uncle took me out into the warehouse anyway to show me what was there. While my uncle spoke to the guards . . . I was able to take some pictures that you need to see."

"Pictures of what, Jamal?"

"I . . . I do not know what they mean."

"Okay, just relax." Bob looked in the rearview mirror, and Kolt checked the passenger-side mirror. Both men were scanning for anyone following them. Bob continued speaking to Jamal in Pashto. "Pull into this parking lot here, and we'll take a look at what you found."

They stopped, and Jamal pulled his mobile phone from his salwar kameez. He started to fiddle with it, but Bob just took it from his hands. Bob had given him the Motorola device because of its high-resolution video and digital still camera, and he'd perfunctorily shown the young Afghan how to use it, but the American intelligence operative knew how to work the thing in his sleep.

Bob downloaded the pictures onto his laptop in only a few seconds. When he double-clicked on the file, he blinked his eyes hard, twice. Over his right shoulder

Raynor muttered in confusion, "Uh . . . are you sure that's what you just downloaded?"

Bob was not sure. He looked at the file on his Toughbook. Finally he said, "I . . . yeah, that's what Jamal gave me. . . . Oh my God."

Both he and Raynor stared at the screen, at a digital photo of a U.S. Army Black Hawk helicopter. The markings, the paint job, were just like on all the Black Hawks crisscrossing the skies back over the border in Afghanistan.

Behind it in the warehouse was another helicopter, a nearly identical Black Hawk.

"Jamal? These two choppers? They are in the warehouse back there?"

"Yes, Mister Bob."

Bob addressed Racer now, incredulity in his voice: "How did you dumb Army fucks manage to lose two helicopters?"

Kolt shook his head, then considered the question seriously. "A Black Hawk is a Sikorsky UH-60. Sikorsky sells UH-60s to Egypt, the UAE, the Philippines, Brazil, and others. A couple of guys with the right equipment could take an Egyptian bird and paint it up like a U.S. bird in nothing flat."

Kopelman nodded. "This is big. These two choppers can carry forty troops."

"Forty bad guys."

"Right. Think about it, Racer. If they find a way to get them over the border, they could land at a FOB or even a full-sized base. There would be confusion, but nobody is going to suspect they're about to get nailed by AQ from inside the base. AQ can wipe out a lot of our guys with a pair of Black Hawks full of shooters."

"I know. And then they can get access to a lot of equipment. A lot of weapons. These two Black Hawks could be a game changer in this fight."

Jamal spoke for the first time. "My uncle . . . he does not like these people. But he likes his money. It is always so with my uncle. He said the two helicopters were not the only things in the warehouse, but trucks came and took the rest away already."

"What else was there?" asked Bob. Kolt quickly asked Jamal to speak more slowly and clearly so he could follow the conversation.

"Crates of goods. He did not know what they were. Never saw inside. But he knew that they came from the German's factory on the other side of Darra Adam Khel."

"And it's all gone now?"

"Yes. My uncle says the factory is no longer producing things. He met a local representative of the German there yesterday to get his payment, and there was only an empty factory floor full of sewing machines and metalworking machines, an upstairs office with a desk and a computer and a cot, this German man living and working there, and some armed foreigners guarding the place. It looks like it is about to close down completely."

Kolt said to Bob in English, "We're running out of time, Bob!"

Kopelman nodded, then asked Jamal, "Can your uncle get us into the factory?"

"No. He got his money. He has no business there now."

Bob blew out a long sigh. "I'd *love* to get a look at that Kraut's computer."

Kolt looked at Jamal. "Your uncle said there were ten guards?"

The young Afghan nodded.

Kopelman raised a hand. "Don't even think about it, Racer. You remember our talk about the definition of the word 'reconnaissance,' don't you? You *aren't* going into that factory."

"Then what are we going to do?"

"We are going to pass all this on to Grauer so he can alert the Agency." Kopelman wasn't going to wait one second. He closed his laptop and powered up the sat phone. Then he sent Jamal over to a small market to buy himself a cup of tea to help him relax. As soon as the young Afghan climbed out of the car Kolt asked Bob, "Do you believe him?"

"I do. I can't always tell when a Pashtun is lying, but I can tell when one is scared. He's scared of us, scared we will think he is somehow involved because his uncle owns the factory. If he had ratted us out, he wouldn't have shared that intel. I mean, what's the point?"

Bob spent the next ten minutes on the phone with Grauer communicating from the Radiance Ops Center over the border in Jalalabad. After Bob stowed the phone, he looked back at Raynor in the backseat. "He's going to inform Langley."

"What about us?"

"We are getting out of here."

Kolt was not satisfied. "Bob. Whatever these guys are going to do . . . they are going to do it soon. They can't fly those choppers once the winter closes in. Plus, just keeping them on hand like that they run the risk of compromise."

"I agree. Something nasty is about to go down, in days, not weeks."

Kolt asked, "Where is the factory?"

"Not far, two klicks to the east of here. Why?"

"Can we drive by? Just to check it out."

Bob strummed his fingers on his closed laptop. He nodded his head. "Okay. Can't hurt. When Jamal gets back we'll head over there before leaving town." He looked back to Kolt. "But I'll tell you one thing, Racer."

"What's that?"

"If I see a German dude out front on smoke break I'm jumping out of this cab and beating the shit out of him."

Kolt nodded appreciatively. "No argument from me."

THIRTY-FIVE

Minutes later Jamal was back behind the wheel and they were headed east, and once again the Hilux was stuck in a traffic jam. Cars, trucks, bicycles, rickshaws, donkey carts, donkeys without carts that had been packed with incredible amounts of bags, boxes, and other items. They crawled along with the rest of the traffic, and Bob began regretting his decision to take a look at Buchwald's factory.

It was almost dark when they reached a wide intersection. Jamal motioned to a compound on the northwest corner. "That's the place." Jamal pointed to a nondescript single-story wall, behind which stood a two-story wood, metal, and sandstone structure. It was the size of a small grocery store, except for the fact it was multilevel.

Two malevolent-looking security guards stood out front. Another sat Indian-style on the roof.

Raynor had no doubt there would be more inside.

Kolt asked Jamal, “No chance you have an uncle that owns this place, too?” He asked it in English, and Bob translated.

Jamal just shook his head. The joke was lost on him.

They found themselves stuck in the intersection. A dispute between truck drivers in front of them delayed everyone in all four directions, first as the two vehicles honked back and forth at one another, and then as the men climbed down from their cabs and began arguing animatedly on the dusty street. Kolt and Bob used the delay to take in as much of the area as possible.

Bob spoke aloud in English as he looked out the grimy window of the car, giving voice to his observations of the compound. “It’s buttoned up pretty tight. Sheet metal fence. Gate wide enough for a semi to get in and out of. Looks like a satellite dish on the roof. Regular phone and electric wires running in and out.”

Kolt was not listening. Instead he had his eyes on the crowd. Dozens of men in salwar kameezes or more Western-style Pakistani dress strode up and down the sidewalks and crossed between narrow spaces between the vehicles on the street, hustling home as night fell. Women were in the crowd too, but they did not walk alone. All the women had male escorts with them, as was the custom here in Taliban-controlled Pashtunistan.

Kolt looked back quickly toward the factory, and he made a decision.

The truck moved forward as traffic rerouted itself around the protracted argument between the truck drivers.

Sixty seconds later they were again stuck in a jam. They'd moved forward only one hundred yards, and now they were a block past the factory. Kolt tapped Jamal on the shoulder. "How do I look?" The young driver turned back from the right-sided steering wheel. He stammered his response in surprise. Raynor had dressed himself head to toe in the blue burka Kopelman had bought earlier.

"You . . . you look like a woman," Jamal said.

"Am I pretty?" Raynor joked.

Jamal just laughed nervously. Pashtun men did not act this way, did not joke like this.

Kopelman turned around in his seat to see what his man was doing. "What the hell is wrong with you? Quit screwing around!"

But Kolt turned serious now. Behind his mesh veil he said, "Bob, you know that any woman not accompanied by a man on the street is going to stand out like a sore thumb around here, right?"

"Absolutely. You wouldn't make it thirty seconds on the street, so don't even think—"

"Then you'd better tell Jamal to come with me." Kolt opened the back door of the cab and climbed out in his burka. In his cloaked arms he held a simple bag with his Pashtun clothing.

"Racer!" Kopelman sounded at once terrified and furious, but he did manage to shout it in a whisper. Raynor stepped down to the pavement and began walking away from the truck as the sun set over the sandstone hills to the west.

Fifteen seconds later, Jamal caught up with him and

walked stiffly beside. Kolt could almost hear the young man's heartbeat.

They walked fifty yards, back in the direction of the factory, past dozens of other pedestrians and shopkeepers out in front of their stores. Raynor remained hunched over to take a few inches off his height, and from seeing women walking with men in the area, he knew to walk behind Jamal, even as he whispered directions to the young Afghan. "Straight ahead. No, let's turn up this pathway with the steps."

He could not see Jamal's face in front of him, could barely make out a damned thing through the obscuring mesh of the burka face hole. But he imagined Jamal was probably in a state of panic.

They walked up stone-and-wooden steps and soon arrived at a part of the arcade that had closed for the evening. They were just one street over from Buchwald's factory now, and the coast seemed to be clear. Raynor reached out and grabbed Jamal by the arm. "I want to walk around the factory, go around to the back, and then head back to the truck. Okay?"

Jamal nodded slowly. "Okay. Please promise me you will not speak, and you will not fight anyone."

"I promise," Kolt said. He hoped like hell it was a promise he could keep.

Jamal turned and headed toward the factory, still walking stiffly and self-consciously. Raynor knew he'd put the helpful young man through a lot in the past few days, and he also knew he would not be alive without him.

Racer followed him toward Buchwald's factory.

* * *

Less than ten minutes later Raynor and Jamal climbed back into the truck. Bob had shifted over behind the wheel, the engine was already running, and he immediately pulled into traffic. Without speaking he headed west back through town and toward the Hayatabad road to the north, the way back to Peshawar.

He looked over to Jamal in the left seat, saw the young man to be sweat covered and white as a ghost. Kopelman just patted him on the shoulder as a way to say both *I understand* and *I'm sorry.*

Then he turned and shouted back to the man in the backseat just now uncovering himself from the blue burka. "Damn it, Racer! I hope you have one hell of a good explanation of why you pulled that stunt!"

Kolt shrugged. "I knew you wouldn't let me go if I asked permission."

"Go *where*?"

"We walked the perimeter of Buchwald's factory. Bob, I figured it out. I know how to get into that place without being sighted by any sentries. If we pick up a couple of items in the market and come back here tomorrow morning, I can get in and get a look at Buchwald's computer."

"The sentries won't see you?"

"They won't see me get in. I'm not saying they won't see me once I'm inside."

"So you are going to kill ten guys?"

"If I have to, you're damned right I am. Anyway, I only saw four on the outside."

Bob drove in silence through the darkness. In minutes they had left the town behind and turned north. With good luck and good traffic flow they'd be in Peshawar in a half hour.

Kopelman thought it over as he drove. Finally he said, "No. No way. Too risky. We found the German, we found the choppers. We've passed that on to Langley. We reconnoitered the factory and confirmed it is still occupied. We've done enough."

Raynor barked back. "Enough for what, Bob? We've found a pair of helos that we can't hit from the air because of collateral damage. We've also found five prisoners that we can't rescue, and potentially forty Taliban about to be used in an al Qaeda plot that could, easily, kill hundreds. An op at an unknown time, an unknown place, and . . . shit, it's an unknown op."

"You're not going into that factory, Racer. It's too dangerous."

"When we get back to Pesh, I want you to call Grauer. We'll see what he says."

"I'm in charge of you while you're in-country."

"And Colonel Grauer is in charge of you! See if he orders you to order me into the factory to get access to Buchwald's computer. I guarantee that he will." He paused. "Grauer won't mind risking my life for that potential intel haul, and I don't mind either."

"I *do* mind, Racer, although at the moment, the thought of you taking a bullet in the ass is pretty damned appealing, I'll have to admit."

"I can do it, Bob. Trust me."

A long pause as the Hilux cleared the gate at the exit to the congested village. There was no checkpoint for those leaving.

"I'll think about calling Grauer. But I'm going to tell him what I saw, and what I saw . . . you can*not* penetrate."

"Pete knows what I can do." Kolt said it in a confident tone, and he was confident Grauer would let him try.

But could he do it? On that question the confidence left him.

Raynor had no idea.

Jamal dropped Raynor and Kopelman off in a square a quarter mile from Bob's apartment. The heavyset American spy had no reason to not trust his Afghani agent now—surely if Jamal was playing for the other team neither Kopelman nor Raynor would still be alive. Nevertheless, there was no operational need for Bob to show the agent exactly where he lived. After parting ways with Jamal, the two Americans walked a circuitous route back to Bob's flat, passing electronics shops, spice shops, auto mechanics working late into the evening. Bob stepped into a small restaurant while Kolt circled the block to keep moving and came back around in front of the eatery just as Bob stepped out with a bag of cooked rice with bits of lamb.

The two men sat down on mats in Bob's living room just after nine in the evening. They ate, mostly in silence, and then after he'd pulled rice and meat from his thick beard and licked his fingers clean, Bob Kopelman turned on the sat phone and called Pete Grauer.

Kolt drank bottled water and listened intently as Kopelman told Grauer about the drive to the factory, and of Kolt's reckless reconnaissance, in drag, no less, of the perimeter. Bob did not protest Raynor's actions to Grauer as much as Kolt had feared, though he did say more than once that Racer was a risk taker.

Then Bob told Pete of Racer's desire to try entering the factory. Bob was still firmly against the attempt, feeling the CIA had enough intel to act against the cell. Even if the Agency did not have the entire operation wrapped up or even a good understanding of the plot, Kopelman argued, the CIA could use their own assets in the area, whatever those might be, to get into the factory and to hit the warehouse. From Bob's side of the conversation Kolt got the impression that Grauer was skeptical of the CIA's understanding of things in and around Peshawar, and to Kolt this meant he'd probably get the go-ahead to attempt to penetrate Buchwald's location.

He was right.

Bob nodded, handed the phone over to Raynor.

"Sir?"

"Can you do it, Kolt?"

"Yes, sir."

"You have one source telling you there are as many as ten armed personnel in the target location. What if he's wrong?"

"There might be fewer."

"And there might be more."

"I'm willing to take that risk. I'm willing to do it alone."

A pause on the other end of the line. "Look. I talked to Langley today. They knew nothing about Buchwald, about the warehouse and factory south of Peshawar, about Chechens in Pakistan, about Turkish and Yemeni AQ operators running an op in Peshawar. You and Bob are the tip of the spear on this."

"Did they listen to you? Are they taking this situation seriously?"

"Very seriously. They are sending a guy over to Pesh tonight—he'll be there first thing tomorrow morning. He's Special Activities Division, a veteran, top-notch by his reputation. He's going to debrief Kopelman."

Kolt looked up at Bob, said into the phone, "The Agency is going to debrief a guy they deemed unreliable, who has been running an agent who they also deemed unreliable?" Bob just rolled his eyes and shrugged. Kolt was more direct: "Assholes."

Grauer's chuckles crackled over the satellite link. "Yeah, hypocritical, but smart on their part. I'm actually a little surprised. They seem really worried about this. Almost like they know something we don't about what's going to go down."

"So, you are saying you are giving me permission to go into the factory?"

Another pause by Grauer. "Racer, what I'm about to say may seem cold, but I'll go ahead and say it anyway. I am willing to risk *you* to do this, but I'm not willing to risk Bob. We can use any info we can get, but not at the risk of the best Radiance human intelligence asset in western Pakistan. Do I make myself clear?"

"Perfectly clear. I just want Bob's agent to drop me

off near the target location tomorrow at noon, and then go someplace to stand off until I call him for the pickup. Bob won't be involved at all. He will stay up here in Pesh and meet the guy from SAD."

The connection hissed for a moment. Kolt imagined Grauer sitting in the Ops Center and running his hand over his razor-short hair. Finally he said, "Your plan is authorized."

"Thank you, sir. Passing you back to Kopelman."

Bob took the phone back, his eyes locked on Raynor's. "Racer looks happy, which means you said yes." He listened, then told Grauer he'd call him after Raynor left with Jamal the next morning, and then meet with the CIA operative for the debriefing. He hung up and then dialed Jamal's mobile phone. As it rang he changed his mind, disconnected the call.

"Might as well let the kid get a good night's rest. If I tell him he'll be going on a mission with you in the morning, he won't sleep a wink."

THIRTY-SIX

Early the next morning Kolt found Kopelman making tea in the kitchen. They sat in silence. The only light in the room was the glow of the hot plate as the chai brewed. Kopelman served it with milk and sugar for them both.

Raynor had slept little. He knew that this morning's mission would be one hell of a risk. He'd be going in alone, one man against unknown odds, but he'd seen no alternative. No one else was here to hit that factory. Maybe this SAD guy coming to talk to Bob could put something together, but Kolt knew there was no time to waste. The al Qaeda op was imminent; if he could glean any intel from Buchwald's place, then he could pass that on to the CIA officer and speed up any counteroperation the Agency would put together.

Just like going into Zar's compound three days ago, he saw no alternative to risking his life.

While he sipped his chai he placed one of the two

Kalashnikov rifles on the tiny kitchen table. In seconds he stripped it down to its component parts. He used a rag to wipe out the insides, inspected the color and the grit in the black grease that covered the rag. He then retrieved a toolbox Bob kept in his garage, and he lubricated the weapon and reassembled it. He slid the magazine back into the well and hooked it into place with a loud click. He racked the bolt and flipped the safety back up into position.

He then placed the weapon back on the table and reached for his tea.

He sipped the lava-hot milky liquid slowly. Bob Kopelman surprised him by breaking the stillness with a powerful voice.

"I'm going with you." It was an announcement. A proclamation.

Kolt lowered his tea. "Into Darra?"

Bob shook his head. "Into the factory."

Kolt laughed in surprise. "No . . . no you're not."

"I know I'm not exactly Delta Force material"—he looked down at his corpulent frame tugging at the fabric of his local clothing—"but in any scenario you'll find yourself in down there in Darra Adam Khel, you will benefit with an extra set of eyes, my language skills, and an extra gun."

"Grauer said he'd sacrifice me, but you were too important."

Kopelman waved the comment away as irrelevant. "Forget Pete. *He* may send men into harm's way to be sacrificed, but you are under *my* care here. If you go, *I* go."

Raynor regarded the comment as he took another sip of tea. "That sounds a bit like Pashtunwali."

Kopelman looked like he was going to disagree. Then he just sighed, said, "What can I say? I *have* gone native. Pashtunwali makes sense in a situation like this."

"You're sure about this?"

"Yes." Bob's eyes turned cold suddenly. "Plus, I have other skills. If you find Buchwald, I may be able to get him to talk."

"You don't think I can be persuasive when necessary?"

"Let's just say my presence may relieve you of that burden."

Kolt did not understand the comment, but he knew when there was no point in arguing. This was one of those times. "All right, Bob. I'll have to go into the factory alone and then open a side door for you. I'm going to have to vault a ten-foot razor-wire fence, and, pardon me, but I don't think you would survive climbing over that fence."

Bob chuckled. "I don't think that fence would survive me climbing over it."

Raynor went into the garage to grab the other Kalashnikov. It could stand for a thorough cleaning, as well.

Bob contacted Jamal at eight in the morning. He'd given him a good night's rest by delaying the call. Bob told him that they would need to go back to the factory. He gave the Afghan his address for the first time, instructed him to come directly to pick them up. Jamal arrived at nine and parked the Hilux in Kopelman's garage. Together the three men set out on foot in Peshawar toward the bazaar, the same market where Jamal Metziel's mother and brother had been killed back in 2010.

Under Kolt's direction Bob bought a thick rug from an old shopkeeper. Raynor stood right there with him, made no eye contact with anyone, kept his head low. A few passing merchants tried to sell him their wares; he waved them away without a glance. Jamal stood close. It was his job to distract anyone here who paid any attention to Racer. He was nervous—Jamal was always nervous when Kolt was around. Kolt understood completely. He knew the danger Kopelman's local agent was in.

After leaving the carpet shop, Raynor carried the heavy rug on his shoulder, used it to shield his face from half of the stalls and the vendors and customers that stood in them. They climbed some steps in the market, passed dozens of little metal-and-concrete shacks selling all types of weapons; swords, knives, guns, even morning stars and maces. The instruments were more decorative than functional. Bob, Kolt, and Jamal scanned each one with bored expressions, though they were, in fact, desperately looking for one item in particular. There were no words between them, and twice Kopelman stopped upon seeing something for sale, but both times Raynor slowed and followed the older man's gaze, then just picked up the pace after determining the items to be unfit for his use.

Finally they hit the jackpot. They'd passed many tiny kiosks selling knives, but all the previous shops' selections had been entirely ornamental, or else cheap jackknives or switchblades made in China. Raynor had given Bob a specific mission to find only quality-made, razor-sharp throwing knives, and he had all but given up hope they'd run across anything worth inspecting further, much less purchasing. But a simple stall nestled near the top of a narrow cul-de-sac of shops at a tiny kiosk all but hidden in deep morning shadow sold all manner of knives, and there, on a table near the back, over one hundred simple, well-made, hand-crafted steel shanks lay on a red cloth.

Kolt spotted them and stopped. Bob noticed his partner's fixed stare, entered the little stall, and a few minutes later walked out with a half dozen of the blades wrapped in a small square of burlap tied with string.

Soon they were heading south in the yellow Hilux, Jamal at the wheel on the right side, Kopelman in the passenger seat on the left, and Kolt Raynor in the backseat with their purchases and other gear. He knew he'd have to crawl back into the tiny metal hellhole that he'd used several days earlier to infiltrate the Tirah Valley. There was a checkpoint at the edge of Darra. He and Bob had managed to bypass it the day before, but the Toyota truck would have to drive on through.

He waited as long as possible, then lowered the rear seat and slid back into the tight confinement. Unlike during his first visit to the metal box, this time Bob was with him, so he *could* cuss out the heavyset spy for making the human-sized stash, at least to Raynor's thinking, significantly less than human-sized.

Bob just chuckled and snapped the rear seat back into place after Kolt slid up the metal door.

The checkpoint came and went, the Hilux was waved through, and Raynor was released from captivity below the truck. Traffic was not one-half of what it had been the previous afternoon, so they made their way quickly to the intersection in front of Buchwald's factory, and found the two guards in front. There was no sentry on the roof at the moment, but that was not necessarily good news. Kolt knew the man could be patrolling the grounds or using the toilet. Jamal dropped the two Americans off at the massive gun market arcade a few blocks away. Here, literally hundreds of kiosks, shops, tiny doorways, and even rolling carts sold the weapons made here and in the villages nearby. Every possible firearm one could imagine was copied here at Darra Adam Khel, and even though tension and fear were at the forefront of Kolt Raynor's mind at the moment, he could not help but stop and look in wonder as he passed huge water-cooled machine guns, ancient Lee Enfields, brand-new HK knockoffs, and dozens of other models hanging from racks on walls or leaning against dirty windows.

And once again gunfire crackled at regular intervals throughout the bazaar as the weapons were tested by fabricators and potential customers alike.

Kolt turned away from the treasure trove of armaments, and Bob followed as they headed east toward their target.

As the first call to the noon prayer emanated from

the loudspeakers of the mosque on the main road, Bob and Kolt moved into position at the rear of the factory's property. The metal fence was ten feet high and capped with razor wire hanging from bars in a V pattern. Attempting to climb it free-handed would be suicide at its most excruciating. When the prayers were well under way, a quick scan of the back alley showed the two Americans that they were alone. Raynor hurriedly unfurled the thick rug and launched it high over the razor wire above him. It hung down several feet on both sides of the fence, covering the sharp barbs at the top.

Next Bob put his back to the fence and knelt down slightly. Kolt put a sandal on the sixty-year-old's thigh and Kopelman braced it with his hands. Then the ex–Delta officer leaped up, launched off Bob's thigh, grasped the fence next to the hand-spun wool, and then rolled himself over the rug.

He dropped inside the factory grounds, quickly spun back around, and climbed up to flip the thick carpet back over the fence.

Bob caught the heavy wool and then ran off to his right. There, a narrow alley ran alongside the building's wall, and a heavy bolted door gave access through the gate. Here, Bob waited.

Within twenty seconds of approaching the fence, Kolt Raynor was over and clear, hidden between two drums of machine oil.

Infiltrating a guarded building at noon, even a guarded building not in use, is rarely an optimal situation, and this proved to be no different. Kolt Raynor picked the lock on the rear door and opened it slowly, sending a long shaft of light into an open metal-walled room the size of a basketball court. All around him in the dusty light coming from windows ringing the building from its open second floor, he saw sewing machines, metal presses, lathes, thick rolls of thread, spools of aluminum, tables, chairs, and other equipment that revealed the location to be a manufacturing plant of items fashioned from fabric and metal. The noonday prayers outside drew to a close—though Kolt could not recite or even mimic the Islamic prayer ritual, he had heard it so many times that he recognized the ending—so Raynor rushed to the side door that led to the alleyway. This door was bolted and chained from the inside, and it took him nearly two minutes to get it opened. Opening the door let more light into the room, but the light was all but blotted out by Bob Kopelman's big form in his salwar kameez, his squat pakol hat, and the bulky rug over his shoulder. He carried the AK-47 in his right hand, but he did not have it up in the ready position. Instead, he focused on hurrying inside the building before anyone noticed his movements in the alleyway, and he let the rifle swing with his rushed steps. Bob dropped the rug on the ground inside the factory door.

Just as Kolt closed the door behind him, blocking out the light from the street and again darkening the large factory floor, the front freight door of the building slid up. It was large enough to accommodate a tractor trailer, and the wide shaft of daylight lit virtually the entire room. Both Americans crouched behind a pallet of gray canvas, their backsides low to the ground and their lower backs pressed against the wall behind them and next to the side door. Two men spoke in Arabic. Kolt could not decipher their words, but thought it sounded like the men spoke a Saudi dialect.

Kopelman leaned close in his ear. "Egyptians," he said confidently.

Kolt chastised himself for not being a better language student, though he was painfully aware just how confounding the different dialects of Arabic could be to even a native speaker, much less a country boy from North Carolina.

Gunfire crackled again from outside. More shopkeepers displaying their wares. Raynor still had to fight the urge to hit the deck.

Kneeling now behind the pallet, they heard the squawking of a walkie-talkie, and then more men checking in over the radios. Presumably this was the rest of the AQ security cordon around the location. Paying close attention to the guard force's comms check, Kolt determined there were a total of eight men in and around the factory.

He wondered where in the hell they all were. Two here, two more at the front gate. According to Jamal's uncle, Buchwald's office was on the upstairs landing, reached by a metal ramp in the northeast corner of the building. He suspected there could be a couple of bodyguards with the German up there, as well as a duo of patrolling guards roaming the perimeter of the property.

He'd love to avoid the security completely, but he did not see that as likely. He held a razor-sharp throwing knife in his right hand, and kept the AK steady and low in his left.

By the sounds of the footsteps, the two men separated. One stepped into a room across the factory floor—Raynor suspected it was a kitchen. The other walked through a door just a few feet from the other side of Bob and Kolt's pallet. The door shut behind him, and Raynor caught a whiff of urine and human feces.

It was the bathroom for the factory floor.

Raynor decided in a heartbeat that he'd take the closest man now while he held an advantage. He neither spoke to nor looked at Kopelman as he rose, rushed past him, and opened the bathroom door.

All his senses were alert, his nerve endings on fire as his heart pounded against his ribs. The light was low. The flooring and walls were gray cinder block. The Egyptian sentry stood at the far wall, his back to Raynor as he urinated into a hole in the floor.

Kolt's jaw flexed as he moved forward quietly and swiftly. The man had heard the door open. He spoke as he faced the wall, but Raynor did not understand. The man was relaxed, obviously assuming his colleague had followed behind to relieve himself.

Kolt reached around the man's head with his left arm, covered his mouth completely. His knife was tight in his right hand, and he brought it up a half second later, just as the man's body tightened in surprise. Kolt jabbed the sharp tip into the Egyptian's neck, an inch or two below his jaw, and pushed the blade in to its metal hilt. At the same time Raynor pushed the man face forward into the wall, and he pinned him there with his body while the Egyptian twitched and writhed in the throes of death.

Blood gushed and sprayed onto Raynor's right hand and arm, ran down to his elbow, and streamed to the floor.

When the Egyptian's legs gave out and Kolt could hold him up no more, he stepped back and let the limp body slide face-first to the floor. The man's head drooped facedown into the toilet hole.

Kolt turned around slowly, wiping the blood off the knife, and the door opened on the other side of the room. It was the other Egyptian. The sentry was not alert. He did not look up for a full second after opening the door, but when he did he saw only the bloody throwing knife spinning through the air, just an instant before it buried itself into his throat, just above his clavicle. The sentry brought his hands up to the pain. Blood sprayed through his fingers as he grasped the knife and pulled it out with a sick gurgle.

Removing the sharp blade only caused the blood flow to increase. The al Qaeda gunman dropped hard to his knees, holding his throat in a futile attempt to contain the spray.

Kolt Raynor drew another knife from his belt and moved across the floor quickly toward the man, ready to finish him off lest he make any noise before he died. But the man crumpled to his left hip and then slumped over, folding peacefully to the floor like a man nodding off to sleep.

The spray of blood slickened the concrete, but within seconds it reduced to a trickle from its source as the man's heart stopped beating.

Kolt stood over the bloody body, looking down at it,

and the door opened again. He launched forward, over the prostrate man, raised the fresh knife high to go after the third man's carotid artery.

But he stopped his attack suddenly. It was Bob. His rifle was up. His eyes were wide. Kolt just patted him on his thick chest and passed him through the doorway.

Bob Kopelman remained behind a moment, his eyes fixed on the carnage in the bathroom.

"I didn't hear a thing," Kolt heard the older man mutter in awe.

Back on the factory floor, the two Americans headed silently toward the ramp up to the landing on the second level. Kolt led the way, the folded Kalashnikov in one hand and a throwing knife in the other. There were four other men somewhere. If they were patrolling the grounds, there was no way to know if they would be close enough to register danger if Kolt started shooting.

Raynor neared the top of the ramp now with Kopelman on his heels. There was an open hallway on his left just ahead. He knelt low and peered around the corner. Bob remained just behind and out of the way. Kolt saw two men down at the end of the hall, maybe thirty feet from him. They stood on either side of a simple wooden door that, Kolt assumed, opened to Helmut Buchwald's office.

Sustained chatter from a light machine gun outside. Five-round bursts, over and over and over.

Kolt Raynor stood suddenly, slid the knife inside his belt, opened the folded wire stock on his weapon, flipped the safety down to the single-shot setting, and stepped into the hallway.

Both men were caught completely by surprise. Raynor raised the rifle to his shoulder, lined up the iron sights, and took each man with a single round to the head.

The guards were dead before their bodies hit the ground.

Four down now, and two out at the main gate. That left two unaccounted for, assuming the eight men who had checked in on the radio were Buchwald's entire protection force. Kolt could not be certain. He was even confused about how many men he'd just disabled—his adrenaline did not help his arithmetic and his quick recall like it did his reflexes and his fight-or-flight response mechanism.

Four. Yes, he'd killed four, he was certain.

Raynor stepped back on the ramp and waved Bob forward. They shouldered up to one another and made for the door at the end of the hallway. Whoever was inside would be very aware that the two shots in the hall outside had nothing to do with gun salesmen showing off their merchandise in the arcade up the street.

Raynor leveled his weapon on his shoulder and kicked open the wooden door.

THIRTY-SEVEN

The office was just a small room with two windows that faced out toward the distant sandstone hills. A desk was centered against the wall opposite the windows, and it faced into the room. The door Raynor entered through was to the left of the desk, and this gave Kolt an easy target, as Helmut Buchwald sat behind the desk, totally exposed to Raynor's Kalashnikov.

There was no one else inside the office.

"Hände hoch, Arschloch," Kolt said. *Hands high, asshole.*

The older German's hands slowly moved skyward as his eyes flitted off toward the doorway. Kolt saw the glance. He spoke English now, principally because he'd exhausted a good portion of his German knowledge in his previous three-word sentence. "Your babysitters are dead. No one is coming to help you."

"Who are you? What are you doing here?" The German's English was clear and idiomatic.

Bob spoke as he stepped into the room behind his partner. "Well, that all depends on your perspective. As far as *you're* concerned, Helmut, we are the bad guys. And just how bad we are all depends on you." Kopelman walked forward, past Raynor, grabbed Buchwald by the collar of his short-sleeved button-down, and rolled the man in his wheeled chair out from behind the desk. While Raynor covered the German with his AK, Kopelman tore wires from a banker's lamp and a telephone on the desk and a space heater in the corner next to a cot. He spent the next two minutes strapping his prisoner to the chair with the wires. The German started to shout but Kopelman just slapped him with an open hand to quiet him. "Knock it off!"

"You are Americans?"

"Who else?" Bob said as he pulled off the German's loafers and his socks and tied his bare ankles to the horizontal legs of the rolling chair. "How about from now on, we ask the questions? Alles klar?" Bob tied the older man's hands behind his back, looping the wire through the metal of the chair back.

Once it was clear that Helmut wasn't going anywhere, Raynor went forward to the windows and looked out into the street. He could not see the two sentries on the other side of the metal gate, but he assumed they were still there. Nothing else looked out of place. No alarm had been sounded as far as he could tell.

Jamal's yellow pickup rolled into view. He was

moving through the streets to avoid suspicion by the factory's sentries.

Kolt turned back and nodded to Bob, then motioned to the far corner of the room.

Several pieces of luggage were there, packed and stacked on the cot. "Going somewhere?" Bob asked Helmut, but the German just looked away.

Bob looked at Kolt now. "Watch the hall." Kolt followed orders, went to the hallway and knelt, kept his rifle's muzzle on the open doorway to the ramp down to the factory floor.

"Now, Helmut," Bob began. "I'll tell you what we *do* know, and you will tell me what we *don't* know. You may not want to, but it's going to be in your best interests to keep this conversation quick, friendly, and painless."

Still nothing from the German.

"We know you were an arms maker and an equipment manufacturer with Heckler & Koch, we know you are working with a Turkish man, and we know he is al Qaeda. We also know al Qaeda is planning an operation to send Chechens posing as American Rangers to infiltrate a coalition location. We know about the Black Hawks at the warehouse that you and your Turkish associate have rented, and we know you met with the American prisoners held in Shataparai to test the authenticity of your phony gear."

Buchwald looked positively poleaxed. "I do not know what you are talking about."

Bob sighed. He did not take his eyes from his captive.

"We *know,* Helmut. And we aren't leaving until we get what we want from you."

"What is it that you want?" Helmut's German accent was more pronounced now, perhaps due to fear or surprise.

Bob ignored this question. Posed one of his own. "What is the target location of the Chechen forces?"

"I told you! I don't know what you're talking about."

Bob punched the sixty-five-year-old German in the jaw.

Buchwald started to scream but Kopelman deftly spun around behind him, wrapped a meaty forearm over the older man's mouth, and stifled his noises. He leaned intimately into the gray-haired man's left ear. "Let's try and keep it down, okay? Can you do that for me?" Slowly the man nodded. Bob pulled his arm away. Stepped back in front and looked the German over. "That was just a love pat. You aren't even bleeding." Kopelman paused, then said, "Yet, anyway."

"Fucking Americans! You think you can do whatever you want! You cowboys are all—"

"Save your spiel for some Berlin coffee shop!" growled Bob. "You tell us what we need to know and we'll let you walk. We don't care about you. We're just trying to stop more bloodshed."

"Nein! *You* are the invaders here. All the bloodshed is the fault of—"

Bob hit him again, harder this time, hard enough for Raynor to look away from the empty hallway and back over his shoulder.

Kolt was a little surprised by the rough stuff so early

in the interrogation, but he understood the haste. They wouldn't be able to make a day out of this, sitting in the middle of an enemy stronghold trying to coax information from a man at the center of an enemy operation. He could not imagine remaining undetected here for more than ten minutes or so. There would be another radio check sooner or later between the sentries, and that would alert the four men still alive to the loss of their comrades.

"I do not know anything except my duties here at the factory. I was hired to oversee local arms makers in the fabrication of some rifles. Also, I was asked to oversee and provide quality control for the design and creation of some American Army uniforms and other personal gear."

"For who?"

"I don't know. I was hired by the Turk. I did not meet anyone else."

"The Turk? That is what they call the man who rented this factory?"

"Yes. I only know him by that name."

"You're lying, Buchwald."

Kopelman and Buchwald stared into one another's eyes for a long moment. Finally Helmut spoke again, his voice soft and plaintive. "I do not know names. . . . But if I tell you anything . . . *anything* at all . . . they will kill me."

Bob knelt, closed the distance between the two men's faces. "You're dead already without our help. I have a network of contacts in the Pashtun community here. If I tell them that I had a long and fruitful conversation with Helmut Buchwald, how long do you think it will be before the wrong guy gets wind of that, and the black turbans show up at your door? Even back home in Germany, it won't be a week before an al Qaeda operative guts you like a fish while you're walking down the street."

"I have told you nothing! I *know* nothing, and they know I do not! The Turk *did* make me go out into the FATA to see some American prisoners. He wanted me to be there when they tested out the equipment on them. I then came back here, worked on refining the guns, and then I finished.

"I did my job, my job is complete, and now I am leaving! You have no right to—"

Kopelman lifted his rifle off the desk, pressed it against Buchwald's forehead. "You aren't going anywhere, asshole."

The German did not even blink. "You won't shoot me. I am not afraid of you." He looked past Kopelman, out the windows across the room. A vista of rooftops in the foreground gave way to brown hills a half mile in the distance. "I am, however, *very* afraid of them."

"I'll have to change that, won't I?" the big American said. He lowered the rifle, placed it back on the desk. Bob punched the German again. Buchwald cried out.

"Bastard! I know nothing! I promise you!"

"What about the laptop?" Kolt asked from his position guarding the hallway. He'd noticed the open MacBook Pro on the desk. If the German wasn't going to reveal details of the plot, perhaps his computer could give them some answers.

Kopelman slid a metal chair up behind the desk, sat down, and played with the keys on the computer. A few seconds later he announced, "Locked. Encrypted." Slowly his head turned to the German seated to his left and staring ahead. "I'm gonna need that password, old buddy. How I get it is entirely up to you."

"I cannot be threatened," Buchwald said, his narrow jaw jutted forward in defiance.

"Yeah, I expect you're right." Bob shrugged. "No time for that, anyway."

Kolt stepped away from the doorway, tried his luck with Buchwald. "We don't have time to dick around. We need the password, right now, or you are going to get hurt."

The German just stared up at him. He was frightened, unquestionably, but he appeared resolute.

Bob walked over to Kolt, and together they stepped to the far side of the office. "His manufacturing operation is shut down. His bags are packed. He's stalling."

"Yep. Which means either he's expecting help to come for him or—"

"Or the op is about to go down and every minute he can buy will help the AQ operation."

The two Americans just looked at one another for a moment, until Bob broke the staring contest. "We can get him to talk."

"How?"

"The question is not How do we get him to talk? The question is How far are you willing to go to get him to talk?"

Raynor's jaw tightened. "Look at me. Do you think

there is *anything* I won't do to stop the infiltration and get Eagle 01 back?"

Kopelman did just what Kolt asked. He looked into Raynor's eyes, measured the younger man's resolve. "I'm going to have to rush this. It might get ugly."

Kolt looked out the window. He didn't like this part of the work. But he looked back at his older associate. His voice was strong. "That asshole over there strapped into his chair is the one driving this boat. My conscience will be clear no matter what he makes us do."

A nod from the big spy. "Good. Now, go downstairs, get the big green contraption sitting in the southwest corner of the factory. I noticed it's on wheels. Roll it up the ramp to me in here."

Kolt Raynor nodded, though there was a flicker of shock on his face. "Okay."

"I don't want you in here when I do it. I told you I would relieve you of that burden. But before I send you out, I need you to haul that thing up here."

Kolt looked at the German, then slowly left the room, hoping like hell the old man would reveal the password before Bob had to resort to desperate measures. He moved down the hallway, across the steel landing, and then down the ramp carefully, his weapon at the low ready all the while.

The factory floor was as dark and quiet as he had left it.

Kolt found the machine, and his stomach turned. It was a German-made one-ton flywheel punch press, a heavy metalworking device that could stamp and pierce holes in steel with its powerful vertical ram.

Damn, Raynor thought. He hung the Kalashnikov around his neck by the sling, unplugged the heavy tool, and began rolling it on its wheels up toward the ramp.

It took a minute to get back in the office. He found the scene to be much the same as he'd left it, Buchwald nervous but defiant, Kopelman composed but resolute. When Helmut saw the big green device roll into the room, he began tugging at his bindings. Sweat drained off his forehead and down onto his shirt and tie.

"You cannot do this! You are mad! You—"

Kopelman smacked him again. Raynor rolled the press over to Kopelman and plugged it into the only 220-volt plug in the wall. Bob deftly flipped two buttons, and the machine burst to life.

Kopelman knew exactly what he was doing, which uneased Kolt even more.

The German started to say something else, fast and frantic, but Bob just covered the man's mouth with his hand while he spoke to Raynor over the buzz of electrical current and the spinning flywheel on the side of the device. "Now, can you give me a few minutes alone with Herr Buchwald? Shut this door behind you, go out to the landing, and cover the front door to the factory. I'll try to stifle the screams, but I can't promise the guards at the gate won't hear this bastard beg for me to kill him when it gets bad."

Kolt nodded, looked at the petrified German for a few seconds, then left the room, shutting the broken door behind him on the way out.

* * *

Kopelman took off the German's tie, then found a roll of packing tape on the desk. He tore off a length of the tape and secured one end to the edge of the desk, letting the rest dangle next to his prisoner. Then he knelt down in front of the seated man. The machine press was to his right. "Listen. This is going to just about kill you, and I can't very well expect you to keep quiet. No, you're going to want to scream bloody murder, and we can't have that. So I'm going to seal your mouth up, which means you won't be able to give me the password to your laptop to stop the pain, even if you want to. We'll work on one of your hands for a minute. I'll punch some holes through the flesh and bone, lop off a finger or two, and then I'll take the tie out, give you another chance before we ruin the other hand. Theoretically we could go on to the toes after that, but by then you'll probably be running out of blood and short on time, so I figure you will give me the password once your hands are useless. Are you understanding my English?" Kopelman's actions and tone were calm and matter-of-fact.

Buchwald's wide eyes dripped tears. "You are bluffing." he said, his voice cracked along with the words.

Bob calmly rolled the black necktie into a ball while he continued speaking. "Only one way to find out, I guess. Don't talk."

Buchwald said, "I don't intend to talk."

Bob nodded, continued rolling the tie tighter into a ball as he spoke. "Once I have the password, and your hands are shredded hunks of torn meat hanging off the ends of your arms, I'll go ahead and shoot you if you want me to. But if, for some unknown reason, you decide you want to live, well, I guess that's all right by me. You're not going to be any good to anyone with a couple of stumps, but I won't kill you unless you beg me to."

"I will never give you the info—"

As his lips formed the o in "information," Bob Kopelman jammed the balled-up necktie ball deep inside the German's mouth. He took the strapping tape off the side of the desk and secured the gag tightly.

Helmut Buchwald screamed through the gag as Bob slid the machine closer, untied the German's left hand. "I hope you're a righty and not a lefty," he said. The German's head jacked back and forth from side to side, as if to say *No! No!*

Bob said, "I hate to do this, really do, Herr Buchwald, but even more than that, I hate to think where those two Black Hawks full of terrorists are heading, and I can rationalize this little descent into Psychoville, because this is the only way I can get a proud and obstinate son of a bitch like you to give me that password."

Kopelman was much stronger than the German. He surprised Buchwald by grabbing his left hand tightly at the wrist and yanking it out straight. With a short struggle he managed to force it onto the floor plate of the machine press under the half-inch-diameter circular ram punch.

Buchwald fought to free his arm from the American's grip, but he could not. He tried to ball his hand into a fist, but the ram was only two inches above the plate, and there was no room.

Kopelman winced with effort as he held the panicked

German's arm steady with his left hand, but still, he looked him in the eyes as his right hand rose slowly to a button on the side of the press.

The German shook his head from side to side so hard it looked like he would break his neck.

"Are you saying 'No, you don't need to do this because I will happily give you that password you politely requested?' "

Buchwald stopped. Looked up at the big American spy through eyes wide with shock and drenched with tears. After a long moment he shook his head again.

"No password?" Bob asked for confirmation.

The German shook his head, but it was tentative. Almost imperceptible.

"Aw, Helmut, dass ist nicht gut." Bob reached for the button.

A sudden scream into the gag, followed by a frantic nod from Buchwald. Then another. Now it looked as if he'd give himself whiplash.

"You gonna give me that password?"

Buchwald hesitated. Blinked more tears of terror from his eyes. Then he nodded again.

Now Bob gently shook his head from side to side. No. "Who's bluffing now?" Bob could see it in the man's eyes. He was stalling. He wasn't going to give him what he wanted.

Not yet, anyway.

Bob Kopelman stabbed the red button with the index finger of his right hand. The clutch on the press released the flywheel and the ram shot down three inches, eviscerating the center of Helmut Buchwald's left hand as it plunged down into the hole in the floor plate. When it recoiled to its previous position it left a perfect half-inch circle in the man's hand. Blood splattered left and right from the wound while the German screamed into his spit-soaked necktie. Every portion of his body that was not strapped tightly to the chair convulsed.

"Let's do a finger next." Bob said it in a normal voice, but Buchwald could not hear him over the mind-numbing agony.

Kolt had pulled a shirt off of one of the bodies in the hallway and exchanged it with his own. The new kameez was relatively clean and white, whereas Raynor's was soaked in blood from the man he'd killed in the bathroom.

He then went out to the landing and covered the entrances to the factory. Raynor heard noises in the office behind him, but they were stifled by a door, the length of the hallway, and, as near as he could tell, some sort of gag over or in the German's mouth. Still, he could plainly hear the torture, and it sickened him as a human being.

But he was one hundred percent certain that this was a necessary measure.

He did his job now, watched the door, hoped the surviving sentries would not initiate a radio comms check anytime soon. He'd taken a walkie-talkie from one of the dead men in the hallway and attached it to his belt so he could listen in on any transmissions.

Raynor did not take his eyes off the big sliding front door. He understood what was happening in the room behind him, and he allowed himself no moral high ground because he wasn't witnessing it himself.

This was the ticking-time-bomb scenario. Untold numbers of his former military colleagues might die without the information in the head of the man whose pathetic grunts, screams, and sobs drifted through the thin paneling of the room behind him.

Torture was an awful, dreadful, sickening device—a device that often did not give good results.

But in this case, Raynor understood with cold clarity, it was worth a shot.

Just then the sentry's radio crackled to life. A man gave a call sign in Arabic. Kolt could not understand it, but he was familiar with the cadence of the radio call of a security detail checking in.

A second man reported in, but then there was a break. A hesitation, then a questioning from the man who spoke first. A further questioning call to report in.

Shit. Time's up.

Kolt stood, considered going back into the office to alert Kopelman.

The door opened suddenly in the hallway behind. Bob stood there, his face placid, though a thick sheen of sweat hung on his forehead.

Raynor looked to him hopefully.

A nod from the big spy. "Got it. Tried it. It works. We're in."

Kolt breathed a sigh of relief. He stepped into the room quickly, told Bob that the surviving security detail had been alerted. Kopelman all but ran to the desk to sit back down at the computer.

Kolt looked at the prisoner. Other than a bloody hand, there was no color whatsoever anywhere else on Buchwald's skin. His face, his arms, the portion of his chest exposed above the sweat-soaked and blood-splattered white short-sleeved shirt, all of his skin was ashen.

He had not passed out from the pain. He had not been so lucky. His eyes were tight from the agony of what had once been his left hand. Kolt looked at it. It was loose and hanging in his lap, covered with the rich blood. Kolt counted only four fingers. The palm bled profusely, and the skin had reddened and swelled, almost like a miniature catcher's mitt.

Bob wasn't thinking about his prisoner. He had moved on. "Okay, the entire hard drive is being dumped to our man's servers over the border. It will take a couple of minutes, tops. Why don't you untie Buchwald? We'll take him with us, just to see if that keeps the sentries from shooting if they see us. I doubt he's that precious to them anymore, but it's worth a try."

Kolt nodded, knelt in front of Buchwald, and began untying his bare ankles.

Bob stood, came from around the desk, and hefted his AK from it. "I'll check the front door. Hurry!"

"Got it."

Buchwald moaned in agony, cradling his hand in his lap while Kolt untied his ankles as quickly as possible. While he did so Kolt said, "You picked the wrong friends, which means you picked the wrong enemies. Can't say I feel sorry for you, but I bet that hurts like a—"

Kolt first heard the crack in the window behind him. Instinctively his neck tucked down into his shoulder. He did not immediately recognize the crack as a steel-jacketed bullet fired from a suppressed sniper rifle, but when the bullet whizzed right past his ear with the sound of a wasp moving at warp speed and hit Helmut Buchwald high on the head, an inch above the hairline, he knew what it was faster than most men.

Buchwald's scalp exploded with a hollow *thunk,* a large piece of his skull slammed into the wall behind the desk, and blood sprayed behind it and speckled the paneled wall in crimson.

Just then, Bob stepped back into the room from the doorway on Raynor's right. He saw the dead man half strapped in the chair, the top of his head cracked wide open. He shouted, "What the hell did you—"

"Get down!" screamed Kolt.

Bob did not understand what was going on, but he followed Raynor to the floor of the office. As he did wood splintered above him where a round pulverized the doorjamb.

"Sniper!" shouted Bob.

"No shit!" shouted Raynor. Bob stayed low, below the line of sight of the hills in the distance through the window.

Suddenly the walkie-talkie crackled to life as a man barked orders.

Raynor did not understand, but Bob translated for him. "It's the shooter! He's calling in reinforcements. There will be guys on us in seconds." And then he asked, "Is the data transfer complete?"

"How the hell do I know?" shouted Kolt from his position flat on the floor. Bob just pointed at the laptop and Kolt crept across the floor on his belly. He grabbed the power cable and pulled it off toward the floor. Then rolled on his back behind the desk and caught the computer before it hit the ground.

The sniper on the hillside must have seen the movement, because just then the banker's lamp on the desk exploded into pulverized bits of metal and glass.

"We've got to get out of here." Again, Bob stated the obvious.

Raynor ignored the debris raining down on top of him. He looked at the computer. "Yeah, 'Transfer Complete and Received.' "

Bob scooted on his big belly to the hallway, shifted to a low crouch, and hurried to the landing, then stood and ran down the ramp. He pulled his radio from his salwar kameez and called Jamal. Raynor was close on his heels. Already he held the AK out in front of him, and he scanned for targets below as he ran down the ramp.

"Jamal, where are you?" Bob asked in Pashto.

Jamal's voice came back over the radio's speaker. "I am in front of the factory. Something is wrong. Two guards entered the gate. They are moving toward the factory with their guns—"

Just then the small door to the right of the main loading bay opened. Kolt knew the two men who'd been guarding the front gate would be the first threats he'd encounter, and he spun toward the sound, the movement, and the light of the opening door. The two men stood in the light with their weapons on their shoulders and peered into the dark, and Raynor shot them both dead. Both rounds passed just over Kopelman's head on their way to their targets.

"Damn it!" Bob shouted. He was on the factory floor now. Kolt was still above. "Watch your fire!"

Kolt ran down to the floor, passed Kopelman, pulled the two dead men inside the building, and then shut and locked the door. He popped the al Qaeda radio off his belt and tossed it to the floor. He knew they'd be out in public in seconds, and he did not want their transmissions coming from his belt.

Jamal's voice came through Bob's walkie-talkie again and echoed in the large room. "Mister Bob. A pickup truck just pulled up out front. Four men, coming toward you. I think these are Taliban!"

Raynor and Kopelman turned and ran for the back door.

THIRTY-EIGHT

A minute later Bob and Kolt were exactly where they did not want to be: moving quickly and purposefully, but not running, through the thick gun bazaar arcade of Darra Adam Khel, trying like hell to get away from the men back at the factory and to somehow link up with Jamal. The Hilux was their way out of town, but Jamal was parked on the other side of the factory. Bob had received one more transmission from his Afghan agent, announcing that two more pickup trucks had arrived and entered the factory gate, but then Bob was forced to turn off the radio and slip it back inside his shirt. He could hardly move through the heavy pedestrian traffic while taking radio calls of that nature.

So he and Kolt moved blindly to the west, sometimes heading a block to the north, other times back down to the south, but generally in a westward direction. They did not speak to one another—they were not once more than five feet away from a passerby or a shopkeeper or a rickshaw driver hawking for a fare. Their weapons hung from their backs, but they drew no special attention on these mean streets of the frontier town.

They'd covered a couple hundred yards without incident, but a pickup truck appeared ahead of them, blocking off the alley of wooden shop stalls. In the bed of the truck two turbaned men stood, their rifles propped on their hips, staring intently out over the crowd of foot traffic and bicycles—scanning faces, clothes, mannerisms of the hundred or so moving men in front of them.

It occurred to Kolt that the sniper must have described them to the enemy chasing them. He wished he'd thought to purchase a new pakol or a shawl or anything that would alter his appearance in any way, but he'd been so intent on just getting the hell away from the factory that the thought of stopping to browse a clothing kiosk had not occurred to him.

Kopelman slowed upon seeing the men thirty yards in front of him. He began to turn into a stall as if to peruse the rifles on sale there, but before his big body disappeared from the view of the two Taliban in the truck, one of them pointed and shouted at him. Bob pretended not to hear. He continued into the little open-front shop, and the two men leaped from the truck and ran forward through the thick afternoon crowd.

Kolt could tell he hadn't yet been made. Bob's large frame surely was the distinguishing characteristic that made the men anxious to check him out. Kolt stepped into a stand right across from Bob that sold decorative medieval weapons—broadswords and maces and battle-axes. He waved a hand to shoo away the teenage shop boy who approached him, and turned back in time to see the two gunmen converge on Kopelman just twenty feet away across the cobblestone alleyway. They looked like Pakistani Taliban, and they were no doubt in communication with the AQ guards in the hills who had sniped at him back at the factory.

"You are looking for a fine weapon, sir?" the shop boy asked in Pashto. Kolt shook his head, kept watch on the growing confrontation in the stall across the way. "Take a look at this beautiful morning star, made by hand with resined walnut and cast iron." Kolt said nothing, just shook his head again and waved an angry hand at the boy.

Bob was speaking to the two Taliban. Raynor could not hear the words, but he could not imagine the gunmen just walking away without taking this man away for the sniper to identify. The boy said something else, words that Kolt could not decipher without concentrating on, and all his concentration was on the other little shop across the alleyway.

One of the Taliban spoke into a walkie-talkie, the same model the al Qaeda men were using back at the factory. Seconds later the horn of a truck began honking up the alley to Raynor's left—he pictured another pickup truck full of trouble making its way slowly through the tight foot traffic of the arcade.

The boy said something else in Kolt's ear. The little salesman was starting to piss Raynor off.

Both Taliban put their hands on Bob Kopelman's shoulders. He protested, in Pashto, of course, but they began leading him out of the little stall.

Kolt gritted his teeth. Tension and adrenaline and the frantic urgency of the moment, the desperate need to make a decision, to find a way out of this situation that was going downhill fast, threatened to overtax Raynor's well-trained brain.

He had to do something. And he had to do something now.

His decision made, his face hardened.

In a blur of perfect execution Kolt unslung the AK-47 from his back, spinning the muzzle-down weapon up in front of him. The shop boy threw his arms up and stepped back quickly, knocking his ass against a wooden table full of decorative swords. The barrel of the Kalashnikov rose, spun, and Raynor's finger dropped to the trigger. He fired two quick rounds into both of the Taliban holding Bob Kopelman, and both men spun around in the middle of the dusty alleyway and dropped dead on their backs amid the crowd.

The pedestrians all around began shouting, running, panicking, knocking over bikes and tables and a metal stove with several teapots on its burners, pushing one another down as they tried to flee the gunfire that had killed men right in front of them. As they leaped, ran, shoved, tumbled, and crawled, many of these men hefted their own weapons from their shoulders or drew them from their belts.

Raynor ran to Bob, grabbed him by the left arm, and

spun him around in the opposite direction, and the two men began running through the crowd, away from the honking horn of the pickup approaching from behind and toward the parked truck at the intersection ahead. The one man in the cab, the driver, quickly climbed out with his AK, stepped forward, and propped his rifle on the hood of his truck.

A three-round burst from Raynor's rifle knocked him backward into a crowd of men running by on the sidewalk.

"Get in the truck!" shouted Kopelman. Raynor saw the vehicle had left-sided steering, so he vaulted the hood, landed by the driver's-side door, and dove behind the wheel. The truck faced up a steep alleyway. Kopelman opened the passenger-side door and lunged inside, reached back and closed the door behind him.

Kolt looked down and saw that the keys were not in the ignition.

A burst of automatic fire came from the crowd back up the alley where the other pickup was pushing its way through the scrambling pedestrians.

"Fuck!" shouted Raynor. He did not have time to get back out of the truck and rifle through the dead man's pockets for the key. Instead, he popped the truck's clutch into neutral, stuck his left foot out the open door, and pushed backward on the ground with all the strength in his leg and back. The small pickup rolled backward down the alleyway, slowly at first, but quickly picking up speed. Some men scrambled out of the way; others, clearly not understanding what was happening and only trying to help, desperately grabbed on to the door and sides of the vehicle to try to arrest its uncontrolled backward descent.

The pickup rolled faster now, and the would-be helpers tumbled away from it. Raynor did not even bother to put his hands on the steering wheel. It would not respond to his commands, and he knew they'd roll back twenty, thirty, fifty yards at most and then crash into a shop or a rickshaw or a truck. They might well hit or run over some pedestrians in the process, but his only objective was to get away from the shoot-out above him and get the hell out of here.

The crash came after thirty-five yards, a jarring rearward slam into the support beam for a plastic tarp awning in the front of an adobe building selling counterfeit versions of Thompson submachine guns. A second support beam was knocked over with the truck's impact, and then the bed smashed through the facade of the building, coming to rest in a cloud of dust.

"Move! Move!" Kolt screamed at Kopelman as he threw open his own door, moved to the hood of the pickup, and immediately picked out targets up the steep alley. Two turning pickup trucks full of armed men had already sighted their weapons on the crash below them. They were preparing to fire over the dozens who had not yet cleared the street, but a long, fully automatic burst from Raynor's AK into the windshield of the first vehicle killed the driver and caused the small truck to swerve violently to the side, sending the men in the cab tipping out into the street and tumbling down the hill.

Rather than open his own door in the direction of

the enemy, Bob had crawled across the cab of the truck, and now he fell out the driver's side onto the street. Quickly he clambered to his feet, and he shouted at Raynor to follow him around the side of the adobe building. Kolt did so, tossing his empty and smoking rifle to the street as he made the turn in a sprint.

They were on a larger street now, two lanes wide, but it was still only made of hard dirt and bits of gravel. It headed downhill. Shops and stalls lined both curbs all the way to a turn in the road thirty yards on. They passed a shop selling a homemade version of the HK MP5 9 mm submachine gun. It was far from Kolt's first choice for a frontline battle rifle, but it was the closest weapon available. One of the small black rifles sat proudly on a stand at the entrance, with two loaded magazines nearby in case a prospective buyer wanted to step into the street to fire some test rounds at the surrounding hills. Raynor scooped up the weapon, grabbed the mags, seated one, and pulled the charging handle back, all just in time, as a half-dozen men on foot appeared around the turn in front of him and Bob. They were armed and clearly part of the force chasing them through the alleyways of the Gun Village. Kolt fired on them immediately, saw his shots hit low into the street and kick up dust. Then he pushed Bob into a wooden kiosk on his right. Raynor followed him into the kiosk but passed him, gained speed with his run, and threw his entire body at the plywood back wall.

With a violent jolt the impact smashed the wood and sent Raynor airborne. He'd expected to land in the dirt of another alley, but instead he found himself spinning through the air, six feet straight down, where he slammed chest-first into the corrugated metal roof of a stall facing the next alleyway over, which was farther down the hill than Kolt had anticipated. His fake MP5 skittered off the side of the roof and fell into the crowd of scrambling men below. The tin roof dented in when Raynor hit it, bending into the general shape of a man impacting from above, but it did not give enough to prevent Kolt from getting the wind knocked out of him. Slowly he rolled to his knees, gasping for any air his lungs could accept, and he looked up at the hole he'd created in the back wall of the tiny shop above.

Bob Kopelman appeared through the opening at high speed. He leaped through the air and came down right next to Kolt feetfirst, and instantly the roof of the stall collapsed, sending both Americans crashing down with it, tumbling through the debris.

Bob was the first to his feet, though he stumbled and staggered out of the dust and wreckage. Raynor was a few steps behind, still gasping for air. He felt pain in his forearm, looked down as he struggled to catch his breath, and saw he'd suffered a foot-long laceration to the inside of his forearm from a sharp corner of the sheet metal roofing.

Blood appeared in a jagged line on his arm.

From out of the foot traffic and the shop workers running in all directions, the owner of the shop the two American spies had just destroyed stepped forward. He was a thin man of fifty. He wore a long neat beard and a long white shirt. In his right hand he held a local copy of a Colt .45 model 1911 with silver etching and faux ivory handgrips. With neither a word nor any visible emotion he leveled the handgun at Bob's chest and pulled the trigger.

Click.

The weapon did not fire.

Bob punched the man in the face with his beefy right hand, sending the shopkeeper's head snapping back and his body falling into the crowd behind him. The pistol fell to the ground.

Another man in the crowd fired a weapon, but Bob did not know if the round had been intended for him or not. The men in the road grew in number by the second. Bob looked around for a gun, then back toward Raynor.

Kolt stepped clear of the wreckage of the shop. In his right hand he held a counterfeit Mossberg 590 shotgun. He racked a shell into the chamber and fired high in the air, pumped the weapon again, and lowered it at the crowd, sweeping the barrel in a wide, wild 180-degree arc. He pushed through the mob. No one else fired again and Raynor managed to fight through, though many men shouted at him now. Bob stayed right on Kolt's heels and they ran up the street, turned a quick left and then a quick left again, finding themselves on a long row of stone stairs bordered on both sides by more shops from the arcade of gun vendors. As they descended the stairs in a run Kolt grabbed a fresh AK-47 from a shop stall and a fully loaded magazine from another, and then tossed the Mossberg pump shotgun to big Bob Kopelman.

"You're hurt, Racer!" Bob was exhausted. His chest

wheezed and he gasped the words as he saw Kolt's bloody arm.

Kolt ignored the comment. "We need to find a place where we can call Jam—"

A vendor from the last kiosk appeared on the road with a machete in his hand. He started chasing Raynor and Kopelman, ready to kill to retrieve his stolen magazine, and he gave up the chase only when Kolt clicked the mag onto his Kalashnikov and chambered a round. Kolt turned and stitched a three-round burst at the feet of the pursuing man, and the man stopped and ran in the other direction, ending his pursuit.

Raynor turned back around and kept running, now just behind Bob.

Gunfire above and behind them caused them to pick up the pace even more. At first Kolt thought the noise might be just guns fired in anger or some other dustup in the area, but after the third burst he saw the stairs below him and to his right crack and tear up with the impact of rifle rounds. Bob turned around and fired the shotgun up at an armed man at the top of the steps. He looked like a shopkeeper but he was clearly trying to kill both of the fleeing Americans. The blast of 12-gauge pellets from twenty-five yards caught the shopkeeper in the midsection and he disappeared over the hill above the steps.

They made it farther down the stairs. In front of them ran the wide road that passed through the center of town. On this street they'd last seen Jamal and his truck, a few hundred yards back to the east, and Kolt hoped to see the old yellow Hilux when he turned the corner, although at this point Kolt couldn't blame the kid if he'd gunned the Toyota's engine and hauled ass halfway to Karachi.

As they ran for the main street they began taking more fire from behind. Bob was only ten yards from the intersection, but Kolt slowed his sprint, stopped, spun, and dropped to his knees. Another pickup truck full of Taliban was fifty yards behind and coming down the hill toward them. Raynor dumped the remainder of the AK's magazine at the truck and it jacked hard to the right, hit a motorized rickshaw, and went up on two wheels. The truck flipped, landed on its roof, and slid off the road, over the descending steps, and into a storefront factory that fabricated rifle ammunition.

An explosion rocked the arcade. Hot metal shards and red flames shot out in all directions, and black smoke mushroomed into the blue afternoon sky. Raynor flattened himself to the ground to avoid the shrapnel. He had no time to alert Kopelman behind him, only hoped the old guy would make it around the corner of the building at the intersection before shrapnel perforated his heavy frame.

Kolt looked back, did not see the sixty-year-old, hoped like hell he'd not run into trouble on the main street. Kolt clambered back to his knees, saw even more blood all over the right side of his shirt now from where he'd slashed his arm in the fall through the kiosk roof. He ignored it—the arm worked and the bleeding hadn't slowed him yet. His adrenaline warded off the exhaustion he'd otherwise suffer from the exertion of the past ten minutes, though it would not protect him from uncontrolled blood loss.

He left the empty rifle in the street and ducked into a nearby stall. There he found one young shopkeeper cowering in the shadows. Kolt just pushed by him and grabbed the only rifle he could find, a long and heavy Lee Enfield bolt-action replica. He hefted it off the wall, turned to the boy, and in Pashto he shouted, "Where are bullets?" The kid pointed to a shelf: leather pouches full of cartridges were stacked three deep. Raynor grabbed one and slung the carry strap over his neck, took the time to load the unfamiliar weapon with five rounds, all the while looking out into the street for more enemy. Blood dripped off his arm as if from a leaky faucet. It drained down his hand and between his fingers, even wetting the cartridges and the breech of the big rifle.

Also in the kiosk, hanging from a nail on a support beam, was a Makarov pistol in a leather holster built into a long bandolier. Kolt slung this over his head as well, turned back to the kid to ask where the bullets were for *this* gun, but caught only a quick glimpse of the boy running away.

He did not take the time to hunt for the handgun ammunition; instead, he ran back out onto the stairs, shouldered up to the corner of the building at the intersection, and looked around it.

Bob was there, in the street, lying on his side. His shotgun was ten feet from his outstretched hand. It looked as if he'd slipped in a puddle there in the dust.

But it was not a puddle of water, it was blood. Bob's blood. He'd been shot through the chest. Kolt had not heard the round, did not know from which direction it had come.

"No!" Raynor shouted, and he ran toward the older man, darted out into the street to grab him and pull him to safety. Immediately the road tore apart in front of him—bullets stitched up the road, and bits of stone and dirt and dust flew into the air between his run and his fallen partner. Raynor spun around and dove back out of the street, back behind the baked-mud building at the corner of the intersection.

On his chest in the alleyway now he crawled back around. Bob was still there, crumpled on his side of the street. He was moving still. His big body twitched and his chest wheezed.

"Bob! Don't move! I'm coming to get you. Just sit tight and I'll—"

Kopelman looked up at Raynor. He did not speak, just blew out one more long breath as his life left his body.

Bob stilled, and his eyes locked open in death, his irises rolled back. Fifteen feet from Raynor.

Kolt stood up. He felt weak and tired suddenly. Slowly he turned away, left Bob's body behind, and began walking back up the hill.

A minute later he'd found a tiny space between two kiosks in the arcade. He pushed through, came out onto another busy alleyway, hid his bloody arm as much as possible from the crowds of agitated locals. He carried his rifle under his arm, business end down. A couple of people looked at him in surprise, noticing the dirt and blood and sweat, but Kolt assumed that the situation had been so chaotic, they could not all know that he had been part of the gunfight. He could just as easily have been an innocent victim of all the shooting or of the explosion to the east. Kolt felt his body tiring quickly. He didn't think he could run again even if his life depended on it, so he just strolled along with the foot traffic, made his way back down to the main road, started to turn to the left because he knew Bob's body would be in the street fifty yards to his right, and he did not want to see it *or* the crowd that inevitably would have formed around it.

But turning left he saw something just as disheartening.

Jamal's yellow Hilux was there, surrounded by a half-dozen Taliban. Jamal was standing outside it, arms high, the muzzle of a Kalashnikov to the back of his head.

No.

Kolt retreated back into the alleyway. He checked behind him—there were a few people walking around, but he didn't see any Taliban.

He looked back around the corner once again. He knew that if he could do anything for the young Afghan who'd saved his life, it would be right now, right this second, before Jamal was led away from the Hilux, taken away in a truck or pushed off for interrogation by more black-turbaned assholes.

Now or never, Raynor said to himself. He raised the heavy rifle, hoped like hell it was accurate at fifty yards, and lined it up on the man with the gun at Jamal's head. Jamal stood right by the open door to his truck. Kolt hoped he could remove the immediate threat to him. Then, if the kid had any sense, he would dive into his Hilux and take off.

It wasn't much of a plan, but Jamal's chances would be zero if the Taliban hustled him away from the scene.

Kolt Raynor fired the Lee Enfield. He did not look to see if his round hit the man covering Jamal. Instead, he racked the bolt of the heavy gun and quickly sighted on the next closest man. Fired again. Racked the bolt again and fired on a third target. He expected, at any moment, to be machine-gunned from behind. But he didn't give a shit. The intel had been sent to the CIA. Bob was dead.

There was nothing else he could do for T.J. and Eagle 01.

Kolt did not give a damn if he lived or died anymore.

He was done.

He manipulated the bolt a third time, and then a fourth, lining up his sights each time on a fresh gunman.

After he fired the fifth round his smoking rifle was spent. He ejected the last empty cartridge, sending it arcing through the air ahead of a stream of gray smoke. Incoming gunfire began pocking the street and the building next to him. He paused only to look at the scene ahead.

Five dead men in the street, more running or crawling for cover.

The Hilux speeding off in the opposite direction.

"Go, kid!" Kolt shouted, hoping Jamal could make it out of town, dump the car, and then find his way out of Peshawar. It would not be safe for him around here, and there wasn't a damned thing Kolt Raynor could do to help him.

Kolt turned back into the alley. Men scattered, hid in their shops or ran like hell into side streets. Others dived into rickshaws or pedaled their bicycles out of the way, desperate to get clear of yet another gun battle.

Kolt dropped the empty rifle, took the leather ammo satchel off his neck, and threw it down as well. He forced himself to jog away, armed now with only an empty Makarov replica.

A minute later he made his way out onto a small side street. A lone taxicab sat parked in the dust. A driver behind the wheel shouted into his cell phone.

Raynor climbed into the back of the taxi. The man turned and looked at him, saw the blood, the sweat, the torn tunic.

The Western features.

"Get out!" he screamed in Pashto.

Kolt pulled the empty Makarov pistol and jabbed the muzzle against the driver's forehead, pressing it hard into the man's black prayer cap. "Drive!" he said in Pashto, and the man spun around to his steering wheel and complied. Kolt kept the weapon in the back of the cab driver's neck as they left Darra Adam Khel, heading back north on the Peshawar–Hayatabad road.

THIRTY-NINE

T.J. and his men had awakened slowly that morning, as usual, and then sat around in the dark talking once again about Racer's visit three nights earlier. Zar and his men had been up that entire night, several times barging in on the chained Americans and standing there silently, glaring at the prisoners as if trying to decide if they really did have no idea what was going on. T.J. found out from a guard the next day that, as far as Zar and company knew, a junior AQ man and one of the local Taliban guards got into a fight with a knife and a gun, and they both lost.

Josh and the boys decided that Kolt must have killed one of the men out of necessity, and then killed the other to stage the crime scene to cover up his presence in the fort. Kolt's ruse had worked, and the Delta men in the tiny cell now only prayed that Raynor had made it all the way to safety.

This morning had continued just as every other morning here at Zar's camp. A breakfast of tea and flatbread, a daily team prayer service led by one of the staff sergeants, some mild calisthenics there on the small dirt floor in the cramped confines of their chamber, and then back to the bunks for discussion and idle conversation.

Lunch came after noon, again, just like every other day. And then after lunch, they returned to the discussion of Racer's visit, and then slept, dreaming of freedom.

Everything changed in the middle of the afternoon. Men entered the cell, Zar's men, and Zar Afridi himself followed behind them. There was a nervousness in the actions of all the visitors. Few words were spoken, the three sergeants were ordered to sit on their cots, and T.J. was ordered out of the cell.

At gunpoint he was led out into the sunny afternoon and then ordered to dunk his long hair and bearded face in a water bucket positioned by a low stepstool. He did as he was told, then sat on the stool. Hurriedly an old man came toward him with a long straight razor.

T.J. shot to his feet, and his arms rose in defense. Zar stepped forward, spoke to his prisoner in Pashto. "No, my friend, it is fine. We have been instructed to cut your hair and to shave you. To put you in new, clean clothes."

"Ordered by who?"

"TTP," Zar said. T.J. knew he was talking about Tehrik-i-Taliban. The Pakistani Taliban.

If this news was supposed to put T.J. at ease, it failed miserably. He asked, "Why?"

"I do not know."

Timble looked over the old man with the razor. He certainly did not appear as if he had nefarious intentions. Josh asked if he could just shave himself and cut his own hair, but no one, Zar Afridi included, was going to let him wield a straight razor.

In ten minutes it was done. He'd had his head shaved just once in the past three years. Up in Hazara the previous summer the prisoners had been so infested with lice that their captors had had to remove all their hair. Otherwise, the men had worn long hair and beards, just like their Pashtun jailers, but only Bouncer, a Puerto Rican staff sergeant named Tony Marquez, looked much like a Pashtun.

T.J. reentered the cell. His men just stared at his thin, bare face, and then Marquez was led out of the room.

The barber made quick work of all the others. One of the men even caught a glimpse of the CIA helicopter pilot, Skip Knighton, as he was led from the main building to get his head shaved.

Afterward, back in the darkness of their cell, the men of Eagle 01 tried to figure out what was going on. Were they to be released? Were they to be involved with the Chechens in the phony American Rangers uniforms? No one knew.

In the early evening, Lieutenant Colonel Josh Timble heard a commotion in the compound outside the walls of his cell. Quickly he and Staff Sergeant Troy "Spike" Kilborn placed the two rope cots on top of one another, and Josh climbed upon them. Staff Sergeant Tony "Bouncer" Marquez, the fittest of the four men housed in the twelve-foot-square hut, hustled onto the shaky contraption and dropped down onto his hands and knees. T.J. climbed onto Marquez, pulled himself up to the vent slat at the top of the wall, and looked out into the compound, while Staff Sergeant Tim "Roscoe" Haynes held him steady from behind.

It was foggy, and the sun's direct light had left the valley for the day. Out of the low light and the mist, three four-wheel-drive Toyota pickup trucks with canvas-covered beds pulled to a stop on the long driveway not fifty feet from the Americans' cell. A dozen men climbed from the vehicles. T.J. tried to identify the new arrivals to Zar's compound from his lousy vantage point. He could tell only that they were all armed and that most wore prayer caps or bare heads. At first glance they did not look like the Pakistani Taliban he had been around the majority of his time in captivity. He noticed Zar Afridi himself come out to greet the men. The warlord walked with several of his militia by his side.

T.J. expected to witness the long and friendly Pashtun greeting, followed by a slow walk either toward the hurja on the far side of the fortress, or at least toward Zar's main building. But there was no greeting, only a rushed conversation while all fifteen men marched directly toward the Americans' cell.

"Down, down," Josh instructed, and Roscoe helped him down from the vent. Spike and Bouncer scrambled to put the cots back in place.

All four men had just made it back to their respective positions when the iron door was unlocked with a series of loud clangs and the gritty sliding of an old iron bolt, and more early-evening light shot into the room in a growing shaft that reached T.J. on his cot against the far wall.

"Everyone up!" The first man through the door shouted it in English. Zar's two sentries held handcuffs and leg irons. They hustled around the men who entered the cell and began restraining the four Americans.

T.J. looked at the English speaker. He was young, early thirties tops, and he wore a long black beard and long black hair. His skin was very fair, his eyes were hazel green, and his posture was proud and erect. His two words of English were surprisingly clear for a Pashtun or an Arab. T.J. wondered if he might be a Westerner.

Next to him stood a man T.J. recognized. He was the AQ man in the glasses who had come in with the German and the Chechen "Rangers" a few weeks back. At the time, Timble had been concentrating on the fake Americans. But now he focused on the al Qaeda operative. He was in his late thirties, had well-manicured hands and a clean bearded face.

And he possessed the coldest black eyes Timble had ever seen.

Spike had commented after this man's last visit to the cell that his accent was certainly Turkish. T.J. hadn't noticed, but Spike knew languages better than anyone else on the team.

As Josh felt the hot metal cuffs snap on his ankles, repeating a miserable process that he'd been subjected to hundreds of times in the past thirty-six months, he suspected that the time for the mysterious operation, in which he and his men would be probably be unwilling participants, had just come.

"Where are we going?" he asked the AQ man in Turkish. He did not know much of the language, but he wanted to assert himself by showing this al Qaeda strongman that he knew the man's country of origin.

But the dark man with the dark eyes and the trim beard did not answer. Instead, the light-skinned long-hair spoke. Again, in English. "You are the officer. I understand you are called T.J.?"

The man spoke with no foreign accent whatsoever. He sounded exactly like an American.

T.J. slowly stammered his response. "That's right. Who are you?"

The bearded man did not answer the question; instead, he said, "There has been an incident in Darra. You are no longer safe here, so I will be taking charge of you."

T.J. looked around the room for Zar Afridi, but he had remained outside. Zar was in control of the captives, and a Pashtun host took responsibility for his guests. T.J. looked at the English speaker and said, "Zar and his militia might have something to say about that."

"Yes. Pashtunwali can be an annoyance when it is used to protect someone other than oneself." He waved a hand in the air. "But there is a way around that. I have personally assured Zar that you and your men will not be harmed. I will ensure your safety during our sojourn. Afterward, I have promised him, I will return you all to his care."

"Our sojourn?"

"We are taking a trip, and we leave immediately. To avoid the prying eyes of coalition drones, a covered truck will be backed up to the door here, and your men will climb into the back. You will ride in the back-seat with me and one of my men. Your helicopter pilot friend will travel in another vehicle. If you or your men make any attempt to escape, the pilot will be shot. Do I make myself clear?"

T.J. just nodded. He slowly looked to his three men, and said, "Do what he says."

T.J. imagined his face showed the same level of shock as the others'. There was no question now. This guy *was* an American. He'd always known there were Americans who belonged to al Qaeda. But he imagined them living in Karachi or Cairo or Berlin or London, working the Internet or drinking tea and smoking hoo-kahs, not actually operating in the field. This fellow countryman seemed to be a full-fledged operative.

Seconds later a truck backed all the way to the cell door, and armed gunmen opened the canvas back of the covered vehicle. They used their rifle barrels to mo-tion the shackled Americans inside.

Once they were chained in the truck, a group of five children, following orders from several armed men, piled into the vehicle. Two more stood on the small run-ning boards and held on to the outside. These were the human shields. T.J. knew that if any drones were watch-ing now they would not strike these vehicles.

T.J. and his men left the relative safety of Zar Afri-di's compound in the custody of al Qaeda.

* * *

Ten minutes later T.J. bounced and bumped in the backseat, jostled with the uneven surface of the broken logging trail. The truck had wasted no time in getting out of Zar's compound and then leaving Shataparai. They'd backed into a small cave in the mountainside, where they'd left the children behind. The truck now crossed the bridge, and T.J. sensed that they were heading northeast along the geographical contours of the floor of the Tirah Valley. His cuffs scratched his ankles and wrists as he bucked in the rear seat, a dark-skinned gunman on his right and the mysterious American on his left.

In the front seat were an armed driver and an armed passenger. They were Pashtun, probably not al Qaeda, but the American spoke to them in Arabic, and they followed his orders.

"Who are you?" T.J. asked in English.

"I am Daoud al-Amriki."

"David the American," Timble translated. "That's a little vague. Who *were* you?"

"A long time ago, before I converted and took this name, I was someone else. That no longer matters to me, nor should it to you."

"You are al Qaeda." It was a statement, not a question. He was here with the Arabs; who else could he be?

Daoud shrugged. "You Americans like to simplify the struggle against the West. To give your enemy a name, like a country you can hate or a city you can attack. I belong, with all of God's followers, to the resistance against you. If you want to call it al Qaeda because you are unable to grasp that we are everything, we are everyone, and we are everywhere . . . then so be it."

T.J. shrugged. "Al Qaeda, *and* a pompous ass." Then he said, "You are a traitor."

"To the country of my birth? Certainly. But not to my religion."

"What's the plan?" asked T.J. now. The vehicle slowed, negotiating a low stream bed. The undercarriage of the truck scraped loudly on a rock, and Daoud shouted at the driver before turning back to T.J.

"You'll know soon enough, Captain Joshua Timble." Daoud al-Amriki smiled. "We know all about you." Josh had not been a captain for nine years. "We know you are a Ranger." He had not been a Ranger for six. Still, for three years here in captivity, neither he nor his men had revealed their real names to their captors. That this American al Qaeda operative knew his name was disquieting, even if he did not know his current rank or organization.

Josh shook it off. He needed intel. "You said something happened. A place called Darra?"

"Darra Adam Khel. South of Peshawar. A German associate working for us was tortured and killed. We have reason to believe it was done by CIA spies."

Josh said nothing. Any inflection, any reaction, any comment, might be recognized by al-Amriki. T.J. could ill afford to give away any knowledge that he knew his fellow countrymen were searching for the German.

Al-Amriki continued: "We killed one of the spies. The other escaped. We don't know what he knows. We don't know who he may be in communication with. Therefore we will be forced to execute our operation at dawn tomorrow." He shrugged. "It is no matter. We are ready."

"Can you give me a hint about your operation?" T.J. had become an expert at getting his captors to talk. He saw in this young man's eyes that he was proud of his plan, and Josh thought he might be able to draw him out in conversation.

It was dark now in the valley. The driver flipped on his headlights, and the beams shone on nothing but dust as the vehicle ahead bottomed out again in the road. Daoud held on to the handle above the door to the backseat. He grimaced after another crashing bounce of the truck. Then he looked back at T.J. in the darkness. "What do you know about the Vietnam War?"

Josh was taken aback. He could hardly imagine the relevance. He replied, "A lot, actually."

"Then you will be familiar with the Tet Offensive, January 1968."

"Of course."

"A single act that changed the course of history."

T.J. cocked his head, slowly. *Where is he going with this?* he wondered. "The Communists lost that battle."

"Yes, but they won the war, didn't they? General Giap and his forces could not defeat the Americans on the field of battle—that was obvious. The Americans had an advantage in numbers, in technology, in resources. So he did not try to beat them on the battlefields. He used guerrilla techniques, the slow boil of harassing operations, and the Americans found themselves fighting an amorphous foe that they could not defeat."

T.J. just looked at al-Amriki in the dark truck cab.

"Does that sound familiar? Afghanistan is Vietnam all over again."

T.J. started to argue, but the American traitor continued. "But Giap did not want America in his country for a hundred years. So he devised a plan to win. He used what resources he had, including irregular forces, the Vietcong, and he ordered a simultaneous attack on all the major cities of the south. Why? He knew he could not hold any of those cities for any length of time. His attack was too broad to do more than cause chaos for a few days at most. But Giap understood the American public. They were weary of war, sick of watching it on their news, watching their money go up in smoke and their young come home in body bags. Giap knew this, and he understood this one event, this Tet Offensive, would be the tipping point, the point at which the American public had finally had enough." He paused for dramatic effect. "Tomorrow, Captain Timble, will be the tipping point in the Afghanistan War. Tomorrow will be *our* Tet."

"You are going to attack all the major cities of Afghanistan? All *three*?" T.J. sniffed, unimpressed with the scheme.

Al-Amriki smiled through his beard. "Don't take the metaphor too literally. I mean that we will, in one act, in one day, with one mission, end this war in the favor of Islam and to the shame of the infidels."

T.J. looked away. That was ridiculous. This guy was delusional. "Then you'd better be prepared to lose a lot of men."

"I am. In fact, that is the plan. But the men who will

be lost will happily lay down their lives to throw the infidels out of Afghanistan and Pakistan."

T.J. looked out the front windshield now. This guy was nuts if he thought he and a few costumed Chechens could accomplish such a feat.

"And that's not all," Daoud al-Amriki said proudly. "We have our eyes on another prize."

Josh smiled a little. "You going to run for president of the United States?" His sarcasm was ignored by the younger man.

"No. But we will, by our actions tomorrow morning, set the wheels in motion for the fall of the Pakistani government. Our friends will take control of the country, and *we* will take control of the nuclear weapons they possess."

"Never," muttered Timble, but his voice betrayed a slight concern.

"Don't worry, Captain," said al-Amriki. "You and your men will be safe as long as you do what you're told."

Josh started to question him some more, but he stopped himself. He needed time to think, to plan. If this operation was something on the scale that Daoud al-Amriki claimed, then he'd need to reevaluate the situation. He sat silently, rocked with the vehicle as it moved through the darkness, a sick ache of dread growing in his stomach along with the nausea caused by the motion.

FORTY

The hands on Kolt's wristwatch displayed 1900 Zulu, midnight local time. He sat at the kitchen table in Bob Kopelman's apartment. His torn, bloody, and filthy clothing lay strewn on the linoleum floor around him. Bandages and antiseptics and ointments and scissors and tape sat on the table in front of him.

Along with a bottle of Jim Beam whiskey he'd found on a shelf in the living room.

He hadn't touched the booze, yet, but he'd stared at the bottle and it had stared back at him while he'd cleaned and dressed the long and deep gouge in his forearm. He'd even stood up on his tired and sore legs, walked doubled over like a hunchback to take the strain off his stiff lower back, just to go to the cupboard to get a teacup with which to drink the whiskey.

The teacup sat next to the bottle untouched.

For now.

Kolt sighed. A long, painful exhalation. He'd pulled the landline telephone into the kitchen and placed it in front of him, had to stretch the cord to its limit for it to reach.

The phone rested in his lap, but he had not yet brought himself to make the call that he knew he'd have to make.

Raynor knew he was acting foolishly now. There was no way to be sure Bob had not had anything on his body that might lead al Qaeda or the Taliban right here to this address. At any moment the garage door downstairs could come crashing down, and the black turbans could come up the stairs. Raynor had found a loaded Smith & Wesson .357 Magnum revolver in Bob's desk drawer, and this now rested on the table next to the Kentucky bourbon and the teacup. The five hollow-point Magnum cartridges in the handgun's cylinder could knock down the first couple of men who charged through the door. But that would not do much more than delay the inevitable. Kolt hoped that if the bad guys *did* come through that door, he'd remember to reserve the fifth round in the revolver for himself, to save himself from being taken alive.

Yes, this was stupid, sitting here tired and spent and hurt and unsure about what to do next, but he'd needed a place to hide and to treat the wound on his forearm and to get out of his bloody clothing and to regroup. He did not know Peshawar, only this apartment, Bob's place. So, for better or worse, he'd come back here.

But he could not stay. With another glance at the bottle and another successful turn away from it, he picked up the phone and dialed the number.

Bob's home phone was clean: Radiance had provided Kopelman with a cable hookup running through his computer that routed calls through an untraceable line that could not be monitored from the outside.

The international connection took forty seconds. During this time Kolt closed his eyes, tried to concentrate and think of *something* to say. When the connection was made, there was no hesitation from the other side.

"Christ, Bob! Thank God! Talk to me! I've been ringing the Thuraya off the hook trying to—"

"It's Racer."

Pete Grauer paused. When he spoke again there was even more concern in his voice. "What the *hell* is going on?"

"Bob's dead, Pete." Kolt almost whispered it.

"Damn it!" Grauer shouted, his rage aimed squarely at Kolt Raynor. "Damn it! Son of a bitch!"

Kolt closed his eyes. Spoke over the curses. "We infiltrated the German's factory, almost made it out, but AQ and Taliban gunners nailed the shit out of us right there in Darra Adam Khel. Bob and I wasted a dozen of them, easy . . . but there were a dozen more."

"Fuck!" Grauer shouted. Then he paused a moment. His voice changed. "I told him not to go with you."

"I know. He insisted. I should have stopped him from—"

"I've known Bob Kopelman twenty years."

"Sorry, sir," was all Kolt could say. Bob's death was not his fault, and he knew it. But merely because he'd survived and the old spy had not, he would never forgive himself.

"What about the contact? Jamal?"

"I'm not sure. I think he might have gotten out of there. I . . . I really don't know."

"Damn it, Kolt!"

"I thought maybe the Agency or the State Department could look for him. Help him out. Jamal risked everything for us. He's compromised and the Taliban will be hunting—"

"Negative," Grauer said firmly.

Kolt knew it had been ridiculous to even suggest that there would be official help from the U.S. government for a foreign national agent of a private company working in the black in Pakistan. "Right."

Pete Grauer was furious. No doubt he was devastated as well. But he remained focused on the mission. "I received the data from Buchwald's laptop, sent it on to the Agency. Their man in Peshawar, the one who was planning to meet with Kopelman—he's calling me frantically trying to get in touch with Bob. There was something on that laptop, apparently, that's scared the shit out of Langley."

"I'll talk to him if you want me to."

Grauer paused. Kolt knew he wasn't Grauer's first choice as a liaison between his organization and the CIA. Still, he was the only one here. Finally, the former Ranger colonel said, "Don't guess there is any other option."

"Where and when?"

"Just tell me where you are and I'll let them know. They'll pick you up and deliver you there."

"I'm at Bob's place."

"His *apartment*?"

"Affirmative."

"Kolt, how do you know it hasn't been compromised?"

"I *don't*." Kolt looked at the door to the garage. Expected it to explode in splinters ahead of a dozen black turbans.

"What is wrong with you?" A slight hesitation. "You're not drinking, are you?"

Kolt looked at the bottle of Jim Beam. As he did so he sat up straighter in the chair. "Of course not. I'm operational."

"Bullshit, Racer."

"Not a drop, sir." Kolt stood, turned from the bottle, and walked the phone back into the apartment's spartan living room.

Grauer either believed him or else just let it go. "Are you wounded?"

Now Kolt glanced at his arm. "Not bad."

"All right. I'll tell the Agency where to pick you up. Watch for them, and don't shoot any white guys that come through the door."

"Roger that."

"Anything else?"

"Yeah, Pete. I'm sorry about Bob. I did my best to—"

Grauer hung up the phone.

Raynor spent the time waiting for the CIA car by staring out the apartment's second-story window at the city of Peshawar. It was one in the morning, and even in the moonlight he found the town to be grimy and filthy. The foreign smells sickened him. And though he was exhausted, he found himself unable to rest or even to relax here, hidden in the sloppy urban sprawl of the big city, the majority of whose inhabitants would, if given half a chance, happily rip someone with his background and origin limb from limb.

A small Mazda minivan pulled up in front of the warehouse. Raynor fingered the Smith & Wesson in his hand—pulled the hammer back with his thumb.

Two men stepped out. As they passed in front of the headlights of their vehicle he could tell they were Westerners, and likely Americans. He could tell from their features, their eyes, the way they wore the local clothing, even in their confident and wide strides as they approached the garage door. He wondered if he fit in around here any better than these guys. No. He was sure of it. In the mountains he had been invisible when he'd wanted to be, but here, in the city, he was not invisible. He did not melt into the texture of his surroundings. No . . . Here he was Kolt Raynor . . . American.

Infidel.

He lowered the hammer back on the pistol and went to the kitchen to open the garage door.

"Racer?" one said. No friendly handshake or bonhomie between fellow countrymen abroad.

Kolt nodded.

"Let's go," said the other. Raynor followed them out to the van, climbed in behind them, and found a third man behind the wheel.

The drive was short, and no words were spoken. Soon they pulled into a dark garage. It reminded Kolt of Bob's house here in the city, but he had no clue where they were. The vehicle's door slid open and Kolt was ushered out. An open stone staircase went up a single flight and he took it. The other men did not follow. He entered a second-story room that was dimly lit by lamps covered with fabric shades. There was no furniture, and the floor was bare except for several small mats and rugs lying around. A glass door to a balcony was centered on the far wall, and on either side of it was a window that was closed and shuttered. A porcelain tea service sat in the middle of the dim room, and a man sat in the corner. In front of him a Nalgene water bottle rested on the cement floor.

"Jeff Hammond. You're Racer?"

"Yes."

Hammond looked at the bandaged forearm of the private operator. "How bad is that?"

Kolt shrugged. "Not bad."

"Looks like it's seeping blood. You need stitches?"

"Not today."

"I can get one of my guys to take a look."

"It's okay."

Hammond motioned for Raynor to sit down on the floor across the tea service from him, and Kolt did so. Raynor looked over the CIA officer and was impressed with what he saw. He was a fit man, fifty or so, dressed in a modified local garb that seemed, to Kolt, to be a more efficient way to blend in than Raynor's own attire. Hammond wore cream-colored pants, not nearly as baggy and loose as his own salwar, and his loose local shirt was hidden under an olive drab military-style jacket that Kolt had seen on the street many times. A short-barreled

AK-74 rifle leaned against the wall behind him. He wore a pakol hat on his curly salt-and-pepper hair. His beard was short, but he would not stand out walking through the market. The only anomaly in the room, the only tip-off that this was not a Pashtun in his simple flat in Peshawar, was the Nalgene water bottle.

Hammond said, "You are Kolt Raynor. Former Ranger, made it into the Unit, then you were bounced out three years ago for an op that went bad in North Waziristan."

Kolt just looked at him. Not a great way to start this meeting, as far as he was concerned.

"You worked for Peter Grauer at Radiance, but you were a drunk, so you got canned from that job after an arguably justified but utterly incompetent shooting in international waters off the coast of Somalia a couple of months back."

Still nothing from Kolt except a blank stare.

"And now you are here. The lone survivor of a bloodbath that took the life of an ex–Agency case officer and compromised a reliable local agent."

Now Raynor looked away, to the empty wall over Hammond's shoulder.

The CIA man asked, "You want to fill me in on your actions since Radiance dropped you into the FATA?"

"Not really, no."

"You could be in a shitload of trouble."

Raynor did not bat an eyelash. "I'm used to it."

Hammond's eyebrows rose, and he smiled a bit. "Well . . . you've done okay. Actually, Langley is impressed with what you've accomplished. There are

Agency operatives and agents running around Peshawar, FATA, and the North-West Frontier Province, but nobody has pulled off anything close to what you've done. We have overhead surveillance, contacts in the Pak army, NOCs and foreign nationals, but you and Grauer and Kopelman were some real studs to get eyes on, and to learn about this impending AQ op."

Raynor just sighed. He was tired.

Hammond stared at Kolt for a long moment. He himself blew out a long sigh that seemed to take some of the bite from his earlier coolness. "I almost made it into Delta. Before your time. I was 5th Group, had a buddy that made it into the Unit. I managed to survive selection for a while, but wandered off a hill at night, broke my foot. Took four men to get me back up and into a truck." Hammond laughed, but Kolt knew there wasn't a damned thing funny about the story.

He did not respond.

"After that I figured, screw it, I'll take the easy road, take a job at the Agency. Work an embassy desk, chat up Russian dignitaries at cocktail parties." He waved his hand at the austere conditions around him. "That plan worked out about as well as my dream to make it into your old outfit."

Kolt started to stand. He wasn't in the mood for small talk right now.

"Look, I can use some help as I try to straighten this out over here. I'd like you on my team."

Kolt settled back down on the mat. "What is your team going to do about the operation al Qaeda is planning?"

"Grauer has us in the loop. We know about the Black Hawks, the fake platoon-sized element of Rangers, the al Qaeda men fighting for control of the Eagle 01 prisoners. Which means, we know something very shitty is going to happen unless we can stop it."

Raynor nodded.

"And I'm guessing you share our concerns."

"I do."

"Then why don't you take it from the top, tell me what you know, what you saw, what you did? And most important, I'd like to know what you think."

Kolt considered it. He didn't know if Hammond was any good, but he did know that Hammond and his three men were the only guys here, so he decided to help him if he could. He spent the next five minutes telling Jeff Hammond about his actions over the past four days. Other than the actual name of Jamal, he left little out.

When he was finished the CIA man leaned his head back against the wall. "So, we can't hit the compound at Shataparai without killing the prisoners, and we can't send a rescue mission in to get them out without heavy losses?"

"Complete losses, as far as I'm concerned."

Hammond nodded. Said, "Don't guess it matters much."

"Why not?"

Hammond picked up the water bottle, stood. Walked over to the balcony of the flat. Looked through the curtains out the window. He changed the subject. "There will be a peace jurga in Kabul in January. A big peace conference with the Afghani government and the Afghani Taliban. Some say this might stop the fighting over there."

"You think the Chechens are going to hit that? That's two months away. These guys aren't going to sit on their hands for two months!"

Hammond looked back to Raynor. "No, they aren't going to hit the peace jurga. We believe al Qaeda is going to try their best to kill it before it happens."

"How can they do that?"

"With an operation that will embarrass the U.S., and thereby weaken the Afghani government. Our allies in the Pakistani government as well."

The stakes were suddenly much larger than Raynor had envisioned. "You must have found something in the data we harvested from the German's laptop."

Hammond nodded. "Yes. That was very helpful. Before we got the computer dump and figured out what they were really up to, we thought they were going to just nail some forward operating base over the border, kill some marines, dance around and proclaim victory for the year by getting in the last hit before the winter comes."

Hammond said nothing else.

"So? What's the plan? How will they prevent this peace conference?"

Hammond's eyes showed worry.

"Talk, man! Look, I want to get Eagle 01 out of this. Anything you can say—"

"We are reasonably certain Eagle 01 was taken from Zar's compound last night, just a few hours after the shoot-out in Darra Adam Khel."

Kolt launched to his feet. "What? Where are they now?"

"We don't know where they are." Hammond hesitated. Then, "But we think we know where the AQ contingent that has them is going."

"Where?"

Hammond looked out the glass door and into the darkness.

"Where?"

Jeff Hammond shook his head. Took a sip from the water bottle. "I've got orders, Racer. You are not cleared for that."

"You've got to be kidding. Thought we were part of a team."

Hammond shrugged now. " 'Need-to-know.' You know how that goes."

Kolt launched across the room, grabbed the operator by both lapels of his military jacket, pulled him to his feet, and pushed him against the wall. The water bottle flew through the air, slammed onto the floor, and bounced across the room. "I've risked my life to get you the intel you have! Kopelman died for it! At this point in the game, asshole, *I* decide if it's something I need to know!"

Hammond looked shocked and angry, but not totally unsympathetic. Still, he did not back down. "Grauer explained your contract status with Radiance to my higher-ups. You've got no security clearance whatsoever. You're just a private citizen. Langley told me to get what I can from you, but under no circumstances was I to pass on classified intel *to* you."

Kolt grabbed the man tighter. Nodded slowly. "It's

true. I'm just a private citizen. Which means I can walk away from this whole thing right now. I can hop a bus for Islamabad and be sitting at a café with a reporter for *The New York Times* before happy hour tonight."

Hammond did not respond to the threat.

Kolt let go of the man's jacket and took a half step back.

"You want me on the team? You have *one* chance to have me on the team. Tell me what the target is."

Jeff Hammond went back to his spot on the floor. Slowly Kolt returned to the mat in front of the CIA officer.

Hammond said, "From Buchwald's laptop we got an account number for a bank in Quetta. We looked into the account. A month ago it was accessed by a high-ranking foreign national intelligence officer, a guy Langley trusted. A guy we've had on payroll for several years. A guy who set up an operation for us, ran it effectively, to the best of our estimation, for some time."

"A guy who was playing you all along," Kolt said.

Hammond shrugged. "Who knows?"

"What was the operation he ran?"

Jeff Hammond looked at his water bottle but did not drink from it. He seemed torn as to what he should say, but finally he looked up into Kolt's eyes, and the words came out with speed and intensity.

"A black site. A secret prison, a place where we could house high-value targets without anyone knowing that we were holding them. A place where the locals could do the interrogation while Agency . . . 'advisers,' shall we say? could help out with the questioning."

"I thought black sites were illegal now," Raynor said, but with no great surprise in his voice.

"There are some gray areas. Still . . . Langley has not read Congress in on the existence of this particular operation."

"Guess there isn't too much of a gray area, then."

Hammond shrugged. "I'm just a grunt on the ground, Raynor. The Sandcastle wasn't my baby."

"The Sandcastle?"

"That's the site."

"So, you think al Qaeda is going to attack this Sandcastle?"

Jeff Hammond just nodded. "Helmut Buchwald, the German guy you iced, took money from the Quetta account to finance his gun-making factory. The guy who ran the Sandcastle made a large withdrawal from the same account just five days ago. He is on leave at the moment, not on duty at the Sandcastle. The only reasonable conclusion is that the Quetta account was some sort of operational slush fund, which suggests the two men were paid by the same masters. If Buchwald was working for al Qaeda, which you and Bob established to Langley's satisfaction . . . then the guy who runs the Sandcastle just got paid by al Qaeda."

"Paid for what?"

"Best guess would be access to his location. Complicity in an op against it. They even gave him time to get out of there before the shit hit the fan, to go on leave."

Kolt asked, "But . . . wherever this Sandcastle is, how the hell are they going to get the Black Hawks there?

They'd show up on radar the moment they left the FATA. If they were heading to Afghanistan we could knock them out of the sky with no problem. If T.J. and the men were in the choppers, then they would be killed, but they'd have to assume we wouldn't let them just fly over the border and—"

Hammond shook his head. "The black site . . . it's here."

"Here? You mean, here in Pakistan?"

"I mean here in Khyber."

Kolt shook his head like he hadn't heard correctly. Then, slowly, he muttered, "Holy shit."

"Fifteen miles west of Peshawar, just outside of Landi Kotal, right smack dab in the Khyber Pass. It was an old British garrison and stockade, a hundred fifty years old. One of dozens of little fortresses overlooking the pass. The al Qaeda Black Hawks can fly fifteen miles low, through the pass, without being picked up on radar."

Raynor's mouth hung open. "Back up a second. You guys are operating an Agency prison in a Taliban-controlled area?"

"Ironic, huh? Actually, the Taliban don't run Landi Kotal." He looked at the floor. "Not yet, anyhow. There is a special ops unit of the Pakistani Khyber Rifles at the black site, the best of their best and all vetted by Langley. The Khyber Rifles hold Landi Kotal itself, although the highway through the pass is full of Taliban ambush sites."

Kolt still could not believe what he was hearing. "Who are the prisoners at the black site?"

"All HVTs. We've gotten more actionable intel out of the Sandcastle than any other source in the past three or four years. That's where we picked up the final pieces of the puzzle that led us to OBL last year in Abbottabad. Right now at the site there are two AQ superheavyweights, a couple of well-informed AQ foot soldiers, and two dozen or so Afghanistan Taliban. Big shots, regional commanders, military wing, even a prominent former spokesperson, kind of a VIP. These are all guys either the Pakistani army picked up in Pakistan and handed over to us, or . . . in some cases—to tell you the truth—in *most* cases . . ."

He paused. Looked off into space for a moment. It was clear Hammond was still struggling with telling secrets. It was hardly standard operating procedure for a man in his profession.

Kolt pressed. "In most cases, what?"

"In most cases the Agency picks up guys on the Afghani side. Guys we know are dirty, guys we need information from, and guys we don't want to hand over to the Justice Department. So we hood them, zip-tie them, drive them over the border, and hand them off to the Khyber Rifles. We just sort of play like these tangos got popped in Pakistan by the Pakistanis, instead of in our area of operations over the border."

"So the Khyber Rifles can interrogate them?"

"The Khyber Rifles have some men that know which side their bread is buttered on. They work for us. They interrogate the prisoners."

"With Agency officers there to observe?"

"You got it."

Kolt's voice turned darker. "You are talking about extraordinary rendition."

Hammond chuckled without smiling. "It's not as extraordinary as you might think. No ghost planes, no secret international treaties or complicated chains of custody. We just toss their asses on a donkey cart and hump them over the border. No muss, no fuss."

"Unless the Sandcastle gets hit by a platoon of al Qaeda operatives posing as Americans. They slaughter the American advisers and then release the HVTs, who then reveal the existence of the black site to the world."

"Yeah . . . unless *that* happens." Hammond blew out a long sigh. "Shit. Can you fucking see the fallout on this? Forget Abu Ghraib. This is *that* times one hundred. Plus the White House is going to go ballistic. Not to mention the Agency men who'll be wiped out in the attack. I've got some good friends at the Sandcastle right now."

"Then pull them out. Leave the prisoners and the Paki guards and just get our boys out of there!"

"It's not that simple."

"Yes, actually, it *is* that simple!"

"Langley has to give the order, and they haven't given the order. They are afraid that without the Agency guys at the Sandcastle, the Pakistani guards will just fold up like a cheap suitcase and let the HVTs go. If they do that, or they kill them, and word leaks out that this was a CIA black site, then that will bite us in the ass. It will hurt our friends in the Pakistani government, which means they could lose their fingernail hold on power. If the extremists take over Pakistan, this is going to turn into a soup sandwich."

"So what are you guys doing to stop them from taking over the Sandcastle?"

"We've alerted the SAD guys at the black site. And I will head over there in the morning as soon as the road opens."

"You and three guys in a minivan?"

"Yeah, for now, basically, that's about it. Langley is working with Colonel Webber at Delta to develop a hit to pull our guys and the HVTs out of there, but again, that would involve the White House, and there is no assurance we're going to get authorization for a ground incursion into Pakistan from the White House. Since the OBL hit, they've pretty much put the kibosh on sending military over the border in any numbers that could be noticed. Hopefully, when they learn what's at stake they will see that pissing off Islamabad is the lesser of two evils."

"Damn." Kolt shook his head in disbelief. "I'll go with you."

Hammond shook his head. "I'd love that—I could definitely use an ex–Delta gun—but I've got orders. We are to have no operational relationship with you."

"Man . . . screw your orders. You weren't supposed to tell me all that shit you just told me."

"Yeah . . . well, I can deny that. But if I put you with my team heading to Landi Kotal . . . can't see how I can keep that from Langley."

Kolt stood. "Then I'll go on my own."

Hammond slowly rose. He lifted his folded Kalashnikov from its resting place leaning against the wall.

"You have gear?"

Kolt shook his head. "Negative."

"You have wheels?"

Again, "Negative."

Hammond clicked his tongue on the roof of his mouth while he thought. Then he said, "Tell you what—I just happen to have a gassed-up Suzuki dirt bike and an AK. A backpack with ammo and water. I just might accidentally leave all that behind in the garage when me and my men leave at six a.m."

Raynor just nodded. "Why don't you leave now?"

"The pass doesn't open until six. Before that we'd get nailed by bandits or Taliban checkpoints within a thousand yards of travel. Anyway, AQ doesn't have the night vision equipment our guys do. They are too smart to hit in darkness. If we leave here at six we'll still be at the site a half hour before first light."

Kolt looked at his watch. "So we sit here for three hours?"

"You can bunk out. I'm going to call Langley. Tell them what I learned from you. Encourage them to talk to the White House and to JSOC, and to fight like hell to get that Delta hit approved. Without Delta, we will do our best. But let's face it . . . if they don't show, we're all dead."

FORTY-ONE

After six hours of driving, the majority of it off-road, T.J., his three men, and the CIA pilot were all led out of the trucks in chains and pushed into a dark warehouse. They were lined up against a wall by their guards, and then their chains were strapped together by lengths of thick hemp and fastened to an iron pipe in the wall.

Here they sat for two hours. Any time one of them tried to speak to another, he was threatened with a rifle butt to his head by the pair of Chechens guarding them.

A light hung from the ceiling and shone directly on Eagle 01, so they could not see more than twenty feet of empty cement warehouse flooring in front of them. But Josh could hear a tremendous bustle outside. Trucks coming and going, the shouting of men, and the clanging of metal. Activity on the far side of the warehouse, out of his view. Shouts in Chechen and Arabic and Pashto. Engines starting up and then stopping.

Finally a Chechen in a salwar kameez ordered the men to their feet, then stepped up to Timble and unlocked his chains. He did not do this to the rest of the men in line.

Across the bare cement floor of the warehouse came the echo of a door opening and then closing again. Timble saw men arrive through the darkness in front of him a few seconds later. Five, then seven figures, all dressed as 75th Ranger Regiment soldiers. They wore their carbines across their chests and Kevlar helmets on their heads, their thick goggles stowed high upon them.

They weren't Rangers, Josh knew. They were just more men in costume. But he also knew they looked close enough to fool most anyone they came across for as long as they would need to wreak havoc.

One of the Rangers stepped forward. He wore a major's insignia, he was clean-shaven, of course, and he was young, perhaps thirty. In the low light and with the change of clothing and the lack of facial hair, it took T.J. several seconds to realize whom he was looking at.

It was Daoud al-Amriki. David the American. He smirked at T.J. "My first shave in six years. How do I look?"

T.J. tried to mask his surprise. Gruffly he responded, "Like a damn fool."

David just smiled as if he had expected the retort. T.J. looked him up and down, saw the mistakes he'd made in wearing his gear. His pants were not tucked into his boots, his goggles on his helmet were stowed upside down, and his kneepads were upside down as well. Still, this was an American, dressed as an American, and

Josh knew this only made the al Qaeda operation more deadly.

A man with a wooden pushcart appeared from the darkness of the far side of the warehouse. On the cart were several more sets of uniforms; boots, rifles, helmets; backpacks. All the same high-quality forgeries.

"Captain Timble. What do you think?" Daoud lifted a tunic from the top of the stack. He unfolded it and held it high. TIMBLE was written on the name tape over the right breast. A captain's bars were on the helmet lying next to it.

T.J. just stared.

"Put it on. There is gear here for you and all your men. They can dress in whatever fits—their name tapes are not accurate."

T.J. made no move toward the clothing. He found himself almost paralyzed with shock. He'd had no idea that the AQ operatives expected him to physically take part in whatever they had planned.

"No fucking way. I'm not wearing that. I don't know what you—"

Daoud cut him off with a shrug. "I expected this, of course." He said something in Arabic that T.J. didn't pick up, but quickly two of the Chechens rushed from behind Daoud al-Amriki and grabbed the last man in the line of prisoners. It was Skip Knighton, the surviving CIA helo pilot. The two big Chechens pushed him to the ground, onto his knees. His bindings were attached to the three Delta sergeants, so the entire row, minus T.J., stumbled. One of the Delta prisoners recovered and went after the Chechens, but quickly a large unit of phony Rangers appeared from the darkness, easily two dozen men now, and they raised weapons high and shouted at the Americans in their own mother tongue. No one in Eagle 01 spoke Chechen, but the words could nevertheless be construed as nothing other than threats.

T.J. and his men backed off.

Through it all Daoud al-Amriki stood by, haughty and confident. When the noise died down, when two men stood over the American helicopter pilot with rifles to his head, when two dozen more stood in a line to the left and right and just behind David the American, when T.J. and his men were standing back against the wall, Daoud al-Amriki said, "For the purposes of today's operation, I need only you, Captain Timble. As you can see, I have plenty of other soldiers who can play the part of an American force. These other four men of yours are absolutely expendable."

Daoud stepped over to Skip Knighton, stood in front of and over him, though his eyes and those of Josh Timble remained locked together. Josh did not speak.

"Expendable, Captain," Daoud repeated, and he quickly drew the replica Beretta pistol in the drop leg holster on his hip. "I am happy to prove that to you now." He raised the weapon and placed it to the helicopter pilot's forehead.

"No!" shouted T.J., just as the pistol cracked and Knighton's head snapped back, a splatter of blood erupted behind him, and he dropped dead on the cold concrete.

All the Delta men began shouting and pulling at

their bindings. They tried to drop to the floor to tend to their fellow prisoner, but they were pushed away by the rifle butts of the two Chechens who'd stood alongside Knighton as he was killed.

"You son of a—"

"Save it, Timble. Save your curses. You will need them after I shoot the next infidel in the row."

The two Chechens pushed Tony Marquez down on his knees now, two feet from the crumpled body of the CIA pilot. "Screw these pricks, boss!" Tony shouted, and Daoud pointed his pistol at the fresh forehead in front of him.

"No!" shouted Josh again. And then, "I'll do it! I'll put on the damn uniform! We all will!"

Daoud al-Amriki seemed pleased with himself. He lowered the pistol, found the safety and engaged it, then reholstered it awkwardly. It was obvious that he was accustomed to neither this weapon nor the holster low on his hip. He had to concentrate on his actions. He then looked back up to Josh, and declared, "As I said, I really don't need these other men. Any delay, any tricks, and I will shoot them all through the head. Are we clear, Captain?"

T.J. just looked down at Skip's dead body. He'd spent three years suffering with the man, and now he was gone. T.J. reached for the uniform. As he did so he barked an order to the remaining prisoners: "Kit up!"

Raynor woke up slowly. His body felt stiff and sore, and his left forearm wound burned with a savage heat. He'd slept for two hours on the mats on the floor of one of the bedrooms of the CIA safe house, and as the events of the previous day came back to him, one at a time, he recognized with a start that there was an important piece of this puzzle that had been eluding him.

Before nodding off he had borrowed Hammond's satellite phone to call Pete Grauer in Jalalabad to let him know what was going on. Hammond had been all for any help Radiance could provide, unofficially, of course. Hammond had made his own appeal to his own masters for a rescue mission to the black site, but the red tape involved with getting that mission approved made it seem damned unlikely that it would happen in time.

Grauer had immediately agreed to have Pam Archer's Predator available to linger over Landi Kotal, and to relay intel to Langley in real time from the Radiance Operations Center. What Langley would do with that information was anyone's guess.

But Kolt had only just now considered another facet of the enemy operation. It was funny how, in his cluttered and weary mind, this one thing somehow became so clear to him.

Raynor sat up now. A couple hours' sleep was not much, not nearly enough, but it would have to do. He was hungry and thirsty. In addition to the injury to his arm from the metal roof, his elbow and knees throbbed from the fight with the Afghani Taliban in the dry creek bed three days ago.

He shook off the aches and pains, and stepped into the sitting room. Hammond and his men were there.

"We leave in twenty," Hammond said. He loaded his carbine and placed it on body armor he had laid out on the cold cement floor. The other paramilitary operations operators were rechecking their own gear.

Raynor said, "I've been thinking. They know we got to the German, so they must assume we know about the choppers."

Hammond nodded. "Probably."

"Which means they know they can't fool us by landing a couple of Black Hawks at the Sandcastle."

Hammond shrugged this time. "So?"

"So, what if they have another plan?"

"Such as?"

"I don't know. I've been trying to figure that out. Maybe some other component to the attack on the black site. They have to assume we will be ready with RPGs or shoulder-fired missiles or something to knock down the choppers."

"Yeah, we are ready. But maybe they think we won't hit the choppers because the missing Delta guys will be on board."

Raynor shook his head. "No. In the past, if they had the boys, they would use them, show them off. But they aren't showing them off now. They may have them on the choppers, but it's not to use them as human shields. There is some other reason the boys are part of this op."

"Well, either way, we are ready for the Black Hawks. I hate to think those poor D-boys will be on board, but we aren't letting those choppers land in the Sandcastle. We'll shoot them down."

Kolt understood, and he knew that T.J. would understand as well. But there was something else. "You are ready for the choppers. Focused on the choppers. But what if they attack from the ground?"

"Do you have reason to believe the attack will come from the ground?"

"No . . . except, when I met with T.J. he said Pakistani Taliban were working with AQ. And in Zar's compound, there were AQ *and* Taliban there. And again, when Bob and I were hit in Darra Adam Khel, we were most definitely hit by AQ *and* Taliban forces, coordinating with one another."

Hammond understood. A distant look glazed over his eyes. "So where are the Pakistani Taliban now? Why aren't they involved in the actual op against the Sandcastle?"

"Maybe they are."

The CIA man agreed. "Maybe they are. The fort is well protected from the road, though. Once we take out the Black Hawks we can concentrate on any ground forces."

Kolt said, "It might help if you had some forewarning."

Hammond nodded forcefully now. "Agreed. If you are so certain the Sandcastle is going to get hit from the ground as well, why don't you go to the one place any ground force will have to pass on its way there?"

"Where is that?"

"Just three klicks east of the Sandcastle, the only two roads out of Peshawar meet. The Khyber Agency Road dead-ends into the Torkham Road, which then passes right by our black site on the way to the Afghani border. If you are right, if the Pakistani Taliban are involved, they will pass through that junction. I'll hook you up with a radio and you can let us know if you spot trouble."

"Roger that."

Kolt took a radio offered by one of Hammond's men. Then he headed for the stairs down to the garage.

"Wait a second, Racer. We have a few minutes before we need to—"

"I'm not waiting for you guys. I'm taking that gun, that bike, and that bag."

"You can follow us."

But Kolt Raynor was already in the cement-block stairway, heading down toward the garage. He called out as he descended, "I know where I'm going. See you when I see you, Hammond."

FORTY-TWO

Dick Nelson stood on the square roof of the central stockade building at the Sandcastle and looked toward the east. Out over the fortress wall, out past the rocky hills. It was not yet dawn, but he'd been up all night, communicating with Langley and the CIA stations in Islamabad and Kabul, bolstering security here at the fort, meeting with the leadership of the Khyber Rifles in charge of perimeter security.

It had been a long night.

Below him, in the offices run by his seven-man CIA staff, men burned documents in a metal can, erased the hard drives of their laptops, and loaded extra magazines with ammunition.

Nelson and his team of operations officers had been stationed here for months, but they knew today would be their last day at the Sandcastle. Either they would be pulled out before the impending attack came, they would be pulled out after repelling the attack, or their bodies would be pulled out of the rubble after the attack.

Whichever way things worked out, they weren't going to need their files or their computers much longer, so the shredding, the burning, and the erasing went on below him at a fever pitch.

Glenn climbed the ladder up from the ground floor of the stockade, lifted himself out of the hole in the roof, and stepped up behind his boss. "Dick?"

Nelson looked away from the eastern sky, toward his security officer. "What's the latest?"

"I've got one of my guys in each tower. Each is armed with a Stinger. Also in each tower are two Khyber Rifles grenadiers with RPGs, and a guy with an RPK. If the choppers come, we'll take them out at distance. You have my personal guarantee."

Nelson nodded. "I just got a call from Hammond. He and his team are on their way from Pesh. He has reason to believe there might be a ground attack heading for us too. He's in radio contact with an asset positioned at the Torkham–Khyber Agency junction, ready to alert us to any approaching troops."

Glenn said, "We have good cover, we have the high ground, we have eight of us and thirty Khyber Rifles. And we have fair warning. I have to like our chances all around on this one, Dick."

"Don't get cocky."

"Never."

Now Chuck, the SAD communications officer, climbed onto the flat roof. It was a cold morning, but he'd been down in a small sandbagged room surrounded by all his warm electronics. Consequently he wore only a T-shirt. An HK MP5 hung from his chest.

Nelson snapped at him before he could speak. "I want you in body armor, damn it!"

"Yes, sir."

"You heard from Langley?"

"Affirmative. No pullout as of yet, but they want us to be ready to go in case the call comes. They are trying to get authorization from the White House to call in Delta Force, either to help us with security or to help us pull up stakes and get the fuck out of here. Either way, we can expect that decision to take a couple of hours, and the execution of that decision to take a couple more, depending on how ready Delta is to move. In the meantime, we are on our own."

Nelson looked back to the east. "We've been on our own here for a long time, gents. I always knew this day would come. Now it's about to get real."

Delta Force Lieutenant Colonel Joshua Timble stood in his ill-fitting uniform with insignia proclaiming him to be a captain in the 75th Ranger Regiment. The boots were several sizes too big and they looked and smelled like rubber from a salvaged truck tire. His body armor was fake, thick quilted padding that wouldn't stop a projectile from a pellet gun. His helmet was plastic, again too large, and it slid down over his eyes when he looked down to cinch his belt.

He checked his empty rifle. It was a replica, but a

damned fine one. Still, even if he scavenged some ammo, this gun wouldn't do him much good. The firing pin was missing.

Despite what he could see through close scrutiny, Josh knew that he, his three men, David the American, and the thirty or so Chechens he now counted around him all looked just like a platoon of Rangers. He imagined they could all walk together across Fort Benning at night and, from a short distance, not reveal themselves to be anything other than a unit geared up like they were ready to deploy.

Al-Amriki began leading the Chechens through the warehouse, and the Delta men fell in with them. Another group of five Chechens in salwar kameezes walked along behind. These troops held AKs on the captives so they would not try to escape or attack.

Halfway across the floor, T.J. found himself walking right next to the American al Qaeda agent.

"I demand that Skip's body be delivered to U.S. forces."

Al-Amriki did not break stride. "You demand?" He laughed. "Is that some Geneva Convention bullshit? Sorry, I didn't sign it. I'll have a couple of guys dig a hole in the dirt deep enough to keep the dogs from pulling him up, but that's as far as I go, Captain Timble."

T.J. fought to keep his fury in check. He changed the subject. "How do you know my name?"

David smiled as he walked. He fumbled with the ammo pouches on his chest rig, fought with the Velcro straps to keep his rifle sling from getting stuck between them. He said, "After you were captured you were photographed by the Pakistani Taliban for proof of life. These pictures were sent to your government. They also sent these pictures to some of my associates in the West who had access to Defense Department databases. They looked at tens of thousands of photos of American soldiers. You and your men are not listed as missing or dead. I suppose your being lost over the border is an embarrassment to your government. Anyway, my associates had to just keep going through pictures to find out who, exactly, the Taliban had in their custody. Looking at pictures of one infidel after another. They found your military photograph, and matched it to your proof-of-life picture. But once you were identified, once my organization realized you were an officer from an elite unit, we realized that a plan that we already had in the works would be helped nicely by your participation."

T.J. still had no idea where they were going. He could not imagine them piling into trucks and driving into Afghanistan, but he could less imagine any other destination. He said, "You really think we all can just waltz over the border and right up to a coalition base?"

Al-Amriki led T.J. out the back door of the warehouse, into the predawn glow of the morning. The Delta officer's eyes were on his captor as he was waiting for an answer. When none came, he turned his head, followed al-Amriki's gaze into the walled parking lot at the back of the warehouse.

His mouth opened in shock.

Daoud said, "We're not going over the border. And we *definitely* are not going to waltz."

T.J. could not believe his eyes. In front of him, two

American-flagged Black Hawk helicopters stood in the dawn's early light. Their crews were inside, the auxiliary power was on in both birds, and the men, the markings, and the cabin lights all looked authentic to the American Delta operator. Above them canvas tarps attached to high poles provided concealment from the air.

"How the hell—?" He did not finish the sentence. Horror coursed through Timble's veins. This operation was showing itself to be more and more sophisticated by the minute.

T.J. walked forward slowly, his empty rifle hanging from his neck and swaying in front of him. He had perfected the art of getting intelligence from his enemy by asking short, simple, to-the-point questions while maintaining both an air of nonchalance and an attitude of impressed awe at the actions of the enemy. For the past three years his captors and would-be killers had found it hard to ignore his innocent queries.

But right now his awe was real.

Daoud spoke proudly. "We had these trucked up from Karachi. They came on a cargo ship from Saudi Arabia. Given to us by our brothers who have infiltrated the Royal Saudi Army. This truly is a worldwide operation you are going to take part in, Captain Timble. I can't expect you to feel pride, but just know you are very important."

"Great," T.J. muttered softly. Behind him his men filed out of the door, and they too stopped and stared in surprise.

"They were hidden in freight containers, unpacked, and reassembled here in Peshawar. They have been flight-tested by their crews, all Pakistani army, but allied with us."

"You said we aren't going over the border. Where are we going?"

"No. We are going to make a short flight through the Khyber Pass. Five kilometers from the border is a CIA secret prison. I believe the term you and your colleagues use is a black site. We will go there, and we will liberate some friends of mine."

T.J. knew nothing of a CIA prison in Khyber. He had no idea if Daoud was even telling him the truth.

Al-Amriki continued: "You and I will go in the lead helicopter, and your men will follow us in the rear helicopter. Remember, if you try anything, anything at all, I only have to make a call to the other Black Hawk and your men will be thrown out the door, down to the rocks."

Timble bit the inside of his lip. Even in his unfit, unhealthy, and thoroughly weakened state he could snap this bastard's neck. But it wouldn't change a damned thing other than getting himself and his men killed. The operation around them looked well organized and 100 percent ready to go. Josh could only go along for the ride now, and hope like hell he and his men could find a way to prevent it from being carried out.

Daoud al-Amriki lifted his rifle high into the air, then motioned toward the helicopters. "My brothers! Allahu Akbar! It is time!"

Hammond and his team arrived at the Sandcastle just after six thirty in the morning. They were stopped by the Khyber Rifle guards at the old fort's main gate, but a call to Dick Nelson by the alert local forces cleared their way forward. Then they drove up the steep gravel road in the dawn's illumination, pulled through the open gate to the inner compound, and stopped in front of the squat stone building at the center of the huge dirt courtyard.

Dick Nelson met Jeff Hammond with a handshake. "What kind of a dumb-ass sneaks *in*to the Alamo right before the Mexicans attack?"

Hammond smiled ruefully, raised his hand, then turned back around to retrieve his weapon and ammunition from the van. His three men were already out and sliding into their chest harnesses, strapping loaded magazines onto their bodies. "I go where they send me, Dick, same as you. Any chance they are going to pull us out in time?"

Nelson shook his head. "Doesn't look good."

Hammond figured as much. "How do you want us deployed?"

"Your team, me, and three of my guys will man the parapets rimming the roof of the stockade, this building behind me in the center of the compound. The rest of my team is set up with Stingers in the four corner towers. The Khyber Rifles are dispersed equally among the towers as well."

Hammond nodded. He had more military experience than Nelson, but Nelson was in charge, and Hammond could see no better plan.

"And the prisoners?"

"The prisoners are directly below us, two flights

belowground. I have five Khyber Rifles down there, too."

"Got it. The bad guys could come at any time, so we'd better hop to it."

"Roger that."

T.J. sat handcuffed to the bench in the cabin of the Black Hawk. The doors were open and the cold morning air blew across his face. Even crammed together with fifteen other men, it felt free and liberating to be on this ride, after so long in confinement.

He looked down at the earth not more than one hundred feet past his right boot. Below him farmland and dry marshes shot by in the low light of the morning. He could tell they were flying to the northwest by the position of the morning sun, but he did not know exactly where they were headed.

Josh Timble made a decision, turned to David the American, and leaned into his ear to be heard. "Amriki?"

"Yes?"

"Your plan isn't going to work!"

The American al Qaeda operative put a radio headset over T.J.'s ears, then put one on himself. He flipped a switch on the communications console in the back of the chopper, then sat back down next to the American operator.

"Really? That's unfortunate. I guess we will all go home and forget about it. But before I do that, can you please tell me why?"

"Look. If the U.S. was going to send someone to this

black site you mentioned, it wouldn't be Rangers. Rangers don't cross the border on a mission like this. Wouldn't happen. And the U.S. personnel at this place are going to know that. They'll shoot down these two birds before we get within a half mile of the front door."

"Rangers don't cross the border, you say?"

"No."

"*You* crossed the border."

Timble didn't want to reveal any information to an al Qaeda operative, but at this point, talking this asshole out of his suicide mission was the best thing he could do for his men *and* for the Americans at this alleged black site.

"I'm not a Ranger. I was, but I haven't been in a long time. That intel you have on me is old. Almost ten years old, as a matter of fact."

Al-Amriki seemed momentarily confused. He'd been wearing a bit of a smart-ass smirk below his thick goggles, but it slipped away while he thought.

"So, you are saying, you and your men are CIA?"

Timble wasn't going to reveal anything else. "We are *not* Rangers. These uniforms aren't going to fool the Americans at the target location."

Al-Amriki thought about it for a long moment. Timble hoped he was considering ordering that the choppers be turned around.

Instead, he just shrugged, leaned back against the cool metal of the helicopter's wall. "The uniforms do not have to fool the men at the Sandcastle. They just have to fool the rest of the world. I am confident they will do just that."

T.J. did not understand. "But how are you going to get into the site?"

"The men who are going to get us into the black site are already *at* the black site."

"Locals?"

"Part of the guard force."

"Why would they let you in?"

"Because they know that their martyrdom will be rewarded in paradise."

Josh Timble looked into the eyes of the American traitor. He knew the man was telling the truth, and he understood now. "You've infiltrated jihadists into the black site?"

"They were already at the black site before they became jihadists. We have taught them the way of the Koran, and we have convinced them that their help will free their people from the poisoning influence of the infidel."

David the American smiled. He was so proud of himself. So smug. T.J. wanted to throw him out of the helicopter, but his handcuffs made this fantasy impossible.

Instead, he just looked back outside at the early dawn while brown hills undulated below him.

Kolt stood in the cold morning, rubbed his arms for warmth, did his best to avoid touching the deep wound to his right forearm. He'd placed his rifle on the ground so he could rub with both hands, and he stomped his feet. Even though he was standing and moving, he was careful to conceal himself from the road junction by the copper-hued boulders around him that glowed in the morning sun. He'd walked the motorbike down in a shallow gully behind him so that its metal did not glint from the rays and give away his position.

But so far, he'd seen not a thing to worry about.

He watched the smattering of traffic fifty yards in front of his hide. Donkeys pulled carts, the occasional jingle bus or merchant truck headed to Torkham or the border. This part of the Khyber Pass was subject to attacks by highway robbers or ambushes by Taliban looking to torch fuel trucks heading from Islamabad to Afghanistan.

But for now, for this morning anyway, Kolt had not seen a damned thing.

He shivered, then glanced back over his left shoulder at the squat fort in the distance, perhaps a mile and a half away. Its walls were the same color as the rocks around it and the hills behind, so it was nearly invisible from the valley floor, although, with its high perch, anyone in the towers of the Sandcastle could see the road below. He knew Agency men were positioned on the roof of the building at the center of the fort.

Kolt stopped stamping his feet.

A low sound, more a perceived vibration than actual noise. He looked at the two roads ahead of him for a clue as to its origin, but only a small white taxi and a pair of donkey carts were in sight. On the far side of the hill, in the town of Landi Kotal, he could hear more engine noise and honking horns, but this low tone was different.

Distinct.

The noise grew slowly, changed from a hum to a soft but steady beat. He continued scanning the vista in front of him, stopped doing so only to kneel down and grab the Kalashnikov.

The thumping grew, began to echo off the walls of the valley, and Raynor knew that sound well. He looked a little longer, toward the rising morning sun, and then he saw them.

A pair of Black Hawks, silhouetted against the orange dawn, moving low and fast.

In seconds they passed by, a hundred yards off his left, streaking directly toward the Sandcastle, and Raynor depressed the button on his walkie-talkie. As he made the call he looked back at the road, scanned the distance for any sign of a follow-on attack from the ground.

"Hammond, birds are inbound, say again, birds are inbound. Approaching from the south—"

A new sound, also low and deep, echoed through the valley in the wake of the passing choppers. It was an explosion. At first he thought a Black Hawk had crashed, but they were still in the air.

But beyond them, at the Sandcastle, a plume of black smoke rose from the building in the center of the compound.

Then another low thump and one of the four towers turned to smoke and dust.

While Kolt Raynor watched, yet another brief flash of fire and black smoke appeared from a tower on the other side of the fort. Seconds later he heard the passing boom of this explosion as well.

"Oh my God," he whispered.

FORTY-THREE

Dick Nelson lay on his back on the roof of the stockade. He'd heard the approaching choppers and run to look out between the battlements on the roof, but a noise behind him, close, had turned his head. One of the Khyber Rifles had appeared on the roof, out of the ladder hole, and shouted, "Allahu Akbar!"

One of Nelson's men dove toward the Pakistani, managed to all but envelop the small man in the salwar kameez just as an explosion turned them both to pink mist.

While Nelson tried to recover his senses the tower on the southeast wall of the compound blew apart, fire and rock and smoke and debris blasting into the air. Before he'd even wiped the blood from his eyes from the first blast he was pelted with debris from the second.

He made his way slowly to his feet to look over the

parapet to seek the origin of the attack, when the tower on the southwest corner exploded in exactly the same fashion. He fell back onto the roof of the stockade, one of Hammond's men fell on top of him, dead, and while he was held down by the other man's body the other two towers exploded, shrapnel flew in all directions above him, and small rocks and burning splinters rained down on his position once more.

Just like that his rooftop citadel and his four antiaircraft positions were down. The enemy helos had not even arrived and already suicide bombers had decimated his defenses and killed most of his men.

Through a ringing in his ears he heard the thumping of the Black Hawks; they appeared overhead a few seconds later. Dick Nelson freed himself, grabbed his M-4 and rolled onto his knees, and now he saw that both birds were flying with their doors open. Men in Ranger uniforms were strapped into the sides of the open craft, and their weapons were raised, and in seconds the roof around Nelson began to pock and shatter with incoming rifle fire from above.

"Everybody off the roof!" he screamed to anyone still alive. He ran to the wooden ladder that led down into the stockade, and he pushed two of his men in front of him. He turned to open fire on the closest Black Hawk, but found it turning away after its strafing run. He then swung his rifle around to the other helicopter, but before he could even line up his weapon's sights on his target he was shot by an automatic rifle. The first couple of rounds clanged off his body armor, but rounds three and four tore through his throat. His body jerked and dropped back off the side of the roof, cartwheeled once before hitting the hard earth of the courtyard.

Raynor gunned the Suzuki out of the gulley, going airborne before crashing down hard on the dirt bike's forgiving suspension. His AK hung from his back, his extra rifle mags were strapped tight to his chest, and though he wanted to get to the black site as fast as possible, he came off the throttle a bit so that he would not lose control on the gravel hillside.

In twenty seconds he was on the Torkham Road, jacking the bike back to the west, gunning the engine now for all he could pull from it. He knew there could still be a ground attack from Taliban forces, but the men at the Sandcastle did not have the luxury of allowing Kolt to hang back to deal with the second wave of threats. They were deep in the shit right now.

For the first kilometer of his race toward the battle on the hillside in front of him he really did not have any plan other than to drive right to the black site and engage whatever targets he could find. But during his ride he had time to think and refine his plan, and just before he arrived at the long gravel road up toward the fort he left the highway and turned in the opposite direction, to the south. He shot up another hillside, tried to get the bike to take him as high as possible before he leaped off it and continued on foot. The helos thumped behind him, the soft crackle of small-arms fire carried to him, but still he trudged up the steep incline, finally tucking behind a large boulder and turning toward the fort on the opposite wall of the valley. This would be a challenging distance for accurate fire from a Kalashnikov, five hundred yards easily. But he thought he could dump rounds into the Black Hawks, maybe get lucky and damage one of the birds or take out one of the pilots. He even hoped they would see his muzzle flashes and attack him, over here, giving Hammond and the others time to regroup and reposition.

Kolt wondered if T.J. and his men would be on board one of the choppers he fired at. He hoped not, but nevertheless, he knew what he had to do.

But by the time he got high enough on the hill, turned back around, and lined his weapon up on the Sandcastle, the Black Hawks had landed in the courtyard on the other side of the wall.

"Shit!" Kolt screamed into the cold morning. "Shit!"

He began sliding back down the rocky hillside, skidding and stumbling down toward his dirt bike.

Pam Archer's arrival over the Khyber Pass had been delayed by the CIA. They had their own Reaper drones taking off at Jalalabad to head into the area, so she had to wait to get clearance to use the runway. At the last minute the two Reapers were ordered back to the hangar, some change ordered to their munitions load from on high, so the Radiance drone flight was approved, and Baby Girl launched into the morning Afghanistan sky and quickly streaked over the border into Pakistan.

Grauer wished he could send something more potent than an unmanned aerial vehicle toward the target, but at this point, that was all he had at his disposal. He had learned all about the Sandcastle during his call with Racer a few hours earlier. Then, just forty-five minutes ago, he'd got a call from Langley, and Langley had laid it all out to him. The black site, the impending hit, etc., etc. He pretended like this was all news to him, but they didn't seem to care what he already knew or how. They had bigger fish to fry now. They were worried. No, they were scared shitless, and they solicited Pete Grauer's help.

Grauer had to suspend disbelief. He found it incredible that this secret interrogation facility had been operating just five klicks from the border for years. He figured the few up on the seventh floor, the top brass who had been read in on the Sandcastle project, must have protected that information like the Holy Grail. But a chain is only as strong as its weakest link, and the weakest link of the Sandcastle had been, apparently, the leader of the Khyber Rifles who gave up the goods to al Qaeda and then split with a fat cash withdrawal from the Quetta slush fund.

Now it was all about damage control. Radiance would fly over the site while the Reapers got armed up. The CIA men at the black site and their loyal guard force would just have to hold back the attack.

And then there was Racer. In all the chaos and confusion of the past few hours Grauer had forgotten to ask him where he would be when the attack came.

No matter. Raynor had done his job. It had been a costly job, true, but they would not have been in a position to thwart the attack if not for the work of Kolt Raynor and Bob Kopelman.

The speaker in the Operations Center came to life with the voice of Pam Archer. "I'm on station, sir."

"Good," Grauer replied, and the room mikes picked up his voice and sent it on to her headset in Baby Girl's trailer. He and his team of analysts turned to the large monitor, watched the image pan slowly in an arc, showing miles and miles of winding brown highway intersecting brown rock-strewn hillside.

The pan stopped suddenly on black smoke rising into the sky. Quickly the camera zoomed in on a low-walled stone fort, where the smoke poured from the four distinct corners of the outer wall. Centered between the billowing columns was a large single-story building with its own fire burning on the roof. Untouched outbuildings dotted the large courtyard in front of it.

The camera zoomed again.

Bodies on the roof. Bodies on the ground in the courtyard. Two Black Hawk helicopters with rotors spinning. Men in U.S. military uniforms moved in teams toward the central building. Gray smoke poured from their rifles as they fired at targets in the dark windows.

"We're too late," Grauer said. "Those are enemy fighters in the open."

"Are there any friendlies at all alive in the courtyard?" someone asked, but no one knew the answer.

Grauer said to Pam, and to the room, "Our feed is going directly to Langley. They are seeing this at the same time we are."

The mobile phone on Pete Grauer's hip rang. He retrieved it distractedly, flashed his eyes down from the monitor to look at the caller ID.

It was Pam.

"Why are you calling me on my mobile?"

"Pete. We need to arm Baby Boy. He has two pylons for Hellfires. I can bring Baby Girl home and then launch Baby—"

"Do you have any Hellfires lying around that I don't know about? Under your bunk maybe?"

"No, sir. But you can talk to Langley. This is a special circumstance."

"Their Reapers will be on their way soon, and they will have air-to-ground munitions."

"We don't even know if they will be cleared to fire. We don't know if Delta will be coming over to rescue our personnel."

"No, Pam, we *don't.* Just keep monitoring the feed."

"But—"

Grauer terminated the call.

T.J. was not particularly impressed with the Pakistani Black Hawk pilots. Gunfire popped and cracked over at the stockade, there were pockets of surviving defenders around the perimeter, and the two choppers landed right in the courtyard, not twenty-five yards from the battle.

But T.J. *was* impressed with the twenty-five Chechens. As soon as the birds landed, the al Qaeda fighters dispersed, headed in small units to take over all the outbuildings while providing covering fire into the stockade.

They were organized, well trained, and seemingly fearless.

As if he could read minds, Daoud al-Amriki spoke into his headset. "Every one of these men has been handpicked. They all have combat experience, either against the Russians in Chechnya and Dagestan, or against coalition forces in Iraq or Afghanistan. These are true fighters, brave warriors."

T.J. did not answer, but he watched their movements and noted the leaders of their unit, and he could tell these men were excellent soldiers. He could also tell they were bloodthirsty. A pair of Khyber Rifles were taken alive at the front gate. While T.J. watched from the seat of the Black Hawk he saw the young Pakistanis kicked to the ground and then riddled with rifle fire at point-blank range. Another injured sentry tried to surrender, raising his bloody hands while leaning against the front bumper of the minivan. He was gunned down where he stood.

The first team of Chechens entered the front door of the stockade in a tactical train. T.J. heard an incredible amount of fire inside the building, and he tried to picture the scene. The American operators here at this black site would be outnumbered, but they would have the best defensive position inside the prison walls.

An explosion blew flame and debris out the open windows. The gunfire stopped, and then a pair of Chechens in Ranger uniforms appeared in the doorway, wobbled slowly back outside on teetering legs. The second man was on fire; his backpack and his left arm were totally engulfed in flames, though he seemed unaware of this fact. Both men were dazed from the blast. They just stood out in the open as another team of five men rushed past them into the smoking entrance to the stockade.

The burning man was knocked to the ground by a pair of his comrades, and he was dragged away from the entrance and rolled around in the dirt to extinguish the flames. The other man who had staggered out after the blast pitched forward into the gravel of the driveway. T.J. could not tell if he was dead or not, but no one came to him to render aid.

The second team of assaulters on the stockade fared better than the first. After a full minute of constant gunfire, the pace and intensity of the firing slowed. Another five-man team was called through the door, and then another.

Al-Amriki spoke into a radio on his shoulder, and seconds later the al Qaeda operative T.J. knew as the Turk appeared in the open door of the Black Hawk. He alone was not dressed as a Ranger. He wore the black salwar kameez uniform of an Arab fighter, and he wore a pistol on his belt, but in his arms he carried only an expensive-looking video camera. He wasn't filming at the moment; instead, he just tucked low as gunfire crackled in the stockade, kept up a conversation for a few minutes in the American al Qaeda operative's ear.

T.J. could not hear a word over the spinning rotors, but soon the gunfire died out completely, and the engines on the two Black Hawks were shut down.

Then T.J. heard the tail end of the conversation in Arabic.

The Turk said, "No more than ten minutes, you understand!"

Al-Amriki replied, "Ten or fifteen, yes." David the American leaped from the helicopter just as the first of the surviving Americans were dragged out of the front door of the stockade.

Kolt made it to his second overlook after ten minutes of scrambling down one hill, racing across the road on the Suzuki, and then dumping the bike and climbing up the hillside just to the west of the black site. The fight had raged for most of this time. But it had since quieted down; even the destroyed towers around the Sandcastle's perimeter had all but stopped disgorging their black smoke into the air.

When he found his new hide, he took just a few seconds to rest, to control his heavy breathing, to allow the sore and strained muscles in his legs and back to replenish their stores of oxygen. Then he looked out across the hillside, one hundred yards away, down into the fort.

He had neither binoculars nor a scope on his rifle, so he used his naked eyes. He could see the Black Hawks—their blades no longer turned. Beyond them was a group of men in Ranger uniforms. These would be the Chechens. Kolt hefted his Kalashnikov, propped the magazine on a rock to steady the weapon, and looked down the iron sights.

He lifted his head.

Where were T.J. and his men? He did not know for sure if they were part of the operation, but he had a feeling they were down there right now, somewhere in the fortress. Kolt did not want to just pepper the Chechens and the choppers with AK rounds and risk taking his old mates out accidentally. Plus, there were likely still Agency men there, either hiding or being held prisoner by the al Qaeda guys.

Kolt squinted. Among the Ranger uniforms he saw one man dressed in black. It was hard to be sure, but he thought the guy held a video camera in his hands.

"What the hell?"

Below him, on his right, commercial traffic passed on the Torkham Road, completely unaware of the danger two hundred yards above.

Kolt knew what he had to do. He *had* to get closer. AQ would set up a perimeter in seconds if they were any good, so he leaped back up on his exhausted legs and started toward the Sandcastle, the western wall covering the enemy's view of his advance.

T.J.'s cuffs had been unfastened and he was led out of the helicopter at gunpoint by one of the Chechen Rangers. He was then reunited with his three colleagues. Troy Kilborn had taken a grazing round to his right hip when the chopper in which he was riding took fire from the CIA men on the roof. He was in pain, and his pants leg was bloody, but he was able to stand.

The four Americans stood together in the dirt, twenty-five yards from the front door of the stockade. Three Chechens guarded them, their weapons pointed directly at the Americans' chests.

From the stockade a man appeared. He was an Arab,

dressed in a white jumpsuit, and he squinted into the sun, shielding his eyes with his hand as he stepped out. He was followed by another man, and then another. Soon a line of Arabs staggered out and stood in the courtyard. They were confused. More like bewildered, but the Chechens who spoke Arabic comforted them, and the Turk aggressively hugged two of the older Arab men in the group.

While this was going on the surviving CIA men were led out under guard and ordered onto the dirt near the shot-up minivan in front of the stockade. All of the Americans were wounded, some gravely.

FORTY-FOUR

Jeff Hammond had taken an AK round in his right forearm and another in his right thigh. He had tried to stanch the heavy bleeding while still two levels down, fighting it out with the al Qaeda attackers. But a flash-bang grenade had so disoriented him that he did not even remember being led up the stairs, pushed out of the building, and dumped down here in the dirt.

He looked around him. Glenn, Nelson's communications man, was still alive. Hammond had yelled at him to put on body armor just before the battle had begun, but apparently he'd never gotten around to it. It looked like Glenn had taken a rifle butt to the face—his nose was clearly broken—but he was sitting up next to Hammond. Next to him was one of Hammond's men. Tyrone. He was unconscious, and bleeding from multiple wounds.

Hammond looked away from his man, up at the sky.

Wished he saw a flight of Chinooks coming out of the blue, laden down with Delta Force assaulters.

But the sky was clear.

"You guys American?"

Hammond turned his head. Twenty feet from him he saw four men in the same phony Ranger gear, but these guys were covered by three tangos with M-4 rifles.

The CIA officer knew exactly who they were. "Yeah. You are the JSOC boys?"

"Yes," said one of the men. "I'm T.J."

Hammond knew he was the missing lieutenant colonel, Joshua Timble. "Thought there were five of you left?" he asked.

"There were."

"Any idea what their plan is?" asked Hammond. He watched the Arab prisoners file out of the stockade. The Chechens led them around the side of the building, positioned them near the wall of the stockade, and began handing them canteens of water, hugging them, and motioning for them to wait right where they were.

T.J. shook his head, then did a quick head count of the al Qaeda forces. He counted al-Amriki and the Turk, and eighteen Chechens. Apparently they'd lost seven men in the attack. There were sixteen prisoners here at the site, all of whom were now standing together by the wall of the stockade.

"No way they can fly out with all these guys," Timble said.

"I was thinking the same thing." Hammond rolled up onto his left elbow, wincing with the pain in his leg. He then made to check on the other two men, but a

Chechen appeared over him and kicked him back onto his back.

The Turk shouted a command and six of the Chechens pulled RPGs from the rear Black Hawk, then ran off in different directions. One man in each tower, and two at the front gate. T.J. assumed it was an attempt at a thin perimeter security. More of a trip-wire setup than an actual guard force. Then one of the men guarding him and his men grabbed T.J. by his fake body armor and pulled him away from the others and closer to the prisoners.

T.J. noticed that four Arab men in prisoner jumpsuits, two older and two younger, had been led to the rear helicopter. These, he determined, were AQ. The remaining prisoners, twelve members of the Afghanistan Taliban, stayed near the wall of the stockade, eagerly drinking water and trying to communicate with the Chechens. Some dropped to pray; others smiled or even laughed.

Al-Amriki was on his walkie-talkie, over by the Black Hawks. He finished his transmission moments later and returned to Timble's side. Together the two men silently looked at the prisoners.

Soon the Turk began filming the scene.

T.J. was beginning to get a bad feeling about where this was all going.

Without warning, Daoud addressed the Taliban arrayed in front of him. Surprisingly, to T.J. anyway, he did so in English. Josh thought it highly unlikely the majority of these men would speak English.

"Gentlemen. We have kept you here, in some circumstances, for years. We, the American government, the Pakistani government, the Pakistani Frontier Corps, and the government of Afghanistan, have all been involved in your capture, your imprisonment, and your torture. Some of your brothers have died here due to this torture."

"What the hell is goin' on, boss?" asked Roscoe, twenty-five feet away. A rifle butt slammed into the back of his head, and Roscoe went down. Timble started to move to help his teammate, but an armed Chechen behind him got in his way, led him back to his place with his rifle. The Turk stepped close to Timble now, panned slowly across his face with the camera, and captured the Black Hawk helicopters squat and still in the courtyard. The other three Delta men were filmed from the shoulders up, just a quick pan, and then the Turk turned around and centered on al-Amriki, who had restarted his speech. The Turk filmed al-Amriki from the back, capturing both his Ranger uniform and the crowd of Taliban prisoners in front of the baked mud wall.

"We will be closing this prison here in the Federally Administered Tribal Areas. Your Taliban brothers have grown too strong for us to hold you here any longer, so we must return to Afghanistan."

Timble noticed the Turkish cameraman had started panning along a neat row of Chechen "Rangers" standing at parade rest in front of the two Black Hawks.

"Unfortunately, men, we cannot take you with us. I have been ordered by the White House, the Pentagon, and the CIA to execute you immediately."

T.J. muttered, "Oh my God."

Al-Amriki stepped back quickly, and the Chechen Rangers stepped forward in their line, raised their weapons at the Taliban. Those who had understood the English were no clearer on what was happening than those who did not.

But Josh understood. He raised his arms and started to shout. The Chechens rushed past him to close the distance.

The Chechen near the Delta team raised his rifle to his shoulder and covered all three operators. Another man placed a rifle barrel to T.J.'s neck.

The camera missed all of this. It was, instead, focused on al-Amriki's back, and on the Chechens on either side of him.

Daoud al-Amriki raised a gloved hand high in the air, brought it down as he shouted, "Fire!"

At a distance of no more than twenty feet, ten Chechens opened up on the stunned Taliban: their counterfeit M-4 rifles barked and snapped, supersonic rounds cracked through the air and burrowed into their targets. The dozen Taliban HVTs began bucking and spinning and falling, their empty hands raised in surrender even as blood shot from their chests and heads and the baked mud wall behind them exploded into dust and shone with crimson splatter.

Every single one of the ten Chechens in the firing squad emptied his weapon into the men. Three hundred rounds, fired from short distance, into the tight mass of a dozen humans, left nothing alive downrange.

A dozen dead bodies, as torn as their torn jumpsuits, red with spilled blood and scattered flesh.

And the Turk recorded it all.

Timble understood. Propaganda. Al Qaeda rescued its four men, yes, but that was probably not even the primary objective here. No . . . this entire operation was to create a film, documentary evidence of America's imprisoning, torturing, and then massacring Afghani Taliban.

And Josh Timble himself was the proof. His face, his name, his career before becoming a black operator with the Unit, this all created the final piece of the puzzle. Without him it could all be just a clever ruse. The choppers and the soldiers and the uniforms and the guns and even the guy speaking flawless English. The Arab world would convict America for much much less, but America could always say it was nothing but an opportunistic and cynical disinformation operation on the part of the enemy. Some of its allies would believe it.

But Captain Josh Timble? An Army Ranger the Pentagon had "erased" when he became a Delta operator? How the hell could the Americans come out now and say, "Oh yes, about Timble. He was captured by the enemy years ago. We just didn't think to mention it."

America had some strong allies in the world, but no relationship was tight enough to believe that transparent lie.

No matter that the transparent lie was the truth.

America's secret prison, in cahoots with the Afghani and Pakistani governments, where the Taliban heavyweights had been tortured for years, and where they were finally executed.

On camera.

Christ almighty.

This would derail any peace in Afghanistan; this would eradicate any working relationship whatsoever between the Pakistani government and the U.S. government. Hell, this could bring thousands, no, tens of thousands of new foot soldiers from around the world into the folds of the jihadists.

Protests and terrorism at every symbol of America in every nation in the Eastern Hemisphere.

America would lose its stomach for this debacle, and America would go home.

The Tet Offensive? No, this would be worse.

The sounds of the gunfire had died out, replaced by the sound of the slowest of the Chechens still reloading their rifles with fresh and full magazines.

Roscoe, Bouncer, and Spike understood, too. They were part of this ruse, part of this setup, the ramifications of which were now becoming clear.

"Holy shit, boss," said Bouncer. "This was the plan all along."

T.J. heard his teammate through the ringing in his ears. He just nodded, looking at the pile of dead men in prison jumpsuits.

Daoud al-Amriki turned toward Timble. He nodded. Proud of himself. "And that's a wrap."

"So you execute your Taliban allies?"

Al-Amriki just shrugged. "Afghani Taliban. Their colleagues are planning on suing America for peace.

These men's deaths are insignificant in comparison to the big picture. This will kill the peace jurga next January. It will reveal the Americans and the Pakistani government to be torturing and murdering Taliban dignitaries, and it will push America out of Pakistan at least, and with some luck, it will push America out of Afghanistan as well."

Obviously he was an architect of this plan, but T.J. suspected that the politics of it were determined by the very top leadership of al Qaeda. Daoud continued: "We fully expect this to weaken the government in Islamabad and to push our allies into power. If and when that happens, we will have access to the nuclear weapons that Pakistan possesses." Al-Amriki could not stop smiling. He looked like a proud young American soldier who'd just taken part in a successful battle.

Josh Timble nodded, sighed, and then launched himself at his fellow countryman with the strength of pure hatred.

Raynor made his way slowly and stealthily through the ruins of the low tower on the Sandcastle's wall. He banged his wounded forearm several times climbing over the broken rocks to make his way into a small blast hole, and then he picked his way forward in the darkness and lingering dust and smoke, finally making it to a staircase that led up to the tower's roof.

Gunfire crackled over at the stockade. It was heavy and protracted. It sounded like a full mag dump by a dozen or so shooters.

It sounded like a firing squad.

Kolt used the noise to rush to the roof. There, at the top, he saw him: a single Chechen standing on the roof. He had looked back to catch a glimpse of the action over by the Black Hawks.

Raynor rose behind him, reached around his body, and grabbed his jaw. Yanked it violently to the right while jacking the man's body harshly to the left. The torsion of the contradictory movements snapped his neck.

The Chechen dropped straight down on the broken stone roof. Kolt followed him, lowering his body between the parapets. He crawled forward, brought his rifle to his shoulder, and looked at the scene.

The two Black Hawks began spooling up.

"What did I miss?" he whispered to himself.

It took two Chechens and their rifle butts ten seconds to get the American prisoner off of al-Amriki. As soon as T.J. leaped on the unsuspecting Daoud, all three of the Delta men closer to the Black Hawks launched on their guards, and the one CIA man in the dirt who was ambulatory scrambled to his feet and charged a Chechen with a rifle.

The CIA man was shot with a three-round burst at point blank range. He flew backward and landed on Jeff Hammond, who could only try to hold pressure on the entry wounds. The three Delta prisoners were beaten down severely. All of them were left facedown in the dirt and gravel, bleeding from their heads and arms and backs.

T.J. was hurt as well, but he was in better shape than

David the American. Daoud had taken a fist to his nose, which gushed blood like a faucet, and his eyes watered and blackened. He'd also been knocked to the ground and kicked and kneed in the groin, and he found it impossible to catch his breath, much less give any orders for thirty seconds. When he did recover, when he finally pulled himself back up to his feet by using his counterfeit M-4 rifle as a crutch, when he did find himself able to suck in enough air to speak loudly enough to be heard by the men around him, he barked a command in Arabic.

"Line them up and kill them all!"

T.J.'s helmet was knocked from his head, and he was dragged by two men over to the pile of Taliban bodies in front of the wall and dropped on top of them.

He turned and saw his three teammates being kicked forward. A Chechen fired a short burst next to Bouncer to get him to his feet and moving, and soon they were shoved down on the dead pile as well. There were only two CIA men remaining, and the unconscious man was shot in the head where he lay. His forehead exploded and tissue splattered on Hammond, who scrambled to his feet and limped slowly over to the rest of his countrymen so that he could share his fate with them.

The five wounded Americans lay in front of the dead bodies, looked with blurred vision through their bruised eyelids at the American traitor who had just ordered their execution. The Turk was at the man's side, encouraging him to hurry up. The chopper blades spun. The AQ men in the rear helo looked on. Dust sandblasted T.J.'s eyes.

Al-Amriki wiped a half cup of blood from his nose and face. “I said kill these infidels!”

A group of Chechens moved forward quickly and raised their rifles.

Kolt Raynor was too far away to see all the action taking place on the other side of the Black Hawks, but he knew he had to do something when he saw the Chechens in view run over toward the wall of the stockade. They moved with purpose—he could tell they were responding to an order, and he saw them raise their rifles as they hustled.

Kolt worried about hitting his own men, killing T.J. and his team, but at this point, he did not see that he had much choice.

“Fuck it.” He sighted on the rear chopper because most of the action was taking place forward of the bird.

He flipped the AK to the fully automatic setting.

And with no real objective other than to send as many al Qaeda men to cover as possible, he put pressure on the trigger.

T.J. reached over and took Tony Marquez’s hand and shook it weakly. He was the closest man to where he lay. “See you around, Bouncer. It’s been an honor serving with—”

Just then came the *snap, snap, snap* of incoming rounds, and the corresponding crack of gunfire from the west. The Chechen guards ducked or dove to the dirt, and the firing squad turned as one toward the threat.

The Turk and al-Amriki cowered low behind the

front Black Hawk. Daoud then ran toward the corner of the stockade and made his way around for cover.

In three seconds Timble had gone from hopelessness to hope. He sat up on the bodies of the dead Taliban and shouted to the Americans around him:

"Everybody in the building!"

FORTY-FIVE

Raynor had emptied his Kalashnikov, but he did not want to let up on his one-man assault for the amount of time it would take to reload it. Instead, he lifted the RPG dropped by the dead Chechen sentry and pointed it at the rear helicopter. He took less than a second to aim—he was more interested in making noise than in hitting his target. He just wanted to create as big a distraction as possible for as long as possible to help any surviving Americans.

Kolt launched the finned grenade, and a black smoke trail streaked away from him and shot toward the Black Hawk. The grenade nailed it just aft of center. The big helicopter shuddered and filled with fire and black smoke. The burning black fuel was caught up in the swirling rotors and shot out in all directions, clouding the entire scene.

Raynor dropped to a knee to reload his AK, but just

then an incoming RPG, fired from one of the other towers, hit the stone wall just below his position. The explosion knocked him off his feet, and he slammed his forehead on the parapet as he fell. He rolled over onto his back, slow to recover from the concussion, and looked up into the air.

His ears rang.

Move! Move! he told himself. He needed to keep up the fire, no matter what. On his back still, he reached a weak hand out, searching for his rifle. It took him a moment, but soon he realized it had fallen over the side of the tower when the RPG hit.

Kolt Raynor was unarmed.

Bits of the parapet a foot above his body cracked and exploded as Kalashnikov fire came from multiple directions.

He stared at the blue sky. He did not think he could get up, did not think he could do anything more for T.J. and his men.

He closed his eyes. He thought it was over.

His ears rang still.

Boom! Another RPG hit his tower. Debris rained down on him. He covered his face with his arms to protect himself, though it hardly mattered.

He knew he would be dead as soon as the Chechens came up the stairs.

Then his eyes opened and his arms lowered to his sides.

His head cocked.

A faint noise overcame the ringing in his ears. A buzzing sound, like an angry bumblebee. On his back

Kolt turned his head from side to side, looking around, as the buzzing grew louder and louder.

The stone tower began to vibrate. Broken bits of rocks shook next to him.

Then, just ten feet or so from the tip of his nose, an MH-6M Little Bird helicopter raced overhead. Kolt could see the ankle-high hiking boots of the men strapped to its two outboard benches, and the untucked MultiCam camo pants whipping in the wind.

There was one unit in the U.S. military whose men wore hiking boots and didn't tuck their pants into them.

Fucking Delta!

Hell yes!

Another Little Bird shot by, just off to his left. Then the ringing in his ears was completely supplanted by the sounds of more propellers, larger machines, the reverberations like jackhammers tearing up the rocky hillsides in all directions.

Kolt Raynor did not move. He was disoriented, but he'd been in the Unit long enough to know that during a Delta hit the last thing you wanted to do was pop your head up and look around, *especially* in a damned guard tower.

Instead, he just lay there, not moving a muscle, and watched the sky. Soon a Black Hawk helicopter chugged overhead. Kolt wanted to stand up and cheer, but he knew better, so he kept still.

As T.J. got the men moving around the corner toward the entrance to the stockade, the rear enemy Black Hawk exploded in smoke and fire. T.J. knew that the al Qaeda prisoners had been in there, and he hoped like hell they'd gone up in the black smoke that obscured the entire area now with the prop wash.

And then, just after he dove through the entrance to the stockade, Timble heard the wheezing sound of the six-bladed propellers of Little Birds. He looked over his shoulder and saw four choppers banking in a tight arc over the highway to the south. Instantly he knew the Unit had come.

It was dark in the stockade. The first room they came to had been blackened with explosives. A pair of Kalashnikovs lay in the shambles of burned and torn furniture. T.J. grabbed a weapon and gave the other to Kilborn, as he was the least injured.

And now, inside the stockade and appreciating the cover it provided, he also knew the Chechens would quickly realize that this baked-mud-and-stone building would be a good refuge for them, too.

"Down the stairs!" he shouted. "We are holding this stairwell!" Kilborn, Marquez, and Haynes shouted their assent. Hammond was helped along by Haynes—the older CIA officer was badly hurt and losing blood.

Together the five Americans headed down the darkened staircase.

When the sky above him cleared, Kolt Raynor, very slowly and very carefully, slid across the gallery of the tower to the stairs that led back down to ground level, and sat on a stone step. The ringing in his ears subsided, and he remembered the radio that Hammond had given him. He doubted Hammond was still alive, but he retrieved it from his vest and depressed the button.

"Hammond, this is Racer. Are you receiving?"

There was a long pause, then a crackle and a response, but it wasn't Hammond's voice.

"Racer? It's T.J. I'm with Hammond in the main building, break. He's injured. I've got three more with me, one is injured. Where the hell are you? Over."

Kolt breathed a sigh of relief. "I can't believe you are still around, dude."

T.J. was all business. "We are on the cell floor of the stockade, covering up the stairwell. There are Chechens above us on both floors. Suggest you guys come flashbang the hell out of that front room and assault simultaneously from the two windows."

"T.J., I'm not part of the hit. I'm kind of off to the side on this. I'm at the southwest tower. I blew up the rear chopper, then the boys came in overhead."

Another slight pause. "Dude, if you blew up the rear chopper, then you just saved our asses and smoked four senior AQ who were ten seconds from freedom. Best you keep your head down till the boys get things cleared up. Don't do anything stupid. Just sight tight."

"You, too, brother."

"Listen, do you guys know about al-Amriki?"

"Al *who*?"

"Shit. Okay, there is an AQ senior operator running this show. He is—"

Gunfire on T.J.'s side of the call interrupted the conversation. Kolt heard the radio go dead as his friend took his hand off the transmit button to return fire.

"T.J.? T.J.?"

FORTY-SIX

The Delta assault was led by Master Sergeant David "Monk" Kraus. He, Colonel Webber, Benji, and others had been studying the satellite photos of the compound for the past three hours, even when it seemed highly unlikely they'd get the go-ahead for the cross-border incursion. Webber knew time would be critical if the call came, so he had the attack force kit up, load into ten helicopters, and head off into the darkness.

The four Little Birds flew to a covert forward refueling point set up just over the border in Afghanistan, not eight miles from the black site. The sixteen assaulters who would fly on the external pods of the Little Birds arrived shortly thereafter, flown to the refueling point in an MH-47J Chinook Dark Horse along with a massive fuel bladder for the choppers. Once the Little Birds gassed up, the assaulters strapped themselves into their outboard positions, and waited. Sixteen more assaulters sat in three MH-60J Black Hawks, waiting on the ground like their mates in the Little Birds.

Webber remained in near-constant contact with Pete Grauer, and he watched the feed from the Radiance UAV that flew over the Sandcastle. CIA Reaper drones were supposedly on the way, but they had been delayed for some inexplicable reason, so Grauer's drone had the only eyes on what was happening. Once Webber saw the live feed of the smoking structures and the assault by the enemy Black Hawks, he radioed Monk at the forward refueling site.

"Monk . . . we're still waiting on word for the hit."

An angry delay. Monk's professional "Yes, sir" was delivered in a clipped tone.

"I'll tell you what," Webber continued. "Nobody said we can't get up in the air, at least. Maybe you guys could head east, straddle the border, be ready to shoot over if we get the call."

Monk liked this order. "Will do, sir."

Forty-five seconds later all nine birds involved in the attack were airborne.

Twenty minutes after this Webber connected with Monk again. The master sergeant's headset broadcast the thumping of the Black Hawk's rotors above him.

"Sir?"

Webber's order was succinct, as there was not a second to waste: "Execute."

Thirty seconds later, a pair of AH-6M Little Birds armed with two 2.75-inch rockets and M-134 7.62 mm miniguns flew into Pakistan, just a couple hundred yards from the Torkham border crossing. The choppers flew below rooftop level—often their skids raced above the N25 highway at no more than four feet off the ground. They shot through the morning traffic of jingle buses, taxis, and private cars and trucks, going around or just above vehicles on their way. They continued hugging the terrain as they left the road and turned up a narrow valley with sheer walls on both sides, streaking through the Khyber Pass at over one hundred miles an hour. The rest of the force crossed the border exactly sixty seconds behind the first helos. They hugged the terrain as well, four Little Birds with four assaulters on each ship, and three Black Hawks with eight men on board each of the first two craft, and only the flight crew on the third. All raced east over Torkham, and over the heads of hundreds of astonished Pakistanis.

The lead pair of Little Bird gunships joined up with the Torkham Road again, followed it for no more than a minute before banking hard to the left, climbing a rocky hill, and "popping up" to one hundred feet above the earth. They appeared simultaneously over the southern wall of the black site just in time to see an explosion at the southwest tower. The pilots turned their attention to the three other towers, where they could see men with RPGs lifting them to fire.

The choppers' noses dropped and they dove at the black site. Rockets poured from their two seven-tube outboard launchers. After a single screaming pass by the gunships, all three occupied towers blazed with fire, and debris rained down around them.

On the second pass the Little Birds switched to miniguns, tearing up anyone who fired on them in the large dirt courtyard of the Sandcastle.

The four small helicopters full of assaulters appeared from the hills to the west now and shot over the compound. The men on the slicks fired their HK416s at targets below and around them.

The assaulters knew their assigned targets—two birds came to a hover low over the stockade, and four men dropped from each, five feet down to the building's roof. The eight men fired through the parapets at enemy near the smoldering UH-60 Black Hawks that were parked in the courtyard.

The other two birds found their landing zones in the courtyard fouled with debris, so they also slowed to a hover at thirty feet. The assaulters reached above them, and each pulled a five-inch silver cotter pin, which released a forty-foot dark green nylon twist fast rope, which dropped to the ground. The men unsnapped their safety lines and slid down the ropes like expert firemen.

Once on the ground the assaulters quickly oriented themselves and sprinted to their designated outbuildings, searching for targets and opening doors at their destinations. The men did not hesitate, they did not confer with one another, they did not stop to find cover.

They were assaulters—they attacked.

The first MH60 Black Hawk landed outside near the main gate. Monk led the way off this helo, his 416 on his shoulder, and he ran forward toward the entrance to the fortress. The second MH60 landed behind the Sandcastle. The third flew above in reserve in case Delta found al Qaeda or Taliban prisoners to evacuate. Both teams of assaulters on the ground offloaded and spread out to secure the areas and to prepare to reinforce the teams inside by blowing the locks off the gates and hitting the courtyard.

Benji led the first Little Bird assault team to hit the stockade. He and the seven men with him tossed flash-bang grenades through the windows and entered the ground floor through these windows.

After the explosions, Benji followed a mate inside. A Chechen in a Ranger uniform had been stunned by the banger—he leaned against the wall, his weapon low and weaving back and forth with his deep breaths.

Benji fired a burst into the man's head, and then another burst into his body after he was down.

They cleared the room counterclockwise, using a technique called "Free Flow Close Quarters Battle on Unknown Floor Plans." The men searched for friendlies, dropped enemies, and made sure every armed Chechen was dead before leaving him behind.

The main room now cleared, Benji's team leapfrogged past him toward the stairwell. At the top of the stairs a Chechen ran away from the Americans. He was shot in the back with an HK416.

The stairwell was tight, so the assault team began heading down single file.

When the courtyard was clear of enemies Monk ordered a pair of assaulters to check each tower for survivors. He then checked on his wounded. He had three injured: two had been slightly hurt when a grenade exploded on the roof of the stockade, and another man had been shot through both legs breaching one of the mud-walled outbuildings. A team medic was already working on him over by the smoldering enemy helicopters.

A pair of young assaulters approached Monk from behind. He hadn't been looking in their direction. "Hey, Monk, this asshole says he knows you."

Monk turned around. He wore his typical game face, but still he cracked a half smile. "I'll be damned. What the fuck you doing here, Racer?"

Kolt was all business. "T.J. is on the cell level with four friendlies. Tell the assaulters."

Monk did not hesitate. He barked the warning into his radio, and Benji transmitted back that he understood.

Monk began heading up to check on the casualties. He said, "You look like shit, Kolt."

Raynor had more intel he was desperate to convey. "Listen, I think you're gonna get hit from the ground."

Monk stopped in his tracks. "More crows coming?" he asked, using the Delta term "crows" to denote enemy forces.

"I . . . I don't know for sure. I figured they'd be here by now. But the Pakistani Taliban were involved in the op, and they haven't shown up yet. They just might be on the way."

Monk looked up at the Black Hawks and the Little Birds circling above. He knew they'd already be monitoring the highway below. Fights like this often turned into "spectator sports," with civilians grabbing guns and running to the battle. But nobody was looking for a planned attack on the Sandcastle. He'd rectify that immediately.

Monk reached for his radio and warned the men circling above. As soon as he ended the transmission another assaulter radioed to him from over by the burned Black Hawks. "Monk, don't know if you want to see this."

"What you got, Sheepdog?"

"I got a dead hajji in black pajamas holding a high-end video camera."

"Is the camera intact?"

"The camera is, but the hajji isn't. Looks like he lost a staring contest with a minigun."

"Secure the camera and I'll come take a look."

Monk wondered if they'd managed to kill a journalist.

FORTY-SEVEN

Daoud al-Amriki had stripped down to his underwear, and now he pulled a pair of jeans and a Banana Republic T-shirt from his backpack. He had made his way through a window in the back of the stockade just as the choppers arrived overhead, and he'd entered the stairwell just as he heard Timble and the other prisoners come through the front door. Now he was in a small dark closet at the end of the hallway on the second level. Timble had passed by the hallway heading down toward the empty cells below, and now the Americans fired up at a group of five surviving Chechens who'd sought refuge on this level. More American soldiers were above on the stairs, firing down on the al Qaeda soldiers. The Chechens were caught in a crossfire, with only this small hallway for cover.

Al-Amriki remained in the closet. He did not go out to fight and die with the doomed Chechens.

He finished changing, then smeared blood from his broken nose all over his face. He hid his rifle and his Ranger uniform under dry goods in the corner of the closet, and he waited for either the Chechens to come down the hall to his position, or the Americans to find him.

Looking across the small closet, he found a breaker for the lights to the building. He pulled it down, and the lights went out. He peeked out into the hallway and saw small emergency lights glow dimly in the stairwell.

As the lights went out Benji ordered two of his team to prepare to toss bangers into the hallway of the second floor. He'd just received word that Eagle 01 was two levels below his position, but between him and them were two levels of Chechens.

"Hit 'em!" Benji ordered, the pins were pulled on the flash-bangs, and the canisters bounced down the stairs. The six Delta men turned away from the blast and noise, actuated their rifles' SureFire flashlights, and then descended hurriedly in a tactical train.

They made it to the first-level basement hallway, exchanging fire as they closed on a group of Chechens. The assaulter in front of Benji lurched back onto his heels and fell to the ground. Benji stepped in front of him and covered him while advancing into the hallway. He moved to the right to get more of his men in with him, and in seconds it was over.

Three Chechens in Ranger uniforms lay facedown in the dark hall. Benji and his men riddled them all with more gunfire, allowing no one to play possum.

Some of the assaulters reloaded while others covered, and then the first group covered while the second got their guns reloaded and back in the fight.

There were two doors at the end of the hall, both closed.

Benji checked his men. Touchdown had been shot several times in his ballistic plate. He lay on his back and struggled to catch his breath, but a medic checking over him wasn't finding any blood.

Benji moved forward through the darkness. "We're going to bang those doors, roger?"

"Roger," came the reply from the three men behind him.

They opened the first door, tossed in a flash-bang, and entered behind the noise and light. One man stayed in the hall to cover the other door.

The room was an empty communications center. Benji and his team exited and approached the other door.

"Don't shoot! Don't shoot!" The voice on the other side of the door was clearly American.

"Come on out, hands high!" Benji shouted. The door opened slowly. A young, clean-shaven American in a T-shirt and jeans, his face streaked with a small amount of blood, stepped out into the dazzling beams of the weapon lights. His eyes blinked with fear.

"Joey Barnes. I'm with the CIA."

Benji nodded to Tomahawk, who stepped forward and grabbed the man by the collar. It was odd that an Agency man would say "I'm with the CIA." It sounded stilted and "Hollywood" to Benji. Normally CIA people would say "Agency" when in the field, if they said anything at all. But Benji had already turned with the rest of his men to head down and clear the next level. The young man behind him had sure as shit been through a lot in the last couple of hours, and he sure as shit would be motivated to get his point across that he wasn't like all the Chechens that Delta were killing around here.

Benji didn't think about it again as he reentered the stairwell with his men.

Tomahawk moved with the CIA operator toward the stairs.

"You hurt?"

"My face, man! It's bad!" Even in the low light Tomahawk didn't think it looked too bad. Maybe a busted nose, tops. Still, he patted the American on the back, then shouted up the stairwell. "Got a wounded friendly, coming up!"

"Roger!" came the reply from the ground-floor room.

Tomahawk pulled the injured American up the darkened stairs, held him by his arm, and led the way with the light on his rifle. At the top of the stairs he handed him off to another man. On the way out the front door of the stockade "Joey Barnes" grabbed a towel from the floor, shook out some bits of stone and broken glass, and then covered his face. He reentered the light of day with all but his eyes covered, and he was led over to a medic set up on the far side of the two burned-out Black Hawks.

The assaulter accompanying him said, "Take a knee here and the medic will check you out. We'll have you over to Bagram in no time, buddy." Then the young Delta man turned away and returned to his mates in the stockade.

Daoud al-Amriki stood there, covering his face with the towel in case any of the CIA men who had seen him before the soldiers appeared were still alive. A few feet in front of him a medic had just finished pushing an IV into the arm of another injured man. Al-Amriki heard the medic talk on his radio, ordering a medevac to land.

"Let me help this helo land, and then I'll take a look, sir," the medic said to al-Amriki.

While the soldier's back was turned, the al Qaeda operator knelt over to the unconscious patient with the IV in his arm, pulled the long combat knife and the tan-colored .40 caliber Glock from his chest rig.

The small helicopter came in for a landing not fifteen yards from the medic in the center of the compound. In the sky above other choppers circled.

The medic turned back around. Said, "Okay. Let me take a look at—"

Daoud al-Amriki rammed the knife into the medic's stomach, just below his body armor.

The man staggered backward, fell back over the other wounded assaulter on the ground.

The Little Bird was, at that moment, landing with its side toward the injured man on the ground. Consequently, neither the pilot nor the copilot witnessed the commotion behind them and to their right. Instead, the copilot jumped out of the left seat and began running around front to help load the casualty. Al-Amriki came around the back of the Little Bird, avoiding the copilot, and climbed into the man's vacated seat.

The pilot saw the stranger climbing in next to him. Over the spinning propeller he shouted, "What the hell do you think—"

Al-Amriki pointed the Glock between his eyes. "Fly! Now!"

The copilot arrived at the two wounded men on the ground. He wondered where in the hell the medic had gone. Looking down at one of the injured, he recognized a soldier named Dice, knew he was the medic who had called for the casualty evacuation not sixty seconds earlier. Dice lifted a hand covered in a bloody latex glove and weakly pointed to the copilot's Little Bird.

The copilot turned around in time to see his small black helicopter rise straight up into the sky.

It took thirty seconds for the other choppers to notice the Little Bird streaking off to the east instead of the west. A radio call from a Delta assaulter on the ground came just after. The other helicopters began broadcasting to one another about the hijacked chopper, and a few seconds after that, both of the circling gunships began giving chase.

Three levels belowground, Benji had made it to T.J. and his men.

"Good to see you, Colonel," Benji said. But T.J. cut him off.

"Did you get the American?"

"What American?"

"Shit! There is an American AQ guy! Dressed as a Ranger. He's the one running this op."

Benji waved away the worry. "All the Rangers are dead. Let's get you up and you can tell Monk what you know."

Hammond was unconscious now, so he had to be carried by a pair of assaulters. Other men began coming down the stairs, causing a logjam.

Finally, as they started up the stairs, Benji's radio came alive with the transmissions about the American CIA man who had stabbed Dice and hijacked a chopper.

T.J. shoved past Delta men trying to help him as he rushed to the surface.

The hijacked Little Bird landed in an intersection in western Peshawar. A gunshot rang out and a man climbed out and ran for his life.

Forty seconds later an identical Little Bird touched down in the intersection just long enough for two Delta assaulters to leap to the ground. The chopper shot back into the air, flew low and fast in a tight circle as the Delta pair moved toward the other chopper with their rifles high. They found the aircraft empty save for the body of the dead pilot. After a brief radio exchange between the men on the ground, the helicopter circling above them, and personnel in a Black Hawk back over the Sandcastle, another Little Bird landed in the street, this time disgorging the copilot. He ran to the copilot's seat of the other Little Bird, and one Delta man boarded each helicopter.

Seconds later both of the helos were back in the air, retreating to the west.

Daoud al-Amriki disappeared into the markets of Peshawar, searching frantically for a telephone.

FORTY-EIGHT

Inside the ground-floor room of the stockade, Monk placed the Turk's camera on a wooden table. He and T.J. looked at it. Timble had explained to the master sergeant the significance of the camera in front of him and the problems it could cause.

Monk's prescription for the problem was succinct. "Thermite?"

"That'll do it," T.J. said.

Monk pulled a thermite grenade and laid the camera and the grenade in an empty metal ammo can. "Fire in the hole!" he shouted as he pulled the pin on the thermite. The men backed out of the room, and a searing heat followed them through the doorway. Sputtering flame shot out of the canister burning everything it touched.

Pam Archer's UAV banked over the eastern outskirts of Landi Kotal, began flying back to the Sandcastle.

She'd been heading toward Peshawar to look for the missing Little Bird, but a pair of CIA Reaper drones had moved into the sector, so she was called back to base by Grauer. On her way back to Jalalabad, she decided to make one final pass over the Delta hit.

All the action was over, as far as she knew. Several men had been injured, but she hadn't heard of any KIAs from Grauer other than the Little Bird pilot. The assault seemed to have had its snags, but, she admitted, it had gone better than she'd expected.

And Racer was still alive.

She eyed the traffic on the N25 highway. It had picked up with the morning—even the huge battle a few hundred meters from the road hadn't halted the flow of trucks heading from Pakistan toward the Afghanistan border. It was amazing how accustomed people around here had become to violence.

Ten thousand feet below Baby Girl she saw the three big Black Hawks descending as they prepared to land to exfiltrate the Delta team. She decided to turn back around, to make one more circuit of the area of operation to keep an eye out while the boys loaded up.

A flash of light in the mountains to the east of the Sandcastle caught her eye. She looked at the area it had come from, but then her eyes changed their focus to the far side of her monitor.

One of the Black Hawks emitted billowing black smoke and began slowly rotating, losing control of its XY axis.

"Holy shit!" she shouted into her mike.

"What the hell was that?" came Grauer's voice in her headset. He had seen it, too.

"That sure looked like a SAM!" As Pam said it she was certain it had, in fact, been a surface-to-air missile. She panned closer to the portion of the hill where she'd seen the flash. There, secreted down in a tiny crevasse that ran parallel to the wall of the Sandcastle, a two-man team hefted a long green tube. She enlarged the image.

One of Grauer's analysts spoke in the OC, and Pam could pick up her voice in the headset. "That's an Anza. Probably a Mark 3. They are Pakistani-made, knockoffs of a Chinese design. Damned effective against choppers out to five kilometers. The Pakistani army has them."

"Guess the Taliban has them, too," Grauer said.

On a hunch Pam decreased the magnification on her camera and began scanning the rocky hills around the Sandcastle.

Two more flashes in the mountains to the east now. A pair of missiles shot into the sky from points a quarter mile apart. Above the brown earth a circling Little Bird dove and banked hard to the right, desperate to avoid them.

Kolt Raynor stood with T.J. and the other ex-prisoners, watching in horror as the big Black Hawk above them spun on its center axis and its nose dipped. In seconds it made a hard, spinning crash landing near the western wall.

Raynor began running toward the wreckage when

he heard another explosion, to his right. A Little Bird helo, just back from Peshawar, had taken a direct hit from a missile and exploded in midair. Burning debris fell five hundred feet and landed in the hills to the north of the Sandcastle.

Behind him Kolt heard Monk shouting, "From the east! SAMs from the east!"

The second and third Black Hawks landed without incident, and men began helping the Eagle 01 survivors aboard.

Raynor saw others ahead of him rushing to look for survivors of the downed Black Hawk, so he turned and ran the other way, toward the eastern wall of the Sandcastle. He knew the attackers would be Pakistani Taliban, but he had not expected them to come from that direction. The terrain on both sides of the Khyber Pass was brutal, but this force of men had managed to make it overland, not via the convenient highway that had been cut right through the mountains.

Kolt, Benji, and Monk all arrived at the wall at the same time. Kolt had picked up an AK from a dead Khyber Rifles guard on the way, and he climbed a wooden ladder to a stone landing that allowed him to look out over the hills to the east. The other two men shouldered up to him, and as they peered through the stone parapets they could see heads peek over rocks in the distance. But there was no gunfire toward their position from the enemy force. It seemed the enemy were concentrating on taking out the air assets.

Kolt understood, and he explained to the others. "This was part of the plan. Al Qaeda knew American choppers would come to sanitize the black site after the AQ hit. These guys must have been camped out here waiting to knock them out of the sky."

Just then, a Little Bird on a strafing run over the hills was hit with a streaking Anza missile. The chopper shuddered and smoked, but it remained airborne. It turned back to the west and began limping for the Afghanistan border.

Benji lifted his HK416 and fired at the cluster of rocks from where the rocket was fired, over three hundred yards away. He stopped firing, doubtful that he'd hit anything. Then he turned to Racer and asked, "Why didn't these guys start shooting the helos as soon as they came? We've had air assets buzzing overhead for twenty minutes. Why did they open up just now?"

Kolt thought for a moment. "Because the AQ guy in charge, this American T.J. told us about, ordered them not to fire until he gave them the signal. He was planning on getting out of here on one of his two Black Hawks. He would have told the Taliban commander to stay concealed until he called him and let him know they could start blasting helos."

"So the American AQ guy just made a phone call to these guys out here."

"That's right."

Benji said, "Shit. How are we going to exfil with all these fucking SAM crews?"

Monk had been on the radio, communicating with the helicopter air support and ordering the Little Birds to move off five kilometers, out of range of the Anza missiles. He turned to Benji and Kolt and said, "We don't have the vehicles to go overland. It's five klicks to the border. We'll have to suppress these crows ourselves with what we've got."

"What about UAVs?" asked Raynor.

Monk shook his head. "There are a pair of Agency Reapers above us, but they aren't authorized to provide close air support."

Kolt turned and looked at the master sergeant. "Then what the fuck *are* they authorized to do?"

"They are here to wipe any evidence away. They are going to level this place as soon as we get out of here."

"Damn it! Can't they make an exception and help us out?"

Monk shrugged. "I'm sure they are knocking that request up the chain of command right now."

"Shit!" shouted Kolt in utter exasperation. "Not a damned thing has changed in the past three years!"

Benji stated the obvious. "Look, Monk. We've lost three choppers already, and we have no idea how many missile launchers are out there. There is no way we can take off without getting nailed."

Monk just nodded, trying to figure a quick way out of this. They could wait for the Reaper drones to get the go-ahead to launch Hellfires on the missile crews, but every second they stayed here at the Sandcastle the danger increased. Monk wanted to get the hell out of here, now.

Kolt turned to Monk. "Listen. When those two Black Hawks take off, every one of those missile crews is going to have to pop up from cover to launch. One man with a scoped rifle, if he's willing to stay behind, can keep those heads down, or blow those heads off."

"Any volunteers?" Monk asked sarcastically.

Raynor answered immediately, "Me. Get me a scoped rifle and I'll keep them occupied."

"And *then* what?"

"Then I head overland toward the border."

Monk shook his head. "That is ridiculous. No way."

"I'm not under your command, remember? You can't stop me."

"The hell I can't! I'll put your ass into one of those helos myself!"

"I'm *not* getting in one of those helos. They are going to get shot down unless I engage the missile crews."

"Staying here is suicide, Racer!"

"I'm not staying here. I'm going to head up into those hills to the west. Give me five minutes to get some high ground, and then you guys take off."

Monk hesitated, only because Kolt was right—he did *not* have the authority to tell Racer he couldn't do whatever the hell he wanted. "If you do this, you are on your own."

Kolt said, "Fine, but don't make me use this damned AK. Give me a *chance*."

Monk reached for his radio. In seconds a sniper appeared. The young man was extremely pissed when ordered to hand his SR-25 over to the American in hajji pajamas, but he did as he was told. While the sniper was busy removing his gear from his body—his gun, his ammo, his ballistic computer from his wrist—Monk took Racer aside. "Nobody's coming back to pick you up. You're clear on that, right?"

Raynor was already slinging the rifle over his shoulder. "I'm clear."

Monk's professional demeanor did not waver for an instant. "Okay. As soon as we're gone, get away from this fort. *Don't* get your ass blown up by the damned CIA."

Kolt nodded, began running toward the western gate.

Monk called after him: "Racer. Go make your own luck." Monk knew better than to wish anyone in the Unit "good luck." He turned and began running toward the choppers, shouting orders into his radio.

FORTY-NINE

Pam fingered a Motorola handheld radio that she kept on her desk near her coffee mug. Through it she could communicate with her ground crew, the six Radiance employees who maintained her two UAVs.

Her hand lingered tentatively over the black walkie-talkie. Finally she lifted it to her mouth. Pressed the transmit button.

Her eyes remained on her monitor. The Sandcastle was in the center; the brown hills around took up much of the screen.

"Joseph, can you please come to Trailer 1?"

"Two minutes, Pammy."

Pam sipped her lukewarm triple mocha while she waited. Looking down at the cup of hot coffee, she noticed that her hands were quivering with trepidation.

She had just heard from Grauer that Racer had insisted on staying behind to fire on the Taliban missile crews as the Black Hawks tried to take off and make their way out of the Khyber Pass. Pete assured her that he was working on a way to help bring Racer out of Pakistan, *if* he managed to survive the next few minutes. But whatever he had cooked up, Grauer didn't sound terribly optimistic about Racer's chances of survival.

Grauer had also told her that the CIA was not likely to use its Reaper drones and Hellfire missiles to do more than its original mission—to vaporize the Sandcastle in order to erase all evidence of the black site.

Pam could not shake the thought that she'd once before held Racer's life in her hands, and she'd once before been given orders that led to disaster for him and others. Once before she had folded in the face of her commander, and many people had paid dearly for her inability to convince others what needed to be done.

As she stirred sugar into her triple mocha her chin rose slightly and her slight shoulders pulled back inside her olive flight suit.

She'd come to a decision.

She'd do what she had to do.

Come what might, she was going to do everything in her power to help Racer survive the day.

Joseph stepped in from the sunny afternoon. His bald black head shone from the sweat of working outside in the Afghanistan autumn. "What can I do you for, my love?"

As usual, Pamela kept her eyes on her monitors and gauges. There was a tiny rearview mirror taped on her console to her right so that she could see who was behind her in the trailer. She looked into it as she asked, "Can you have Baby Boy towed into the hangar?"

"The hangar? We've got the Falcon in there now. I can fit Baby Boy, but it will be a tight squeeze."

"That's fine."

"There's no wind today," he added, confused by her request to bring the bird indoors.

"I need him out of view."

"'Kay. Why?"

"Because I need him prepped for flight."

Joseph cocked his head. "Something wrong with Baby Girl?"

Pam turned away from her monitors and faced the man standing at the door to the trailer. Her doing so was a rare enough occurrence that the engineer knew something was up.

"No. I'm going to launch him. Have them both up at the same time."

Joseph stared at her for several seconds. "Grauer knows about this?"

"No, he does not. But I want you to tell him that I told you he ordered it. That should cover your ass, at least."

"What the hell are you planning—"

"Trust me. It will be better for you if you don't know."

Joseph nodded slowly. "How soon till launch?"

"Twenty minutes at the outside. Ten would be better. I need full fuel. Every last drop."

"Wow, Pam." He shook his head. "I'll get the team together and start work on it now." He pulled his radio from his belt.

"You're my hero, Joseph." Pam turned back to her monitor.

Kolt Raynor squeezed the trigger on his rifle. The recoil blurred his vision through the scope for an instant, but he had already refocused on his target by the time the turbaned man's head jerked back and blood shot into the air.

Raynor had no time to congratulate himself. He heard the Black Hawks' propellers churning the thin mountain air as they gained altitude ahead and to his right. He scanned quickly with his rifle's optics and found another crew, stepping out from behind a revetment far on the other side of the Sandcastle. Raynor fired twice. The first round missed high, but the second spun the man with the missile tube on his shoulder down to the ground.

His scope panned again. Another crew of two men, ready to fire. Kolt cracked off another round of Hornady Black Hills Gold .308 Winchester ammo, and another Taliban doubled over dead.

The Black Hawks were high in the air now. A missile launched from the far side of the Sandcastle—Raynor had missed this crew. He listened for the sounds of the impact with one of the big birds as he traced the smoke from the launch. Finding two men who had already ducked deep into a thicket of brush, Raynor fired five rounds in rapid succession from his twenty-round magazine, right where the brush moved.

He was certain he'd hit the men.

The missile missed the chopper and exploded into a

hillside south of Torkham. The Black Hawk's various antimissile countermeasures had done their job.

Kolt emptied his rifle at a group of Taliban who fired RPK rifles at his hillside. They had not seen his exact position, but he had seen theirs, so his last eight bullets sent the machine gunners back to the cover of a large boulder.

He dumped another full magazine at various gunners and missile crews in the next two minutes. He stopped shooting only when the heavy *thump thump* of the Black Hawk propellers had melted away from his sector of the Khyber Pass.

And then, with no warning whatsoever, an air-to-ground missile slammed dead center into the stockade of the Sandcastle. Kolt was a good two hundred yards away, but still well within the radius for flying bits of shrapnel to tear him apart. He dove to the ground, grabbed the SR-25, and began running, crawling, and scrambling around the side of the hill, staying low to avoid the now continual missile strikes back at the black site.

Shrapnel pinged off boulders around him as he moved.

"Thanks, assholes!" Kolt shouted, directing his rage at the CIA suits in Virginia who had ordered the demolition operation to proceed right on top of him.

Ten minutes later Raynor ran down a hill a half mile to the southwest of the Sandcastle. There was enough traffic below him on the road to keep him from heading for the Suzuki bike he'd left there. It had probably already been stolen, but if not, he would find himself surrounded by civilians that he could not trust to be friendly, and he knew he couldn't just start shooting people who weren't shooting at him. Behind him the explosions had died off. He knew there would be Taliban still alive back there, and he assumed they would be well aware that a sniper had foiled their plan to take down the departing transport helicopters.

Raynor would love to hide out in the mountains of the Khyber Pass until nightfall, use his skills in escape and evasion to make his way west and over the border through the rugged backcountry.

But he saw no way that was going to happen, since the only way off the hill he was now on was to go down directly to the road. A road full of Taliban who were, no doubt, hot on his heels. The only option he saw was to get to the road before the Taliban knew what he was doing, and then run, bike, or drive like hell to get to the border town of Torkham, a few kilometers up the road. Only there would he have any chance of hiding out till nightfall.

It was not even a real plan, more like a fantasy, but it was all Kolt had.

So he ran on, hoping his depleted stores of strength and adrenaline would last a while longer.

He had made it to within one hundred yards of the road when the ground around him began kicking up violently. The all too familiar sound of clattering AK-47s firing on full auto came from his right, up the highway, and bounced off the steep cliffs and dry hillsides of the Khyber Pass.

The Taliban had spotted him.

Kolt dove to the ground for cover.

Pam Archer received the call from Joseph that Baby Boy had been prepped and pulled back out of the hangar, and he was now ready to go. She put down her radio, got up from her seat, took the three steps over to the door of the trailer, and opened it. She popped her head out and called to the Radiance security guard standing just a few feet away. "Jay, can you come in here a sec?"

Jay entered the darkened trailer. His M-4 rifle scratched against the doorjamb. "Hey, Pam, what's up?" Jay knew there was an intense operation under way—Archer had been in one of the trailers virtually twenty hours a day for the past week. But he was just site security, so he knew nothing about the mission over the border.

"I've got one helluva favor to ask of you."

"Anything for a fellow Browns fan."

Pam smiled. She pointed to her seat. "Sit down."

Jay smiled. Laughed nervously. "Sit at the . . . controls? Really?"

"Yeah. I just need to run out and check something. I'll be back in a few."

Jay's jaw dropped. He looked around to see if his buddies were involved in this practical joke. "You want me to fly the Predator?"

"No, silly. It's on autopilot. Wide circles. It will fly itself. I just need you to watch the monitor, the system's console. If something weird happens, a systems failure or some other anomoly, use the joystick to do your best to keep her level and call me on the Motorola. Otherwise, don't touch anything." She had already pushed him gently forward in the tight confines of the trailer. His eyes were wide and focused on the chair in front of all the controls. Pam pushed him again, less gently this time. Not unlike a mother prodding her child to encourage him to sit in the dentist's chair.

"Grauer will have my ass if I fly the UAV."

"Yes, but just think what he'll do to you if you *crash* the UAV. Good luck." Pam Archer shot out the door and shut it behind her.

Alone in the dark room, security officer Jay unslung his rifle and scrambled into the big-backed chair. "Holy shit," he said in awe at everything in front of him.

He kept his hands in his lap and his eyes on the monitor in front of him.

This was a good spot. It would end here.

Raynor sighed.

He'd run back up the hill, two hundred yards above the winding Torkham Road, and found decent cover behind a boulder. He'd peered over it at the two large flatbed trucks that had stopped. Armed men had dismounted, a dozen at least, and clearly they'd seen him run to this position.

At that point he'd decided to look for another spot. Then he'd realized he'd boxed himself in. There was nowhere to go but back down the hill to the highway, and he did *not* want to do that.

Kolt looked through his scope, searching for targets, and was certain now that there were twenty-five men down there, all after him. They obviously knew he had a sniper rifle—they were staying low and behind cover for now. But Kolt knew they would advance slowly but surely on his hide.

One man against twenty-five. He would not survive this fight.

At least he was the one who had the long-range weapon.

A supersonic crack passed on his right, less than a foot from his throat. He threw himself back down into the dirt. His day-old forearm wound screamed at him when he hit the ground.

"Son of a bitch!" *They* had a sniper too. Kolt knew he needed to keep his head down now, and while he did, the Taliban forces would be converging on him, flanking him.

He tried twice more to pop his head back up to fire, but each time, the sniper sent a round his way. As he was boxed in from behind, his options were few and dwindling.

A third time he stood, determined to get a round off this time, but a shape appeared in the near distance. Instinctively he ducked, but it bounced on the boulder in front of him, ricocheted off to his left. His subconscious brain told him it was a grenade before any conscious understanding had been formed in his mind.

He dove again for the ground, landed hard on his wounded arm, just as the grenade exploded twenty feet away. He'd been shielded by a boulder on his left, but debris and shrapnel rained down on him. A sharp rock hit him hard, slicing open the back of his head and dazing him slightly.

Just then staccato bursts from AK-47s barked on his left, in front of him, and to his right. Behind him the boulders were impassable. He rolled to his knees, wincing with pain, rose to a standing position, and began running toward the road.

There was a small goat trail and he took it, his long scoped rifle out in front of him. Two men with AKs had just begun climbing a boulder to try to get a glimpse of the American infidel's position. Kolt shot both men without breaking stride. He kept running past, picking up speed as the gradient of the hill increased.

Gunfire trailed off as the Taliban on the Torkham highway climbed back into their two flatbed trucks to give chase.

FIFTY

Pam stared intently at the monitor in front of her as Baby Boy crossed the border, one thousand feet above Torkham. Quickly she scanned readouts on the heads-up display to ensure all systems were operating nominally.

Her mobile phone rang. She pulled it out and looked at it.

It was Grauer.

"Hi, Pete," she said.

"Pamela, what the hell is going on?"

"Everything is fine."

"No, Pam, everything is *not* fine. I just got a call from Jalalabad tower. They want to know why I have two Predators flying. Since I have only one Predator pilot, I regard having two Predators in the air as a serious problem."

"It's going to be okay, Pete. I have a plan."

"Which you will now tell me about."

A slight pause. "Can you come to Baby Girl's trailer?"

"I'll be there in three minutes."

She closed her phone and leaned forward toward the monitor.

Raynor found himself sprinting through late-morning traffic on the Torkham Road. Cars were stopped just around the bend from where he had been shooting it out with the Taliban. Men stood outside their vehicles; jingle trucks had disgorged their passengers to smoke and wait for the battle to end so they could safely restart their journey to the east.

Kolt jogged now, exhausted, blood dripping freely from the back of his head. He looked back over his shoulder and saw the two Taliban transport trucks rounding the bend slowly. They were three hundred yards back, searching for him up in the hills and rocks, apparently not taking into consideration that he'd actually be dumb enough to run down the middle of the highway.

A group of malicious-looking Pakistani men in turbans shouted at Kolt as he ran by their car. He held the semiautomatic sniper rifle, but he did not wave it at them. He just ignored their curses and kept going. Just ahead of them a small scooter pulled out of oncoming traffic and turned around, facing back to the west. Raynor glanced back over his shoulder again, and saw the Taliban trucks picking up speed, closing on him with purpose.

He'd been seen.

Cars parked on the highway began pulling off the road, getting out of the way of the charging trucks.

Kolt staggered forward, weakening by the step.

"Mister Racer! Mister Racer!"

Raynor stumbled as he stopped and looked at the man on the scooter.

Jamal stared back at him with his customary terrified expression.

Kolt just mumbled in English, "How the fuck . . ."

"Get on!"

Kolt climbed on the back of the scooter and Jamal lurched forward, racing up the empty western lane of the Torkham Road.

"Those trucks behind. They are coming after you?" Jamal asked as he looked at his rearview mirror.

Raynor needed a minute to catch his breath before he could answer. Finally, in Pashto, Kolt said, "Well, actually *now* they are coming after *us.* What are you doing here?"

Jamal stepped on the gas, but the tiny bike would never outrun the big trucks. The two vehicles loaded with gunmen closed quickly. "Mister Bob gave me a number to call if something happened to him. I called it last night. A man named Pete said that I should go to Torkham and wait for his instructions. He called me one hour ago and said that if I wanted to come to Afghanistan, where I will be safe and have a good job, I had to come and pick you up on the road from Landi Kotal. He did not say men would be chasing you!"

Kolt looked back over his shoulder. The two trucks were less than one hundred yards back.

"Go faster!"

"I can go faster only if you get off!" screamed Jamal.

A gun barked behind them. The highway on their right exploded into broken rock as rounds stitched up it.

Kolt knew they would not make it. The town of Torkham was just ahead. He could see the dust and haze in the distance. If they could get there they could find a place to hide, but they could not outrun the trucks behind them.

There was no way. The town was five minutes away and the trucks would be on them in one minute.

The bullets from the Talibani rifles were on them now. Another burst screamed through the air by Raynor's ear.

He squinted ahead at the town before him. Willed it to come closer.

Then his eyebrows furrowed. "What the *hell* is that?"

Jamal looked up too now, and he almost lost control of his scooter.

A sleek white Predator unmanned aerial vehicle shot up the road right toward them, not fifty feet in the air.

With blurring speed it streaked over their heads. The thin white starboard wing tipped slightly, and the craft seemed to yaw to the right. Five seconds after passing directly over Kolt and Jamal's position the big, buzzing drone had lined up perfectly on the first of the speeding trucks.

"Pam." Kolt muttered the name with stunned admiration, transfixed by the craziest thing he had ever seen in his life.

Pam Archer kept a steady left hand on the joystick, an impassive face, her eyes locked on her main monitor. She went to full throttle, twitched down to ten feet over the highway. With the slight tailwind and the descent, her heads-up display read 162 miles an hour.

Pam's drone was no longer a passive monitor of events.

Baby Boy was now a huge kinetic missile.

The first truck saw the aircraft and jacked out of the way, ran off the road, and kicked up dust as the driver fought to keep the vehicle on its tires. The driver tried to pull it back onto the road, but he fishtailed, swerved, crossed the highway, and came to a jolting stop in the low boulders on the south side. The dozen men in the back were tossed all over the highway.

The second truck was not nearly so lucky. With a combined speed of over 210 miles an hour the UAV and the cab of the flatbed slammed together. A fireball erupted as the gas tanks ruptured amid torn electrical wires and the resultant sparks of metal on metal. Most men in the vehicle were incinerated instantly. A few Taliban burned and flailed as they flew through the air, their bodies landing and shredding into burning bits of flesh and clothing and battle gear on a long scatter path up the road.

Kolt and Jamal slowed slightly as they both looked back in awe at the smoke and flames and wreckage behind them. Kolt just shook his head in disbelief.

It was the craziest damned thing he'd ever seen.

"A kamikaze Predator," he mumbled to himself.

He thought of Pam, and smiled.

But Jamal quickly brought him back to the here and now. "Mister Racer. What do we do now?"

Kolt patted the young Afghan on his shoulder as they closed on the border town of Torkham. He shrugged. "How 'bout I buy you a cup of tea?"

Archer ran from Trailer 1 to Trailer 2. Just as she made it to Baby Girl's trailer, Pete Grauer arrived and stepped inside with her. Pam helped Jay out of the cockpit seat. The young security guard looked relieved at first, but then he turned ashen-faced upon seeing the ex–Ranger colonel.

"Enjoy yourself, son?" Grauer asked.

"No! No, sir!"

"Out." Grauer waved the man out of the trailer.

Pam settled in and disengaged the autopilot, taking control of Baby Girl, turning her back over the Torkham Road.

Grauer said, "You crashed the UAV, didn't you?"

"Yes, sir. We needed to buy Racer some time."

Thirty seconds of silence ensued. "Do you think I just get the Predators insured with collision coverage at State Farm?"

Archer cleared her throat nervously. "No, sir." She did not look back, only focused more intently on her work.

Another thirty seconds of silence other than the various mechanical hums of the trailer.

Grauer spoke again. “Archer.”

“Sir?”

A sigh from the man behind. “That was incredible. Nice work.”

“Thank you, sir.”

“And Archer?”

“Sir?”

“*Never* again.”

“No, sir. Absolutely not.”

EPILOGUE

Delta Force Colonel Jeremy Webber's Chinook helicopter landed at 1300 hours. He climbed out of the side door and was followed by an eight-man contingent of snipers, spotters, and assaulters. The men took up positions on the hill overlooking the Torkham border crossing. Two more assaulters, Benji and Monk, stepped out of the helicopter as well, and they followed their commander down the steep road toward the crossing point.

Webber carried a leather satchel under his arm.

The road was congested with travelers, merchants, kids, goats, trucks, rickshaws, and taxis. Several U.S. Army Humvees were parked on the Afghani side. Webber, Monk, and Benji walked past them without a glance, though the young soldiers in the Humvees stared at the odd clothing of the three Americans, tactical attire that proclaimed the men to be of no particular branch of service or specific unit. They looked more like private bodyguards, but they appeared to be unarmed, and they had arrived in a Chinook and not an SUV.

The three men made their way to the Pakistani checkpoint and asked to speak to the official in charge. With stern glares and serious voices the men commanded attention. The border crossing's officer in charge appeared. He wore the attractive beret and uniform of the Pakistani Frontier Corps and sported a mustache that made him a dead ringer for the late Saddam Hussein, apart from his much ruddier complexion.

Colonel Webber extended a hand. "Good afternoon, Major. I wonder if I could have a moment of your time."

"What can I do for you?"

"Is there someplace quiet we can go? Your office, perhaps?"

Monk and Benji stood silently behind as the two men walked off down a hall.

Fifteen minutes later a scooter pulled up to the Pakistani side of the border crossing. On it sat a thin Afghan and another man, lighter-complected, with a scruffy beard and a filthy face. The man on the back of the scooter wore a brown turban, but a splotch of red blood could be seen soaking through it. His right arm was bandaged. He seemed almost asleep.

A guard asked them for their papers. The two men on the scooter did not move. As the guard began to speak to them again, the officer in charge came out of the customs shack, walked up to his young soldier, and told him that the two men on the scooter were permitted to exit the Islamic Republic of Pakistan. The guard shrugged, the scooter drove forward, and the major returned to his building.

When the OIC returned to his office the Americans were gone, but the older man's satchel remained on his desk. Upon opening it the major found five thousand dollars.

He'd hoped for a little more.

Minutes later he heard the helicopter taking off over on the Afghanistan side.

Daoud al-Amriki was proud that he was to die in the presence of his leader. It had been two weeks of hard travel from Pakistan to Yemen, and at each stop along the route, at each safe house or conveyance along the way, a little more of Daoud al-Amriki's free will and liberty had been taken from him. They'd taken his gun in Karachi, his documents and phone on the boat to Aden, his wallet and his money on the road into Sanaa, and then they'd removed his clothing as he went into the hills to the north, replacing them with a peasant's rags.

The chains came on soon after, and the hood not long after that.

Now he sat, hooded and chained, in a room on a farm somewhere near Sa'dah. He knew this only because he'd been here once before, under different circumstances, of course. He remembered the smells of the tea and the baked bread. The scents of the Red Sea and the desert mixing with one another.

On that visit, he'd come to seek audience with his

leader. To lay out his brave plan, and to promise a great victory against the infidels.

This time he had come in chains. In defeat.

He had come, inshallah, to die.

Men entered the room and stood around him. He thought they would remove his hood but they did not. Instead, they lifted him to his feet and led him to another room in the same building, where they pushed him down onto his haunches, and only then did they remove his hood.

He blinked in the fresh light, taking it into his sore eyes in doses as his head hung toward the floor.

Finally, when he was ready, he lifted his head. In front of him, just as he had expected, was Anwar al-Awlaki.

The American-born operational leader of al Qaeda looked healthy and tan. He sat in clean, flowing white robes and a simple cream-colored turban. His black beard, flecked with bits of gray, and his wire-rimmed eyeglasses did not obstruct the serious expression on his face.

Sitting around Awlaki in a semicircle were a half-dozen other men. Al-Amriki did not know any of them.

Daoud al-Amriki greeted them all with a blessing, and a blessing was returned.

Then the young American looked to his leader and said, "I failed you in Pakistan. I will not blame anyone but myself for what happened. I failed to prepare, to anticipate. I failed to—"

Al-Awlaki lifted a hand. Al-Amriki went silent. "You will go to America," he said in perfect English.

Daoud cocked his head. He could not believe he understood the soft voice of the man in front of him. "I? *I* will go?"

"You will attack the infidels from within. You will make a great victory for the believers."

"Yes." Al-Amriki looked to the other men. One of them gave him a curt nod, as if to say, *This will all be explained later.*

"Yes." Daoud al-Amriki said it again, louder, with passion.

A man crawled over to him with a key, and unlocked Daoud's chains.

The bearded man in the flowing white robes spoke once more. "And this time you will not fail. Inshallah."

"Inshallah," said David the American, rubbing his wrists. He looked up at his leader and he smiled.

Inshallah.

ACKNOWLEDGMENTS

I hated Mrs. Johnson's English class. In fact, I applied most of my time to figuring ways to avoid the work and work the system.

We had it all figured out. We matched test days to our skip days. We infiltrated school grounds the same afternoon, usually about twenty minutes after Mrs. Johnson had headed for her faded yellow station wagon with the simulated wood grain side panels and just before the coach expected us on the ball field. After all, at our high school it was often said we worked ball and played school.

We set our cover for action and proceeded cautiously but deliberately to the locked cabinet. Mrs. Johnson never took the tests home the same day to grade. We posted lookouts to cover the doors and windows. One of us would surreptitiously breach the cabinet—jimmy the dime-store lock—or the kid with the skinniest arm would reach down from the top through the small gap of the locked cabinet doors and delicately pull out the appropriate folder—the one holding our fourth-period classmates' completed grammar tests—the master answer sheet always at the top.

If it was multiple choice or fill in the blanks, we were in for an easy make-up exam. If it required some comprehensive writing, the kid with the quickest and neatest handwriting went to work. From execute authority to mission complete—five minutes tops. Even though we had no clue, we were executing a low-visibility hit using the same instincts, thought process, and tactical patience used by our nation's most skilled black ops units.

Unfortunately, as much as those snippets of adolescent action provided a foundation for what I'd eventually be doing as a Delta Force operator, the lack of grounding in proper sentence structure and point of view made life miserable as I wrote *Kill Bin Laden*. I needed a ton of help. In fact, I needed an entire team of professionals. I learned quickly that there is absolutely no intrinsic crossover between leading commandos and writing about commandos.

Shifting from nonfiction to the fictional world that Kolt Raynor rolls in, things only got worse. The team of professionals, again expertly led like a SEAL Team Six commander by my editor, Marc Resnick of St. Martin's Press, and my world-class agent, Scott Miller of Trident Media Group, took a chance on me. Like good general officers, they issued me intent and provided a task and purpose. Then they got out of the way. Write what you know, they said. No limitations, no constraints. Easy enough.

But there was still that high school English class issue. And just like a new Delta Force troop commander needs the institutional knowledge and operational mentoring of a seasoned Delta troop sergeant major, Marc and Scott went to work. In short order, the battle turned as the incredibly talented Mark Greaney joined the team.

If *Black Site* is a success, pin the medals on Marc, Scott, and Mark. They are the best in the business, passionate professionals, and they personify the *Life is good* attitude that makes the daily grind seem more pleasant than painful. Of course, if *Black Site* doesn't get it for you, spare the team, but consider me PNG—persona non grata.

Truth be told, I was not too keen on Dalton Fury adding to the already overcrowded action thriller bookshelves. But when two high school–aged girls say "go for it," and a wonderful wife cuts me some slack on the yard work, selling excuses is a bust. I am equally grateful and forever indebted to my family as I am to the writing team responsible for what you are holding in your hands.

Importantly, Dalton Fury and Kolt Raynor may have served in Delta's ranks together, sneaking into one place over here and blowing the doors down at that place over there, but the similarities aren't exact. The knock on both is that they were impetuous, leaned a little to the arrogant side, and probably never should have slipped by the shrinks in the first place. But they made the best of what God gave them, respected and relied on support personnel as much as fellow operators, and always believed that serving in Delta came with a price. Expectations that you will push the envelope, take the risk, get on target, and develop the situation: it's a mantra that frowns on hand-wringing, hesitation, and overthinking it. I fully embraced it in the real-world Delta Force. And even though I am not Kolt Raynor, he proudly lives it in *Black Site*.

Read on for an excerpt from Dalton Fury's next book

TIER ONE WILD

Available in hardcover from St. Martin's Press

Tier One Wild (1) Using common sense over process, getting away with more than the other guy, and possessing a bit of an attitude. (2) The mindset that all Tier One (Delta Force and SEAL Team 6) operators roll with, encompassing the idea that someone who is specially assessed and selected to serve in the ranks of a special missions unit (DF and ST6) has the mental and physical capacity to perform to a much higher standard, to accept more risk, to march to a different drummer, and to tell a general officer that he is full of shit (with slightly more tact but with absolutely no fear of retribution).

PROLOGUE

New Delhi, India

The dead lay throughout the first-class cabin. Their bodies stank in the still air.

Four men, two women. A flight attendant. An air marshal. A man who had looked like he might start trouble. An Indian diplomat from the Punjab. A German woman who had been shot for screaming.

And one martyr.

Unlike the five dead nonbelievers, Marwan's body had not been dumped across the seats. No, his men had laid him gently on his back, his arms positioned across his chest, a clean starched napkin from a first-class dining cart draped over his face, the two running ends of his red headband just visible. Marwan had been the leader of the six-strong cell of Lashkar-e-Taiba fighters. He and his men had boarded this aircraft two days earlier dressed like businessmen returning from a telemarketing conference in Mumbai. Marwan had gone to the rear galley shortly after takeoff, while the rest of the passengers sat strapped into their seats, compliant like lambs chained to posts in the marketplace. He'd found the case left for him by a Jordanian brother who worked in food service at the Chatrapati Shivaji International Airport in Mumbai, and from it Marwan quietly and efficiently passed the Skorpion machine pistols out to his men. He donned the bulletproof vest left in the bag and slipped the hand grenade into his pocket, and then the seven Pakistani Lashkar-e-Taiba operatives rushed up the aisles and took over the plane.

Twenty-five seconds after they thought they had control, Marwan fell to the aisle dead, killed by a pistol shot to the back of the head, fired by an air marshal. The marshal was himself killed by Skorpion fire in the next moment, which immediately put Jellock in charge of an operation that still had not recovered from the death of its leader.

Jellock was not Marwan. He was scared and uncertain. He was tired and hot and sick of the strange food on the aircraft and the overflowing toilets and the bodies putrefying up in first class. The ballistic vest he now wore dug into his skin and weighed him down as he ran the length of the plane shouting orders.

In the past fifty-five hours he'd forced the 767's American flight crew to fly to New Delhi, then back to Mumbai, then to Bangalore, and now back to New Delhi. Jellock had been afraid to keep the aircraft in one place for too long while he waited for his demands to be met. In the meantime, the Indian government had stalled and his men had threatened and killed passengers and crew.

He wished Marwan were here to tell him what to do, where to go, how to keep order among the other five men in the cell.

But Marwan was dead in first class, and the others looked to Jellock for direction while they bickered among themselves and beat on the passengers in frustration.

What do I do? This is taking too long!

The twenty-three-year-old's exhausted and stressed mind focused quickly. *Too long.* Yes! Too long they had been on the ground here in New Delhi. He felt the government's delays had been trickery, that he'd been played for a fool.

Too long.

Jellock stood, stormed into the cockpit, found the flight crew sleeping in their seats, and he screamed at them. "We leave New Delhi! We fly away!"

"Where?" asked the pilot wearily.

Jellock thought a moment. He needed a safe place. Someplace where the aircraft could remain for enough hours for him to get some rest. "Quetta!"

"Pakistan." The pilot said it as a groan. A statement of frustration.

"Yes!" Jellock screamed every word he said to the pilots, thinking it would make him appear authoritative.

The pilot shrugged. "When?"

"Now! Take off!"

"Son, you don't understand. We have to go through a preflight checklist and pull our maps for the route we—"

"Take off now or I kill a passenger!" Jellock turned to yell out into the cabin. "Mohammed!"

The pilot rubbed his eyes and reached for his case containing his maps and charts. "Okay! Okay. Just give me five minutes to—"

"One minute!" Jellock yelled, certain of the deceit of this nonbeliever. "In one minute we are moving to the runway or I kill one passenger every minute!"

"Three minutes! You've got to give us at least—"

"Two minutes! No more!"

"I need three!"

"You can have three, but I kill one passenger." He turned back to the cabin. "Mohammed! Bring me the first child you see!"

"All right! Calm down! We're moving in two!" shouted the pilot, before tuning out the terrorist and focusing on his aircraft.

ONE

The hazy night sky was cool three thousand feet above and aft of the Boeing 767, but Delta Force Major Kolt "Racer" Raynor perspired into his goggles. Rivulets of sweat ran down the back of his black Nomex suit as he hung under the taut canopy of his square parachute and focused on the scene below.

It had been nearly four years since he'd led other men into battle. He had been assessed as ready by both his superiors and his peers, and he felt ready, but still, he was human.

And this shit was scary as hell.

Two more canopies drifted down through the darkness near him. The three chutes were stacked—teammates Digger and Slapshot were strapped together in a tandem rig below and fifty feet ahead of Kolt, and Stitch was positioned slightly above and fifty feet behind.

All four men floated with the wind down toward their drop zone, a few hundred feet aft of the hijacked American Airlines flight.

Digger spoke into his radio from his position up front, hanging in front of Slapshot. “Hey, boss. That plane looks like it’s ready to depart. There’s no auxiliary power attached. Aft stairs are up, too.”

“Guess they aren’t gonna wait around for us to sneak up all ninja-like,” Slapshot mumbled into his mic. The big man always injected humor when no one else was in the mood.

And Kolt was not in the mood. “Damn,” he said.

Next Stitch came over the radio: “Back to me a bit, boss,” and Racer immediately realized he had drifted a little too close to the men in front of him. Calmly he adjusted his toggles to remedy the error.

The plan had been to land and then link up with other Americans on the ground—CIA case officers and military types from the embassy here—and then they would decide how to proceed. They’d set their drop zone as a spot on the tarmac behind the hijacked aircraft, out of sight from the terminal, because the Agency boys on site had said TV cameras were positioned all over the terminal, and no one at Delta wanted the cameras to get a shot of a team of commandos dropping in from the sky at 0330 hours.

As he hung twenty-five hundred feet above the ground, Kolt eyed the plane, keeping it between his stack and the cameras.

He hoped like hell he and his mates would get a crack at taking the jet down before this was all over. He reasoned that, if the plane stayed put in New Delhi for just a few hours more, there was a decent chance he would get the order from the Joint Operations Center to hit the target.

But as he was thinking this, below his boots red and green indicator lights began blinking on the wingtips of the 767. Almost instantly the two Pratt & Whitney engines on the aircraft began to roar. Seconds later the nose of the craft turned slightly to the left, centering on the long runway that ran off to the west.

The 767 began to move as the engines pitched higher.

Kolt Raynor groaned in frustration. "You've got to be kidding."

Digger shouted into his radio, "Son of a bitch is rolling."

"Repositioning on the tarmac or heading to the runway?" Stitch asked from the back. He could not see past Racer's chute.

"Bet they're flying out of here. They've been doing a lot of erratic shit like that."

"Suggestions?" Kolt asked quickly into his mic. He knew to get the input of his sergeants at a critical moment like this.

Slapshot said, "There isn't much sense in linking up with officials if the hijacked plane isn't gonna hang around."

And then Stitch chimed in, "Racer, you have execute authority. Why don't we hit it?"

It was true, Raynor had pried execute authority from Colonel Webber, the head of Delta Force. This allowed Raynor, as the military commander at the scene, the flexibility to call for a hasty in-extremis takedown of the aircraft if he saw the opportunity to do so or if he felt the necessity to try, like if the terrorists, or "crows" in Delta parlance, started shooting hostages before official approval for Delta's mission came from the JOC.

Still, Kolt wasn't sure what Stitch was getting at. He keyed his mic. "*Hit* it? While it's moving?"

"We can land on the roof and head for the cockpit. I've got the harpoon. If we go in single file we can breach the escape hatch. If we increase our descent speed we can be inside before they go throttle-up."

"Have you guys done that before?" Kolt asked incredulously.

"Not a moving aircraft, and only in training back at Bragg, boss," Slapshot answered. But he agreed with his fellow sergeant's assessment. "We aren't going to get another chance at this. If the plane isn't there, then the TV crews might see us, and if they film us dropping on the tarmac that will get back to the crows in the jet. Might just piss them off enough to kill some more passengers."

"Now or never," Stitch said. "What's the call, Racer?"

Kolt asked, "What about Digger?"

Now Digger chimed in. Though he was the youngest of the team and perhaps the most fit overall, he possessed one potential handicap to the operation.

Where his lower right leg used to be, he now wore a titanium prosthesis. Kolt could not imagine how he could run along the roof of a moving aircraft with a leg made out of metal.

"No sweat, boss. I've got this," Digger said. He sounded confident and eager.

Kolt's operational brain trust had spoken and their vote was unanimous. Still, this was his first hit since returning to the Unit just two months prior, and Colonel Webber had made it crystal clear to Raynor that he needed to change his ways. There was no room in the modern Delta Force for the Tier One Wild antics that had gotten him in hot water in the past, and Webber had reminded Kolt numerous times that he was on incredibly thin ice. Nevertheless, Kolt and his boys had been the alert squadron at Fort Bragg when this hostage crisis unfolded, so Kolt and his team had been called to bat.

Make your decision, Raynor! He said it to himself in a silent shout.

Three seconds later he pressed the push-to-talk button on his chest rig again. "Let's hit it." *Webber's gonna have my ass,* he thought, but right now he had *much* bigger fish to fry.

In the Joint Operations Center at Forward Operating Base Yukon in Bagram, Afghanistan, the chow hall, the gym, and the movie tent stood empty. Right now everyone with access was stacked at the back of the JOC watching the shocking footage displayed on a single large plasma screen at the front of the room. A Predator drone's night-vision camera caught the huge commercial aircraft moving slowly through the darkness toward the runway, and its satellite uplink broadcast the ghostly images to the screen at the JOC. Racer and his team were not in the picture, they were still high in the air on their descent, and their drop zone was out of the camera's current field of view.

The Agency guys at the airfield in New Delhi were on the other end of a Thuraya sat phone and their running commentary was piped through the speakers of the JOC. The CIA's liaison officer stood near Colonel Jeremy Webber, holding a phone to his ear and passing on additional information to the head of Delta Force.

The tension in the air infected everyone. All were frozen in amazement at the huge plasma monitor, referred to in the JOC as "Kill TV."

The men and women stood in rapt attention as the hijacked aircraft rolled steadily down the taxiway, clearly moving for takeoff on Runway 29. A few seconds later, the Predator downlink went fuzzy. The "eye in the sky" had blinked. It was a mechanical glitch that seemed to be common with that aerial asset at exactly those moments when clear observation was desperately needed.

The Kill TV feed came back up a moment later, just as the silhouetted figures of four men under three parachutes passed between the 767 and the camera's lens. Black hot figures flying through the air with the heat off their bodies trapped in the chutes above them, creating a faint umbrella shape.

"Holy shit. There they are!" exclaimed the operations sergeant major, breaking the silence that had fallen over the JOC. They should have been landing far back on the tarmac, but it looked to everyone at Bagram as if the Delta team were making for the runway itself. "What the hell are they doing?"

The three chutes sailed purposefully toward the plane on the ground, which meant only one thing to Colonel Jeremy Webber. The men were *not* continuing on to the drop zone on the now-empty tarmac.

No. It looked like . . .

Webber cocked his head slightly. "Racer is assaulting." He said it in a clipped voice that indicated to everyone in the room that he was pissed.

No one in the JOC was new to special operations or terrorist interdictions, but still many gasped in shock. Assaulting an aircraft as it sat at the end of the runway, seconds from takeoff?

Colonel Webber sat back in his chair. He *was* pissed, but he was not surprised. Kolt fucking Raynor, his man on the scene, had been a pseudo-insubordinate troop commander before he'd been kicked out of Delta four years ago. Now that he was back in the Unit, there was little reason to expect anything but pseudo-insubordination now, even with all Webber's "personal counseling" of his wayward major.

He stared silently at the downlink screen. Webber would have stopped Racer and the others if he had any control over this situation. But the Delta operators' audacious and daring actions effectively neutered any long-arm leadership—or micromanagement—since the JOC was 220 miles away from the action.

Colonel Webber cleared his throat and in a confident and booming voice said, "All right, we seem to have a common operating picture and are now in a current operation with operators on target. Push the QRF to the airspace and air-loiter twenty minutes out, spin up the extraction fixed-wing aircraft ASAP, and get me the SECDEF on the red line."

Immediately several of the staff in the JOC went from statues of stone to blurs of activity—the Quick Reaction Force choppers were ordered into the theater, the extraction aircraft were ordered ready, and secure comms with the Pentagon were established.

Webber's confident orders, tuned to just the right authoritative tenor by decades of command, sounded confident and certain, but that was just for public consumption.

Silently to himself the colonel breathed softly, "Dammit, Racer, you'd better not dick this up."

Even though they had not expected to drop right into combat, the four men six hundred feet above the aircraft were geared up for battle. Kolt "Racer" Raynor and Master Sergeant Clay "Stitch" Vickery wore individual MC-4 HALO rigs while Master Sergeant Peter "Digger" Chambliss hung behind Master Sergeant Jason "Slapshot" Holcomb in a HALO tandem rig. These were not the best parachute rigs available to Delta, but they were the best rigs they had been able to grab as they raced onto the MC-130H Combat Talon II at the intermediate staging base at Masirah Air Base off the coast of Oman. As this was an in-extremis op, they only had time to bring in the best gear they could amass on the fly. All four operators wore the Ops-Core FAST ballistic helmet with infrared strobes activated and blinking on top. Under the helmet all wore dark brown Peltor ear protection and radio headsets. The team would be going in light, protectionwise; three wore just chest plates, which would stop a frontal pistol or rifle round to their center mass; only Racer wore hard protection on both his chest and his back.

Each operator had a .40-caliber Glock 23 with a tan grip and a SureFire tactical light attached to a rail under its barrel. These pistols were secured in rigs on their chests, not on their hips. In the tight aisles of a commercial aircraft, the chest holsters allowed for faster deployment of the combat handguns than a belt rig would. Only Slapshot and Stitch brought rifles along—each carried an HK416 strapped barrel-down on their left side. Extra ammo was secured in their chest rigs, which also held their MBITR MX radios in nylon side pouches.

The radios were wired to their Peltor headsets so that they could communicate effectively during the assault.

All four men were dressed in black flight suits with an American flag, subdued gray and black in color, on the left shoulder. On the right shoulder a call sign patch was affixed . . . a black border with a luminous tape letter/number combo. Kolt's read MI1, as he was a troop commander in Mike Squadron. As a troop sergeant major of Mike, Slapshot was MI2. Stitch and Digger were, respectively, team leader and second-in-command of Mike's Alpha team, so their patches read MA1 and MA2. Three of them were wearing desert tan and black Salomon trail shoes, while Kolt wore the same old tan leather combat boots he'd had since the invasion of Iraq nearly ten years earlier. The shoes were worn and torn, but he still loved them, old school though they were.

They had exited the MC-130 Talon II at twenty thousand feet wearing Gentex oxygen masks with a hose attached to a Twin 53 bailout bottle inside a pouch on the right hip. Once they descended below ten thousand feet they disconnected their masks and let them hang to the side. All wore thermal underwear and black balaclavas to maintain body heat during the descent. On their hands were black Mechanix M-Pact Covert gloves with plastic knuckle protectors, and digital altimeters were strapped to the back of each of their hands.

Each man also carried a pair of nine-banger flash-bang grenades and a personal first aid pouch with one-hand tourniquet rigs.

At four hundred feet above the target, Slapshot, with Digger riding in the front of his rig, maneuvered to line up his approach angle to the rear of the 767, which was now turning off the taxiway and onto the runway. All Kolt and Stitch had to do was follow the red and green chemlites on the pack tray of their teammates to the target while maintaining safe separation. Racer, the least experienced jumper in the bunch, struggled to keep in formation with the other two chutes.

Kolt said, "Our spot is the long axis of the fuselage. We'll harpoon the escape hatch above the cockpit, depressurize the plane, and enter. We're going to have to do this fast and dirty before they take off. Once inside, haul ass aft and make friends in the rear. Remember, there are a hundred forty souls on board, plus at least six crows."

"One four zero souls, six assholes, roger," said Stitch.

"One-forty poor SOBs. Six bad guys. Got it," replied Digger.

"One four zero live. Six die. Then breakfast. Roger," said Slapshot, interjecting his trademark nonchalance into the tension.

"Boss, I have the harpoon," Stitch reminded his team leader.

To this Kolt replied, "Pull around to my left and take the base."

"Roger that," Stitch said, and seconds later he glided past his major, and then past the tandem team in front. He corrected back to the right and moved to the head of the line. Now it was Stitch's job to lead the others. He had red and green chemlites on the back of his pack, and the men behind him kept their eyes locked firmly on those lights as they neared the target.

Kolt struggled to keep his place in the stack as they neared the landing, but he managed to touch down on the slick aircraft roof just a few steps behind the others. He, Slapshot, and Stitch pulled their harness release pins and the three parachutes floated off the right side of the plane, just clearing the wing's edge before drifting softly to the tarmac.

All four men were prone on top of the aircraft now, and they fought to stay atop the slick and sloping surface, knowing they needed to get off the roof and inside the plane before the pilot applied takeoff thrust and jetted down the runway. Stitch and Kolt hugged the skin of the aircraft, something akin to balancing on a giant basketball, while Slapshot, still attached and lying on top of Digger, pulled the tandem chute's quick release to disconnect himself from his mate.

Inside the cockpit the two-man American flight crew had no idea that four Delta Force commandos were crawling toward the cockpit along the aircraft's fuselage. Both the pilot and copilot sat strapped to their seats with their headsets on, and they concentrated on the rushed takeoff sequence, manipulating the appropriate buttons.

The leader of the terrorists, the jittery man-child with the bulletproof vest who called himself Jellock, leaned into the cockpit. "One minute we are in air or boy die!"

The copilot held out a placating hand to the armed gunman, then turned to the captain. "We ready to go?"

"I have no idea," the pilot replied as he turned to the runway in front of him. "But we're outta here before they shoot that kid."

He reached for the throttle, and the copilot did the same.